THE CASE-BOOK OF
SHERLOCK HOLMES

THE CASE-BOOK OF
SHERLOCK HOLMES

Sir Arthur Conan Doyle

WORDSWORTH CLASSICS

This edition published 1993 by
Wordsworth Editions Limited
8b East Street, Ware,
Hertfordshire SG12 9HJ

ISBN 1 85326 070 3

Printed and bound in Great Britain by
Mackays of Chatham plc, Chatham Kent

INTRODUCTION

THIS VOLUME COMPLETES the canon of the illustrated Sherlock Holmes stories reprinted from *The Strand Magazine*. It contains the short story series *Reminiscences of Sherlock Holmes*, *The Valley of Fear*, a sinister novella which appeared in 1914–15, *His Last Bow: The War Service of Sherlock Holmes* and the last twelve stories *The Case-Book of Sherlock Holmes*.

Sherlock Holmes is perhaps the best-known of all fictional characters. From the first appearance of the short staories in the *Strand Magazine* chronicling his extraordinary deductive powers, Holmes became a larger-than-life figure whose devotees were stricken when it seemed that the great detective had perished at the Reichenbach Falls in *The Adventure of the Final Problem*. Young men put mourning crêpe in their hats, and the author was forced by public demand to resurrect his hero. From that day, a literary cult was born and continues unabated to this day. Perhaps it is best exemplified by the Baker Street Irregulars, who exist to perpetuate the memory, methods and iconography of the great detective. Its members comprise diplomats, judges, academics as well as great numbers of ordinary readers who enjoy the romance and atmosphere of Conan Doyle's creation.

Sherlock Holmes' methods can be traced back to one of Doyle's teachers at the Edinburgh Infirmary. Joseph Bell used to enliven his lectures by encouraging students to recognise a patient as a left-handed cobbler or as a retired sergeant of a Highland regiment who had served in Barbados, by the simple process of accurate observation and rational deduction. This inclined Doyle to attribute these qualities to a detective as a hero, which was unusual, if not unique, in English stories of the time.

The first appearance of Sherlock Holmes was in 1887, in *A Study in Scarlet*, which was presented as 'a reprint from the reminiscences of John H. Watson, late of the Army Medical Department', and so the happy pairing of the deductive Holmes with the down-to-earth Dr Watson as foil was established. *The Sign of Four* followed in 1890, but Holmes did not really catch the public imagination until the first of the short stories, *A Scandal in Bohemia*, was published in the July issue of the *Strand Magazine* in 1891. These stories were illustrated by the remarkable Sidney Paget, who used his brother Walter as model for 'the tall, spare figure of Holmes', standing before the Baker Street fireplace, looking down on Watson in his 'singular introspective fashion'. It was Paget who equipped Holmes with the famous deerstalker hat, though he never gave him the meerschaum pipe which became an icon following a stage production of one of the stories in the 1920's.

As well as being fast-paced detective stories, the Sherlock Holmes adventures provide a fascinating glimpse into 1890's London. The domestic arrangements at 221b Baker Street are the focal point of the metropolitan civilisation that encompasses November fogs and hansom cabs, frock coats, silk hats and hurried railway journeys on trains that run on time, scandal in high places and murder in low ones.

From textual evidence, Sir Sidney Roberts concluded that Sherlock Holmes was born in 1854 of an English father and a mother descended from a line of French painters. He seems to have been something of an asthete at university, probably Oxford, but certainly not Cambridge. On coming down from university he took rooms near the British Museum to study those sciences relevant to his subsequent career. In 1881, in a laboratory at St Bartholomew's Hospital, he met Dr Watson, and they decided to share the rooms in Baker Street. We know that Holmes refused a knighthood, but he did accept the *Légion d'honneur*. He retired to Sussex and kept bees, but of his life after 1914, there exists no record.

Arthur Conan Doyle was born in Edinburgh in 1859. He was educated at Stonyhurst and Edinburgh University where he qualified as a doctor. He practised at Southsea from 1882-1890, but from that date he devoted himself entirely to writing. Without doubt, the Sherlock Holmes stories are his finest work, but Doyle himself always preferred his other writing, especially the historical romances such as Micah Clarke, Sir Nigel *and* The White Company. *He had considerable success with these, as he did with* The Exploits of Brigadier Gerard *which recount the preposterous adventures of a vainglorious officer of Napoleon's cavalry, and the Professor Challenger stories, the first of which was* The Lost World *(1912). In later years, Doyle's increasing obsession with spiritualism clouded his judgement. He was knighted in 1902 and died in 1930.*

Further reading:
J D Carr: *The Life of Conan Doyle*
R Pearsall: *Conan Doyle: A Biographical Solution*
S C Roberts: *Holmes and Watson*

CONTENTS

Reminiscences of Sherlock Holmes
(1908-13)

The Valley of Fear
(1914-15)

Part I: The Tragedy of Birlstone

Part II: The Scowrers

His Last Bow
(1917)

The Case-Book of Sherlock Holmes
(1921-27)

THE CASE-BOOK
OF SHERLOCK HOLMES

Facsimile from the Strand Magazine
Volumes LXII, LXIII, LXV, LXVII, LXIX, LXXII, and LXXIII
October 1921 – April 1927

"THIS IS AWFUL! YOU DON'T MEAN—YOU DON'T MEAN THAT
I AM SUSPECTED?"

THE STRAND MAGAZINE.

Vol. xxxv   SEPTEMBER, 1908.   No. 213.

A Reminiscence of Mr. Sherlock Holmes.

By ARTHUR CONAN DOYLE.

I.—The Singular Experience of Mr. John Scott Eccles.

 FIND it recorded in my note-book that it was a bleak and windy day towards the end of March in the year 1892. Holmes had received a telegram whilst we sat at our lunch, and he had scribbled a reply. He made no remark, but the matter remained in his thoughts, for he stood in front of the fire afterwards with a thoughtful face, smoking his pipe, and casting an occasional glance at the message. Suddenly he turned upon me with a mischievous twinkle in his eyes.

"I suppose, Watson, we must look upon you as a man of letters," said he. "How do you define the word 'grotesque'?"

"Strange—remarkable," I suggested.

He shook his head at my definition.

"There is surely something more than that," said he; "some underlying suggestion of the tragic and the terrible. If you cast your mind back to some of those narratives with which you have afflicted a long-suffering public, you will recognise how often the grotesque has deepened into the criminal. Think of that little affair of the red-headed men. That was grotesque enough in the outset, and yet it ended in a desperate attempt at robbery. Or, again, there was that most grotesque affair of the five orange pips, which led straight to a murderous conspiracy. The word puts me on the alert."

"Have you it there?" I asked.

He read the telegram aloud.

"Have just had most incredible and grotesque experience. May I consult you?—Scott Eccles, Post Office, Charing Cross."

"Man or woman?" I asked.

"Oh, man, of course. No woman would ever send a reply-paid telegram. She would have come."

"Will you see him?"

"My dear Watson, you know how bored I have been since we locked up Colonel Carruthers. My mind is like a racing engine, tearing itself to pieces because it is not connected up with the work for which it was built. Life is commonplace, the papers are sterile; audacity and romance seem to have passed for ever from the criminal world. Can you ask me, then, whether I am ready to look into any new problem, however trivial it may prove? But here, unless I am mistaken, is our client."

A measured step was heard upon the stairs, and a moment later a stout, tall, grey-whiskered and solemnly respectable person was ushered into the room. His life history was written in his heavy features and pompous manner. From his spats to his gold-rimmed spectacles he was a Conservative, a Churchman, a good citizen, orthodox and conventional to the last degree. But some amazing experience had disturbed his native composure and left its traces in his bristling hair, his flushed, angry cheeks, and his flurried, excited manner. He plunged instantly into his business.

"I have had a most singular and unpleasant experience, Mr. Holmes," said he. "Never in my life have I been placed in such a situation. It is most improper—most outrageous. I must insist upon some explanation." He swelled and puffed in his anger.

"Pray sit down, Mr. Scott Eccles," said Holmes, in a soothing voice. "May I ask, in the first place, why you came to me at all?"

"Well, sir, it did not appear to be a matter which concerned the police, and yet, when you have heard the facts, you must admit that I could not leave it where it was. Private detectives are a class with whom I have absolutely no sympathy, but none the less, having heard your name——"

"Quite so. But, in the second place, why did you not come at once?"

"What do you mean?"

Holmes glanced at his watch.

"It is a quarter-past two," he said. "Your telegram was dispatched about one. But no one can glance at your toilet and attire without seeing that your disturbance dates from the moment of your waking."

Our client smoothed down his unbrushed hair and felt his unshaven chin.

"You are right, Mr. Holmes. I never gave a thought to my toilet. I was only too glad to get out of such a house. But I have been running round making inquiries before I came to you. I went to the house agents, you know, and they said that Mr. Garcia's rent was paid up all right, and that everything was in order at Wistaria Lodge."

"Come, come, sir," said Holmes, laughing. "You are like my friend Dr. Watson, who has a bad habit of telling his stories wrong end foremost. Please arrange your thoughts and let me know, in their due sequence, exactly what those events are which have sent you out unbrushed and unkempt, with dress boots and waistcoat buttoned awry, in search of advice and assistance."

Our client looked down with a rueful face at his own unconventional appearance.

"I HAVE BEEN RUNNING ROUND MAKING INQUIRIES BEFORE I CAME TO YOU."

"I'm sure it must look very bad, Mr. Holmes, and I am not aware that in my whole life such a thing has ever happened before. But I will tell you the whole queer business, and when I have done so you will admit, I am sure, that there has been enough to excuse me."

But his narrative was nipped in the bud. There was a bustle outside, and Mrs. Hudson opened the door to usher in two robust and official-looking men, one of whom was well known to us as Inspector Gregson of Scotland Yard, an energetic, gallant, and, within his limitations, a capable officer. He shook hands with Holmes, and introduced his comrade as Inspector Baynes of the Surrey Constabulary.

"We are hunting together, Mr. Holmes, and our trail lay in this direction." He turned his bulldog eyes upon our visitor. "Are you Mr. John Scott Eccles, of Popham House, Lee?"

"I am."

"We have been following you about all the morning."

"You traced him through the telegram, no doubt," said Holmes.

"Exactly, Mr. Holmes. We picked up the scent at Charing Cross Post Office and came on here."

"But why do you follow me? What do you want?"

"We wish a statement, Mr. Scott Eccles, as to the events which led up to the death last night of Mr. Aloysius Garcia, of Wistaria Lodge, near Esher."

Our client had sat up with staring eyes and every tinge of colour struck from his astonished face.

"Dead? Did you say he was dead?"

"Yes, sir, he is dead."

"But how? An accident?"

"Murder, if ever there was one upon earth."

"Good God! This is awful! You don't mean—you don't mean that I am suspected?"

"A letter of yours was found in the dead man's pocket, and we know by it that you had planned to pass last night at his house."

"So I did."

"Oh, you did, did you?"

Out came the official note-book.

"Wait a bit, Gregson," said Sherlock Holmes. "All you desire is a plain statement, is it not?"

"And it is my duty to warn Mr. Scott Eccles that it may be used against him."

"Mr. Eccles was going to tell us about it when you entered the room. I think, Watson,

a brandy and soda would do him no harm. Now, sir, I suggest that you take no notice of this addition to your audience, and that you proceed with your narrative exactly as you would have done had you never been interrupted."

Our visitor had gulped off the brandy and the colour had returned to his face. With a dubious glance at the inspector's note-book, he plunged at once into his extraordinary statement.

"I am a bachelor," said he, "and, being of a sociable turn, I cultivate a large number of friends. Among these are the family of a retired brewer called Melville, living at Albemarle Mansion, Kensington. It was at his table that I met some weeks ago a young fellow named Garcia. He was, I understood, of Spanish descent and connected in some way with the Embassy. He spoke perfect English, was pleasing in his manners, and as good-looking a man as ever I saw in my life.

"In some way we struck up quite a friendship, this young fellow and I. He seemed to take a fancy to me from the first, and within two days of our meeting he came to see me at Lee. One thing led to another, and it ended in his inviting me out to spend a few days at his house, Wistaria Lodge, between Esher and Oxshott. Yesterday evening I went to Esher to fulfil this engagement.

"He had described his household to me before I went there. He lived with a faithful servant, a countryman of his own, who looked after all his needs. This fellow could speak English and did his housekeeping for him. Then there was a wonderful cook, he said, a half-breed whom he had picked up in his travels, who could serve an excellent dinner. I remember that he remarked what a queer household it was to find in the heart of Surrey, and that I agreed with him, though it has proved a good deal queerer than I thought.

"I drove to the place—about two miles on the south side of Esher. The house was a fair-sized one, standing back from the road, with a curving drive which was banked with high evergreen shrubs. It was an old, tumble-down building in a crazy state of disrepair. When the trap pulled up on the grass-grown drive in front of the blotched and weather-stained door, I had doubts as to my wisdom in visiting a man whom I knew so slightly. He opened the door himself, however, and greeted me with a great show of cordiality. I was handed over to the man-servant, a melancholy, swarthy individual, who led the way, my bag in his hand, to my bedroom. The whole place was depressing. Our dinner was *tête-à-tête*, and though my host did his best to be entertaining, his thoughts seemed to continually wander, and he talked so vaguely and wildly that I could hardly understand him. He continually drummed his fingers on the table, gnawed his nails, and gave other signs of nervous impatience. The dinner itself was neither well served nor well cooked, and the gloomy presence of the taciturn servant did not help to enliven us. I can assure you that many times in the course of the evening I wished that I could invent some excuse which would take me back to Lee.

"One thing comes back to my memory which may have a bearing upon the business that you two gentlemen are investigating. I thought nothing of it at the time. Near the end of dinner a note was handed in by the servant. I noticed that after my host had read it he seemed even more distrait and strange than before. He gave up all pretence of conversation and sat, smoking endless cigarettes, lost in his own thoughts, but he made no remark as to the contents. About eleven I was glad to go to bed. Some time later Garcia looked in at my door—the room was dark at the time—and asked me if I had rung. I said that I had not. He apologized for having disturbed me so late, saying that it was nearly one o'clock. I dropped off after this and slept soundly all night.

"And now I come to the amazing part of my tale. When I awoke it was broad daylight. I glanced at my watch, and the time was nearly nine. I had particularly asked to be called at eight, so I was very much astonished at this forgetfulness. I sprang up and rang for the servant. There was no response. I rang again and again, with the same result. Then I came to the conclusion that the bell was out of order. I huddled on my clothes and hurried downstairs in an exceedingly bad temper to order some hot water. You can imagine my surprise when I found that there was no one there. I shouted in the hall. There was no answer. Then I ran from room to room. All were deserted. My host had shown me which was his bedroom the night before, so I knocked at the door. No reply. I turned the handle and walked in. The room was empty, and the bed had never been slept in. He had gone with the rest. The foreign host, the foreign footman, the foreign cook, all had vanished in the night! That was the end of my visit to Wistaria Lodge."

Sherlock Holmes was rubbing his hands and chuckling as he added this bizarre incident to his collection of strange episodes.

"Your experience is, so far as I know, perfectly unique," said he. "May I ask, sir, what you did then?"

"I was furious. My first idea was that I had been the victim of some absurd practical joke. I packed my things, banged the hall door behind me, and set off for Esher, with my bag in my hand. I called at Allan Brothers', the chief land agents in the village, and found that it was from this firm that the villa had been rented. It struck me that the whole proceeding could hardly be for the purpose of making a fool of me, and that the main object must be to get out of the rent. It is late in March, so quarter-day is at hand. But this theory would not work. The agent was obliged to me for my warning, but told me that the rent had been paid in advance. Then I made my way to town and called at the Spanish Embassy. The man was unknown there. After this I went to see Melville, at whose house I had first met Garcia, but I found that he really knew rather less about him than I did. Finally, when I got your reply to my wire I came out to you, since I understand that you are a person who gives advice in difficult cases. But now, Mr. Inspector, I understand, from what you said when you entered the room, that you can carry the story on, and that some tragedy has occurred. I can assure you that every word I have said is the truth, and that, outside of what I have told you, I know absolutely nothing about the fate of this man. My only desire is to help the law in every possible way."

"I am sure of it, Mr. Scott Eccles—I am sure of it," said Inspector Gregson, in a very amiable tone. "I am bound to say that everything which you have said agrees very closely with the facts as they have come to our notice. For example, there was that note which arrived during dinner. Did you chance to observe what became of it?"

"Yes, I did. Garcia rolled it up and threw it into the fire."

"What do you say to that, Mr. Baynes?"

The country detective was a stout, puffy, red man, whose face was only redeemed from grossness by two extraordinarily bright eyes, almost hidden behind the heavy creases of cheek and brow. With a slow smile he drew a folded and discoloured scrap of paper from his pocket,

"It was a dog-grate, Mr. Holmes, and he overpitched it. I picked this out unburned from the back of it."

Holmes smiled his appreciation.

"You must have examined the house very carefully, to find a single pellet of paper."

right, green baize. God speed. D.' It is a woman's writing, done with a sharp-pointed pen, but the address is either done with another pen or by someone else. It is thicker and bolder, as you see."

"A very remarkable note," said Holmes,

"IT WAS A DOG-GRATE, MR. HOLMES, AND HE OVERPITCHED IT. I PICKED THIS OUT UNBURNED FROM THE BACK OF IT."

"I did, Mr. Holmes. It's my way. Shall I read it, Mr. Gregson?"

The Londoner nodded.

"The note is written upon ordinary cream-laid paper without watermark. It is a quarter sheet. The paper is cut off in two snips with a short-bladed scissors. It has been folded over three times and sealed with purple wax, put on hurriedly and pressed down with some flat, oval object. It is addressed to Mr. Garcia, Wistaria Lodge. It says: 'Our own colours, green and white. Green open, white shut. Main stair, first corridor, seventh

glancing it over. "I must compliment you, Mr. Baynes, upon your attention to detail in your examination of it. A few trifling points might be added. The oval seal is undoubtedly a plain sleeve-link—what else is of such a shape? The scissors were bent nail-scissors. Short as the two snips are, you can distinctly see the same slight curve in each."

The country detective chuckled.

"I thought I had squeezed all the juice out of it, but I see there was a little over," he said. "I'm bound to say that I make nothing of the note except that there was something on hand, and that a woman, as usual, was at the bottom of it."

Mr. Scott Eccles had fidgeted in his seat during this conversation.

"I am glad you found the note, since it corroborates my story," said he. "But I beg to point out that I have not yet heard what has happened to Mr. Garcia, nor what has become of his household."

"As to Garcia," said Gregson, "that is easily answered. He was found dead this morning upon Oxshott Common, nearly a mile from his home. His head had been smashed to pulp by heavy blows of a sand-bag or some such instrument, which had crushed rather than wounded. It is a lonely corner, and there is no house within a quarter of a mile of the spot. He had apparently been struck down first from behind, but his assailant had gone on beating him long after he was dead. It was a most furious assault. There are no foot-steps nor any clue to the criminals."

"Robbed?"

"No, there was no attempt at robbery."

"This is very painful—very painful and terrible," said Mr. Scott Eccles, in a querulous voice; "but it is really uncommonly hard upon me. I had nothing to do with my host going off upon a nocturnal excursion and meeting so sad an end. How do I come to be mixed up with the case?"

"Very simply, sir," Inspector Baynes answered. "The only document found in the pocket of the deceased was a letter from you saying that you would be with him on the night of his death. It was the envelope of this letter which gave us the dead man's name and address. It was after nine this morning when we reached his house and found neither you nor anyone else inside it. I wired to Mr. Gregson to run you down in London while I examined Wistaria Lodge. Then I came into town, joined Mr. Gregson, and here we are."

"I think now," said Gregson, rising, "we had best put this matter into an official shape. You will come round with us to the station, Mr. Scott Eccles, and let us have your state-ment in writing."

"Certainly, I will come at once. But I retain your services, Mr. Holmes. I desire you to spare no expense and no pains to get at the truth."

My friend turned to the country inspector.

"I suppose that you have no objection to my collaborating with you, Mr. Baynes?"

"Highly honoured, sir, I am sure."

"You appear to have been very prompt and businesslike in all that you have done. Was there any clue, may I ask, as to the exact hour that the man met his death?"

"He had been there since one o'clock. There was rain about that time, and his death had certainly been before the rain."

"But that is perfectly impossible, Mr. Baynes," cried our client. "His voice is un-mistakable. I could swear to it that it was he who addressed me in my bedroom at that very hour."

"Remarkable, but by no means impos-sible," said Holmes, smiling.

"You have a clue?" asked Gregson.

"On the face of it the case is not a very complex one, though it certainly presents some novel and interesting features. A further knowledge of facts is necessary before I would venture to give a final and definite opinion. By the way, Mr. Baynes, did you find anything remarkable besides this note in your examination of the house?"

The detective looked at my friend in a singular way.

"There were," said he, "one or two *very* remarkable things. Perhaps when I have finished at the police-station you would care to come out and give me your opinion of them."

"I am entirely at your service," said Sherlock Holmes, ringing the bell. "You will show these gentlemen out, Mrs. Hudson, and kindly send the boy with this telegram. He is to pay a five-shilling reply."

We sat for some time in silence after our visitors had left. Holmes smoked hard, with his brows drawn down over his keen eyes, and his head thrust forward in the eager way characteristic of the man.

"Well, Watson," he asked, turning suddenly upon me, "what do you make of it?"

"I can make nothing of this mystification of Scott Eccles."

"But the crime?"

"Well, taken with the disappearance of the man's companions, I should say that they were in some way concerned in the murder and had fled from justice."

"That is certainly a possible point of view. On the face of it you must admit, however, that it is very strange that his two servants should have been in a conspiracy against him and should have attacked him on the one night when he had a guest. They had him alone at their mercy every other night in the week."

"Then why did they fly?"

"Quite so. Why did they fly? There is

a big fact. Another big fact is the remarkable experience of our client, Scott Eccles. Now, my dear Watson, is it beyond the limits of human ingenuity to furnish an explanation which would cover both these big facts? If it were one which would also admit of the mysterious note with its very curious phraseology, why, then it would be worth accepting as a temporary hypothesis. If the fresh facts which come to our knowledge all fit themselves into the scheme, then our hypothesis may gradually become a solution."

" But what is our hypothesis?"

Holmes leaned back in his chair with half-closed eyes.

"You must admit, my dear Watson, that the idea of a joke is impossible. There were grave events afoot, as the sequel showed, and the coaxing of Scott Eccles to Wistaria Lodge had some connection with them."

"But what possible connection?"

"Let us take it link by link. There is, on the face of it, something unnatural about this strange and sudden friendship between the young Spaniard and Scott Eccles. It was the former who forced the pace. He called upon Eccles at the other end of London on the very day after he first met him, and he kept in close touch with him until he got him down to Esher. Now, what did he want with Eccles? What could Eccles supply? I see no charm in the man. He is not particularly intelligent—not a man likely to be congenial to a quick-witted Latin. Why, then, was he picked out from all the other people whom Garcia met as particularly suited to his purpose? Has he any one outstanding quality? I say that he has. He is the very type of conventional British respectability; and the very man as a witness to impress another Briton. You saw yourself how neither of the inspectors dreamed of questioning his statement, extraordinary as it was."

"But what was he to witness?"

"Nothing, as things turned out, but everything had they gone another way. That is how I read the matter."

"I see, he might have proved an alibi."

"Exactly, my dear Watson; he might have proved an alibi. We will suppose, for argument's sake, that the household of Wistaria Lodge are confederates in some design. The attempt, whatever it may be, is to come off, we will say, before one o'clock. By some juggling of the clocks it is quite possible that they may have got Scott Eccles to bed earlier than he thought, but in any case it is likely that when Garcia went out of his way to tell him that it was one it was

really not more than twelve. If Garcia could do whatever he had to do and be back by the hour mentioned he had evidently a powerful reply to any accusation. Here was this irreproachable Englishman ready to swear in any court of law that the accused was in his house all the time. It was an insurance against the worst."

" Yes, yes, I see that. But how about the disappearance of the others?"

"I have not all my facts yet, but I do not think there are any insuperable difficulties. Still, it is an error to argue in front of your data. You find yourself insensibly twisting them round to fit your theories."

"And the message?"

"How did it run? 'Our own colours, green and white.' Sounds like racing. 'Green open, white shut.' That is clearly a signal. 'Main stair, first corridor, seventh right, green baize.' This is an assignation. We may find a jealous husband at the bottom of it all. It was clearly a dangerous quest. She would not have said 'God speed' had it not been so. 'D.' — that should be a guide."

"The man was a Spaniard. I suggest that 'D' stands for Dolores, a common female name in Spain."

"Good, Watson, very good — but quite inadmissible. A Spaniard would write to a Spaniard in Spanish. The writer of this note is certainly English. Well, we can only possess our souls in patience, until this excellent inspector comes back for us. Meanwhile we can thank our lucky fate which has rescued us for a few short hours from the insufferable fatigues of idleness."

An answer had arrived to Holmes's telegram before our Surrey officer had returned. Holmes read it, and was about to place it in his note-book when he caught a glimpse of my expectant face. He tossed it across with a laugh.

"We are moving in exalted circles," said he.

The telegram was a list of names and addresses: " Lord Harringby, The Dingle; Sir George Ffolliott, Oxshott Towers; Mr. Hynes Hynes, J.P., Purdey Place; Mr. James Baker Williams, Forton Old Hall; Mr. Henderson, High Gable; Rev. Joshua Stone, Nether Walsling."

"This is a very obvious way of limiting our field of operations," said Holmes. "No doubt Baynes, with his methodical mind, has already adopted some similar plan."

" I don't quite understand."

"HE TOSSED IT ACROSS WITH A LAUGH."

"Well, my dear fellow, we have already arrived at the conclusion that the message received by Garcia at dinner was an appointment or an assignation. Now, if the obvious reading of it is correct, and in order to keep this tryst one has to ascend a main stair and seek the seventh door in a corridor, it is perfectly clear that the house is a very large one. It is equally certain that this house cannot be more than a mile or two from Oxshott, since Garcia was walking in that direction, and hoped, according to my reading of the facts, to be back in Wistaria Lodge in time to avail himself of an alibi, which would only be valid up to one o'clock. As the number of large houses close to Oxshott must be limited, I adopted the obvious method of sending to the agents mentioned by Scott Eccles and obtaining a list of them. Here they are in this telegram, and the other end of our tangled skein must lie among them."

It was nearly six o'clock before we found ourselves in the pretty Surrey village of Esher, with Inspector Baynes as our companion.

Holmes and I had taken things for the night, and found comfortable quarters at the Bull. Finally we set out in the company of the detective on our visit to Wistaria Lodge. It was a cold, dark March evening, with a sharp wind and a fine rain beating upon our faces, a fit setting for the wild common over which our road passed and the tragic goal to which it led us.

II. — The Tiger of San Pedro.

A COLD and melancholy walk of a couple of miles brought us to a high wooden gate which opened into a gloomy avenue of chestnuts. The curved and shadowed drive led us to a low, dark house, pitch - black against a slate-coloured sky. From the front window upon the left of the door there peeped the glimmer of a feeble light.

"There's a constable in possession," said Baynes. "I'll knock at the window." He stepped across the grass plot and tapped with his hand on the pane. Through the fogged glass I dimly saw a man spring up from a chair beside the fire, and heard a sharp cry from within the room. An instant later a white - faced, hard-breathing policeman had opened the door, the candle wavering in his trembling hand.

"What's the matter, Walters?" asked Baynes, sharply.

The man mopped his forehead with his handkerchief and gave a long sigh of relief.

"I am glad you have come, sir. It has been a long evening, and I don't think my nerve is as good as it was."

"Your nerve, Walters? I should not have thought you had a nerve in your body."

"Well, sir, it's this lonely, silent house and the queer thing in the kitchen. Then, when you tapped at the window I thought it had come again."

"That what had come again?"

"The devil, sir, for all I know. It was at the window."

"What was at the window, and when?"

"It was about two hours ago. The light was just fading. I was sitting reading in the chair. I don't know what made me look up, but there was a face looking in at me through the lower pane. Lord, sir, what a face it was! I'll see it in my dreams."

"Tut, tut, Walters! This is not talk for a police-constable."

"I know, sir, I know; but it shook me, sir, and there is no use to deny it. It wasn't black, sir, nor was it white, nor any colour that I know, but a kind of queer shade like clay with a splash of milk in it. Then there was the size of it—it was twice yours, sir. And the look of it—the great staring goggle eyes, and the line of white teeth like a hungry beast. I tell you, sir, I couldn't move a finger, nor get my breath, till it whisked away and was gone. Out I ran, and through the shrubbery, but thank God there was no one there."

"If I didn't know you were a good man, Walters, I should put a black mark against you for this. If it *were* the devil himself, a constable on duty should never thank God that he could not lay his hands upon him. I suppose the whole thing is not a vision and a touch of nerves?"

"That at least is very easily settled," said Holmes, lighting his little pocket lantern. "Yes," he reported, after a short examination of the grass bed, "a number twelve shoe, I should say. If he was all on the same scale as his foot he must certainly have been a giant."

"What became of him?"

"He seems to have broken through the shrubbery and made for the road."

"Well," said the inspector, with a grave and thoughtful face, "whoever he may have been, and whatever he may have wanted, he's gone for the present, and we have more immediate things to attend to. Now, Mr. Holmes, with your permission, I will show you round the house."

The various bedrooms and sitting-rooms

"'VERY INTERESTING INDEED,' SAID HOLMES,"

754

'THERE WAS A FACE LOOKING IN AT ME THROUGH THE LOWER PANE.'

"Look at this," said Baynes. "What do you make of it?"

He held up his candle before an extraordinary object which stood at the back of the dresser. It was so wrinkled and shrunken and withered that it was difficult to say what it might have been. One could but say that it was black and leathery, and that it bore some resemblance to a dwarfish human figure. At first, as I examined it, I thought that it was a mummified negro baby, and then it seemed a very twisted and ancient monkey. Finally, I was left in doubt as to whether it was animal or human. A double band of white shells was strung round the centre of it.

had yielded nothing to a careful search. Apparently the tenants had brought little or nothing with them, and all the furniture down to the smallest details had been taken over with the house. A good deal of clothing with the stamp of Marx and Co., High Holborn, had been left behind. Telegraphic inquiries had been already made which showed that Marx knew nothing of his customer save that he was a good payer. Odds and ends, some pipes, a few novels, two of them in Spanish, an old-fashioned pinfire revolver, and a guitar were amongst the personal property.

"Nothing in all this," said Baynes, stalking, candle in hand, from room to room. "But now, Mr. Holmes, I invite your attention to the kitchen."

It was a gloomy, high-ceilinged room at the back of the house, with a straw litter in one corner, which served apparently as a bed for the cook. The table was piled with half-eaten dishes and dirty plates, the *débris* of last night's dinner.

"Very interesting — very interesting indeed!" said Holmes, peering at this sinister relic. "Anything more?"

In silence Baynes led the way to the sink and held forward his candle. The limbs and body of some large white bird, torn savagely to pieces with the feathers still on, were littered all over it. Holmes pointed to the wattles on the severed head.

"A white cock," said he; "most interesting! It is really a very curious case."

But Mr. Baynes had kept his most sinister exhibit to the last. From under the sink he drew a zinc pail which contained a quantity of blood. Then from the table he took a platter heaped with small pieces of charred bone.

"Something has been killed and something has been burned. We raked all these out of the fire. We had a doctor in this morning. He says that they are not human."

Holmes smiled and rubbed his hands.

"I must congratulate you, inspector, on handling so distinctive and instructive a case.

Your powers, if I may say so without offence, seem superior to your opportunities."

Inspector Baynes's small eyes twinkled with pleasure.

"You're right, Mr. Holmes. We stagnate in the provinces. A case of this sort gives a man a chance, and I hope that I shall take it. What do you make of these bones?"

"A lamb, I should say, or a kid."

"And the white cock?"

"Curious, Mr. Baynes, very curious. I should say almost unique."

"Yes, sir, there must have been some very strange people with some very strange ways in this house. Did his companions follow him and kill him? If they did we should have them, for every port is watched. But my own views are different. Yes, sir, my own views are very different."

"You have a theory, then?"

"And I'll work it myself, Mr. Holmes. It's only

due to my own credit to do so. Your name is made, but I have still to make mine. I should be glad to be able to say afterwards that I had solved it without your help."

Holmes laughed good-humouredly.

"Well, well, inspector," said he. "Do you follow your path and I will follow mine. My results are always very much at your service if you care to apply to me for them. I think that I have seen all that I wish in this house, and that my time may be more profitably employed elsewhere. *Au revoir* and good luck!"

I could tell by numerous subtle signs, which might have been lost upon anyone but myself, that Holmes was on a hot scent.

"FROM UNDER THE SINK HE DREW A ZINC PAIL."

As impassive as ever to the casual observer, there were none the less a subdued eagerness and a suggestion of tension in his brightened eyes and brisker manner which assured me that the game was afoot. After his habit he said nothing, and after mine I asked no questions. Sufficient for me to share the sport and lend my humble help to the capture without distracting that intent brain with needless interruption. All would come round to me in due time.

I waited, therefore — but, to my ever-deepening disappointment, I waited in vain. Day succeeded day, and my friend took no step forward. One morning he spent in town, and I learned from a casual reference that he had visited the British Museum. Save for this one excursion, he spent his days in long, and often solitary, walks, or in chatting with a number of village gossips whose acquaintance he had cultivated.

" I'm sure, Watson, a week in the country will be invaluable to you," he remarked. " It is very pleasant to see the first green shoots upon the hedges and the catkins on the hazels once again. With a spud, a tin box, and an elementary book on botany, there are instructive days to be spent." He prowled about with this equipment himself, but it was a poor show of plants which he would bring back of an evening.

Occasionally in our rambles we came across Inspector Baynes. His fat, red face wreathed itself in smiles and his small eyes glittered as he greeted my companion. He said little about the case, but from that little we gathered that he also was not dissatisfied at the course of events. I must admit, however, that I was somewhat surprised when, some five days after the crime, I opened my morning paper to find in large letters :—

" THE OXSHOTT MYSTERY.
A SOLUTION.
ARREST OF SUPPOSED ASSASSIN."

Holmes sprang in his chair as if he had been stung when I read the head-lines.

" By Jove!" he cried. " You don't mean that Baynes has got him ? "

" Apparently," said I, as I read the following report :—

" Great excitement was caused in Esher and the neighbouring district when it was learned late last night that an arrest had been effected in connection with the Oxshott murder. It will be remembered that Mr. Garcia, of Wistaria Lodge, was found dead on Oxshott Common, his body showing signs of extreme violence, and that on the same night his servant and his cook fled, which appeared to show their participation in the crime. It was suggested, but never proved, that the deceased gentleman may have had valuables in the house, and that their abstraction was the motive of the crime. Every effort was made by Inspector Baynes, who has the case in hand, to ascertain the hiding-place of the fugitives, and he had good reason to believe that they had not gone far, but were lurking in some retreat which had been already prepared. It was certain from the first, however, that they would eventually be detected, as the cook, from the evidence of one or two tradespeople who have caught a glimpse of him through the window, was a man of most remarkable appearance—being a huge and hideous mulatto, with yellowish features of a pronounced negroid type. This man has been seen since the crime, for he was detected and pursued by Constable Walters on the same evening, when he had the audacity to revisit Wistaria Lodge. Inspector Baynes, considering that such a visit must have some purpose in view, and was likely therefore to be repeated, abandoned the house, but left an ambuscade in the shrubbery. The man walked into the trap, and was captured last night after a struggle, in which Constable Downing was badly bitten by the savage. We understand that when the prisoner is brought before the magistrates a remand will be applied for by the police, and that great developments are hoped from his capture."

" Really we must see Baynes at once," cried Holmes, picking up his hat. " We will just catch him before he starts." We hurried down the village street and found, as we had expected, that the inspector was just leaving his lodgings.

" You've seen the paper, Mr. Holmes ? " he asked, holding one out to us.

" Yes, Baynes, I've seen it. Pray don't think it a liberty if I give you a word of friendly warning."

" Of warning, Mr. Holmes ? "

" I have looked into this case with some care, and I am not convinced that you are on the right lines. I don't want you to commit yourself too far, unless you are sure."

" You're very kind, Mr. Holmes."

" I assure you I speak for your good."

It seemed to me that something like a wink quivered for an instant over one of Mr. Baynes's tiny eyes.

" We agreed to work on our own lines, Mr. Holmes. That's what I am doing."

" Oh, very good," said Holmes. " Don't blame me,"

"No, sir; I believe you mean well by me. But we all have our own systems, Mr. Holmes. You have yours, and maybe I have mine."

"Let us say no more about it."

"You're welcome always to my news. This fellow is a perfect savage, as strong as a cart-horse and as fierce as the devil. He chewed Downing's thumb nearly off before they could master him. He hardly speaks a word of English, and we can get nothing out of him but grunts."

"And you think you have evidence that he murdered his late master?"

"I didn't say so, Mr. Holmes; I didn't say so. We all have our little ways. You try yours and I will try mine. That's the agreement."

Holmes shrugged his shoulders

"THE MAN WALKED INTO THE TRAP AND WAS CAPTURED."

as we walked away together. "I can't make the man out. He seems to be riding for a fall. Well, as he says, we must each try our own way and see what comes of it. But there's something in Inspector Baynes which I can't quite understand."

"Just sit down in that chair, Watson," said Sherlock Holmes, when we had returned to our apartment at the Bull. "I want to put you in touch with the situation, as I may need your help to-night. Let me show you the evolution of this case, so far as I have been able to follow it. Simple as it has been in its leading features, it has none the less presented surprising difficulties in the way of an arrest. There are gaps in that direction which we have still to fill.

"We will go back to the note which was handed in to Garcia upon the evening of his death. We may put aside this idea of Baynes's that Garcia's servants were concerned in the matter. The proof of this lies in the fact that it was *he* who had arranged for the presence of Scott Eccles, which could only have been done for the purpose of an alibi. It was Garcia, then, who had an enterprise, and apparently a criminal enterprise, in hand that night, in the course of which he met his death. I say criminal because only a man with a criminal enterprise desires to establish an alibi. Who, then, is most likely to have taken his life? Surely the person against whom the criminal enterprise was directed. So far it seems to me that we are on safe ground,

"We can now see a reason for the disappearance of Garcia's household. They were *all* confederates in the same unknown crime. If it came off then Garcia returned, any possible suspicion would be warded off by the Englishman's evidence, and all would be well. But the attempt was a dangerous one, and if Garcia did *not* return by a certain hour it was probable that his own life had been sacrificed. It had been arranged, therefore, that in such a case his two subordinates were to make for some prearranged spot, where they could escape investigation and be in a position afterwards to renew their attempt. That would fully explain the facts, would it not?"

The whole inexplicable tangle seemed to straighten out before me. I wondered, as I always did, how it had not been obvious to me before.

"But why should one servant return?"

"We can imagine that, in the confusion of flight, something precious, something which he could not bear to part with, had been left behind. That would explain his persistence, would it not?"

"Well, what is the next step?"

"The next step is the note received by Garcia at the dinner. It indicates a confederate at the other end. Now, where was the other end? I have already shown you that it could only lie in some large house, and that the number of large houses is limited. My first days in this village were devoted to a series of walks, in which in the intervals of my botanical researches I made a reconnaissance of all the large houses and an examination of the family history of the occupants. One house, and only one, riveted my attention. It is the famous old Jacobean grange of High Gable, one mile on the farther side of Oxshott, and less than half a mile from the scene of the tragedy. The other mansions belonged to prosaic and respectable people who live far aloof from romance. But Mr. Henderson, of High Gable, was by all accounts a curious man, to whom curious adventures might befall. I concentrated my attention, therefore, upon him and his household.

"A singular set of people, Watson—the man himself the most singular of them all. I managed to see him on a plausible pretext, but I seemed to read in his dark, deep-set, brooding eyes that he was perfectly aware of my true business. He is a man of fifty, strong, active, with iron-grey hair, great bunched black eyebrows, the step of a deer, and the air of an emperor—a fierce, master-ful man, with a red-hot spirit behind his parchment face. He is either a foreigner or has lived long in the Tropics, for he is yellow and sapless, but tough as whipcord. His friend and secretary, Mr. Lucas, is undoubtedly a foreigner, chocolate brown, wily, suave, and cat-like, with a poisonous gentleness of speech. You see, Watson, we have come already upon two sets of foreigners—one at Wistaria Lodge and one at High Gable—so our gaps are beginning to close.

"These two men, close and confidential friends, are the centre of the household; but there is one other person, who for our immediate purpose may be even more important. Henderson has two children—girls of eleven and thirteen. Their governess is a Miss Burnet, an Englishwoman of forty or thereabouts. There is also one confidential man-servant. This little group forms the real family, for they travel about together, and Henderson is a great traveller, always on the move. It is only within the last few weeks that he has returned, after a year's absence, to High Gable. I may add that he is enormously rich, and whatever his whims may be he can very easily satisfy them. For the rest, his house is full of butlers, footmen, maid-servants, and the usual overfed, underworked staff of a large English country-house.

"So much I learned partly from village gossip and partly from my own observation. There are no better instruments than discharged servants with a grievance, and I was lucky enough to find one. I call it luck, but it would not have come my way had I not been looking out for it. As Baynes remarks, we all have our systems. It was my system which enabled me to find John Warner, late gardener of High Gable, sacked in a moment of temper by his imperious employer. He in turn had friends among the indoor servants, who unite in their fear and dislike of their master. So I had my key to the secrets of the establishment.

"Curious people, Watson! I don't pretend to understand it all yet, but very curious people anyway. It's a double-winged house, and the servants live on one side, the family on the other. There's no link between the two save for Henderson's own servant, who serves the family's meals. Everything is carried to a certain door, which forms the one connection. Governess and children hardly go out at all, except into the garden. Henderson never by any chance walks alone. His dark secretary is like his shadow. The gossip among the servants is that their master is terribly afraid of something. 'Sold his soul to the devil in exchange for money,' says Warner, 'and expects his creditor to come up and claim his own.' Where they came from or who they are nobody has an idea. They are very violent. Twice Henderson has lashed at folk with his dog-whip, and only his long purse and heavy compensation have kept him out of the courts.

"Well, now, Watson, let us judge the situation by this new information. We may take it that the letter came out of this strange household, and was an invitation to Garcia to carry out some attempt which had already been planned. Who wrote the note? It was someone within the citadel, and it was a woman. Who, then, but Miss Burnet, the governess? All our reasoning seems to point that way. At any rate, we may take it as a hypothesis, and see what consequences it would entail. I may add that Miss Burnet's age and character make it certain that my first idea that there might be a love interest in our story is out of the question.

"If she wrote the note she was presumably the friend and confederate of Garcia. What, then, might she be expected to do if she heard of his death? If he met it in some nefarious enterprise her lips might be sealed. Still, in her heart she must retain bitterness and hatred against those who had killed him, and would presumably help so far as she could to have revenge upon them. Could we see her, then, and try to use her? That was my first thought. But now we come to a sinister fact. Miss Burnet has not been seen by any human eye since the night of the murder. From that evening she has utterly vanished. Is she alive? Has she perhaps met her end on the same night as the friend whom she had summoned? Or is she merely a prisoner? There is the point which we still have to decide.

"You will appreciate the difficulty of the situation, Watson. There is nothing upon which we can apply for a warrant. Our whole scheme might seem fantastic if laid before a magistrate. The woman's disappearance counts for nothing, since in that extraordinary household any member of it might be invisible for a week. And yet she may at the present moment be in danger of her life. All I can do is to watch the house and leave my agent, Warner, on guard at the gates. We can't let such a situation continue. If the law can do nothing we must take the risk ourselves."

"What do you suggest?"

"I know which is her room. It is accessible from the top of an outhouse. My suggestion is that you and I go to-night and see if we can strike at the very heart of the mystery."

It was not, I must confess, a very alluring prospect. The old house with its atmosphere of murder, the singular and formidable inhabitants, the unknown dangers of the approach, and the fact that we were putting ourselves legally in a false position, all combined to damp my ardour. But there was something in the ice-cold reasoning of Holmes which made it impossible to shrink from any adventure which he might recommend. One knew that thus, and only thus, could a solution be found. I clasped his hand in silence, and the die was cast.

But it was not destined that our investigation should have so adventurous an ending. It was about five o'clock, and the shadows of the March evening were beginning to fall, when an excited rustic rushed into our room.

"They've gone, Mr. Holmes. They went by the last train. The lady broke away, and I've got her in a cab downstairs."

"Excellent, Warner!" cried Holmes, springing to his feet. "Watson, the gaps are closing rapidly."

In the cab was a woman, half-collapsed from nervous exhaustion. She bore upon her aquiline and emaciated face the traces of some recent tragedy. Her head hung listlessly upon her breast, but as she raised it and turned her dull eyes upon us I saw that her pupils were dark dots in the centre of the broad grey iris. She was drugged with opium.

"I watched at the gate, same as you advised, Mr. Holmes," said our emissary, the discharged gardener. "When the carriage came out I followed it to the station. She was like one walking in her sleep; but when they tried to get her into the train she came to life and struggled. They pushed her into the carriage. She fought her way out again. I took her part, got her into a cab, and here we are. I sha'n't forget the face at the carriage window as I led her away. I'd have a short life if he had his way—the black-eyed, scowling yellow devil."

We carried her upstairs, laid her on the sofa, and a couple of cups of the strongest coffee soon cleared her brain from the mists of the drug. Baynes had been summoned by Holmes, and the situation rapidly explained to him.

"Why, sir, you've got me the very evidence I want," said the inspector, warmly, shaking

"SHE FOUGHT HER WAY OUT AGAIN."

"You will rise high in your profession. You have instinct and intuition," said he.

Baynes flushed with pleasure.

"I've had a plain-clothes man waiting at the station all the week. Wherever the High Gable folk go he will keep them in sight. But he must have been hard put to it when Miss Burnet broke away. However, your man picked her up, and it all ends well. We can't arrest without her evidence, that is clear, so the sooner we get a statement the better."

"Every minute she gets stronger," said Holmes, glancing at the governess. "But tell me, Baynes, who is this man Henderson?"

"Henderson," the inspector answered, "is Don Murillo, once called the Tiger of San Pedro."

The Tiger of San Pedro! The whole history of the man came back to me in a flash. He had made his name as the most lewd and bloodthirsty tyrant that had ever governed any country with a pretence to civilization. Strong, fearless, and energetic, he had sufficient virtue to enable him to impose his odious vices upon a cowering people for ten or twelve years. His name was a terror through all Central America. At the end of that time there was a universal rising against him. But he was as cunning as he was cruel, and at the first whisper of coming trouble he had secretly conveyed his treasures aboard a ship which was manned by devoted adherents. It was an empty palace which was stormed by the insurgents next day. The Dictator, his two children, his secretary, and his wealth had all escaped them. From that moment he had vanished from the world, and his identity had been a

my friend by the hand. "I was on the same scent as you from the first."

"What! You were after Henderson?"

"Why, Mr. Holmes, when you were crawling in the shrubbery at High Gable I was up one of the trees in the plantation and saw you down below. It was just who would get his evidence first."

"Then why did you arrest the mulatto?"

Baynes chuckled.

"I was sure Henderson, as he calls himself, felt that he was suspected, and that he would lie low and make no move so long as he thought he was in any danger. I arrested the wrong man to make him believe that our eyes were off him. I knew he would be likely to clear off then and give us a chance of getting at Miss Burnet."

Holmes laid his hand upon the inspector's shoulder.

frequent subject for comment in the European Press.

"Yes, sir; Don Murillo, the Tiger of San Pedro," said Baynes. "If you look it up you will find that the San Pedro colours are green and white, same as in the note, Mr. Holmes. Henderson he called himself, but I traced him back, Paris and Rome and Madrid to Barcelona, where his ship came in in '86. They've been looking for him all the time for their revenge, but it is only now that they have begun to find him out."

"They discovered him a year ago," said Miss Burnet, who had sat up and was now intently following the conversation. "Once already his life has been attempted; but some evil spirit shielded him. Now, again, it is the noble, chivalrous Garcia who has fallen, while the monster goes safe. But another will come, and yet another, until some day justice will be done; that is as certain as the rise of to-morrow's sun." Her thin hands clenched, and her worn face blanched with the passion of her hatred.

"But how come you into this matter, Miss Burnet?" asked Holmes. "How can an English lady join in such a murderous affair?"

"I join in it because there is no other way in the world by which justice can be gained. What does the law of England care for the rivers of blood shed years ago in San Pedro, or for the ship-load of treasure which this man has stolen? To you they are like crimes committed in some other planet. But *we* know. We have learned the truth in sorrow and in suffering. To us there is no fiend in hell like Juan Murillo, and no peace in life while his victims still cry for vengeance."

"No doubt," said Holmes, "he was as you say. I have heard that he was atrocious. But how are you affected?"

"I will tell you it all. This villain's policy was to murder, on one pretext or another, every man who showed such promise that he might in time come to be a dangerous rival. My husband—yes, my real name is Signora Victor Durando — was the San Pedro Minister in London. He met me and married me there. A nobler man never lived upon earth. Unhappily, Murillo heard of his excellence, recalled him on some pretext, and had him shot. With a premonition of his fate he had refused to take me with him. His estates were confiscated, and I was left with a pittance and a broken heart.

"Then came the downfall of the tyrant. He escaped as you have just described. But the many whose lives he had ruined, whose nearest and dearest had suffered torture and death at his hands, would not let the matter rest. They banded themselves into a society which should never be dissolved until the work was done. It was my part, after we had discovered in the transformed Henderson the fallen despot, to attach myself to his household and keep the others in touch with his movements. This I was able to do by securing the position of governess in his family. He little knew that the woman who faced him at every meal was the woman whose husband he had hurried at an hour's notice into eternity. I smiled on him, did my duty to his children, and bided my time. An attempt was made in Paris, and failed. We zigzagged swiftly here and there over Europe, to throw off the pursuers, and finally returned to this house, which he had taken upon his first arrival in England.

"But here also the ministers of justice were waiting. Knowing that he would return there, Garcia, who is the son of the former highest dignitary in San Pedro, was waiting with two trusty companions of humble station, all three fired with the same reasons for revenge. He could do little during the day, for Murillo took every precaution, and never went out save with his satellite Lucas, or Lopez as he was known in the days of his greatness. At night, however, he slept alone, and the avenger might find him. On a certain evening, which had been prearranged, I sent my friend final instructions, for the man was for ever on the alert, and continually changed his room. I was to see that the doors were open, and the signal of a green or white light in a window which faced the drive was to give notice if all was safe, or if the attempt had better be postponed.

"But everything went wrong with us. In some way I had excited the suspicion of Lopez, the secretary. He crept up behind me, and sprang upon me just as I had finished the note. He and his master dragged me to my room, and held judgment upon me as a convicted traitress. Then and there they would have plunged their knives into me, could they have seen how to escape the consequences of the deed. Finally, after much debate, they concluded that my murder was too dangerous. But they determined to get rid for ever of Garcia. They had gagged me, and Murillo twisted my arm round until I gave him the address. I swear that he might have twisted it off had I understood what it would mean to Garcia.

"HE AND HIS MASTER DRAGGED ME TO MY ROOM."

Lopez addressed the note which I had written, sealed it with his sleeve-link, and sent it by the hand of the servant, José. How they murdered him I do not know, save that it was Murillo's hand who struck him down, for Lopez had remained to guard me. I believe he must have waited among the gorse bushes through which the path winds and struck him down as he passed. At first they were of a mind to let him enter the house and to kill him as a detected burglar; but they argued that if they were mixed up in an inquiry their own identity would at once be publicly disclosed and they would be open to further attacks. With the death of Garcia the pursuit might cease, since

such a death might frighten others from the task.

"All would now have been well for them had it not been for my knowledge of what they had done. I have no doubt that there were times when my life hung in the balance. I was confined to my room, terrorized by the most horrible threats, cruelly ill-used to break my spirit—see this stab on my shoulder and the bruises from end to end of my arms—and a gag was thrust into my mouth on the one occasion when I tried to call from the window. For five days this cruel imprisonment continued, with hardly enough food to hold body and soul together. This afternoon a good lunch was brought me, but the moment after I took it I knew that I had been drugged. In a sort of dream I remember being half-led, half-carried to the carriage; in the same state I was conveyed to the train. Only then, when the wheels were almost moving, did I suddenly realize that my liberty lay in my own hands. I sprang out, they tried to drag me back, and had it not been for the help of this good man, who led me to the cab, I should never have broken away. Now, thank God, I am beyond their power for ever."

We had all listened intently to this remarkable statement. It was Holmes who broke the silence.

"Our difficulties are not over," he remarked, shaking his head. "Our police work ends, but our legal work begins."

"Exactly," said I., "A plausible lawyer could make it out as an act of self-defence. There may be a hundred crimes in the background, but it is only on this one that they can be tried."

"Come, come," said Baynes, cheerily; "I think better of the law than that. Self-defence is one thing. To entice a man in cold blood with the object of murdering him is another, whatever danger you may fear from him. No, no; we shall all be justified when we see the tenants of High Gable at the next Guildford Assizes."

It is a matter of history, however, that a little time was still to elapse before the Tiger of San Pedro should meet with his deserts. Wily and bold, he and his companion threw their pursuer off their track by entering a lodging-house in Edmonton Street and leaving by the back-gate into Curzon Square. From that day they were seen no more in England. Some six months afterwards the Marquess of Montalva and Signor Rulli, his secretary, were both murdered in their rooms at the Hotel Escurial at Madrid. The crime was ascribed to Nihilism, and the murderers were never arrested. Inspector Baynes visited us at Baker Street with a printed description of the dark face of the secretary, and of the masterful features, the magnetic black eyes, and the tufted brows of his master. We could not doubt that justice, if belated, had come at last.

"A chaotic case, my dear Watson," said Holmes, over an evening pipe. "It will not be possible for you to present it in that compact form which is dear to your heart. It covers two continents, concerns two groups of mysterious persons, and is further complicated by the highly respectable presence of our friend Scott Eccles, whose inclusion shows me that the deceased Garcia had a scheming mind and a well-developed instinct of self-preservation. It is remarkable only for the fact that amid a perfect jungle of possibilities we, with our worthy collaborator the inspector, have kept our close hold on the essentials and so been guided along the crooked and winding path. Is there any point which is not quite clear to you?"

"The object of the mulatto cook's return?"

"I think that the strange creature in the kitchen may account for it. The man was a primitive savage from the backwoods of San Pedro, and this was his fetish. When his companion and he had fled to some prearranged retreat—already occupied, no doubt, by a confederate—the companion had persuaded him to leave so compromising an article of furniture. But the mulatto's heart was with it, and he was driven back to it next day, when, on reconnoitring through the window, he found policeman Walters in possession. He waited three days longer, and then his piety or his superstition drove him to try once more. Inspector Baynes, who, with his usual astuteness, had minimized the incident before me, had really recognised its importance, and had left a trap into which the creature walked. Any other point, Watson?"

"The torn bird, the pail of blood, the charred bones, all the mystery of that weird kitchen?"

Holmes smiled as he turned up an entry in his note-book.

"I spent a morning in the British Museum reading up that and other points. Here is a quotation from Eckermann's 'Voodooism and the Negroid Religions':—

"'The true Voodoo-worshipper attempts nothing of importance without certain sacrifices which are intended to propitiate his unclean gods. In extreme cases these rites take the form of human sacrifices followed by cannibalism. The more usual victims are a white cock, which is plucked in pieces alive, or a black goat, whose throat is cut and body burned.'

"So you see our savage friend was very orthodox in his ritual. It is grotesque, Watson," Holmes added, as he slowly fastened his note-book; "but, as I have had occasion to remark, there is but one step from the grotesque to the horrible."

The Adventure of the Bruce=Partington Plans.

N the third week of November, in the year 1895, a dense yellow fog settled down upon London. From the Monday to the Thursday I doubt whether it was ever possible from our windows in Baker Street to see the loom of the opposite houses. The first day Holmes had spent in cross-indexing his huge book of references. The second and third had been patiently occupied upon a subject which he had recently made his hobby—the music of the Middle Ages. But when, for the fourth time, after pushing back our chairs from breakfast we saw the greasy, heavy brown swirl still drifting past us and condensing in oily drops upon the window-panes, my comrade's impatient and active nature could endure this drab existence no longer. He paced restlessly about our sitting-room in a fever of suppressed energy, biting his nails, tapping the furniture, and chafing against inaction.

"Nothing of interest in the paper, Watson?" he asked.

I was aware that by anything of interest Holmes meant anything of criminal interest. There was the news of a revolution, of a possible war, and of an impending change of Government ; but these did not come within the horizon of my companion. I could see nothing recorded in the shape of crime which was not commonplace and futile. Holmes groaned and resumed his restless meanderings.

"The London criminal is certainly a dull fellow," said he, in the querulous voice of the sportsman whose game has failed him. "Look out of this window, Watson. See how the figures loom up, are dimly seen, and then blend once more into the cloud-bank. The thief or the murderer could roam London on such a day as the tiger does the jungle, unseen until he pounces, and then evident only to his victim."

"There have," said I, "been numerous petty thefts."

Holmes snorted his contempt.

"This great and sombre stage is set for something more worthy than that," said he. "It is fortunate for this community that I am not a criminal."

"It is indeed !" said I, heartily.

"Suppose that I were Brooks or Woodhouse, or any of the fifty men who have good reason for taking my life, how long could I survive against my own pursuit? A summons, a bogus appointment, and all would be over. It is well they don't have days of fog in the Latin countries—the countries of assassination. By Jove ! here comes something at last to break our dead monotony."

It was the maid with a telegram. Holmes tore it open and burst out laughing.

"Well, well ! What next ?" said he. "Brother Mycroft is coming round."

"Why not ?" I asked.

"Why not ? It is as if you met a tram-car coming down a country lane. Mycroft has his rails and he runs on them. His Pall Mall lodgings, the Diogenes Club, Whitehall—that is his cycle. Once, and only once, he has been here. What upheaval can possibly have derailed him ?"

"Does he not explain ?"

Holmes handed me his brother's telegram.

"Must see you over Cadogan West. Coming at once—MYCROFT."

"Cadogan West ? I have heard the name."

"It recalls nothing to my mind. But that Mycroft should break out in this erratic fashion ! A planet might as well leave its orbit. By the way, do you know what Mycroft is ?"

I had some vague recollection of an explanation at the time of the Adventure of the Greek Interpreter.

"You told me that he had some small office under the British Government."

Holmes chuckled.

"I did not know you quite so well in those days. One has to be discreet when one talks of high matters of State. You are right in thinking that he is under the British

Government. You would also be right in a sense if you said that occasionally he *is* the British Government."

"My dear Holmes!"

"I thought I might surprise you. Mycroft draws four hundred and fifty pounds a year, remains a subordinate, has no ambitions of any kind, will receive neither honour nor title, but remains the most indispensable man in the country."

"But how?"

"Well, his position is unique. He has made it for himself. There has never been anything like it before, nor will be again. He has the tidiest and most orderly brain, with the greatest capacity for storing facts, of any man living. The same great powers which I have turned to the detection of crime he has used for this particular business. The conclusions of every department are passed to him, and he is the central exchange, the clearing-house, which makes out the balance. All other men are specialists, but his specialism is omniscience. We will suppose that a Minister needs information as to a point which involves the Navy, India, Canada, and the bimetallic question; he could get his separate advices from various departments upon each, but only Mycroft can focus them all, and say offhand how each factor would affect the other. They began by using him as a short-cut, a convenience; now he has made himself an essential. In that great brain of his everything is pigeon-holed, and can be handed out in an instant. Again and again his word has decided the national policy. He lives in it. He thinks of nothing else save when, as an intellectual exercise, he unbends if I call upon him and ask him to advise me on one of my little problems. But Jupiter is descending to-day. What on earth can it mean? Who is Cadogan West, and what is he to Mycroft?"

"I have it!" I cried, and plunged among the litter of papers upon the sofa. "Yes, yes, here he is, sure enough! Cadogan West was the young man who was found dead on the Underground on Tuesday morning."

Holmes sat up at attention, his pipe half-way to his lips.

"This must be serious, Watson. A death which has caused my brother to alter his habits can be no ordinary one. What in the world can he have to do with it? The case was featureless as I remember it. The young man had apparently fallen out of the train and killed himself. He had not been robbed, and there was no particular reason to suspect violence. Is that not so?"

"There has been an inquest," said I, "and a good many fresh facts have come out. Looked at more closely, I should certainly say that it was a curious case."

"Judging by its effect upon my brother, I should think it must be a most extraordinary one." He snuggled down in his arm-chair. "Now, Watson, let us have the facts."

"The man's name was Arthur Cadogan West. He was twenty-seven years of age, unmarried, and a clerk at Woolwich Arsenal."

"Government employ. Behold the link with brother Mycroft!"

"He left Woolwich suddenly on Monday night. Was last seen by his *fiancée*, Miss Violet Westbury, whom he left abruptly in the fog about 7.30 that evening. There was no quarrel between them and she can give no motive for his action. The next thing heard of him was when his dead body was discovered by a plate-layer named Mason, just outside Aldgate Station on the Underground system in London."

"When?"

"The body was found at six on the Tuesday morning. It was lying wide of the metals upon the left hand of the track as one goes eastward, at a point close to the station, where the line emerges from the tunnel in which it runs. The head was badly crushed—an injury which might well have been caused by a fall from the train. The body could only have come on the line in that way. Had it been carried down from any neighbouring street, it must have passed the station barriers, where a collector is always standing. This point seems absolutely certain."

"Very good. The case is definite enough. The man, dead or alive, either fell or was precipitated from a train. So much is clear to me. Continue."

"The trains which traverse the lines of rail beside which the body was found are those which run from west to east, some being purely Metropolitan, and some from Willesden and outlying junctions. It can be stated for certain that this young man, when he met his death, was travelling in this direction at some late hour of the night, but at what point he entered the train it is impossible to state."

"His ticket, of course, would show that."

"There was no ticket in his pockets."

"No ticket! Dear me, Watson, this is really very singular. According to my experience it is not possible to reach the platform of a Metropolitan train without exhibiting one's ticket. Presumably, then, the young man had one. Was it taken from him in order to conceal the station from which he came? It is possible. Or did he drop it in the carriage? That also is possible. But the point is of curious interest. I understand that there was no sign of robbery?"

"Apparently not. There is a list here of his possessions. His purse contained two pounds fifteen. He had also a cheque-book on the Woolwich branch of the Capital and Counties Bank. Through this his identity was established. There were also two dress-circle tickets for the Woolwich Theatre, dated for that very evening. Also a small packet of technical papers."

Holmes gave an exclamation of satisfaction.

"There we have it at last, Watson! British Government—Woolwich Arsenal— Technical papers—Brother Mycroft, the chain is complete. But here he comes, if I am not mistaken, to speak for himself."

A moment later the tall and portly form of Mycroft Holmes was ushered into the room. Heavily built and massive, there was a suggestion of uncouth physical inertia in the figure, but above this unwieldy frame there was perched a head so masterful in its brow, so alert in its steel-grey, deep-set eyes, so firm in its lips, and so subtle in its play of expression, that after the first glance one forgot the gross body and remembered only the dominant mind.

At his heels came our old friend Lestrade, of Scotland Yard—thin and austere. The gravity of both their faces foretold some weighty quest. The detective shook hands without a word. Mycroft Holmes struggled out of his overcoat and subsided into an arm-chair.

"A most annoying business, Sherlock," said he. "I extremely dislike altering my habits, but the powers that be would take no denial. In the present state of Siam it is most awkward that I should be away from the office. But it is a real crisis. I have never seen the Prime Minister so upset. As

"THE TALL AND PORTLY FORM OF MYCROFT HOLMES WAS USHERED INTO THE ROOM."

to the Admiralty—it is buzzing like an over-turned bee-hive. Have you read up the case?"

"We have just one so. What were the technical papers?"

"Ah, there's the point! Fortunately, it has not come out. The Press would be furious if it did. The papers which this wretched youth had in his pocket were the plans of the Bruce-Partington submarine."

Mycroft Holmes spoke with a solemnity which showed his sense of the importance of the subject. His brother and I sat expectant.

"Surely you have heard of it? I thought everyone had heard of it."

"Only as a name."

"Its importance can hardly be exaggerated. It has been the most jealously guarded of all Government secrets. You may take it from me that naval warfare becomes impossible within the radius of a Bruce-Partington's operations. Two years ago a very large sum was smuggled through the Estimates and was expended in acquiring a monopoly of the invention. Every effort has been made to keep the secret. The plans, which are exceedingly intricate, comprising some thirty separate patents, each essential to the working of the whole, are kept in an elaborate safe in a confidential office adjoining the Arsenal, with burglar-proof doors and windows. Under no conceivable circumstances were the plans to be taken from the office. If the Chief Constructor of the Navy desired to consult them, even he was forced to go to the Woolwich office for the purpose. And yet here we find them in the pockets of a dead junior clerk in the heart of London. From an official point of view it's simply awful."

"But you have recovered them?"

"No, Sherlock, no! That's the pinch. We have not. Ten papers were taken from Woolwich. There were seven in the pockets of Cadogan West. The three most essential are gone—stolen, vanished. You must drop everything, Sherlock. Never mind your usual petty puzzles of the police-court. It's a vital international problem that you have to solve. Why did Cadogan West take the papers, where are the missing ones, how did he die, how came his body where it was found, how can the evil be set right? Find an answer to all these questions, and you will have done good service for your country."

"Why do you not solve it yourself, Mycroft? You can see as far as I."

"Possibly, Sherlock. But it is a question of getting details. Give me your details, and from an arm-chair I will return you an excellent expert opinion. But to run here and run there, to cross-question railway-guards, and lie on my face with a lens to my eye—it is not my *métier*. No, you are the one man who can clear the matter up. If you have a fancy to see your name in the next honours list——"

My friend smiled and shook his head.

"I play the game for the game's own sake," said he. "But the problem certainly presents some points of interest, and I shall be very pleased to look into it. Some more facts, please."

"I have jotted down the more essential ones upon this sheet of paper, together with a few addresses which you will find of service. The actual official guardian of the papers is the famous Government expert, Sir James Walter, whose decorations and sub-titles fill two lines of a book of reference. He has grown grey in the Service, is a gentle-man, a favoured guest in the most exalted houses, and above all a man whose patriotism is beyond suspicion. He is one of two who have a key of the safe. I may add that the papers were undoubtedly in the office during working hours on Monday, and that Sir James left for London about three o'clock, taking his key with him. He was at the house of Admiral Sinclair at Barclay Square during the whole of the evening when this incident occurred."

"Has the fact been verified?"

"Yes; his brother, Colonel Valentine Walter, has testified to his departure from Woolwich, and Admiral Sinclair to his arrival in London; so Sir James is no longer a direct factor in the problem."

"Who was the other man with a key?"

"The senior clerk and draughtsman, Mr. Sidney Johnson. He is a man of forty, married, with five children. He is a silent, morose man, but he has, on the whole, an excellent record in the public service. He is unpopular with his colleagues, but a hard worker. According to his own account, corroborated only by the word of his wife, he was at home the whole of Monday evening after office hours, and his key has never left the watch-chain upon which it hangs."

"Tell us about Cadogan West."

"He has been ten years in the Service, and has done good work. He has the repu-tation of being hot-headed and impetuous, but a straight, honest man. We have nothing against him. He was next Sidney Johnson in the office. His duties brought him into daily personal contact with the plans. No one else had the handling of them."

" Who locked the plans up that night ? "

" Mr. Sidney Johnson, the senior clerk."

" Well, it is surely perfectly clear who took them away. They are actually found upon the person of this junior clerk, Cadogan West. That seems final, does it not ? "

" It does, Sherlock, and yet it leaves so much unexplained. In the first place, why did he take them ? "

" I presume they were of value ? "

" He could have got several thousands for them very easily."

" Can you suggest any possible motive for taking the papers to London except to sell them ? "

" No, I cannot."

" Then we must take that as our working hypothesis. Young West took the papers. Now this could only be done by having a false key——"

" Several false keys. He had to open the building and the room."

" He had, then, several false keys. He took the papers to London to sell the secret, intending, no doubt, to have the plans themselves back in the safe next morning before they were missed. While in London on this treasonable mission he met his end."

" How ? "

" We will suppose that he was travelling back to Woolwich when he was killed and thrown out of the compartment."

" Aldgate, where the body was found, is considerably past the station for London Bridge, which would be his route to Woolwich."

" Many circumstances could be imagined under which he would pass London Bridge. There was someone in the carriage, for example, with whom he was having an absorbing interview. This interview led to a violent scene, in which he lost his life. Possibly he tried to leave the carriage, fell out on the line, and so met his end. The other closed the door. There was a thick fog, and nothing could be seen."

" No better explanation can be given with our present knowledge ; and yet consider, Sherlock, how much you leave untouched. We will suppose, for argument's sake, that young Cadogan West *had* determined to convey these papers to London. He would naturally have made an appointment with the foreign agent and kept his evening clear. Instead of that, he took two tickets for the theatre, escorted his *fiancée* half-way there, and then suddenly disappeared."

" A blind," said Lestrade, who had sat listening with some impatience to the conversation.

" A very singular one. That is objection No. 1. Objection No. 2 : We will suppose that he reaches London and sees the foreign agent. He must bring back the papers before morning or the loss will be discovered. He took away ten. Only seven were in his pocket. What had become of the other three ? He certainly would not leave them of his own free will. Then, again, where is the price of his treason ? One would have expected to find a large sum of money in his pocket."

" It seems to me perfectly clear," said Lestrade. " I have no doubt at all as to what occurred. He took the papers to sell them. He saw the agent. They could not agree as to price. He started home again, but the agent went with him. In the train the agent murdered him, took the more essential papers, and threw his body from the carriage. That would account for everything, would it not ? "

" Why had he no ticket ? "

" The ticket would have shown which station was nearest the agent's house. Therefore he took it from the murdered man's pocket."

" Good, Lestrade, very good," said Holmes. " Your theory holds together. But if this is true, then the case is at an end. On the one hand the traitor is dead. On the other the plans of the Bruce-Partington submarine are presumably already on the Continent. What is there for us to do ? "

" To act, Sherlock—to act!" cried Mycroft, springing to his feet. " All my instincts are against this explanation. Use your powers ! Go to the scene of the crime ! See the people concerned ! Leave no stone unturned ! In all your career you have never had so great a chance of serving your country."

" Well, well !" said Holmes, shrugging his shoulders. " Come, Watson ! And you, Lestrade, could you favour us with your company for an hour or two ? We will begin our investigation by a visit to Aldgate Station. Good-bye, Mycroft. I shall let you have a report before evening, but I warn you in advance that you have little to expect."

An hour later Holmes, Lestrade, and I stood upon the Underground railroad at the point where it emerges from the tunnel immediately before Aldgate Station. A courteous, red faced old gentleman represented the railway company.

" This is where the young man's body lay," said he, indicating a spot about three feet from the metals. "It could not have fallen from above, for these, as you see, are all blank walls. Therefore it could only have come from a train, and that train, so far as we can trace it, must have passed about midnight on Monday."

"Have the carriages been examined for any sign of violence?"

"There are no such signs, and no ticket has been found."

"No record of a door being found open?"

"None."

"We have had some fresh evidence this morning," said Lestrade. "A passenger who passed Aldgate in an ordinary Metropolitan train about 11.40 on Monday night declares that he heard a heavy thud, as of a body striking the line, just before the train reached the station. There was dense fog, however, and nothing could be seen. He made no report of it at the time. Why, whatever is the matter with Mr. Holmes?"

My friend was standing with an expression of strained intensity upon his face, staring at

"MY FRIEND WAS STANDING WITH AN EXPRESSION OF STRAINED INTENSITY UPON HIS FACE."

the railway metals where they curved out of the tunnel. Aldgate is a junction, and there was a network of points. On these his eager, questioning eyes were fixed, and I saw on his keen, alert face that tightening of the lips, that quiver of the nostrils, and concentration of the heavy tufted brows which I knew so well.

"Points," he muttered; "the points."

"What of it? What do you mean?"

"I suppose there are no great number of points on a system such as this?"

"No; there are very few."

"And a curve, too. Points, and a curve. By Jove! if it were only so."

"What is it, Mr. Holmes? Have you a clue?"

"An idea—an indication, no more. But the case certainly grows in interest. Unique, perfectly unique, and yet why not? I do not see any indications of bleeding on the line."

"There were hardly any."

"But I understand that there was a considerable wound."

"The bone was crushed, but there was no great external injury."

"And yet one would have expected some bleeding. Would it be possible for me to inspect the train which contained the passenger who heard the thud of a fall in the fog?"

"I fear not, Mr. Holmes. The train has been broken up before now, and the carriages redistributed."

"I can assure you, Mr. Holmes," said Lestrade, "that every carriage has been carefully examined. I saw to it myself."

It was one of my friend's most obvious weaknesses that he was impatient with less alert intelligences than his own.

"Very likely," said he, turning away. "As it happens, it was not the carriages which I desired to examine. Watson, we have done all we can here. We need not trouble you any further, Mr. Lestrade. I think our investigations must now carry us to Woolwich."

At London Bridge Holmes wrote a telegram to his brother, which he handed to me before dispatching it. It ran thus:—

"See some light in the darkness, but it may possibly flicker out. Meanwhile, please send by messenger, to await return at Baker Street, a complete list of all foreign spies or international agents known to be in England, with full address.—SHERLOCK."

"That should be helpful, Watson," he remarked, as we took our seats in the Woolwich train. "We certainly owe brother Mycroft a debt for having introduced us to what promises to be a really very remarkable case."

His eager face still wore that expression of intense and high-strung energy, which showed me that some novel and suggestive circumstance had opened up a stimulating line of thought. See the foxhound with hanging ears and drooping tail as it lolls about the kennels, and compare it with the same hound as, with gleaming eyes and straining muscles, it runs upon a breast-high scent—such was the change in Holmes since the morning. He was a different man to the limp and lounging figure in the mouse-coloured dressing-gown who had prowled so restlessly only a few hours before round the fog-girt room.

"There is material here. There is scope," said he. "I am dull indeed not to have understood its possibilities."

"Even now they are dark to me."

"The end is dark to me also, but I have hold of one idea which may lead us far. The man met his death elsewhere, and his body was on the *roof* of a carriage."

"On the roof!"

"Remarkable, is it not? But consider the facts. Is it a coincidence that it is found at the very point where the train pitches and sways as it comes round on the points? Is not that the place where an object upon the roof might be expected to fall off? The points would affect no object inside the train. Either the body fell from the roof, or a very curious coincidence has occurred. But now consider the question of the blood. Of course, there was no bleeding on the line if the body had bled elsewhere. Each fact is suggestive in itself. Together they have a cumulative force."

"And the ticket, too!" I cried.

"Exactly. We could not explain the absence of a ticket. This would explain it. Everything fits together."

"But suppose it were so, we are still as far as ever from unravelling the mystery of his death. Indeed, it becomes not simpler, but stranger."

"Perhaps," said Holmes, thoughtfully; "perhaps." He relapsed into a silent reverie, which lasted until the slow train drew up at last in Woolwich Station. There he called a cab and drew Mycroft's paper from his pocket.

"We have quite a little round of afternoon calls to make," said he. "I think that Sir James Walter claims our first attention."

The house of the famous official was a fine villa with green lawns stretching down to the Thames. As we reached it the fog was lifting, and a thin, watery sunshine was breaking through. A butler answered our ring.

"Sir James, sir!" said he, with solemn face. "Sir James died this morning."

"Good heavens!" cried Holmes, in amazement. "How did he die?"

"Perhaps you would care to step in, sir, and see his brother, Colonel Valentine?"

"Yes, we had best do so."

We were ushered into a dim-lit drawing-room, where an instant later we were joined by a very tall, handsome, light-bearded man of fifty, the younger brother of the dead scientist. His wild eyes, stained cheeks, and unkempt hair all spoke of the sudden blow which had fallen upon the household. He was hardly articulate as he spoke of it.

"It was this horrible scandal," said he. "My brother, Sir James, was a man of very sensitive honour, and he could not survive such an affair. It broke his heart. He was always so proud of the efficiency of his department, and this was a crushing blow."

"We had hoped that he might have given us some indications which would have helped us to clear the matter up."

"I assure you that it was all a mystery to him as it is to you and to all of us. He had already put all his knowledge at the disposal of the police. Naturally, he had no doubt that Cadogan West was guilty. But all the rest was inconceivable."

"You cannot throw any new light upon the affair?"

"I know nothing myself save what I have read or heard. I have no desire to be discourteous, but you can understand, Mr. Holmes, that we are much disturbed at present, and I must ask you to hasten this interview to an end."

"This is indeed an unexpected development," said my friend when we had regained the cab. "I wonder if the death was natural, or whether the poor old fellow killed himself! If the latter, may it be taken as some sign of self-reproach for duty neglected? We must leave that question to the future. Now we shall turn to the Cadogan Wests."

A small but well-kept house in the outskirts of the town sheltered the bereaved mother. The old lady was too dazed with grief to be of any use to us, but at her side was a white-faced young lady, who introduced herself as Miss Violet Westbury, the *fiancée* of the dead man, and the last to see him upon that fatal night.

"I cannot explain it, Mr. Holmes," she said. "I have not shut an eye since the tragedy, thinking, thinking, thinking, night and day, what the true meaning of it can be. Arthur was the most single-minded, chivalrous, patriotic man upon earth. He would have cut his right hand off before he would sell a State secret confided to his keeping. It is absurd, impossible, preposterous to anyone who knew him."

"But the facts, Miss Westbury?"

"Yes, yes; I admit I cannot explain them."

"Was he in any want of money?"

"No; his needs were very simple and his salary ample. He had saved a few hundreds, and we were to marry at the New Year."

"No signs of any mental excitement? Come, Miss Westbury, be absolutely frank with us."

The quick eye of my companion had noted some change in her manner. She coloured and hesitated.

"Yes," she said, at last. "I had a feeling that there was something on his mind."

"For long?"

"Only for the last week or so. He was thoughtful and worried. Once I pressed him about it. He admitted that there was something, and that it was concerned with his official life. 'It is too serious for me to speak about, even to you,' said he. I could get nothing more."

Holmes looked grave.

"Go on, Miss Westbury. Even if it seems to tell against him, go on. We cannot say what it may lead to."

"Indeed, I have nothing more to tell. Once or twice it seemed to me that he was on the point of telling me something. He spoke one evening of the importance of the secret, and I have some recollection that he said that no doubt foreign spies would pay a great deal to have it."

My friend's face grew graver still.

"Anything else?"

"He said that we were slack about such matters—that it would be easy for a traitor to get the plans."

"Was it only recently that he made such remarks?"

"Yes, quite recently."

"Now tell us of that last evening."

"We were to go to the theatre. The fog was so thick that a cab was useless. We walked, and our way took us close to the office. Suddenly he darted away into the fog."

"Without a word?"

"He gave an exclamation; that was all. I waited, but he never returned. Then I walked home. Next morning, after the office opened, they came to inquire. About twelve o'clock we heard the terrible news. Oh, Mr. Holmes, if you could only, only save his honour! It was so much to him."

Holmes shook his head sadly.

"Come, Watson," said he, "our ways lie elsewhere. Our next station must be the office from which the papers were taken.

"It was black enough before against this young man, but our inquiries make it blacker," he remarked, as the cab lumbered off. "His coming marriage gives a motive for the crime. He naturally wanted money. The idea was in his head, since he spoke about it. He nearly made the girl an accomplice in the treason by telling her his plans. It is all very bad."

"But surely, Holmes, character goes for something? Then, again, why should he leave the girl in the street and dart away to commit a felony?"

"Exactly! There are certainly objections. But it is a formidable case which they have to meet."

Mr. Sidney Johnson, the senior clerk, met us at the office, and received us with that respect which my companion's card always commanded. He was a thin, gruff, bespectacled man of middle age, his cheeks haggard, and his hands twitching from the nervous strain to which he had been subjected.

"It is bad, Mr. Holmes, very bad! Have you heard of the death of the chief?"

"We have just come from his house."

"The place is disorganized. The chief dead, Cadogan West dead, our papers stolen. And yet, when we closed our door on Monday evening we were as efficient an office as any in the Government service. Good God, it's dreadful to think of! That West, of all men, should have done such a thing!"

"You are sure of his guilt, then?"

"I can see no other way out of it. And yet I would have trusted him as I trust myself."

"At what hour was the office closed on Monday?"

"At five."

"Did you close it?"

"I am always the last man out."

"Where were the plans?"

"In that safe. I put them there myself."

"Is there no watchman to the building?"

"There is; but he has other departments to look after as well. He is an old soldier and a most trustworthy man. He saw nothing that evening. Of course, the fog was very thick."

"Suppose that Cadogan West wished to make his way into the building after hours; he would need three keys, would he not, before he could reach the papers?"

"Yes, he would. The key of the outer door, the key of the office, and the key of the safe."

"Only Sir James Walter and you had those keys?"

"I had no keys of the doors—only of the safe."

"Was Sir James a man who was orderly in his habits?"

"Yes, I think he was. I know that so far as those three keys are concerned he kept them on the same ring. I have often seen them there."

"And that ring went with him to London?"

"He said so."

"And your key never left your possession?"

"Never."

"Then West, if he is the culprit, must have had a duplicate. And yet none was found upon his body. One other point: if a clerk in this office desired to sell the plans, would it not be simpler to copy the plans for himself than to take the originals, as was actually done?"

"It would take considerable technical knowledge to copy the plans in an effective way."

"But I suppose either Sir James, or you, or West had that technical knowledge?"

"No doubt we had, but I beg you won't try to drag me into the matter, Mr. Holmes. What is the use of our speculating in this way when the original plans were actually found on West?"

"Well, it is certainly singular that he should run the risk of taking originals if he could safely have taken copies, which would have equally served his turn."

"Singular, no doubt — and yet he did so."

"Every inquiry in this case reveals something inexplicable. Now there are three papers still missing. They are, as I understand, the vital ones?"

"Yes, that is so."

"Do you mean to say that anyone holding these three papers, and without the seven others, could construct a Bruce-Partington submarine?"

"I reported to that effect to the Admiralty. But to-day I have been over the drawings again, and I am not so sure of it. The double valves with the automatic self-adjusting slots are drawn in one of the papers which have been returned. Until the foreigners had invented that for themselves

"DO YOU MEAN TO SAY THAT ANYONE HOLDING THESE THREE PAPERS, AND WITHOUT THE SEVEN OTHERS, COULD CONSTRUCT A BRUCE-PARTINGTON SUBMARINE?"

they could not make the boat. Of course, they might soon get over the difficulty."

"But the three missing drawings are the most important?"

"Undoubtedly."

"I think, with your permission, I will now take a stroll round the premises. I do not recall any other question which I desired to ask."

He examined the lock of the safe, the door of the room, and finally the iron shutters of the window. It was only when we were on the lawn outside that his interest was strongly excited. There was a laurel bush outside the window, and several of the branches bore signs of having been twisted or snapped. He examined them carefully with his lens, and then some dim and vague marks upon the earth beneath. Finally he asked the chief clerk to close the iron shutters, and he pointed out to me that they hardly met in the centre, and that it would be possible for anyone outside to see what was going on within the room.

"The indications are ruined by the three days' delay. They may mean something or nothing. Well, Watson, I do not think that Woolwich can help us further. It is a small crop which we have gathered. Let us see if we can do better in London."

Yet we added one more sheaf to our harvest before we left Woolwich Station. The clerk in the ticket office was able to say with confidence that he saw Cadogan West—whom he knew well by sight—upon the Monday night, and that he went to London by the 8.15 to London Bridge. He was alone, and took a single third-class ticket. The clerk was struck at the time by his excited and nervous manner. So shaky was he that he could hardly pick up his change, and the clerk had helped him with it. A reference to a time-table showed that the 8.15 was the first train which it was possible for West to take after he had left the lady about 7.30.

"Let us reconstruct, Watson," said Holmes, after half an hour of silence. "I am not aware that in all our joint researches we have ever had a case which was more difficult to get at. Every fresh advance which we make only reveals a fresh ridge beyond. And yet we have surely made some appreciable progress.

"The effect of our inquiries at Woolwich has in the main been against young Cadogan West; but the indications at the window would lend themselves to a more favourable hypothesis. Let us suppose, for example, that he had been approached by some foreign agent. It might have been done under such pledges as would have prevented him from speaking of it, and yet would have affected his thoughts in the direction indicated by his remarks to his *fiancée*. Very good. We will now suppose that as he went to the theatre with the young lady he suddenly, in the fog, caught a glimpse of this same agent going in the direction of the office. He was an impetuous man, quick in his decisions. Everything gave way to his duty. He followed the man, reached the window, saw the abstraction of the documents, and pursued the thief. In this way we get over the objection that no one would take originals when he could make copies. This outsider had to take originals. So far it holds together."

" What is the next step? "

" Then we come into difficulties. One would imagine that under such circumstances the first act of young Cadogan West would be to seize the villain and raise the alarm. Why did he not do so? Could it have been an official superior who took the papers? That would explain West's conduct. Or could the thief have given West the slip in the fog, and West started at once to London to head him off from his own rooms, presuming that he knew where the rooms were? The call must have been very pressing, since he left his girl standing in the fog, and made no effort to communicate with her. Our scent runs cold here, and there is a vast gap between either hypothesis and the laying of West's body, with seven papers in his pocket, on the roof of a Metropolitan train. My instinct now is to work from the other end. If Mycroft has given us the list of addresses we may be able to pick our man, and follow two tracks instead of one."

Surely enough, a note awaited us at Baker Street. A Government messenger had brought it post-haste. Holmes glanced at it and threw it over to me.

" There are numerous small fry, but few who would handle so big an affair. The only men worth considering are Adolph Meyer, of 13, Great George Street, Westminster; Louis La Rothière, of Campden Mansions, Notting Hill; and Hugo Oberstein, 13, Caulfield Gardens, Kensington. The latter was known to be in town on Monday, and is now reported as having left. Glad to hear you have seen some light. The Cabinet awaits your final report with the utmost anxiety. Urgent representations have arrived from the very highest quarter. The whole force of the State is at your back if you should need it.—MYCROFT."

" I'm afraid," said Holmes, smiling, " that all the Queen's horses and all the Queen's men cannot avail in this matter." He had spread out his big map of London, and leaned eagerly over it. "Well, well," said he, presently, with an exclamation of satisfaction, "things are turning a little in our direction at last. Why, Watson, I do honestly believe that we are going to pull it off after all." He slapped me on the shoulder with a sudden burst of hilarity. "I am going out now. It is only a reconnaissance. I will do nothing serious without my trusted comrade and biographer at my elbow. Do you stay here, and the odds are that you will see me again in an hour or two. If time hangs heavy get foolscap and a pen, and begin your narrative of how we saved the State."

I felt some reflection of his elation in my own mind, for I knew well that he would not depart so far from his usual austerity of demeanour unless there was good cause for exultation. All the long November evening I waited, filled with impatience for his return. At last, shortly after nine o'clock there arrived a messenger with a note :—

" Am dining at Goldini's Restaurant, Gloucester Road, Kensington. Please come at once and join me there. Bring with you a jemmy, a dark lantern, a chisel, and a revolver.—S. H."

It was a nice equipment for a respectable citizen to carry through the dim, fog-draped streets. I stowed them all discreetly away in my overcoat, and drove straight to the address given. There sat my friend at a little round table near the door of the garish Italian restaurant.

" Have you had something to eat? Then join me in a coffee and curaçoa. Try one of the proprietor's cigars. They are less poisonous than one would expect. Have you the tools? "

" They are here, in my overcoat."

" Excellent. Let me give you a short sketch of what I have done, with some indication of what we are about to do. Now it must be evident to you, Watson, that this young man's body was *placed* on the roof of the train. That was clear from the instant that I determined the fact that it was from the roof and not from a carriage that he had fallen."

" Could it not have been dropped from a bridge? "

" I should say it was impossible. If you examine the roofs you will find that they are slightly rounded, and there is no railing round them. Therefore, we can say for certain that young Cadogan West was placed on it."

"How could he be placed there?"

"That was the question which we had to answer. There is only one possible way. You are aware that the Underground runs clear of tunnels at some points in the West-end. I had a vague memory that as I have travelled by it I have occasionally seen windows just above my head. Now, suppose that a train halted under such a window, would there be any difficulty in laying a body upon the roof?"

"It seems most improbable."

"We must fall back upon the old axiom that when all other contingencies fail, whatever remains, however improbable, must be the truth. Here all other contingencies *have* failed. When I found that the leading international agent, who had just left London, lived in a row of houses which abutted upon the Underground, I was so pleased that you were a little astonished at my sudden frivolity."

"Oh, that was it, was it?"

"Yes, that was it. Mr. Hugo Oberstein, of 13, Caulfield Gardens, had become my objective. I began my operations at Gloucester Road Station, where a very helpful official walked with me along the track, and allowed me to satisfy myself not only that the back-stair windows of Caulfield Gardens open on the line, but the even more essential fact that, owing to the intersection of one of the larger railways, the Underground trains are frequently held motionless for some minutes at that very spot."

"Splendid, Holmes! You have got it!"

"So far—so far, Watson. We advance, but the goal is afar. Well, having seen the back of Caulfield Gardens, I visited the front and satisfied myself that the bird was indeed flown. It is a considerable house, unfurnished, so far as I could judge, in the upper rooms. Oberstein lived there with a single valet, who was probably a confederate entirely in his confidence. We must bear in mind that Oberstein has gone to the Continent to dispose of his booty, but not with any idea of flight; for he had no reason to fear a warrant, and the idea of an amateur domiciliary visit would certainly never occur to him. Yet that is precisely what we are about to make."

"Could we not get a warrant and legalize it?"

"Hardly on the evidence."

"What can we hope to do?"

"We cannot tell what correspondence may be there."

"I don't like it, Holmes."

"My dear fellow, you shall keep watch in the street. I'll do the criminal part. It's not a time to stick at trifles. Think of Mycroft's note, of the Admiralty, the Cabinet, the exalted person who waits for news. We are bound to go."

My answer was to rise from the table.

"You are right, Holmes. We are bound to go."

He sprang up and shook me by the hand.

"I knew you would not shrink at the last," said he, and for a moment I saw something in his eyes which was nearer to tenderness than I had ever seen. The next instant he was his masterful, practical self once more.

"It is nearly half a mile, but there is no hurry. Let us walk," said he. "Don't drop the instruments, I beg. Your arrest as a suspicious character would be a most unfortunate complication."

Caulfield Gardens was one of those lines of flat-faced, pillared, and porticoed houses which are so prominent a product of the middle Victorian epoch in the West-end of London. Next door there appeared to be a children's party, for the merry buzz of young voices and the clatter of a piano resounded through the night. The fog still hung about and screened us with its friendly shade. Holmes had lit his lantern and flashed it upon the massive door.

"This is a serious proposition," said he. "It is certainly bolted as well as locked. We would do better in the area. There is an excellent archway down yonder in case a too zealous policeman should intrude. Give me a hand, Watson, and I'll do the same for you."

A minute later we were both in the area. Hardly had we reached the dark shadows before the step of the policeman was heard in the fog above. As its soft rhythm died away Holmes set to work upon the lower door. I saw him stoop and strain until with a sharp crash it flew open. We sprang through into the dark passage, closing the area door behind us. Holmes led the way up the curving, uncarpeted stair. His little fan of yellow light shone upon a low window.

"Here we are, Watson—this must be the one." He threw it open, and as he did so there was a low, harsh murmur, growing steadily into a loud roar as a train dashed past us in the darkness. Holmes swept his light along the window-sill. It was thickly coated with soot from the passing engines, but the black surface was blurred and rubbed in places.

"You can see where they rested the body. Halloa, Watson! what is this? There can be no doubt that it is a blood mark." He was pointing to faint discolorations along the woodwork of the window. "Here it is on the stone of the stair also. The demonstration is complete. Let us stay here until a train stops."

We had not long to wait. The very next train roared from the tunnel as before, but slowed in the open, and then, with a creaking of brakes, pulled up immediately beneath us. It was not four feet from the window-ledge to the roof of the carriages. Holmes softly closed the window.

"HALLOA, WATSON! WHAT IS THIS?"

"So far we are justified," said he. "What do you think of it, Watson?"

"A masterpiece. You have never risen to a greater height."

"I cannot agree with you there. From the moment that I conceived the idea of the body being upon the roof, which surely was not a very abstruse one, all the rest was inevitable. If it were not for the grave interests involved the affair up to this point would be insignificant. Our difficulties are still before us. But perhaps we may find something here which may help us."

We had ascended the kitchen stair and entered the suite of rooms upon the first floor. One was a dining-room, severely furnished and containing nothing of interest. A second was a bedroom, which also drew blank. The remaining room appeared more promising, and my companion settled down to a systematic examination. It was littered with books and papers, and was evidently used as a study. Swiftly and methodically Holmes turned over the contents of drawer after drawer and cupboard after cupboard, but no gleam of success came to brighten his austere face. At the end of an hour he was no further than when he started.

"The cunning dog has covered his tracks," said he. "He has left nothing to incriminate him. His dangerous correspondence has been destroyed or removed. This is our last chance."

It was a small tin cash-box which stood upon the writing-desk. Holmes prised it open with his chisel. Several rolls of paper were within, covered with figures and calculations, without any note to show to what they referred. The recurring words, "Water pressure" and "Pressure to the square inch" suggested some possible relation to a submarine. Holmes tossed them all impatiently aside. There only remained an envelope with some small newspaper slips inside it. He shook them out on the table, and at once

I saw by his eager face that his hopes had been raised.

"What's this, Watson? Eh? What's this? Record of a series of messages in the advertisements of a paper. *Daily Telegraph* agony column by the print and paper. Right-hand top corner of a page. No dates—but messages arrange themselves. This must be the first:—

"'Hoped to hear sooner. Terms agreed to. Write fully to address given on card.—Pierrot.'

"Next comes: 'Too complex for description. Must have full report. Stuff awaits you when goods delivered.—Pierrot.'

"Then comes: 'Matter presses. Must withdraw offer unless contract completed. Make appointment by letter. Will confirm by advertisement.—Pierrot.'

"Finally: 'Monday night after nine. Two taps. Only ourselves. Do not be so suspicious. Payment in hard cash when goods delivered.—Pierrot.'

"A fairly complete record, Watson! If we could only get at the man at the other end!" He sat lost in thought, tapping his fingers on the table. Finally he sprang to his feet.

"Well, perhaps it won't be so difficult after all. There is nothing more to be done here, Watson. I think we might drive round to the offices of the *Daily Telegraph*, and so bring a good day's work to a conclusion."

Mycroft Holmes and Lestrade had come round by appointment after breakfast next day, and Sherlock Holmes had recounted to them our proceedings of the day before. The professional shook his head over our confessed burglary.

"We can't do these things in the force, Mr. Holmes," said he. "No wonder you get results that are beyond us. But some of these days you'll go too far, and you'll find yourself and your friend in trouble."

"For England, home, and beauty—eh, Watson? Martyrs on the altar of our country. But what do you think of it, Mycroft?"

"Excellent, Sherlock! Admirable! But what use will you make of it?"

Holmes picked up the *Daily Telegraph* which lay upon the table.

"Have you seen Pierrot's advertisement to-day?"

"What! Another one?"

"Yes, here it is: 'To-night. Same hour. Same place. Two taps. Most vitally important. Your own safety at stake.—Pierrot.'"

"By George!" cried Lestrade. "If he answers that we've got him!"

"That was my idea when I put it in. I think if you could both make it convenient to come with us about eight o'clock to Caulfield Gardens we might possibly get a little nearer to a solution."

One of the most remarkable characteristics of Sherlock Holmes was his power of throwing his brain out of action and switching all his thoughts on to lighter things whenever he had convinced himself that he could no longer work to advantage. I remember that during the whole of that memorable day he lost himself in a monograph which he had undertaken upon the Polyphonic Motets of Lassus. For my own part I had none of this power of detachment, and the day, in consequence, appeared to be interminable. The great national importance of the issue, the suspense in high quarters, the direct nature of the experiment which we were trying, all combined to work upon my nerves. It was a relief to me when at last, after a light dinner, we set out upon our expedition. Lestrade and Mycroft met us by appointment at the outside of Gloucester Road Station. The area door of Oberstein's house had been left open the night before, and it was necessary for me, as Mycroft Holmes absolutely and indignantly declined to climb the railings, to pass in and open the hall door. By nine o'clock we were all seated in the study, waiting patiently for our man.

An hour passed and yet another. When eleven struck, the measured beat of the great church clock seemed to sound the dirge of our hopes. Lestrade and Mycroft were fidgeting in their seats and looking twice a minute at their watches. Holmes sat silent and composed, his eyelids half shut, but every sense on the alert. He raised his head with a sudden jerk.

"He is coming," said he.

There had been a furtive step past the door. Now it returned. We heard a shuffling sound outside, and then two sharp taps with the knocker. Holmes rose, motioning to us to remain seated. The gas in the hall was a mere point of light. He opened the outer door, and then as a dark figure slipped past him he closed and fastened it. "This way!" we heard him say, and a moment later our man stood before us. Holmes had followed him closely, and as the man turned with a cry of surprise and alarm he caught him by the collar and threw him back into the room. Before our prisoner had recovered his balance the door was shut and Holmes standing with his back against

"BEFORE OUR PRISONER HAD RECOVERED HIS BALANCE THE DOOR WAS SHUT AND HOLMES STANDING WITH HIS BACK AGAINST IT."

it. The man glared round him, staggered, and fell senseless upon the floor. With the shock, his broad-brimmed hat flew from his head, his cravat slipped down from his lips, and there was the long light beard and the soft, handsome, delicate features of Colonel Valentine Walter.

Holmes gave a whistle of surprise.

"You can write me down an ass this time, Watson," said he. "This was not the bird that I was looking for."

"Who is he?" asked Mycroft, eagerly.

"The younger brother of the late Sir James Walter, the head of the Submarine Department. Yes, yes; I see the fall of the cards. He is coming to. I think that you had best leave his examination to me."

We had carried the prostrate body to the sofa. Now our prisoner sat up, looked round him with a horror-stricken face, and passed his hand over his forehead, like one who cannot believe his own senses.

"What is this?" he asked. "I came here to visit Mr. Oberstein."

"Everything is known, Colonel Walter," said Holmes. "How an English gentleman could behave in such a manner is beyond my comprehension. But your whole correspondence and relations with Oberstein are within our knowledge. So also are the circumstances connected with the death of young Cadogan West. Let me advise you to gain at least the small credit for repentance and confession, since there are still some details which we can only learn from your lips."

The man groaned and sank his face in his hands. We waited, but he was silent.

"I can assure you," said Holmes, "that every essential is already known. We know that you were pressed for money; that you took an impress of the keys which your brother held; and that you entered into a correspondence with Oberstein, who answered your letters through the advertisement columns of the *Daily Telegraph.* We are aware that you went down to the office in the fog on Monday night, but that you were seen and followed by young Cadogan West, who had probably some previous reason to suspect you. He saw your theft, but could not give the alarm, as it was just possible that you were taking the papers to your brother in London. Leaving all his private concerns, like the good citizen that he was, he followed you closely in the fog, and kept at your heels until you reached this very house. There he intervened, and then it was, Colonel Walter, that to treason you added the more terrible crime of murder."

"I did not! I did not! Before God I swear that I did not!" cried our wretched prisoner.

"Tell us, then, how Cadogan West met his end before you laid him upon the roof of a railway carriage."

"I will. I swear to you that I will. I did the rest. I confess it. It was just as you say. A Stock Exchange debt had to be paid. I needed the money badly. Oberstein offered me five thousand. It was to save myself from ruin. But as to murder, I am as innocent as you."

"What happened, then?"

"He had his suspicions before, and he followed me as you describe. I never knew it until I was at the very door. It was thick fog, and one could not see three yards. I had given two taps and Oberstein had come to the door. The young man rushed up and demanded to know what we were about to do with the papers. Oberstein had a short life-preserver. He always carried it with him. As West forced his way after us into the house Oberstein struck him on the head. The blow was a fatal one. He was dead within five minutes. There he lay in the

hall, and we were at our wits' end what to do. Then Oberstein had this idea about the trains which halted under his back window. But first he examined the papers which I had brought. He said that three of them were essential, and that he must keep them. 'You cannot keep them,' said I. 'There will be a dreadful row at Woolwich if they are not returned.' 'I must keep them,' said he, 'for they are so technical that it is impossible in the time to make copies.' 'Then they must all go back together to-night,' said I. He thought for a little, and then he cried out that he had it. 'Three I will keep,' said he. 'The others we will stuff into the pocket of this young man. When he is found the whole business will assuredly be put to his account.' I could see no other way out of it, so we did as he suggested. We waited half an hour at the window before a train stopped. It was so thick that nothing could be seen, and we had no difficulty in lowering West's body on to the train. That was the end of the matter so far as I was concerned."

"And your brother?"

"He said nothing, but he had caught me once with his keys, and I think that he suspected. I read in his eyes that he suspected. As you know, he never held up his head again."

There was silence in the room. It was broken by Mycroft Holmes.

"Can you not make reparation? It would ease your conscience, and possibly your punishment."

"What reparation can I make?"

"Where is Oberstein with the papers?"

"I do not know."

"Did he give you no address?"

"He said that letters to the Hôtel du Louvre, Paris, would eventually reach him."

"Then reparation is still within your power," said Sherlock Holmes.

"I will do anything I can. I owe this fellow no particular good-will. He has been my ruin and my downfall."

"Here are paper and pen. Sit at this desk and write to my dictation. Direct the envelope to the address given. That is right. Now the letter: 'Dear Sir,—With regard to our transaction, you will no doubt have observed by now that one essential detail is missing. I have a tracing which will make it complete. This has involved me in extra trouble, however, and I must ask you for a further advance of five hundred pounds. I will not trust it to the post, nor will I take anything but gold or notes. I would come to you abroad, but it would excite remark if I left the country at present. Therefore I shall expect to meet you in the smoking-room of the Charing Cross Hotel at noon on Saturday. Remember that only English notes or gold will be taken.' That will do very well. I shall be very much surprised if it does not fetch our man."

And it did! It is a matter of history — that secret history of a nation which is often so much more intimate and interesting than its public chronicles — that Oberstein, eager to complete the coup of his lifetime, came to the lure and was safely engulfed for fifteen years in a British prison. In his trunk were found the invaluable Bruce - Partington plans, which he had put up for auction in all the naval centres of Europe.

Colonel Walter died in prison towards the end of the second year of his sentence. As to Holmes, he returned refreshed to his monograph upon the Polyphonic Motets of Lassus, which has since been printed for private circulation, and is said by experts to be the last word upon the subject. Some weeks afterwards I learned incidentally that my friend spent a day at Windsor, whence he returned with a remarkably fine emerald tie-pin. When I asked him if he had bought it, he answered that it was a

"THAT WAS THE END OF THE MATTER."

present from a certain gracious lady in whose interests he had once been fortunate enough to carry out a small commission. He said no more; but I fancy that I could guess at that lady's august name, and I have little doubt that the emerald pin will for ever recall to my friend's memory the adventure of the Bruce-Partington plans.

" 'THE MOST EXTRAORDINARY AND TRAGIC AFFAIR HAS OCCURRED
DURING THE NIGHT,' SAID THE VICAR."

Vol. xl. No. 240.

DECEMBER, 1910.

A REMINISCENCE OF
SHERLOCK HOLMES.

The Adventure of the Devil's Foot.

By ARTHUR CONAN DOYLE.

Illustrated by Gilbert Holiday.

IN recording from time to time some of the curious experiences and interesting recollections which I associate with my long and intimate friendship with Mr. Sherlock Holmes, I have continually been faced by difficulties caused by his own aversion to publicity. To his sombre and cynical spirit all popular applause was always abhorrent, and nothing amused him more at the end of a successful case than to hand over the actual exposure to some orthodox official, and to listen with a mocking smile to the general chorus of misplaced congratulation. It was indeed this attitude upon the part of my friend, and certainly not any lack of interesting material, which has caused me of late years to lay very few of my records before the public. My participation in some of his adventures was always a privilege which entailed discretion and reticence upon me.

It was, then, with considerable surprise that I received a telegram from Holmes last Tuesday—he has never been known to write where a telegram would serve—in the following terms : " Why not tell them of the Cornish horror—strangest case I have handled." I have no idea what backward sweep of memory had brought the matter fresh to his mind, or what freak had caused him to desire that I should recount it ; but I hasten, before another cancelling telegram may arrive, to hunt out the notes which give me the exact details of the case, and to lay the narrative before my readers.

It was, then, in the spring of the year 1897 that Holmes's iron constitution showed some symptoms of giving way in the face of constant hard work of a most exacting kind, aggravated, perhaps, by occasional indiscretions of his own. In March of that year Dr. Moore Agar, of Harley Street, whose dramatic introduction to Holmes I may some day recount, gave positive injunctions that the famous private agent should lay aside all his cases and surrender himself to complete rest if he wished to avert an absolute break-down. The state of his health was not a matter in which he himself took the faintest interest, for his mental detachment was absolute, but he was induced at last, on the threat of being permanently disqualified from work, to give himself a complete change of scene and air. Thus it was that in the early spring of that year we found ourselves together in a small cottage near Poldhu Bay, at the farther extremity of the Cornish peninsula.

It was a singular spot, and one peculiarly well suited to the grim humour of my patient. From the windows of our little whitewashed house, which stood high upon a grassy head-land, we looked down upon the whole sinister semicircle of Mounts Bay, that old death-trap of sailing vessels, with its fringe of black

cliffs and surge-swept reefs on which innumer-able seamen have met their end. With a northerly breeze it lies placid and sheltered, inviting the storm-tossed craft to tack into it for rest and protection. Then comes the sudden swirl round of the wind, the bluster-ing gale from the south-west, the dragging anchor, the lee shore, and the last battle in the creaming breakers. The wise mariner stands far out from that evil place.

On the land side our surroundings were as sombre as on the sea. It was a country of rolling moors, lonely and dun-coloured, with an occasional church tower to mark the site of some old-world village. In every direction upon these moors there were traces of some vanished race which had passed utterly away, and left as its sole record strange monuments of stone, irregular mounds which contained the burned ashes of the dead, and curious earthworks which hinted at prehistoric strife.

The glamour and mystery of the place, with its sinister atmosphere of forgotten nations, appealed to the imagination of my friend, and he spent much of his time in long walks and soli-tary meditations upon the moor. The ancient Cornish language had also arrested his attention, and he had, I remember, conceived the idea that it was akin to the Chaldean, and had been largely derived from the Phoenician traders in tin. He had received a consign-ment of books upon philo-logy and was settling down to develop this thesis, when suddenly to my sorrow, and to his unfeigned delight, we found ourselves, even in that land of dreams, plunged into a problem at our very doors which was more intense, more engross-ing, and infinitely more mysterious than any of those which had driven us from London. Our simple life and peaceful, healthy routine were violently in-terrupted, and we were precipitated into the midst of a series of events which caused the utmost excite-ment not only in Cornwall,

"HOLMES SPENT MUCH OF HIS TIME IN LONG WALKS AND SOLITARY MEDITATIONS."

but throughout the whole West of England. Many of my readers may retain some recollection of what was called at the time "The Cornish Horror," though a most imperfect account of the matter reached the London Press. Now, after thirteen years, I will give the true details of this inconceivable affair to the public.

I have said that scattered towers marked the villages which dotted this part of Cornwall. The nearest of these was the hamlet of Tredannick Wollas, where the cottages of a couple of hundred inhabitants clustered round an ancient, moss-grown church. The vicar of the parish, Mr. Roundhay, was something of an archæologist, and as such Holmes had made his acquaintance. He was a middle-aged man, portly and affable, with a considerable fund of local lore. At his invitation we had taken tea at the vicarage, and had come to know, also, Mr. Mortimer Tregennis, an independent gentleman, who increased the clergyman's scanty resources by taking rooms in his large, straggling house. The vicar, being a bachelor, was glad to come to such an arrangement, though he had little in common with his lodger, who was a thin, dark, spectacled man, with a stoop which gave the impression of actual physical deformity. I remember that during our short visit we found the vicar garrulous, but his lodger strangely reticent, a sad-faced, introspective man, sitting with averted eyes, brooding apparently upon his own affairs.

These were the two men who entered abruptly into our little sitting-room on Tuesday, March the 16th, shortly after our breakfast hour, as we were smoking together, preparatory to our daily excursion upon the moors.

"Mr. Holmes," said the vicar, in an agitated voice, "the most extraordinary and tragic affair has occurred during the night. It is the most unheard-of business. We can only regard it as a special Providence that you should chance to be here at the time, for in all England you are the one man we need."

I glared at the intrusive vicar with no very friendly eyes; but Holmes took his pipe from his lips and sat up in his chair like an old hound who hears the view-halloo. He waved his hand to the sofa, and our palpitating visitor with his agitated companion sat side by side upon it. Mr. Mortimer Tregennis was more self-contained than the clergyman, but the twitching of his thin hands and the brightness of his dark eyes showed that they shared a common emotion.

"Shall I speak or you?" he asked of the vicar.

"Well, as you seem to have made the discovery, whatever it may be, and the vicar to have had it second-hand, perhaps you had better do the speaking," said Holmes.

I glanced at the hastily-clad clergyman, with the formally-dressed lodger seated beside him, and was amused at the surprise which Holmes's simple deduction had brought to their faces.

"Perhaps I had best say a few words first," said the vicar, "and then you can judge if you will listen to the details from Mr. Tregennis, or whether we should not hasten at once to the scene of this mysterious affair. I may explain, then, that our friend here spent last evening in the company of his two brothers, Owen and George, and of his sister Brenda, at their house of Tredannick Wartha, which is near the old stone cross upon the moor. He left them shortly after ten o'clock, playing cards round the dining-room table, in excellent health and spirits. This morning, being an early riser, he walked in that direction before breakfast, and was overtaken by the carriage of Dr. Richards, who explained that he had just been sent for on a most urgent call to Tredannick Wartha. Mr. Mortimer Tregennis naturally went with him. When he arrived at Tredannick Wartha he found an extraordinary state of things. His two brothers and his sister were seated round the table exactly as he had left them, the cards still spread in front of them and the candles burned down to their sockets. The sister lay back stone-dead in her chair, while the two brothers sat on each side of her laughing, shouting, and singing, the senses stricken clean out of them. All three of them, the dead woman and the two demented men, retained upon their faces an expression of the utmost horror—a convulsion of terror which was dreadful to look upon. There was no sign of the presence of anyone in the house, except Mrs. Porter, the old cook and housekeeper, who declared that she had slept deeply and heard no sound during the night. Nothing had been stolen or disarranged, and there is absolutely no explanation of what the horror can be which has frightened a woman to death and two strong men out of their senses. There is the situation, Mr. Holmes, in a nutshell, and if you can help us to clear it up you will have done a great work."

I had hoped that in some way I could coax my companion back into the quiet which had been the object of our journey; but one glance at his intense face and contracted eyebrows told me how vain was now the expectation. He sat for some little time in silence, absorbed in the strange drama which had broken in upon our peace.

"I will look into this matter," he said at last. "On the face of it, it would appear to be a case of a very exceptional nature. Have you been there yourself, Mr. Roundhay?"

"No, Mr. Holmes. Mr. Tregennis brought back the account. to the vicarage, and I at once hurried over with him to consult you."

"How far is it to the house where this singular tragedy occurred?"

"About a mile inland."

"Then we shall walk over together. But, before we start, I must ask you a few questions, Mr. Mortimer Tregennis."

The other had been silent all this time, but I had observed that his more controlled excitement was even greater than the obtrusive emotion of the clergyman. He sat with a pale, drawn face, his anxious gaze fixed upon Holmes, and his thin hands clasped convulsively together. His pale lips quivered as he listened to the dreadful experience which had befallen his family, and his dark eyes seemed to reflect something of the horror of the scene.

"Ask what you like, Mr. Holmes," said he, eagerly. "It is a bad thing to speak of, but I will answer you the truth."

"Tell me about last night."

"Well, Mr. Holmes, I supped there, as the vicar has said, and my elder brother George proposed a game of whist afterwards. We sat down about nine o'clock. It was a quarter-past ten when I moved to go. I left them all round the table, as merry as could be."

"Who let you out?"

"Mrs. Porter had gone to bed, so I let myself out. I shut the hall door behind me. The window of the room in which they sat was closed, but the blind was not drawn down. There was no change in door or window this morning, nor any reason to think that any stranger had been to the house. Yet there they sat, driven clean mad with terror, and Brenda lying dead of fright, with her head hanging over the arm of the chair. I'll never get the sight of that room out of my mind so long as I live."

"The facts, as you state them, are certainly most remarkable," said Holmes. "I take it that you have no theory yourself which can in any way account for them?"

"It's devilish, Mr. Holmes; devilish!" cried Mortimer Tregennis. "It is not of this world. Something has come into that room which has dashed the light of reason from their minds. What human contrivance could do that?"

"I fear," said Holmes, "that if the matter is beyond humanity it is certainly beyond me. Yet we must exhaust all natural explanations before we fall back upon such a theory as this. As to yourself, Mr. Tregennis, I take it you were divided in some way from your family, since they lived together and you had rooms apart?"

"That is so, Mr. Holmes, though the matter is past and done with. We were a family of tin-miners at Redruth, but we sold out our venture to a company, and so retired with enough to keep us. I won't deny that there was some feeling about the division of the money and it stood between us for a time, but it was all forgiven and forgotten, and we were the best of friends together."

"Looking back at the evening which you spent together, does anything stand out in your memory as throwing any possible light upon the tragedy? Think carefully, Mr. Tregennis, for any clue which can help me."

"There is nothing at all, sir."

"Your people were in their usual spirits?"

"Never better."

"Were they nervous people? Did they ever show any apprehension of coming danger?"

"Nothing of the kind."

"You have nothing to add, then, which could assist me?"

Mortimer Tregennis considered earnestly for a moment.

"There is one thing occurs to me," said he at last. "As we sat at the table my back was to the window, and my brother George, he being my partner at cards, was facing it. I saw him once look hard over my shoulder, so I turned round and looked also. The blind was up and the window shut, but I could just make out the bushes on the lawn, and it seemed to me for a moment that I saw something moving among them. I couldn't even say if it were man or animal, but I just thought there was something there. When I asked him what he was looking at, he told me that he had the same feeling. That is all that I can say."

"Did you not investigate?"

"No; the matter passed as unimportant."

"You left them, then, without any pre-monition of evil?"

"None at all."

"I am not clear how you came to hear the news so early this morning."

"I am an early riser, and generally take a walk before breakfast. This morning I had hardly started when the doctor in his carriage overtook me. He told me that old

Mrs. Porter had sent a boy down with an urgent message. I sprang in beside him and we drove on. When we got there we looked into that dreadful room. The candles and the fire must have burned out hours before, and they had been sitting there in the dark until dawn had broken. The doctor said Brenda must have been dead at least six hours. There were no signs of violence. She just lay across the arm of the chair with that look on her face. George and Owen were singing snatches of songs and gibbering like two great apes. Oh, it was awful to see! I couldn't stand it, and the doctor was as white as a sheet. Indeed, he fell into a chair in a sort of faint, and we nearly had him on our hands as well."

"Remarkable—most remarkable!" said Holmes, rising and taking his hat. "I think perhaps we had better go down to Tredannick Wartha without further delay. I confess that I have seldom known a case which at first sight presented a more singular problem."

Our proceedings of that first morning did little to advance the investigation. It was marked, however, at the outset by an incident which left the most sinister impression upon my mind. The approach to the spot at which the tragedy occurred is down a narrow, winding country lane. While we made our way along it we heard the rattle of a carriage coming towards us, and stood aside to let it pass. As it drove by us I caught a glimpse through the closed window of a horribly-contorted, grinning face glaring out at us. Those staring eyes and gnashing teeth flashed past us like a dreadful vision.

"My brothers!" cried Mortimer Tregennis, white to his lips. "They are taking them to Helston."

We looked with horror after the black carriage, lumbering upon its way. Then we

"THOSE STARING EYES AND GNASHING TEETH FLASHED PAST US LIKE A DREADFUL VISION."

turned our steps towards this ill-omened house in which they had met their strange fate.

It was a large and bright dwelling, rather a villa than a cottage, with a considerable garden which was already, in that Cornish air, well filled with spring flowers. Towards this garden the window of the sitting-room fronted, and from it, according to Mortimer Tregennis, must have come that thing of evil which had by sheer horror in a single instant blasted their minds. Holmes walked slowly and thoughtfully among the flower-plots and along the path before we entered the porch. So absorbed was he in his thoughts, I remember, that he stumbled over the watering-pot, upset its contents, and deluged both our feet and the garden path. Inside the house we were met by the elderly Cornish housekeeper, Mrs. Porter, who, with the aid of a young girl, looked after the wants of the family. She readily answered all Holmes's questions. She had heard nothing in the night. Her employers had all been in excellent spirits lately, and she had never known them more cheerful and prosperous. She had fainted with horror upon entering the room in the morning and seeing that dreadful

emotion. From her bedroom we descended to the sitting-room where this strange tragedy had actually occurred. The charred ashes of the overnight fire lay in the grate. On the table were the four guttered and burned-out candles, with the cards scattered over its surface. The chairs had been moved back against the walls, but all else was as it had been the night before. Holmes paced with light, swift steps about the room; he sat in the various chairs, drawing them up and reconstructing their positions. He tested how much of the garden was

"WE ASCENDED THE STAIRS AND VIEWED THE BODY."

company round the table. She had, when she recovered, thrown open the window to let the morning air in, and had run down to the lane, whence she sent a farm-lad for the doctor. The lady was on her bed upstairs, if we cared to see her. It took four strong men to get the brothers into the asylum carriage. She would not herself stay in the house another day, and was starting that very afternoon to rejoin her family at St. Ives.

We ascended the stairs and viewed the body. Miss Brenda Tregennis had been a very beautiful girl, though now verging upon middle age. Her dark, clear-cut face was handsome, even in death, but there still lingered upon it something of that convulsion of horror which had been her last human

visible; he examined the floor, the ceiling, and the fireplace; but never once did I see that sudden brightening of his eyes and tightening of his lips which would have told me that he saw some gleam of light in this utter darkness.

"Why a fire?" he asked once. "Had they always a fire in this small room on a spring evening?"

Mortimer Tregennis explained that the night was cold and damp. For that reason, after his arrival, the fire was lit. "What are you going to do now, Mr. Holmes?" he asked.

My friend smiled and laid his hand upon my arm. "I think, Watson, that I shall resume that course of tobacco-poisoning

which you have so often and so justly condemned," said he. "With your permission,
gentlemen, we will now return to our cottage,
for I am not aware that any new factor is
likely to come to our notice here. I will turn
the facts over in my mind, Mr. Tregennis,
and should anything occur to me I will
certainly communicate with you and the
vicar. In the meantime I wish you both
good morning."

It was not until long after we were back in
Poldhu Cottage that Holmes broke his complete and absorbed silence. He sat coiled
in his arm-chair, his haggard and ascetic face
hardly visible amid the blue swirl of his
tobacco smoke, his black brows drawn down,
his forehead contracted, his eyes vacant and
far away. Finally, he laid down his pipe and
sprang to his feet.

"It won't do, Watson!" said he, with a
laugh. "Let us walk along the cliffs together
and search for flint arrows. We are more
likely to find them than clues to this problem.
To let the brain work without sufficient
material is like racing an engine. It racks
itself to pieces. The sea air, sunshine, and
patience, Watson—all else will come.

"Now, let us calmly define our position,
Watson," he continued, as we skirted the
cliffs together. "Let us get a firm grip of
the very little which we *do* know, so that
when fresh facts arise we may be ready to fit
them into their places. I take it, in the first
place, that neither of us is prepared to admit
diabolical intrusions into the affairs of men.
Let us begin by ruling that entirely out of
our minds. Very good. There remain three
persons who have been grievously stricken
by some conscious or unconscious human
agency. That is firm ground. Now, when
did this occur? Evidently, assuming his
narrative to be true, it was immediately after
Mr. Mortimer Tregennis had left the room.
That is a very important point. The pre-
sumption is that it was within a few minutes
afterwards. The cards still lay upon the
table. It was already past their usual hour
for bed. Yet they had not changed their
position or pushed back their chairs. I
repeat, then, that the occurrence was immediately after his departure, and not later than
eleven o'clock last night.

"Our next obvious step is to check, so
far as we can, the movements of Mortimer
Tregennis after he left the room. In this
there is no difficulty, and they seem to be
above suspicion. Knowing my methods as
you do, you were, of course, conscious of the
somewhat clumsy water-pot expedient by

which I obtained a clearer impress of his
foot than might otherwise have been possible.
The wet, sandy path took it admirably. Last
night was also wet, you will remember, and
it was not difficult—having obtained a sample
print—to pick out his track among others
and to follow his movements. He appears
to have walked away swiftly in the direction
of the vicarage.

"If, then, Mortimer Tregennis disappeared
from the scene, and yet some outside person
affected the card-players, how can we reconstruct that person, and how was such an
impression of horror conveyed? Mrs. Porter
may be eliminated. She is evidently harmless. Is there any evidence that someone
crept up to the garden window and in some
manner produced so terrific an effect that he
drove those who saw it out of their senses?
The only suggestion in this direction comes
from Mortimer Tregennis himself, who says
that his brother spoke about some movement in the garden. That is certainly
remarkable, as the night was rainy, cloudy,
and dark. Anyone who had the design
to alarm these people would be compelled
to place his very face against the glass
before he could be seen. There is a three-
foot flower-border outside this window, but
no indication of a footmark. It is difficult
to imagine, then, how an outsider could have
made so terrible an impression upon the
company, nor have we found any possible
motive for so strange and elaborate an
attempt. You perceive our difficulties,
Watson?"

"They are only too clear," I answered,
with conviction.

"And yet, with a little more material, we
may prove that they are not insurmountable,"
said Holmes. "I fancy that among your
extensive archives, Watson, you may find
some which were nearly as obscure. Meanwhile, we shall put the case aside until more
accurate data are available, and devote the
rest of our morning to the pursuit of neolithic
man."

I may have commented upon my friend's
power of mental detachment, but never have
I wondered at it more than upon that spring
morning in Cornwall when for two hours he
discoursed upon celts, arrowheads, and shards
as lightly as if no sinister mystery was waiting
for his solution. It was not until we had
returned in the afternoon to our cottage that
we found a visitor awaiting us, who soon
brought our minds back to the matter in
hand. Neither of us needed to be told who
that visitor was. The huge body, the craggy

and deeply-seamed face with the fierce eyes and hawk-like nose, the grizzled hair which nearly brushed our cottage ceiling, the beard —golden at the fringes and white near the lips, save for the nicotine stain from his perpetual cigar—all these were as well known in London as in Africa, and could only be associated with the tremendous personality of Dr. Leon Sterndale, the great lion-hunter and explorer.

We had heard of his presence in the district, and had once or twice caught sight of his tall figure upon the moorland paths. He made no advances to us, however, nor would we have dreamed of doing so to him, as it was well known that it was his love of seclusion which caused him to spend the greater part of the intervals between his journeys in a small bungalow buried in the lonely wood of Beauchamp Arriance. Here, amid his books and his maps, he lived an absolutely lonely life, attending to his own simple wants, and paying little apparent heed to the affairs of his neighbours. It was a surprise to me, therefore, to hear him asking Holmes, in an eager voice, whether he had made any advance in his reconstruction of this mysterious episode. "The county police are utterly at fault," said he; "but perhaps your wider experience has suggested some conceivable explanation. My only claim to being taken into your confidence is that during my many residences here I have come to know this family of Tregennis very well—indeed, upon my Cornish mother's side I could call them cousins—and their strange fate has naturally been a great shock to me. I may tell you that I had got as far as Plymouth upon my way to Africa, but the news reached me this morning, and I came straight back again to help in the inquiry."

Holmes raised his eyebrows.

"Did you lose your boat through it?"

"I will take the next."

"Dear me! that is friendship indeed."

"I tell you they were relatives."

"Quite so—cousins of your mother. Was your baggage aboard the ship?"

"Some of it, but the main part at the hotel."

"I see. But surely this event could not have found its way into the Plymouth morning papers?"

"No, sir; I had a telegram."

"Might I ask from whom?"

A shadow passed over the gaunt face of the explorer.

"You are very inquisitive, Mr. Holmes."

"It is my business."

With an effort, Dr. Sterndale recovered his ruffled composure.

"I have no objection to telling you," he said. "It was Mr. Roundhay, the vicar, who sent me the telegram which recalled me."

"Thank you," said Holmes. "I may say, in answer to your original question, that I have not cleared my mind entirely on the subject of this case, but that I have every hope of reaching some conclusion. It would be premature to say more."

"Perhaps you would not mind telling me if your suspicions point in any particular direction?"

"No, I can hardly answer that."

"Then I have wasted my time, and need not prolong my visit." The famous doctor strode out of our cottage in considerable ill-humour, and within five minutes Holmes had followed him. I saw him no more until the evening, when he returned with a slow step and haggard face which assured me that he had made no great progress with his investigation. He glanced at a telegram which awaited him, and threw it into the grate.

"From the Plymouth hotel, Watson," he said. "I learned the name of it from the vicar and I wired to make certain that Dr. Leon Sterndale's account was true. It appears that he did indeed spend last night there, and that he has actually allowed some of his baggage to go on to Africa, while he returned to be present at this investigation. What do you make of that, Watson?"

"He is deeply interested."

"Deeply interested — yes. There is a thread here which we have not yet grasped, and which might lead us through the tangle. Cheer up, Watson, for I am very sure that our material has not yet all come to hand. When it does, we may soon leave our difficulties behind us."

Little did I think how soon the words of Holmes would be realized, or how strange and sinister would be that new development which opened up an entirely fresh line of investigation. I was shaving at my window in the morning when I heard the rattle of hoofs, and, looking up, saw a dogcart coming at a gallop down the road. It pulled up at our door, and our friend the vicar sprang from it and rushed up our garden path. Holmes was already dressed, and we hastened down to meet him.

Our visitor was so excited that he could hardly articulate, but at last in gasps and bursts his tragic story came out of him.

"We are devil-ridden, Mr. Holmes! My poor parish is devil-ridden!" he cried.

"Satan himself is loose in it! We are given over into his hands!" He danced about in his agitation, a ludicrous object if it were not for his ashy face and startled eyes. Finally he shot out his terrible news.

"Mr. Mortimer Tregennis has died during the night, and with exactly the same symptoms as the rest of his family."

Holmes sprang to his feet, all energy in an instant.

"Can you fit us both into your dogcart?"

"Yes, I can."

"Then, Watson, we will postpone our breakfast. Mr. Roundhay, we are entirely at your disposal. Hurry—hurry, before things get disarranged."

The lodger occupied two rooms at the vicarage, which were in an angle by themselves, the one above the other. Below was a large sitting-room; above, his bedroom. They looked out upon a croquet-lawn which came up to the windows. We had arrived before the doctor or the police, so that everything was absolutely undisturbed. Let me describe exactly the scene as we saw it upon that misty March morning. It has left an impression which can never be effaced from my mind.

The atmosphere of the room was of a horrible and depressing stuffiness. The

"BESIDE IT SAT THE DEAD MAN, LEANING BACK IN HIS CHAIR."

servant who had first entered had thrown up the window, or it would have been even more intolerable. This might partly be due to the fact that a lamp stood flaring and smoking on the centre table. Beside it sat the dead man, leaning back in his chair, his thin beard projecting, his spectacles pushed up on to his forehead, and his lean, dark face turned towards the window and twisted into the same distortion of terror which had marked the features of his dead sister. His limbs were convulsed and his fingers contorted, as though he had died in a very paroxysm of fear. He was fully clothed, though there were signs that his dressing had been done in a hurry.

We had already learned that his bed had been slept in, and that the tragic end had come to him in the early morning.

One realized the red hot energy which underlay Holmes's phlegmatic exterior when one saw the sudden change which came over him from the moment that he entered the fatal apartment. In an instant he was tense and alert, his eyes shining, his face set, his limbs quivering with eager activity. He was out on the lawn, in through the window, round the room, and up into the bedroom, for all the world like a dashing foxhound drawing a cover. In the bedroom he made a rapid cast around, and ended by throwing open the window, which appeared to give him some fresh cause for excitement, for he leaned out of it with loud ejaculations of interest and delight. Then he rushed down the stair, out through the open window, threw himself upon his face on the lawn, sprang up and into the room once more, all with the energy of the hunter who is at the very heels of his quarry. The lamp, which was an ordinary standard, he examined with minute care, making certain measurements upon its bowl. He carefully scrutinized with his lens the talc shield which covered the top of the chimney, and scraped off some ashes which adhered to its upper surface, putting some of them into an envelope, which he placed in his pocket-book. Finally, just as the doctor and the official police put in an appearance, he beckoned to the vicar and we all three went out upon the lawn.

"I am glad to say that my investigation has not been entirely barren," he remarked. "I cannot remain to discuss the matter with the police, but I should be exceedingly obliged, Mr. Roundhay, if you would give the inspector my compliments and direct his attention to the bedroom window and to the sitting-room lamp. Each is suggestive, and together they are almost conclusive. If the police would desire further information I shall be happy to see any of them at the cottage. And now, Watson, I think that perhaps we shall be better employed elsewhere."

It may be that the police resented the intrusion of an amateur, or that they imagined themselves to be upon some hopeful line of investigation; but it is certain that we heard nothing from them for the next two days. During this time Holmes spent some of his time smoking and dreaming in the cottage; but a greater portion in country walks which he undertook alone, returning after many hours without remark as to where he had been. One experiment served to show me the line of his investigation. He had bought a lamp which was the duplicate of the one which had burned in the room of Mortimer Tregennis on the morning of the tragedy. This he filled with the same oil as that used at the vicarage, and he carefully timed the period which it would take to be exhausted. Another experiment which he made was of a more unpleasant nature, and one which I am not likely ever to forget.

"You will remember, Watson," he remarked one afternoon, "that there is a single common point of resemblance in the varying reports which have reached us. This concerns the effect of the atmosphere of the room in each case upon those who had first entered it. You will recollect that Mortimer Tregennis, in describing the episode of his last visit to his brothers' house, remarked that the doctor on entering the room fell into a chair? You had forgotten? Well, I can answer for it that it was so. Now, you will remember also that Mrs. Porter, the housekeeper, told us that she herself fainted upon entering the room and had afterwards opened the window. In the second case—

that of Mortimer Tregennis himself—you cannot have forgotten the horrible stuffiness of the room when we arrived, though the servant had thrown open the window. That servant, I found upon inquiry, was so ill that she had gone to her bed. You will admit, Watson, that these facts are very suggestive. In each case there is evidence of a poisonous atmosphere. In each case, also, there is combustion going on in the room—in the one case a fire, in the other a lamp. The fire was needed, but the lamp was lit—as a comparison of the oil consumed will show—long after it was broad daylight. Why? Surely because there is some connection between three things—the burning, the stuffy atmosphere, and, finally, the madness or death of those unfortunate people. That is clear, is it not?"

"It would appear so."

"At least we may accept it as a working hypothesis. We will suppose, then, that something was burned in each case which produced an atmosphere causing strange toxic effects. Very good. In the first instance —that of the Tregennis family—this substance was placed in the fire. Now, the window was shut, but the fire would naturally carry fumes to some extent up the chimney. Hence, one would expect the effects of the poison to be less than in the second case, where there was less escape for the vapour. The result seems to indicate that it was so, since in the first case only the woman, who had presumably the more sensitive organism, was killed, the others exhibiting that temporary or permanent lunacy which is evidently the first effect of the drug. In the second case the result was complete. The facts, therefore, seem to bear out the theory of a poison which worked by combustion.

"With this train of reasoning in my head I naturally looked about in Mortimer Tregennis's room to find some remains of this substance. The obvious place to look was the talc shield or smoke-guard of the lamp. There, sure enough, I perceived a number of flaky ashes, and round the edges a fringe of brownish powder, which had not yet been consumed. Half of this I took, as you saw, and I placed it in an envelope."

"Why half, Holmes?"

"It is not for me, my dear Watson, to stand in the way of the official police force. I leave them all the evidence which I found. The poison still remained upon the talc, had they the wit to find it. Now, Watson, we will light our lamp; we will, however, take the precaution to open our window to avoid the premature decease of two deserving members of society, and you will seat yourself near that open window in an arm-chair—unless, like a sensible man, you determine to have nothing to do with the affair. Oh, you will see it out, will you? I thought I knew my Watson. This chair I will place opposite yours, so that we may be the same distance from the poison, and face to face. The door we will leave ajar. Each is now in a position to watch the other and to bring the experiment to an end should the symptoms seem alarming. Is that all clear? Well, then, I take our powder—or what remains of it—from the envelope, and I lay it above the burning lamp. So! Now, Watson, let us sit down and await developments."

They were not long in coming. I had hardly settled in my chair before I was conscious of a thick, musky odour, subtle and nauseous. At the very first whiff of it my brain and my imagination were beyond all control. A thick black cloud swirled before my eyes, and my mind told me that in this cloud, unseen as yet, but about to spring out upon my appalled senses, lurked all that was vaguely horrible, all that was monstrous and inconceivably wicked in the universe. Vague shapes swirled and swam amid the dark cloud-bank, each a menace and a warning of something coming, the advent of some unspeakable dweller upon the threshold, whose very shadow would blast my soul. A freezing horror took possession of me. I felt that my hair was rising, that my eyes were protruding, that my mouth was opened, and my tongue like leather. The turmoil within my brain was such that something must surely snap. I tried to scream, and was vaguely aware of some hoarse croak which was my own voice, but distant and detached from myself. At the same moment, in some effort of escape, I broke through that cloud of despair, and had a glimpse of Holmes's face, white, rigid, and drawn with horror—the very look which I had seen upon the features of the dead. It was that vision which gave me an instant of sanity and of

"WE LURCHED THROUGH THE DOOR, AND AN INSTANT AFTERWARDS HAD THROWN OURSELVES DOWN UPON THE GRASS PLOT."

strength. I dashed from my chair, threw my arms round Holmes, and together we lurched through the door, and an instant afterwards had thrown ourselves down upon the grass plot and were lying side by side, conscious only of the glorious sunshine which was bursting its way through the hellish cloud of terror which had girt us in. Slowly it rose from our souls like the mists from a landscape, until peace and reason had returned, and we were sitting up on the grass, wiping our clammy foreheads, and looking with apprehension at each other to mark the last traces of that terrific experience which we had undergone.

"Upon my word, Watson!" said Holmes at last, with an unsteady voice, "I owe you both my thanks and an apology. It was an unjustifiable experiment even for oneself, and doubly so for a friend. I am really very sorry."

"You know," I answered, with some emotion, for I had never seen so much of Holmes's heart before, "that it is my greatest joy and privilege to help you."

He relapsed at once into the half-humorous, half-cynical vein which was his habitual attitude to those about him. "It would be superfluous to drive us mad, my dear Watson," said he. "A candid observer would certainly declare that we were so already before we embarked upon so wild an experiment. I confess that I never imagined that the effect could be so sudden and so severe." He dashed into the cottage, and, reappearing with the burning lamp held at full arm's length, he threw it among a bank of brambles. "We must give the room a little time to clear. I take it, Watson, that you have no longer a shadow of a doubt as to how these tragedies were produced?"

"None whatever.'

"But the cause remains as obscure as before. Come into the arbour here, and let us discuss it together. That villainous stuff seems still to linger round my throat. I think we must admit that all the evidence points to this man, Mortimer Tregennis, having been the criminal in the first tragedy, though he was the victim in the second one. We must remember, in the first place, that there is some story of a family quarrel, followed by a reconciliation. How bitter that quarrel may have been, or how hollow the reconciliation, we cannot tell. When I think of Mortimer Tregennis, with the foxy face and the small, shrewd, beady eyes behind the spectacles, he is not a man whom I should judge to be of a particularly forgiving disposition. Well, in the next place, you will remember that this idea of someone moving in the garden, which took our attention for a moment from the real cause of the tragedy, emanated from him. He had a motive in misleading us. Finally, if he did not throw this substance into the fire at the moment of leaving the room, who did do so? The affair happened immediately after his departure. Had anyone else come in, the family would certainly have risen from the table. Besides, in peaceful Cornwall, visitors do not arrive after ten o'clock at night. We may take it, then, that all the evidence points to Mortimer Tregennis as the culprit."

"Then his own death was suicide!"

"Well, Watson, it is on the face of it a not impossible supposition. The man who had the guilt upon his soul of having brought such a fate upon his own family might well be driven by remorse to inflict it upon himself. There are, however, some cogent reasons against it. Fortunately, there is one man in England who knows all about it, and I have made arrangements by which we shall hear the facts this afternoon from his own lips. Ah! he is a little before his time. Perhaps you would kindly step this way, Dr. Leon Sterndale. We have been conducting a chemical experiment indoors which has left our little room hardly fit for the reception of so distinguished a visitor."

I had heard the click of the garden gate, and now the majestic figure of the great African explorer appeared upon the path. He turned in some surprise towards the rustic arbour in which we sat.

"You sent for me, Mr. Holmes. I had your note about an hour ago, and I have come, though I really do not know why I should obey your summons."

"Perhaps we can clear the point up before we separate," said Holmes. "Meanwhile, I am much obliged to you for your courteous acquiescence. You will excuse this informal reception in the open air, but my friend Watson and I have nearly furnished an additional chapter to what the papers call the Cornish Horror, and we prefer a clear atmosphere for the present. Perhaps, since the matters which we have to discuss will affect you personally in a very intimate fashion, it is as well that we should talk where there can be no eavesdropping."

The explorer took his cigar from his lips and gazed sternly at my companion.

"I am at a loss to know, sir," he said, "what you can have to speak about which affects me personally in a very intimate fashion."

"The killing of Mortimer Tregennis," said Holmes.

For a moment I wished that I were armed. Sterndale's fierce face turned to a dusky red, his eyes glared, and the knotted, passionate veins started out in his forehead, while he sprang forward with clenched hands towards my companion. Then he stopped, and with a violent effort he resumed a cold, rigid calmness which was, perhaps, more suggestive of danger than his hot-headed outburst.

"I have lived so long among savages and beyond the law," said he, "that I have got into the way of being a law to myself. You would do well, Mr. Holmes, not to forget it, for I have no desire to do you an injury."

"Nor have I any desire to do you an injury, Dr. Sterndale. Surely the clearest proof of it is that, knowing what I know, I have sent for you and not for the police."

Sterndale sat down with a gasp, overawed for, perhaps, the first time in his adventurous life. There was a calm assurance of power in Holmes's manner which could not be withstood. Our visitor stammered for a moment, his great hands opening and shutting in his agitation.

"HE SPRANG FORWARD WITH CLENCHED HANDS TOWARDS MY COMPANION."

"What do you mean?" he asked, at last. "If this is bluff upon your part, Mr. Holmes, you have chosen a bad man for your experiment. Let us have no more beating about the bush. What *do* you mean?"

"I will tell you," said Holmes, "and the reason why I tell you is that I hope frankness may beget frankness. What my next step may be will depend entirely upon the nature of your own defence."

"My defence?"

"Yes, sir."

"My defence against what?"

"Against the charge of killing Mortimer Tregennis."

Sterndale mopped his forehead with his handkerchief. "Upon my word, you are getting on," said he. "Do all your successes depend upon this prodigious power of bluff?"

"The bluff," said Holmes, sternly, "is upon your side, Dr. Leon Sterndale, and not upon mine. As a proof I will tell you some of the facts upon which my conclusions are based. Of your return from Plymouth, allowing much of your property to go on to Africa, I will say nothing save that it first informed me that you were one of the factors which had to be taken into account in reconstructing this drama——"

"I came back——"

"I have heard your reasons and regard them as unconvincing and inadequate. We will pass that. You came down here to ask me whom I suspected. I refused to answer you. You then went to the vicarage, waited outside it for some time, and finally returned to your cottage."

"How do you know that?"

"I followed you."

"I saw no one."

"That is what you may expect to see when I follow you. You spent a restless night at your cottage, and you formed certain plans, which in the early morning you proceeded to put into execution. Leaving your door just as day was breaking, you filled your pocket with some reddish gravel which was lying heaped beside your gate."

Sterndale gave a violent start and looked at Holmes in amazement.

"You then walked swiftly for the mile which separated you from the vicarage. You were wearing, I may remark, the same pair of ribbed tennis shoes which are at the present moment upon your feet. At the vicarage you passed through the orchard and the side hedge, coming out under the window of the lodger, Tregennis. It was now daylight, but the household was not yet stirring. You drew some of the gravel from your pocket, and you threw it up at the window above you——"

Sterndale sprang to his feet.

"I believe that you are the devil himself!" he cried.

Holmes smiled at the compliment. "It took two, or possibly three, handfuls before the lodger came to the window. You beckoned him to come down. He dressed hurriedly and descended to his sitting-room. You entered by the window. There was an interview—a short one—during which you walked up and down the room. Then you passed out and closed the window, standing on the lawn outside smoking a cigar and watching what occurred. Finally, after the death of Tregennis, you withdrew as you had come. Now, Dr. Sterndale, how do you justify such conduct, and what were the motives for your actions? If you prevaricate or trifle with me, I give you my assurance that the matter will pass out of my hands for ever."

Our visitor's face had turned ashen grey as he listened to the words of his accuser. Now he sat for some time in thought with his face sunk in his hands. Then, with a sudden impulsive gesture, he plucked a photograph from his breast-pocket and threw it on the rustic table before us.

"That is why I have done it," said he.

It showed the bust and face of a very beautiful woman. Holmes stooped over it.

"Brenda Tregennis," said he.

"Yes, Brenda Tregennis," repeated our visitor. "For years I have loved her. For years she has loved me. There is the secret of that Cornish seclusion which people have marvelled at. It has brought me close to the one thing on earth that was dear to me. I could not marry her, for I have a wife who has left me for years, and yet whom, by the deplorable laws of England, I could not divorce. For years Brenda waited. For years I waited. And this is what we have waited for." A terrible sob shook his great frame, and he clutched his throat under his brindled beard. Then with an effort he mastered himself and spoke on.

"The vicar knew. He was in our confidence. He would tell you that she was an angel upon earth. That was why he telegraphed to me and I returned. What was my baggage or Africa to me when I learned that such a fate had come upon my darling? There you have the missing clue to my action, Mr. Holmes."

"Proceed," said my friend.

Dr. Sterndale drew from his pocket a paper packet and laid it upon the table. On the outside was written, "*Radix pedis diaboli*," with a red poison label beneath it. He pushed it towards me. "I understand that you are a doctor, sir. Have you ever heard of this preparation?"

"Devil's-foot root! No, I have never heard of it."

"It is no reflection upon your professional knowledge," said he, "for I believe that, save for one sample in a laboratory at Buda, there is no other specimen in Europe. It has not yet found its way either into the pharmacopœia or into the literature of toxicology. The root is shaped like a foot, half human, half goatlike; hence the fanciful name given by a botanical missionary. It is used as an ordeal poison by the medicine-men in certain districts of West Africa, and is kept as a secret among them. This particular specimen I obtained under very extraordinary circumstances in the Ubanghi country." He opened the paper as he spoke, and disclosed a heap of reddish-brown, snuff-like powder.

"Well, sir?" asked Holmes, sternly.

"I am about to tell you, Mr. Holmes, all that actually occurred, for you already know so much that it is clearly to my interest that you should know all. I have already explained the relationship in which I stood to the Tregennis family. For the sake of the sister I was friendly with the brothers. There was a family quarrel about money which estranged this man Mortimer, but it was supposed to be made up, and I afterwards met him as I did the others. He was a sly, subtle, scheming man, and several things arose which gave me a suspicion of him, but I had no cause for any positive quarrel.

"One day, only a couple of weeks ago, he came down to my cottage and I showed him some of my African curiosities. Among other things, I exhibited this powder, and I told him of its strange properties, how it stimulates those brain centres which control the emotion of fear, and how either madness or death is the fate of the unhappy native who is subjected to the ordeal by the priest of his tribe. I told him also how powerless European science would be to detect it. How he took it I cannot say, for I never left the room, but there is no doubt that it was then, while I was opening cabinets and stooping to boxes, that he managed to abstract some of the devil's-foot root. I well remember how he plied me with questions as to the amount and the time that was needed for its effect, but I little dreamed that he could have a personal reason for asking.

"I thought no more of the matter until the vicar's telegram reached me at Plymouth. This villain had thought that I would be at sea before the news could reach me, and that I should be lost for years in Africa. But I returned at once. Of course, I could not listen to the details without feeling assured that my poison had been used. I came round to see you on the chance that some other explanation had suggested itself to you. But there could be none. I was convinced that Mortimer Tregennis was the murderer; that for the sake of money, and with the idea, perhaps, that if the other members of his family were all insane he would be the sole guardian of their joint property, he had used the devil's-foot powder upon them, driven two of them out of their senses, and killed his sister Brenda, the one human being whom I have ever loved or who has ever loved me. There was his crime; what was to be his punishment?

"Should I appeal to the law? Where were my proofs? I knew that the facts were true, but could I help to make a jury of countrymen believe so fantastic a story? I might or I might not. But I could not afford to fail. My soul cried out for revenge. I have said to you once before, Mr. Holmes, that I have spent much of my life outside the law, and that I have come at last to be a law to myself. So it was now. I determined that the fate which he had given to others should be shared by himself. Either that, or I would do justice upon him with my own hand. In all England there can be no man who sets less value upon his own life than I do at the present moment.

"Now I have told you all. You have yourself supplied the rest. I did, as you say, after a restless night, set off early from my cottage. I foresaw the difficulty of arousing him, so I gathered some gravel from the pile which you have mentioned, and I used it to throw up to his window. He came down and admitted me through the window of the sitting-room. I laid his offence before him. I told him that I had come both as judge and executioner. The wretch sank into a chair paralyzed at the sight of my revolver.

I lit the lamp, put the powder above it, and stood outside the window, ready to carry out my threat to shoot him should he try to leave the room. In five minutes he died. My God! how he died! But my heart was flint, for he endured nothing which my innocent darling had not felt before him. There is my story, Mr. Holmes. Perhaps, if you loved a woman, you would have done as much yourself. At any rate, I am in your hands. You can take what steps you like. As I have already said, there is no man living who can fear death less than I do."

Holmes sat for some little time in silence.

"What were your plans?" he asked, at last.

"I had intended to bury myself in Central Africa. My work there is but half finished."

"Go and do the other half," said Holmes. "I, at least, am not prepared to prevent you."

Dr. Sterndale raised his giant figure, bowed gravely, and walked from the arbour. Holmes lit his pipe and handed me his pouch.

"Some fumes which are not poisonous would be a welcome change," said he. "I think you must agree, Watson, that it is not a case in which we are called upon to interfere. Our investigation has been independent, and our action shall be so also. You would not denounce the man?"

"Certainly not," I answered.

"I have never loved, Watson, but if I did, and if the woman I loved had met such an end, I might act even as our lawless lion-hunter has done. Who knows? Well, Watson, I will not offend your intelligence by explaining what is obvious. The gravel upon the window-sill was, of course, the starting-point of my research. It was unlike anything in the vicarage garden. Only when my attention had been drawn to Dr. Sterndale and his cottage did I find its counterpart. The lamp shining in broad daylight and the remains of powder upon the shield were successive links in a fairly obvious chain. And now, my dear Watson, I think we may dismiss the matter from our mind, and go back with a clear conscience to the study of those Chaldean roots which are surely to be traced in the Cornish branch of the great Celtic speech."

The Second Stain

The Solitary Cyclist

The Dancing Men

The Hound of the Baskervilles

The Speckled Band

The Reigate Squires

The Boscombe Valley Mystery

The Red-Headed League

The Norwood Builder

The Abbey Grange

The Final Problem

The Bruce-Partington Plans

A REVERIE.

THE STRAND MAGAZINE

Vol. xli. No. 243.

MARCH, 1911.

A REMINISCENCE OF
SHERLOCK HOLMES.

The Adventure of the Red Circle.

By ARTHUR CONAN DOYLE.

Illustrated by H. M. Brock, R.I., & Joseph Simpson, R.B.A.

"WELL, Mrs. Warren, I cannot see that you have any particular cause for uneasiness, nor do I understand why I, whose time is of some value, should interfere in the matter. I really have other things to engage me." So spoke Sherlock Holmes, and turned back to the great scrapbook in which he was arranging and indexing some of his recent material.

But the landlady had the pertinacity, and also the cunning, of her sex. She held her ground firmly.

"You arranged an affair for a lodger of mine last year," she said—" Mr. Fairdale Hobbs."

"Ah, yes—a simple matter."

"But he would never cease talking of it—your kindness, sir, and the way in which you brought light into the darkness. I remembered his words when I was in doubt and darkness myself. I know you could if you only would."

Holmes was accessible upon the side of flattery, and also, to do him justice, upon the side of kindliness. The two forces made him lay down his gum-brush with a sigh of resignation and push back his chair.

"Well, well, Mrs. Warren, let us hear about it, then. You don't object to tobacco, I take it? Thank you, Watson—the matches! You are uneasy, as I understand, because your new lodger remains in his room and you cannot see him. Why, bless you, Mrs. Warren, if I were your lodger you often would not see me for weeks on end."

"No doubt, sir; but this is different. It frightens me, Mr. Holmes. I can't sleep for fright. To hear his quick step moving here and moving there from early morning to late at night, and yet never to catch so much as a glimpse of him—it's more than I can stand. My husband is as nervous over it as I am, but he is out at his work all day, while I get no rest from it. What is he hiding for? What has he done? Except for the girl, I am all alone in the house with him, and it's more than my nerves can stand."

Holmes leaned forward and laid his long, thin fingers upon the woman's shoulder. He had an almost hypnotic power of soothing when he wished. The scared look faded from her eyes, and her agitated features smoothed into their usual commonplace. She sat down in the chair which he had indicated.

"If I take it up I must understand every detail," said he. "Take time to consider. The smallest point may be the most essential. You say that the man came ten days ago, and paid you for a fortnight's board and lodging?"

"He asked my terms, sir. I said fifty shillings a week. There is a small sitting-room and bedroom, and all complete, at the top of the house."

"Well?"

"He said, 'I'll pay you five pounds a week if I can have it on my own terms.' I'm a poor woman, sir, and Mr. Warren earns little, and the money meant much to me. He took out a ten-pound note, and he held it out to me then and there. 'You can have the same every fortnight for a long time to come if you keep the terms,' he said. 'If not, I'll have no more to do with you.'"

"What were the terms?"

"Well, sir, they were that he was to have a key of the house. That was all right. Lodgers often have them. Also, that he was to be left entirely to himself, and never, upon any excuse, to be disturbed."

"Nothing wonderful in that, surely?"

"Not in reason, sir. But this is out of all reason. He has been there for ten days, and neither Mr. Warren, nor I, nor the girl has once set eyes upon him. We can hear that quick step of his pacing up and down, up and down, night, morning, and noon; but except on that first night he has never once gone out of the house."

"Oh, he went out the first night, did he?"

"Yes, sir, and returned very late—after we were all in bed. He told me after he had taken the rooms that he would do so, and

asked me not to bar the door. I heard him come up the stair after midnight."

"But his meals?"

"It was his particular direction that we should always, when he rang, leave his meal upon a chair outside his door. Then he rings again when he has finished, and we take it down from the same chair. If he wants anything else he prints it on a slip of paper and leaves it."

"Prints it?"

"Yes, sir; prints it in pencil. Just the word, nothing more. Here's one I brought to show you—SOAP. Here's another—MATCH. This is one he left the first morning—DAILY GAZETTE. I leave that paper with his breakfast every morning."

"Dear me, Watson," said Holmes, staring with great curiosity at the slips of foolscap which the landlady had handed to him, "this is certainly a little unusual. Seclusion I can understand; but why print? Printing is a clumsy process. Why not write? What would it suggest, Watson?"

"That he desired to conceal his handwriting."

"But why? What can it matter to him that his landlady should have a word of his writing? Still, it may be as you say. Then, again, why such laconic messages?"

"I cannot imagine."

"It opens a pleasing field for intelligent speculation. The words are written with a broad-pointed, violet-tinted pencil of a not unusual pattern. You will observe that the paper is torn away at the side here after the printing was done, so that the 'S' of 'SOAP' is partly gone. Suggestive, Watson, is it not?"

"Of caution?"

"Exactly. There was evidently some mark, some thumb-print, something which might give a clue to the person's identity. Now, Mrs. Warren, you say that the man was of middle size, dark, and bearded. What age would he be?"

"Youngish, sir—not over thirty."

"Well, can you give me no further indications?"

"He spoke good English, sir, and yet I thought he was a foreigner by his accent."

"And he was well dressed?"

"Very smartly dressed, sir—quite the gentleman. Dark clothes — nothing you would note."

"He gave no name?"

"No, sir."

"And has had no letters or callers?"

"None."

"But surely you or the girl enter his room of a morning?"

"No, sir; he looks after himself entirely."

"Dear me! that is certainly remarkable. What about his luggage?"

The landlady drew an envelope from her bag; from it she shook out two burnt matches and a cigarette-end upon the table.

"They were on his tray this morning. I

"HOLMES STARED WITH GREAT CURIOSITY AT THE SLIPS OF FOOLSCAP."

"He had one big brown bag with him—nothing else."

"Well, we don't seem to have much material to help us. Do you say nothing has come out of that room—absolutely nothing?"

brought them because I had heard that you can read great things out of small ones."

Holmes shrugged his shoulders.

"There is nothing here," said he. "The matches have, of course, been used to light cigarettes. That is obvious from the shortness of the burnt end. Half the match is consumed in lighting a pipe or a cigar. But, dear me! this cigarette stub is certainly remarkable. The gentleman was bearded and moustached, you say?"

"Yes, sir."

"I don't understand that. I should say that only a clean-shaven man could have smoked this. Why, Watson, even your modest moustache would have been singed."

"A holder?" I suggested.

"No, no; the end is matted. I suppose there could not be two people in your rooms, Mrs. Warren?"

"No, sir. He eats so little that I often wonder it can keep life in one."

"Well, I think we must wait for a little more material. After all, you have nothing to complain of. You have received your rent, and he is not a troublesome lodger, though he is certainly an unusual one. He pays you well, and if he chooses to lie concealed it is no direct business of yours. We have no excuse for an intrusion upon his privacy until we have some reason to think that there is a guilty reason for it. I've taken up the matter, and I won't lose sight of it. Report to me if anything fresh occurs, and rely upon my assistance if it should be needed.

"There are certainly some points of interest in this case, Watson," he remarked, when the landlady had left us. "It may, of course, be trivial—individual eccentricity; or it may be very much deeper than appears on the surface. The first thing that strikes one is the obvious possibility that the person now in the rooms may be entirely different from the one who engaged them."

"Why should you think so?"

"Well, apart from this cigarette-end, was it not suggestive that the only time the lodger went out was immediately after his taking the rooms? He came back—or someone came back—when all witnesses were out of the way. We have no proof that the person who came back was the person who went out. Then, again, the man who took the rooms spoke English well. This other, however, prints 'match' when it should have been 'matches.' I can imagine that the word was taken out of a dictionary, which would give the noun but not the plural. The laconic style may be to conceal the absence of knowledge of English. Yes, Watson, there are good reasons to suspect that there has been a substitution of lodgers."

"But for what possible end?"

"Ah! there lies our problem. There is one rather obvious line of investigation." He took down the great book in which, day by day, he filed the agony columns of the various London journals. "Dear me!" said he, turning over the pages, "what a chorus of groans, cries, and bleatings! What a rag-bag of singular happenings! But surely the most valuable hunting-ground that ever was given to a student of the unusual! This person is alone, and cannot be approached by letter without a breach of that absolute secrecy which is desired. How is any news or any message to reach him from without? Obviously by advertisement through a newspaper. There seems no other way, and fortunately we need concern ourselves with the one paper only. Here are the *Daily Gazette* extracts of the last fortnight. 'Lady with a black boa at Prince's Skating Club'—that we may pass. 'Surely Jimmy will not break his mother's heart'—that appears to be irrelevant. 'If the lady who fainted in the Brixton bus'—she does not interest me. 'Every day my heart longs——' Bleat, Watson—unmitigated bleat! Ah! this is a little more possible. Listen to this: 'Be patient. Will find some sure means of communication. Meanwhile, this column.—G.' That is two days after Mrs. Warren's lodger arrived. It sounds plausible, does it not? The mysterious one could understand English, even if he could not print it. Let us see if we can pick up the trace again. Yes, here we are—three days later. 'Am making successful arrangements. Patience and prudence. The clouds will pass.—G.' Nothing for a week after that. Then comes something much more definite: 'The path is clearing. If I find chance signal message remember code agreed—one A, two B, and so on. You will hear soon.—G.' That was in yesterday's paper, and there is nothing in to-day's. It's all very appropriate to Mrs. Warren's lodger. If we wait a little, Watson, I don't doubt that the affair will grow more intelligible."

So it proved; for in the morning I found my friend standing on the hearthrug with his back to the fire, and a smile of complete satisfaction upon his face.

"How's this, Watson?" he cried, picking up the paper from the table. "'High red house with white stone facings. Third floor. Second window left. After dusk.—G.' That is definite enough. I think after breakfast we must make a little reconnaissance of Mrs. Warren's neighbourhood. Ah, Mrs. Warren! what news do you bring us this morning?"

Our client had suddenly burst into the room with an explosive energy which told of some new and momentous development.

"It's a police matter, Mr. Holmes!" she cried. "I'll have no more of it! He shall pack out of that with his baggage. I would have gone straight up and told him so, only I thought it was but fair to you to take your opinion first. But I'm at the end of my patience, and when it comes to knocking my old man about——"

"Knocking Mr. Warren about?"

"Using him roughly, anyway."

so he took a bus home, and there he lies now on the sofa, while I came straight round to tell you what had happened."

"Most interesting," said Holmes. "Did he observe the appearance of these men—did he hear them talk?"

"No; he is clean dazed. He just knows that he was lifted up as if by magic and dropped as if by magic. Two at least were in it, and maybe three."

"And you connect this attack with your lodger?"

"Well, we've lived there fifteen years and

"THEY BUNDLED HIM INTO A CAB THAT WAS BESIDE THE KERB."

"But who used him roughly?"

"Ah! that's what we want to know! It was this morning, sir. Mr. Warren is a time-keeper at Morton and Waylight's, in Tottenham Court Road. He has to be out of the house before seven. Well, this morning he had not got ten paces down the road when two men came up behind him, threw a coat over his head, and bundled him into a cab that was beside the kerb. They drove him an hour, and then opened the door and shot him out. He lay in the roadway so shaken in his wits that he never saw what became of the cab. When he picked himself up he found he was on Hampstead Heath;

no such happenings ever came before. I've had enough of him. Money's not everything. I'll have him out of my house before the day is done."

"Wait a bit, Mrs. Warren. Do nothing rash. I begin to think that this affair may be very much more important than appeared at first sight. It is clear now that some danger is threatening your lodger. It is equally clear that his enemies, lying in wait for him near your door, mistook your husband for him in the foggy morning light. On discovering their mistake they released him. What they would have done had it not been a mistake, we can only conjecture."

"Well, what am I to do, Mr. Holmes?"

"I have a great fancy to see this lodger of yours, Mrs. Warren."

"I don't see how that is to be managed, unless you break n the door. I always hear him unlock it as I go down the stair after I leave the tray."

"He has to take the tray in. Surely we could conceal ourselves and see him do it."

The landlady thought for a moment.

"Well, sir, there's the box-room opposite. I could arrange a looking-glass, maybe, and if you were behind the door——"

"Excellent!" said Holmes. "When does he lunch?"

"About one, sir."

"Then Dr. Watson and I will come round in time. For the present, Mrs. Warren, good-bye."

At half-past twelve we found ourselves upon the steps of Mrs. Warren's house—a high, thin, yellow-brick edifice in Great Orme Street, a narrow thoroughfare at the north-east side of the British Museum. Standing as it does near the corner of the street, it commands a view down Howe Street, with its more pretentious houses. Holmes pointed with a chuckle to one of these, a row of residential flats, which projected so that they could not fail to catch the eye.

"See, Watson!" said he. "'High red house with stone facings.' There is the signal station all right. We know the place, and we know the code; so surely our task should be simple. There's a 'To Let' card in that window. It is evidently an empty flat to which the confederate has access. Well, Mrs. Warren, what now?"

"I have it all ready for you. If you will both come up and leave your boots below on the landing, I'll put you there now."

It was an excellent hiding-place which she had arranged. The mirror was so placed that, seated in the dark, we could very plainly see the door opposite. We had hardly settled down in it, and Mrs. Warren left us, when a distant tinkle announced that our mysterious neighbour had rung. Presently the landlady appeared with the tray, laid it down upon a chair beside the closed door, and then, treading heavily, departed. Crouching together in the angle of the door, we kept our eyes fixed upon the mirror. Suddenly, as the landlady's footsteps died away, there was the creak of a turning key, the handle revolved, and two thin hands darted out and lifted the tray from the chair. An instant later it was hurriedly replaced, and I caught

a glimpse of a dark, beautiful, horrified face glaring at the narrow opening of the box-room. Then the door crashed to, the key turned once more, and all was silence. Holmes twitched my sleeve, and together we stole down the stair.

"I will call again in the evening," said he to the expectant landlady. "I think, Watson, we can discuss this business better in our own quarters."

"My surmise, as you saw, proved to be correct," said he, speaking from the depths of his easy-chair. "There has been a substitution of lodgers. What I did not foresee is that we should find a woman, and no ordinary woman, Watson."

"She saw us."

"Well, she saw something to alarm her. That is certain. The general sequence of events is pretty clear, is it not? A couple seek refuge in London from a very terrible and instant danger. The measure of that danger is the rigour of their precautions. The man, who has some work which he must do, desires to leave the woman in absolute safety while he does it. It is not an easy problem, but he solved it in an original fashion, and so effectively that her presence was not even known to the landlady who supplies her with food. The printed messages, as is now evident, were to prevent her sex being discovered by her writing. The man cannot come near the woman, or he will guide their enemies to her. Since he cannot communicate with her direct, he has recourse to the agony column of a paper. So far all is clear."

"But what is at the root of it?"

"Ah, yes, Watson—severely practical, as usual! What is at the root of it all? Mrs. Warren's whimsical problem enlarges somewhat and assumes a more sinister aspect as we proceed. This much we can say: that it is no ordinary love escapade. You saw the woman's face at the sign of danger. We have heard, too, of the attack upon the landlord, which was undoubtedly meant for the lodger. These alarms, and the desperate need for secrecy, argue that the matter is one of life or death. The attack upon Mr. Warren further shows that the enemy, whoever they are, are themselves not aware of the substitution of the female lodger for the male. It is very curious and complex, Watson."

"Why should you go further in it? What have you to gain from it?"

"What, indeed? It is Art for Art's sake, Watson. I suppose when you doctored

"I CAUGHT A GLIMPSE OF A DARK, BEAUTIFUL, HORRIFIED FACE GLARING AT THE NARROW
OPENING OF THE BOX-ROOM."

you found yourself studying cases without thought of a fee ? "

" For my education, Holmes."

" Education never ends, Watson. It is a series of lessons with the greatest for the last. This is an instructive case. There is neither money nor credit in it, and yet one would wish to tidy it up. When dusk comes we should find ourselves one stage advanced in our investigation."

When we returned to Mrs. Warren's rooms, the gloom of a London winter evening had thickened into one grey curtain, a dead monotone of colour, broken only by the sharp yellow squares of the windows and the blurred haloes of the gas - lamps. As we peered from the darkened sitting-room of the lodging-house, one more dim light glimmered high up through the obscurity.

" Someone is moving in that room," said Holmes in a whisper, his gaunt and eager face thrust forward to the window-pane. " Yes, I can see his shadow. There he is again ! He has a candle in his hand. Now he is peering across. He wants to be sure that she is on the look-out. Now he begins to flash. Take the message also, Watson, that we may check each other. A single flash—that is ' A,' surely. Now, then. How many did you make it ? Twenty. So did I. That should mean ' T.' A T—that's intelligible enough ! Another ' T.' Surely this is the beginning of a second word. Now, then—T E N T A. Dead stop. That can't be all, Watson ? ' A T T E N T A ' gives no sense. Nor is it any better as three words—' A T. T E N. T A,' unless ' T.A.' are a person's initials. There he goes again ! What's that ? A T T E—why, it is the same message over again. Curious, Watson, very curious ! Now he is off once more ! A T—why, he is repeating it for the third time. ' A T T E N T A ' three times ! How often will he repeat it ? No, that seems to be the finish. He has withdrawn from the window. What do you make of it, Watson ? "

" A cipher message, Holmes."

My companion gave a sudden chuckle of comprehension. " And not a very obscure cipher, Watson," said he. " Why, of course, it is Italian ! The ' A ' means that it is addressed to a woman. ' Beware ! Beware ! Beware ! ' How's that, Watson ? "

" I believe you have hit it."

" Not a doubt of it. It is a very urgent message, thrice repeated to make it more so. But beware of what ? Wait a bit ; he is coming to the window once more."

Again we saw the dim silhouette of a crouching man and the whisk of the small flame across the window, as the signals were renewed. They came more rapidly than before—so rapid that it was hard to follow them.

" ' P E R I C O L O ' — ' pericolo ' —Eh, what's that, Watson ? Danger, isn't it ? Yes, by Jove, it's a danger signal. There he goes again ! ' P E R I.' Halloa, what on earth——"

The light had suddenly gone out, the glimmering square of window had disappeared, and the third floor formed a dark band round the lofty building, with its tiers of shining casements. That last warning cry had been suddenly cut short. How, and by whom ? The same thought occurred on the instant to us both. Holmes sprang up from where he crouched by the window.

" This is serious, Watson," he cried. " There is some devilry going forward ! Why should such a message stop in such a way ? I should put Scotland Yard in touch with this business—and yet, it is too pressing for us to leave."

" Shall I go for the police ? "

" We must define the situation a little more clearly. It may bear some more innocent interpretation. Come, Watson, let us go across ourselves and see what we can make of it."

A REMINISCENCE OF
SHERLOCK HOLMES.

The Adventure of the Red Circle.

By ARTHUR CONAN DOYLE.

Illustrated by H. M. Brock, R.I.

PART II.

AS we walked rapidly down Howe Street I glanced back at the building which we had left. There, dimly outlined at the top window, I could see the shadow of a head, a woman's head, gazing tensely, rigidly, out into the night, waiting with breathless suspense for the renewal of that interrupted message. At the doorway of the Howe Street flats a man, muffled in a cravat and great-coat, was leaning against the railing. He started as the hall-light fell upon our faces.

"Holmes!" he cried.

"Why, Gregson!" said my companion, as he shook hands with the Scotland Yard detective. "Journeys end with lovers' meetings. What brings you here?"

"The same reasons that bring you, I expect," said Gregson. "How you got on to it I can't imagine."

"Different threads, but leading up to the same tangle. I've been taking the signals."

"Signals?"

"Yes, from that window. They broke off in the middle. We came over to see the reason. But since it is safe in your hands I see no object in continuing the business."

"Wait a bit!" cried Gregson, eagerly. "I'll do you this justice, Mr. Holmes, that I was never in a case yet that I didn't feel stronger for having you on my side. There's only the one exit to these flats, so we have him safe."

"Who is he?"

"Well, well, we score over you for once, Mr. Holmes. You must give us best this time." He struck his stick sharply upon the ground, on which a cabman, his whip in his hand, sauntered over from a four-wheeler which stood on the far side of the street. "May I introduce you to Mr. Sherlock Holmes?" he said to the cabman. "This is Mr. Leverton, of Pinkerton's American Agency."

"The hero of the Long Island Cave mystery?" said Holmes. "Sir, I am pleased to meet you."

The American, a quiet, businesslike young man, with a clean-shaven, hatchet face, flushed up at the words of commendation. "I am on the trail of my life now, Mr. Holmes," said he. "If I can get Gorgiano——"

"What! Gorgiano of the Red Circle?"

"Oh, he has a European fame, has he? Well, we've learned all about him in America. We *know* he is at the bottom of fifty murders, and yet we have nothing positive we can take him on. I tracked him over from New York, and I've been close to him for a week in London, waiting some excuse to get my hand on his collar. Mr. Gregson and I ran him to ground in that big tenement house, and there's only the one door, so he can't slip us. There's three folk come out since he went in, but I'll swear he wasn't one of them."

"Mr. Holmes talks of signals," said Gregson. "I expect, as usual, he knows a good deal that we don't."

In a few clear words Holmes explained the situation as it had appeared to us. The American struck his hands together with vexation.

"He's on to us!" he cried.

"Why do you think so?"

"Well, it figures out that way, does it not? Here he is, sending out messages to an accomplice — there are several of his gang in London. Then suddenly, just as by your own account he was telling them that there was danger, he broke short off. What could it mean except that from the window he had suddenly either caught sight of us in the street, or in some way come to understand how close the danger was, and that he must act right away if he was to avoid it? What do you suggest, Mr. Holmes?"

"That we go up at once and see for ourselves."

"But we have no warrant for his arrest."

"He is in unoccupied premises under suspicious circumstances," said Gregson. "That is good enough for the moment. When we have him by the heels we can see if New York can't help us to keep him. I'll take the responsibility of arresting him now."

Our official detectives may blunder in the matter of intelligence, but never in that of courage. Gregson climbed the stair to arrest this desperate murderer with the same absolutely quiet and businesslike bearing with which he would have ascended the official staircase of Scotland Yard. The Pinkerton man had tried to push past him, but Gregson had firmly elbowed him back. London dangers were the privilege of the London force.

The door of the left-hand flat upon the third landing was standing ajar. Gregson pushed it open. Within all was absolute silence and darkness. I struck a match, and lit the detective's lantern. As I did so, and as the flicker steadied into a flame, we all gave a gasp of surprise. On the deal boards of the carpetless floor there was outlined a fresh track of blood. The red steps pointed towards us, and led away from an inner room, the door of which was closed. Gregson flung

"HOLMES WAS PASSING THE CANDLE BACKWARDS AND FORWARDS ACROSS THE WINDOW-PANES."

it open and held his light full blaze in front of him, whilst we all peered eagerly over his shoulders.

In the middle of the floor of the empty room was huddled the figure of an enormous man, his clean-shaven, swarthy face grotesquely horrible in its contortion, and his head encircled by a ghastly crimson halo of blood, lying in a broad wet circle upon the white woodwork. His knees were drawn up, his hands thrown out in agony, and from the centre of his broad, brown, upturned throat there projected the white haft of a knife driven blade-deep into his body. Giant as he was, the man must have gone down like a pole-axed ox before that terrific blow. Beside his right hand a most formidable horn-handled, two-edged dagger lay upon the floor, and near it a black kid glove.

" By George ! it's Black Gorgiano himself ! " cried the American detective. " Someone has got ahead of us this time."

" Here is the candle in the window, Mr. Holmes," said Gregson. " Why, whatever are you doing ? "

Holmes had stepped across, had lit the candle, and was passing it backwards and forwards across the window-panes. Then he peered into the darkness, blew the candle out, and threw it on the floor,

" I rather think that will be helpful," said he. He came over and stood in deep thought, while the two professionals were examining the body. " You say that three people came out from the flat while you were waiting downstairs," said he, at last. " Did you observe them closely ? "

" Yes, I did."

" Was there a fellow about thirty, black-bearded, dark, of middle size ? "

" Yes ; he was the last to pass me."

" That is your man, I fancy. I can give you his description, and we have a very excellent outline of his footmark. That should be enough for you."

" Not much, Mr. Holmes, among the millions of London."

" Perhaps not. That is why I thought it best to summon this lady to your aid."

We all turned round at the words. There, framed in the doorway, was a tall and beautiful woman—the mysterious lodger of Bloomsbury. Slowly she advanced, her face pale and drawn with a frightful apprehension, her eyes fixed and staring, her terrified gaze riveted upon the dark figure on the floor.

" You have killed him ! " she muttered. " Oh, *Dio mio*, you have killed him ! " Then I heard a sudden sharp intake of her breath, and she sprang into the air with a cry of joy. Round and round the room she danced, her hands clapping, her dark eyes gleaming with delighted wonder, and a thousand pretty Italian exclamations pouring from her lips. It was terrible and amazing to see such a woman so convulsed with joy at such a sight. Suddenly she stopped and gazed at us all with a questioning stare.

" But you ! You are police, are you not ? You have killed Giuseppe Gorgiano. Is it not so ? "

" We are police, madam."

She looked round into the shadows of the room.

" But where, then, is Gennaro ? " she asked. " He is my husband, Gennaro Lucca. I am Emilia Lucca, and we are both from New York. Where is Gennaro ? He called me this moment from this window, and I ran with all my speed."

" It was I who called," said Holmes.

" You ! How could you call ? "

" Your cipher was not difficult, madam. Your presence here was desirable. I knew that I had only to flash ' *Vieni*' and you would surely come."

The beautiful Italian looked with awe at my companion.

" I do not understand how you know these things," she said. " Giuseppe Gorgiano— how did he——" She paused, and then suddenly her face lit up with pride and delight. " Now I see it ! My Gennaro ! My splendid, beautiful Gennaro, who has guarded me safe from all harm, he did it, with his own strong hand he killed the monster ! Oh, Gennaro, how wonderful you are ! What woman could ever be worthy of such a man ? "

" Well, Mrs. Lucca," said the prosaic Gregson, laying his hand upon the lady's sleeve with as little sentiment as if she were a Notting Hill hooligan, " I am not very clear yet who you are or what you are ; but you've said enough to make it very clear that we shall want you at the Yard."

" One moment, Gregson," said Holmes. " I rather fancy that this lady may be as anxious to give us information as we can be to get it. You understand, madam, that your husband will be arrested and tried for the death of the man who lies before us ? What you say may be used in evidence. But if you think that he has acted from motives which are not criminal, and which he would wish to have known, then you cannot serve him better than by telling us the whole story."

" Now that Gorgiano is dead we fear nothing," said the lady. " He was a devil and a monster, and there can be no judge in the world who would punish my husband for having killed him."

" In that case," said Holmes, " my suggestion is that we lock this door, leave things as we found them, go with this lady to her room, and form our opinion after we have heard what it is that she has to say to us."

Half an hour later we were seated, all four, in the small sitting-room of Signora Lucca, listening to her remarkable narrative of those sinister events, the ending of which we had

"'BY GEORGE! IT'S BLACK GORGIANO HIMSELF!' CRIED THE AMERICAN DETECTIVE."

chanced to witness. She spoke in rapid and fluent but very unconventional English, which, for the sake of clearness, I will make grammatical.

" I was born in Posilippo, near Naples," said she, " and was the daughter of Augusto Barelli, who was the chief lawyer and once the deputy of that part. Gennaro was in my father's employment, and I came to love him, as any woman must. He had neither money nor position—nothing but his beauty and strength and energy—so my father forbade the match. We fled together, were married at Bari, and sold my jewels to gain the money which would take us to America. This was four years ago, and we have been in New York ever since.

" Fortune was very good to us at first. Gennaro was able to do a service to an Italian gentleman—he saved him from some ruffians in the place called the Bowery, and so made a powerful friend. His name was Tito Castalotte, and he was the senior partner of the great firm of Castalotte and Zamba, who are the chief fruit importers of New York. Signor Zamba is an invalid, and our new friend Castalotte has all power within the firm, which employs more than three hundred men. He took my husband into his employment, made him head of a department, and showed his goodwill towards him in every way. Signor Castalotte was a bachelor, and I believe that he felt as if Gennaro was his son, and both my husband and I loved him as if he were our father. We had taken and furnished a little house in Brooklyn, and our whole future seemed assured, when that black cloud appeared which was soon to overspread our sky.

" One night, when Gennaro returned from his work, he brought a fellow-countryman back with him. His name was Gorgiano, and he had come also from Posilippo. He was a huge man, as you can testify, for you have looked upon his corpse. Not only was his body that of a giant, but everything about him was grotesque, gigantic, and terrifying. His voice was like thunder in our little house. There was scarce room for the whirl of his great arms as he talked. His thoughts, his emotions, his passions, all were exaggerated and monstrous. He talked, or rather roared, with such energy that others could but sit and listen, cowed with the mighty stream of words. His eyes blazed at you and held you at his mercy. He was a terrible and wonderful man. I thank God that he is dead !

" He came again and again. Yet I was aware that Gennaro was no more happy than I was in his presence. My poor husband would sit pale and listless, listening to the endless ravings upon politics and upon social questions which made up our visitor's conversation. Gennaro said nothing, but I who knew him so well could read in his face some emotion which I had never seen there before. At first I thought that it was dislike. And then, gradually, I understood that it was more than dislike. It was fear—a deep, secret, shrinking fear. That night—the night that I read his terror—I put my arms round him and I implored him by his love for me and by all that he held dear to hold nothing from me, and to tell me why this huge man overshadowed him so.

" He told me, and my own heart grew cold as ice as I listened. My poor Gennaro, in his wild and fiery days, when all the world seemed against him and his mind was driven half mad by the injustices of life, had joined a Neapolitan society, the Red Circle, which was allied to the old Carbonari. The oaths and secrets of this brotherhood were frightful ; but once within its rule no escape was possible. When we had fled to America Gennaro thought that he had cast it all off for ever. What was his horror one evening to meet in the streets the very man who had initiated him in Naples, the giant Gorgiano, a man who had earned the name of ' Death ' in the South of Italy, for he was red to the elbow in murder ! He had come to New York to avoid the Italian police, and he had already planted a branch of this dreadful society in his new home. All this Gennaro told me, and showed me a summons which he had received that very day, a Red Circle drawn upon the head of it, telling him that a lodge would be held upon a certain date, and that his presence at it was required and ordered.

" That was bad enough, but worse was to come. I had noticed for some time that when Gorgiano came to us, as he constantly did, in the evening, he spoke much to me ; and even when his words were to my husband those terrible, glaring, wild-beast eyes of his were always turned upon me. One night his secret came out. I had awakened what he called ' love ' within him—the love of a brute—a savage. Gennaro had not yet returned when he came. He pushed his way in, seized me in his mighty arms, hugged me in his bear's embrace, covered me with kisses, and implored me to come away with him. I was struggling and screaming when Gennaro entered and attacked him. He struck Gennaro senseless and fled from the house which he was never more to enter. It was a deadly enemy that we made that night.

"SLOWLY SHE ADVANCED, HER FACE PALE AND DRAWN WITH A FRIGHTFUL APPREHENSION."

"A few days later came the meeting. Gennaro returned from it with a face which told me that something dreadful had occurred. It was worse than we could have imagined possible. The funds of the society were raised by blackmailing rich Italians and threatening them with violence should they refuse the money. It seems that Castalotte, our dear friend and benefactor, had been approached. He had refused to yield to threats, and he had handed the notices to the police. It was resolved now that such an example should be made of him as would prevent any other victim from rebelling. At the meeting it was arranged that he and his house should be blown up with dynamite. There was a drawing of lots as to who should carry out the deed. Gennaro saw our enemy's cruel face smiling at him as he dipped his hand in the bag. No doubt it had been prearranged in some fashion, for it was the fatal disc with the Red Circle upon it, the mandate for murder, which lay upon his palm. He was to kill his best friend, or he was to expose himself and me to the vengeance of his comrades. It was part of their fiendish system to punish those whom they feared or hated by injuring not only their own persons, but those whom they loved, and it was the knowledge of this which hung as a terror over my poor Gennaro's head and drove him nearly crazy with apprehension.

"All that night we sat together, our arms round each other, each strengthening each for the troubles that lay before us. The very next evening had been fixed for the attempt. By midday my husband and I were on our way to London, but not before he had given our benefactor full warning of his danger, and had also left such information for the police as would safeguard his life for the future.

"The rest, gentlemen, you know for yourselves. We were sure that our enemies would be behind us like our own shadows. Gorgiano had his private reasons for vengeance, but in any case we knew how ruthless, cunning, and untiring he could be. Both Italy and America are full of stories of his dreadful powers. If ever they were exerted it would be now. My darling made use of the few clear days which our start had given us in arranging for a refuge for me in such a fashion that no possible danger could reach me. For his own part, he wished to be free that he might communicate both with the American and with the Italian police. I do not myself know where he lived, or how. All that I learned was through the columns of a newspaper. But once, as I looked through my window, I saw two Italians watching the house, and I understood that in some way Gorgiano had found out our retreat. Finally Gennaro told me, through the paper, that he would signal to me from a certain window, but when the signals came they were nothing but warnings, which were suddenly interrupted. It is very clear to me now that he knew Gorgiano to be close upon him, and that, thank God ! he was ready for him when he came. And now, gentlemen, I would ask you whether we have anything to fear from the Law, or whether any judge upon earth would condemn my Gennaro for what he has done ? "

"Well, Mr. Gregson," said the American, looking across at the official, " I don't know what your British point of view may be, but I guess that in New York this lady's husband will receive a pretty general vote of thanks."

"She will have to come with me and see the Chief," Gregson answered. " If what she says is corroborated, I do not think she or her husband has much to fear. But what I can't make head or tail of, Mr. Holmes, is how on earth *you* got yourself mixed up in the matter."

"Education, Gregson, education. Still seeking knowledge at the old university. Well, Watson, you have one more specimen of the tragic and grotesque to add to your collection. By the way, it is not eight o'clock, and a Wagner night at Covent Garden ! If we hurry, we might be in time for the second act."

"THE FELLOW GAVE A BELLOW OF ANGER AND SPRANG UPON ME
LIKE A TIGER."

THE STRAND MAGAZINE

Vol. xlii.   DECEMBER, 1911.   No. 252.

A NEW ADVENTURE OF

Sherlock Holmes.

The Disappearance of Lady Frances Carfax.

By ARTHUR CONAN DOYLE.

Illustrated by Alec Ball.

"BUT why Turkish?" asked Mr. Sherlock Holmes, gazing fixedly at my boots. I was reclining in a cane-backed chair at the moment, and my protruded feet had attracted his ever-active attention.

"English," I answered, in some surprise. "I got them at Latimer's, in Oxford Street."

Holmes smiled with an expression of weary patience.

"The bath!" he said; "the bath! Why the relaxing and expensive Turkish rather than the invigorating home-made article?"

"Because for the last few days I have been feeling rheumatic and old. A Turkish bath is what we call an alterative in medicine—a fresh starting-point, a cleanser of the system.

"By the way, Holmes," I added, "I have no doubt the connection between my boots and a Turkish bath is a perfectly self-evident one to a logical mind, and yet I should be obliged to you if you would indicate it."

"The train of reasoning is not very obscure, Watson," said Holmes, with a mischievous twinkle. "It belongs to the same elementary class of deduction which I should illustrate if I were to ask you who shared your cab in your drive this morning."

"I don't admit that a fresh illustration is an explanation," said I, with some asperity.

"Bravo, Watson! A very dignified and logical remonstrance. Let me see, what were the points? Take the last one first—the cab. You observe that you have some splashes on the left sleeve and shoulder of your coat. Had you sat in the centre of a hansom you would probably have had no splashes, and if you had they would certainly have been symmetrical. Therefore it is clear that you sat at the side. Therefore it is equally clear that you had a companion."

"That is very evident."

"Absurdly commonplace, is it not?"

"But the boots and the bath?"

"Equally childish. You are in the habit of doing up your boots in a certain way. I see them on this occasion fastened with an elaborate double bow, which is not your usual method of tying them. You have, therefore, had them off. Who has tied them? A bootmaker—or the boy at the bath. It is unlikely that it is the bootmaker, since your boots are nearly new. Well, what remains? The bath. Absurd, is it not? But, for all that, the Turkish bath has served a purpose."

"What is that?"

"You say that you have had it because you need a change. Let me suggest that you take one. How would Lausanne do, my dear Watson—first-class tickets and all expenses paid on a princely scale?"

"Splendid! But why?"

Holmes leaned back in his armchair and took his notebook from his pocket.

"One of the most dangerous classes in the world," said he, "is the drifting and friendless woman. She is the most harmless, and often the most useful of mortals, but she is the inevitable inciter of crime in others. She is helpless. She is migratory. She has sufficient means to take her from country to country and from hotel to hotel. She is lost, as often as not, in a maze of obscure *pensions* and boarding-houses. She is a stray chicken in a world of foxes. When she is gobbled up she is hardly missed. I much fear that some evil has come to the Lady Frances Carfax."

I was relieved at this sudden descent from the general to the particular. Holmes consulted his notes.

"Lady Frances," he continued, "is the sole survivor of the direct family of the late Earl of Rufton. The estates went, as you may remember, in the male line. She was left with limited means, but with some very remarkable old Spanish jewellery of silver and curiously-cut diamonds to which she was fondly attached—too attached, for she refused to leave it with her banker and always carried it about with her. A rather pathetic figure, the Lady Frances, a beautiful woman, still in fresh middle age, and yet, by a strange chance, the last derelict of what only twenty years ago was a goodly fleet."

"What has happened to her, then ? "

"Ah, what has happened to the Lady Frances ? Is she alive or dead ? There is our problem. She is a lady of precise habits, and for four years it has been her invariable custom to write every second week to Miss Dobney, her old governess, who has long retired, and lives in Camberwell. It is this Miss Dobney who has consulted me. Nearly five weeks have passed without a word. The last letter was from the Hôtel National at Lausanne. Lady Frances seems to have left there and given no address. The family are anxious, and, as they are exceedingly wealthy, no sum will be spared if we can clear the matter up."

"Is Miss Dobney the only source of information ? Surely she had other correspondents ? "

"There is one correspondent who is a sure draw, Watson. That is the bank. Single ladies must live, and their pass-books are compressed diaries. She banks at Silvester's. I have glanced over her account. The last cheque but one paid her bill at Lausanne, but it was a large one and probably left her with cash in hand. Only one cheque has been drawn since."

"To whom, and where ? "

"To Miss Marie Devine. There is nothing to show where the cheque was drawn. It was cashed at the Crédit Lyonnais at Montpelier less than three weeks ago. The sum was fifty pounds."

"And who is Miss Marie Devine ? "

"That also I have been able to discover. Miss Marie Devine was the maid of Lady Frances Carfax. Why she should have paid her this cheque we have not yet determined. I have no doubt, however, that your researches will soon clear the matter up."

"*My* researches ! "

"Hence the health-giving expedition to Lausanne. You know that I cannot possibly leave London while old Abrahams is in such mortal terror of his life. Besides, on general principles it is best that I should not leave the country. Scotland Yard feels lonely without me, and it causes an unhealthy excitement among the criminal classes. Go, then, my dear Watson, and if my humble counsel can ever be valued at so extravagant a rate as twopence a word, it waits your disposal night and day at the end of the Continental wire."

Two days later found me at the National Hotel at Lausanne, where I received every courtesy at the hands of M. Moser, the well-known manager. Lady Frances, as he informed me, had stayed there for several weeks. She had been much liked by all who met her. Her age was not more than forty. She was still handsome, and bore every sign of having in her youth been a very lovely woman. M. Moser knew nothing of any valuable jewellery, but it had been remarked by the servants that the heavy trunk in the lady's bedroom was always scrupulously locked. Marie Devine, the maid, was as popular as her mistress. She was actually engaged to one of the head waiters in the hotel, and there was no difficulty in getting her address. It was 11, Rue de Trajan, Montpelier. All this I jotted down, and felt that Holmes himself could not have been more adroit in collecting his facts.

Only one corner still remained in the shadow. No light which I possessed could clear up the cause for the lady's sudden departure. She was very happy at Lausanne. There was every reason to believe that she intended to remain for the season in her luxurious rooms overlooking the lake. And yet she had left at a single day's notice, which involved her in the useless payment of a week's rent. Only Jules Vibart, the lover of the maid, had any suggestion to offer.

He connected the sudden departure with the visit to the hotel a day or two before of a tall, dark, bearded man. "*Un sauvage—un véritable sauvage !*" cried Jules Vibart. The man had rooms somewhere in the town. He had been seen talking earnestly to madame on the promenade by the lake. Then he had called. She had refused to see him. He was English, but of his name there was no record. Madame had left the place immediately afterwards. Jules Vibart, and, what was of more importance, Jules Vibart's sweetheart, thought

At Baden the track was not difficult to follow. Lady Frances had stayed at the Englischer Hof for a fortnight. Whilst there she had made the acquaintance of a Dr. Shlessinger and his wife, a missionary from South America. Like most lonely ladies, Lady Frances found her comfort and occupation in religion. Dr. Shlessinger's remarkable personality, his whole-hearted devotion, and the fact that he was recovering from a disease contracted in the exercise of his

"HE SPENT HIS DAY UPON A LOUNGE-CHAIR ON THE VERANDA, WITH AN ATTENDANT LADY UPON EITHER SIDE OF HIM."

that this call and this departure were cause and effect. Only one thing Jules could not discuss. That was the reason why Marie had left her mistress. Of that he could or would say nothing. If I wished to know, I must go to Montpelier and ask her.

So ended the first chapter of my inquiry. The second was devoted to the place which Lady Frances Carfax had sought when she left Lausanne. Concerning this there had been some secrecy, which confirmed the idea that she had gone with the intention of throwing someone off her track. Otherwise why should not her luggage have been openly labelled for Baden ? Both she and it reached the Rhenish spa by some circuitous route. Thus much I gathered from the manager of Cook's local office. So to Baden I went, after dispatching to Holmes an account of all my proceedings, and receiving in reply a telegram of half-humorous commendation.

apostolic duties, affected her deeply. She had helped Mrs. Shlessinger in the nursing of the convalescent saint. He spent his day, as the manager described it to me, upon a lounge-chair on the veranda, with an attendant lady upon either side of him. He was preparing a map of the Holy Land, with special reference to the kingdom of the Midianites, upon which he was writing a monograph. Finally, having improved much in health, he and his wife had returned to London, and Lady Frances had started thither in their company. This was just three weeks before, and the manager had heard nothing since. As to the maid, Marie, she had gone off some days beforehand in floods of tears, after informing the other maids that she was leaving service for ever. Dr. Shlessinger had paid the bill of the whole party before his departure.

" By the way," said the landlord, in conclusion, " you are not the only friend of Lady Frances Carfax who is inquiring after her just now. Only a week or so ago we had a man here upon the same errand."

" Did he give a name ? " I asked.

" None ; but he was an Englishman, though of an unusual type."

" A savage ? " said I, linking my facts after the fashion of my illustrious friend.

" Exactly. That describes him very well. He is a bulky, bearded, sunburned fellow, who looks as if he would be more at home in a farmers' inn than in a fashionable hotel. A hard, fierce man, I should think, and one whom I should be sorry to offend."

Already the mystery began to define itself, as figures grow clearer with the lifting of a fog. Here was this good and pious lady pursued from place to place by a sinister and unrelenting figure. She feared him, or she would not have fled from Lausanne. He had still followed. Sooner or later he would overtake her. Had he already overtaken her ? Was *that* the secret of her continued silence ? Could the good people who were her companions not screen her from his violence or his blackmail ? What horrible purpose, what deep design, lay behind this long pursuit ? There was the problem which I had to solve.

To Holmes I wrote showing how rapidly and surely I had got down to the roots of the matter. In reply I had a telegram asking for a description of Dr. Shlessinger's left ear. Holmes's ideas of humour are strange and occasionally offensive, so I took no notice of his ill-timed jest—indeed, I had already reached Montpelier in my pursuit of the maid, Marie, before his message came.

I had no difficulty in finding the ex-servant and in learning all that she could tell me. She was a devoted creature, who had only left her mistress because she was sure that she was in good hands, and because her own approaching marriage made a separation inevitable in any case. Her mistress had, as she confessed with distress, shown some irritability of temper towards her during their stay in Baden, and had even questioned her once as if she had suspicions of her honesty, and this had made the parting easier than it would otherwise have been. Lady Frances had given her fifty pounds as a wedding-present. Like me, Marie viewed with deep distrust the stranger who had driven her mistress from Lausanne. With her own eyes she had seen him seize the lady's wrist with great violence on the public promenade by the lake. He was a fierce and terrible man.

She believed that it was out of dread of him that Lady Frances had accepted the escort of the Shlessingers to London. She had never spoken to Marie about it, but many little signs had convinced the maid that her mistress lived in a state of continual nervous apprehension. So far she had got in her narrative, when suddenly she sprang from her chair and her face was convulsed with surprise and fear. "See!" she cried. "The miscreant follows still ! There is the very man of whom I speak."

Through the open sitting-room window I saw a huge, swarthy man with a bristling black beard walking slowly down the centre of the street and staring eagerly at the numbers of the houses. It was clear that, like myself, he was on the track of the maid. Acting upon the impulse of the moment, I rushed out and accosted him.

" You are an Englishman," I said.

" What if I am ? " he asked, with a most villainous scowl.

" May I ask what your name is ? "

" No, you may not," said he, with decision.

The situation was awkward, but the most direct way is often the best.

" Where is the Lady Frances Carfax ? " I asked.

He stared at me in amazement.

" What have you done with her ? Why have you pursued her ? I insist upon an answer ! " said I.

The fellow gave a bellow of anger and sprang upon me like a tiger. I have held my own in many a struggle, but the man had a grip of iron and the fury of a fiend. His hand was on my throat and my senses were nearly gone before an unshaven French *ouvrier*, in a blue blouse, darted out from a *cabaret* opposite, with a cudgel in his hand, and struck my assailant a sharp crack over the forearm, which made him leave go his hold. He stood for an instant fuming with rage and uncertain whether he should not renew his attack. Then, with a snarl of anger, he left me and entered the cottage from which I had just come. I turned to thank my preserver, who stood beside me in the roadway.

" Well, Watson," said he, " a very pretty hash you have made of it ! I rather think you had better come back with me to London by the night express."

An hour afterwards Sherlock Holmes, in his usual garb and style, was seated in my private room at the hotel. His explanation of his sudden and opportune appearance was simplicity itself, for, finding that he could get away from London, he determined to head me off at the next obvious point of my travels. In the disguise of a working-man he had sat in the *cabaret* waiting for my appearance.

" And a singularly consistent investigation you have made, my dear Watson," said he. " I cannot at the moment recall any possible blunder which you have omitted. The total effect of your proceedings has been to give the alarm everywhere and yet to discover nothing."

" Perhaps you would have done no better," I answered, bitterly.

" There is no ' perhaps ' about it. I *have* done better. Here is the Hon. Philip Green, who is a fellow-lodger with you in this hotel, and we may find in him the starting-point for a more successful investigation."

A card had come up on a salver, and it was followed by the same bearded ruffian who had attacked me in the street. He started when he saw me.

" What is this, Mr. Holmes ? " he asked. " I had your note and I have come. But what has this man to do with the matter ? "

" This is my old friend and associate, Dr. Watson, who is helping us in this affair."

The stranger held out a huge, sunburned hand, with a few words of apology.

" I hope I didn't harm you. When you accused me of hurting her I lost my grip of myself. Indeed, I'm not responsible in these days. My nerves are like live wires. But this situation is beyond me. What I want to know, in the first place, Mr. Holmes, is, how in the world you came to hear of my existence at all."

" I am in touch with Miss Dobney, Lady Frances's governess."

" Old Susan Dobney with the mob cap ! I remember her well."

" And she remembers you. It was in the days before — before you found it better to go to South Africa."

" Ah, I see you know my whole story. I need hide nothing from you. I swear to you, Mr. Holmes, that there never was in this world a man who loved a woman with a more whole-hearted love than I had for Frances. I was a wild youngster, I know—not worse than others of my class. But her mind was pure as snow. She could not bear a shadow of coarseness. So, when she came to hear of things that I had done, she would have no more to say to me. And yet she loved me— that is the wonder of it !—loved me well enough to remain single all her sainted days just for my sake alone. When the years had passed and I had made my money at Barberton I thought perhaps I could seek her

out and soften her. I had heard that she was still unmarried. I found her at Lausanne, and tried all I knew. She weakened, I think, but her will was strong, and when next I called she had left the town. I traced her to Baden, and then after a time heard that her maid was here. I'm a rough fellow, fresh from a rough life, and when Dr. Watson spoke to me as he did I lost hold of myself for a moment. But for God's sake tell me what has become of the Lady Frances."

" That is for us to find out," said Sherlock Holmes, with peculiar gravity. " What is your London address, Mr. Green ? "

" The Langham Hotel will find me."

" Then may I recommend that you return there and be on hand in case I should want you ? I have no desire to encourage false hopes, but you may rest assured that all that can be done will be done for the safety of Lady Frances. I can say no more for the instant. I will leave you this card so that you may be able to keep in touch with us. Now, Watson, if you will pack your bag I will cable to Mrs. Hudson to make one of her best efforts for two hungry travellers at seven-thirty to-morrow."

A telegram was awaiting us when we reached our Baker Street rooms, which Holmes read with an exclamation of interest and threw across to me. " Jagged or torn " was the message, and the place of origin Baden.

" What is this ? " I asked.

" It is everything," Holmes answered. " You may remember my seemingly irrelevant question as to this clerical gentleman's left ear. You did not answer it."

" I had left Baden, and could not inquire."

" Exactly. For this reason I sent a duplicate to the manager of the Englischer Hof, whose answer lies here."

" What does it show ? "

" It shows, my dear Watson, that we are dealing with an exceptionally astute and dangerous man. The Rev. Dr. Shlessinger, missionary from South America, is none other than Holy Peters, one of the most unscrupulous rascals that Australia has ever evolved—and for a young country it has turned out some very finished types. His particular speciality is the beguiling of lonely ladies by playing upon their religious feelings, and his so-called wife, an Englishwoman named Fraser, is a worthy helpmate. The nature of his tactics suggested his identity to me, and this physical peculiarity—he was badly bitten in a saloon-fight at Adelaide in

'89—confirmed my suspicion. This poor lady is in the hands of a most infernal couple, who will stick at nothing, Watson. That she is already dead is a very likely supposition. If not, she is undoubtedly in some sort of confinement, and unable to write to Miss Dobney or her other friends. It is always possible that she never reached London, or that she has passed through it, but the former is improbable, as, with their system of registration, it is not easy for foreigners to play tricks with the Continental police ; and the latter is also unlikely, as these rogues could not hope to find any other place where it would be as easy to keep a person under restraint. All my instincts tell me that she is in London, but, as we have at present no possible means of telling where, we can only take the obvious steps, eat our dinner, and possess our souls in patience. Later in the evening I will stroll down and have a word with friend Lestrade at Scotland Yard."

But neither the official police nor Holmes's own small, but very efficient, organization sufficed to clear away the mystery. Amid the crowded millions of London the three persons we sought were as completely obliterated as if they had never lived. Advertisements were tried, and failed. Clues were followed, and led to nothing. Every criminal resort which Shlessinger might frequent was drawn in vain. His old associates were watched, but they kept clear of him. And then suddenly, after a week of helpless suspense, there came a flash of light. A silver-and-brilliant pendant of old Spanish design had been pawned at Bevington's, in Westminster Road. The pawner was a large, clean-shaven man of clerical appearance. His name and address were demonstrably false. The ear had escaped notice, but the description was surely that of Shlessinger.

Three times had our bearded friend from the Langham called for news—the third time within an hour of this fresh development. His clothes were getting looser on his great body. He seemed to be wilting away in his anxiety. " If you will only give me something to do ! " was his constant wail. At last Holmes could oblige him.

" He has begun to pawn the jewels. We should get him now."

" But does this mean that any harm has befallen the Lady Frances ? "

Holmes shook his head very gravely.

" Supposing that they have held her prisoner up to now, it is clear that they cannot let her loose without their own destruction. We must prepare for the worst."

" What can I do ? "

" These people do not know you by sight ? "

" No."

" It is possible that he will go to some other pawnbroker in the future. In that case, we must begin again. On the other hand, he has had a fair price and no questions asked, so if he is in need of ready-money he will probably come back to Bevington's. I will give you a note to them, and they will let you wait in the shop. If the fellow comes you will follow him home. But no indiscretion, and, above all, no violence. I put you on your honour that you will take no step without my knowledge and consent."

For two days the Hon. Philip Green (he was, I may mention, the son of the famous admiral of that name who commanded the Sea of Azof fleet in the Crimean War) brought us no news. On the evening of the third he rushed into our sitting-room pale, trembling, with every muscle of his powerful frame quivering with excitement.

" We have him ! We have him ! ' he cried.

He was incoherent in his agitation. Holmes soothed him with a few words, and thrust him into an armchair.

" Come, now, give us the order of events," said he.

" She came only an hour ago. It was the wife, this time, but the pendant she brought was the fellow of the other. She is a tall, pale woman, with ferret eyes."

" That is the lady," said Holmes.

" She left the office and I followed her. She walked up the Kennington Road, and I kept behind her. Presently she went into a shop. Mr. Holmes, it was an undertaker's."

My companion started. " Well ? " he asked, in that vibrant voice which told of the fiery soul behind the cold, grey face.

" She was talking to the woman behind the counter. I entered as well. ' It is late,' I heard her say, or words to that effect. The woman was excusing herself. ' It should be there before now,' she answered. ' It took longer, being out of the ordinary.' They both stopped and looked at me, so I asked some question and then left the shop."

" You did excellently well. What happened next ? "

" The woman came out, but I had hid myself in a doorway. Her suspicions had been aroused, I think, for she looked round her. Then she called a cab and got in. I was lucky enough to get another and so to follow her. She got down at last at No. 36, Poultney Square, Brixton. I drove past,

"'WE HAVE HIM! WE HAVE HIM!' HE CRIED."

left my cab at the corner of the square, and watched the house."

"Did you see anyone?"

"The windows were all in darkness save one on the lower floor. The blind was down, and I could not see in. I was standing there, wondering what I should do next, when a covered van drove up with two men in it. They descended, took something out of the van, and carried it up the steps to the hall door. Mr. Holmes, it was a coffin."

"Ah!"

"For an instant I was on the point of rushing in. The door had been opened to admit the men and their burden. It was the woman who had opened it. But as I stood there she caught a glimpse of me, and I think that she recognized me. I saw her start, and she hastily closed the door. I remembered my promise to you, and here I am."

"You have done excellent work," said Holmes, scribbling a few words upon a half-sheet of paper. "We can do nothing legal without a warrant, and you can serve the cause best by taking this note down to the authorities and getting one. There may be some difficulty, but I should think that the sale of the jewellery should be sufficient. Lestrade will see to all details."

"But they may murder her in the meanwhile. What could the coffin mean, and for whom could it be but for her?"

"We will do all that can be done, Mr. Green. Not a moment will be lost. Leave it in our hands. Now, Watson," he added, as our client hurried away, "he will set the regular forces on the move. We are, as usual, the irregulars, and we must take our own line of action. The situation strikes me as so desperate that the most extreme measures are justified. Not a moment is to be lost in getting to Poultney Square.

" Let us try to reconstruct the situation," said he, as we drove swiftly past the Houses of Parliament and over Westminster Bridge. " These villains have coaxed this unhappy lady to London, after first alienating her from her faithful maid. If she has written any letters they have been intercepted. Through some confederate they have engaged a furnished house. Once inside it, they have made her a prisoner, and they have become possessed of the valuable jewellery which has been their object from the first. Already they have begun to sell part of it, which seems safe enough to them, since they have no reason to think that anyone is interested in the lady's fate. When she is released she will, of course, denounce them. Therefore, she must not be released. But they cannot keep her under lock and key for ever. So murder is their only solution."

" That seems very clear."

" Now we will take another line of reasoning. When you follow two separate chains of thought, Watson, you will find some point of intersection which should approximate to the truth. We will start now, not from the lady, but from the coffin, and argue backwards. That incident proves, I fear, beyond all doubt that the lady is dead. It points also to an orthodox burial with proper accompaniment of medical certificate and official sanction. Had the lady been obviously murdered, they would have buried her in a hole in the back garden. But here all is open and regular. What does that mean? Surely that they have done her to death in some way which has deceived the doctor, and simulated a natural end—poisoning, perhaps. And yet how strange that they should ever let a doctor approach her unless he were a confederate, which is hardly a credible proposition."

" Could they have forged a medical certificate ? "

" Dangerous, Watson, very dangerous. No, I hardly see them doing that. Pull up, cabby ! This is evidently the undertaker's, for we have just passed the pawnbroker's. Would you go in, Watson ? Your appearance inspires confidence. Ask what hour the Poultney Square funeral takes place to-morrow."

The woman in the shop answered me without hesitation that it was to be at eight o'clock in the morning.

" You see, Watson, no mystery ; everything above-board ! In some way the legal forms have undoubtedly been complied with, and they think that they have little to

fear. Well, there's nothing for it now but a direct frontal attack. Are you armed ? "

" My stick ! "

" Well, well, we shall be strong enough. ' Thrice is he armed who hath his quarrel just.' We simply can't afford to wait for the police, or to keep within the four corners of the law. You can drive off, cabby. Now, Watson, we'll just take our luck together, as we have occasionally done in the past."

He had rung loudly at the door of a great dark house in the centre of Poultney Square. It was opened immediately, and the figure of a tall woman was outlined against the dim-lit hall.

" Well, what do you want ? " she asked, sharply, peering at us through the darkness.

" I want to speak to Dr. Shlessinger," said Holmes.

" There is no such person here," she answered, and tried to close the door, but Holmes had jammed it with his foot.

" Well, I want to see the man who lives here, whatever he may call himself," said Holmes, firmly.

She hesitated. Then she threw open the door. " Well, come in ! " said she. " My husband is not afraid to face any man in the world." She closed the door behind us, and showed us into a sitting-room on the right side of the hall, turning up the gas as she left us. " Mr. Peters will be with you in an instant," she said.

Her words were literally true, for we had hardly time to look round the dusty and moth-eaten apartment in which we found ourselves before the door opened and a big, clean-shaven, bald-headed man stepped lightly into the room. He had a large red face, with pendulous cheeks, and a general air of superficial benevolence which was marred by a cruel, vicious mouth.

" There is surely some mistake here, gentlemen," he said, in an unctuous, make-everything-easy voice. " I fancy that you have been misdirected. Possibly if you tried farther down the street——"

" That will do ; we have no time to waste," said my companion, firmly. " You are Henry Peters, of Adelaide, late the Rev. Dr. Shlessinger, of Baden and South America. I am as sure of that as that my own name is Sherlock Holmes."

Peters, as I will now call him, started and stared hard at his formidable pursuer. " I guess your name does not frighten me, Mr. Holmes," said he, coolly. " When a man's conscience is easy you can't rattle him. What is your business in my house ? "

"I want to know what you have done with the Lady Frances Carfax, whom you brought away with you from Baden."

"I'd be very glad if you could tell me where that lady may be," Peters answered, coolly. "I've a bill against her for nearly a hundred pounds, and nothing to show for it but a couple of trumpery pendants that the dealer would hardly look at. She attached herself

pocket. "This will have to serve till a better one comes."

"Why, you are a common burglar."

"So you might describe me," said Holmes, cheerfully. "My companion is also a dangerous ruffian. And together we are going through your house."

Our opponent opened the door.

"Fetch a policeman, Annie!" said he.

"HOLMES HALF DREW A REVOLVER FROM HIS POCKET."

to Mrs. Peters and me at Baden (it is a fact that I was using another name at the time), and she stuck on to us until we came to London. I paid her bill and her ticket. Once in London, she gave us the slip, and, as I say, left these out-of-date jewels to pay her bills. You find her, Mr. Holmes, and I'm your debtor."

"I *mean* to find her," said Sherlock Holmes. "I'm going through this house till I do find her."

"Where is your warrant?"

Holmes half drew a revolver from his

There was a whisk of feminine skirts down the passage, and the hall door was opened and shut.

"Our time is limited, Watson," said Holmes. "If you try to stop us, Peters, you will most certainly get hurt. Where is that coffin which was brought into your house?"

"What do you want with the coffin? It is in use. There is a body in it."

"I must see that body."

"Never with my consent."

"Then without it." With a quick movement Holmes pushed the fellow to one side and passed into the hall. A door half open stood immediately before us. We entered. It was the dining-room. On the table, under a half-lit chandelier, the coffin was lying. Holmes turned up the gas and raised the lid. Deep down in the recesses of the coffin lay an emaciated figure. The glare from the lights above beat down upon an aged and withered face. By no possible process of cruelty, starvation, or disease could this worn-out wreck be the still beautiful Lady Frances. Holmes's face showed his amazement, and also his relief.

" Thank God ! " he muttered. " It's some-one else."

" Ah, you've blundered badly for once, Mr. Sherlock Holmes," said Peters, who had followed us into the room.

" Who is this dead woman ? "

" Well, if you really must know, she is an old nurse of my wife's, Rose Spender her name, whom we found in the Brixton Work-house Infirmary. We brought her round here, called in Dr. Horsom, of 13, Firbank Villas—mind you take the address, Mr. Holmes—and had her carefully tended, as Christian folk should. On the third day she died—certificate says senile decay—but that's only the doctor's opinion, and, of course, you know better. We ordered her funeral to be carried out by Stimson and Co., of the Ken-nington Road, who will bury her at nine o'clock to-morrow morning. Can you pick any hole in that, Mr. Holmes ? You've made a silly blunder, and you may as well own up to it. I'd give something for a photograph of your gaping, staring face when you pulled aside that lid expecting to see the Lady Frances Carfax, and only found a poor old woman of ninety."

Holmes's expression was as impassive as ever under the jeers of his antagonist, but his clenched hands betrayed his acute annoyance.

" I am going through your house," said he.

" Are you, though ! " cried Peters, as a woman's voice and heavy steps sounded in the passage. " We'll soon see about that. This way, officers, if you please. These men have forced their way into my house, and I cannot get rid of them. Help me to put them out."

A sergeant and a constable stood in the doorway. Holmes drew his card from his case.

" This is my name and address. This is my friend, Dr. Watson."

" Bless you, sir, we know you very well," said the sergeant, " but you can't stay here without a warrant."

" Of course not. I quite understand that."

" Arrest him ! " cried Peters.

" We know where to lay our hands on this gentleman if he is wanted," said the sergeant, majestically, " but you'll have to go, Mr. Holmes."

" Yes, Watson, we shall have to go."

A minute later we were in the street once more. Holmes was as cool as ever, but I was hot with anger and humiliation. The sergeant had followed us.

" Sorry, Mr. Holmes, but that's the law."

" Exactly, sergeant ; you could not do otherwise."

" I expect there was good reason for your presence there. If there is anything I can do——"

" It's a missing lady, sergeant, and we think she is in that house. I expect a warrant presently."

" Then I'll keep my eye on the parties, Mr. Holmes. If anything comes along, I will surely let you know."

It was only nine o'clock, and we were off full cry upon the trail at once. First we drove to Brixton Workhouse Infirmary, where we found that it was indeed the truth that a charitable couple had called some days before, that they had claimed an imbecile old woman as a former servant, and that they had obtained permission to take her away with them. No surprise was expressed at the news that she had since died.

The doctor was our next goal. He had been called in, had found the woman dying of pure senility, had actually seen her pass away, and had signed the certificate in due form. " I assure you that everything was perfectly normal and there was no room for foul play in the matter," said he. Nothing in the house had struck him as suspicious, save that for people of their class it was remarkable that they should have no servant. So far and no farther went the doctor.

Finally, we found our way to Scotland Yard. There had been difficulties of pro-cedure in regard to the warrant. Some delay was inevitable. The magistrate's signature might not be obtained until next morning. If Holmes would call about nine he could go down with Lestrade and see it acted upon. So ended the day, save that near midnight our friend, the sergeant, called to say that he had seen flickering lights here and there in the windows of the great dark house, but that no one had left it and none had entered. We could but pray for patience, and wait for the morrow.

Sherlock Holmes was too irritable for

conversation and too restless for sleep. I left him smoking hard, with his heavy, dark brows knotted together, and his long, nervous fingers tapping upon the arms of his chair, as he turned over in his mind every possible solution of the mystery. Several times in the course of the night I heard him prowling about the house. Finally, just after I had been called in the morning, he rushed into my room. He was in his dressing-gown, but his pale, hollow-eyed face told me that his night had been a sleepless one.

"What time was the funeral? Eight, was it not?" he asked, eagerly. "Well, it is seven-twenty now. Good heavens, Watson, what has become of any brains that God has given me? Quick, man, quick! It's life or death—a hundred chances on death to one on life. I'll never forgive myself, never, if we are too late!"

Five minutes had not passed before we were flying in a hansom down Baker Street. But even so it was twenty-five to eight as we passed Big Ben, and eight struck as we tore down the Brixton Road. But others were late as well as we. Ten minutes after the hour the hearse was still standing at the door of the house, and even as our foaming horse came to a halt the coffin, supported by three men, appeared on the threshold. Holmes darted forward and barred their way.

"Take it back!" he cried, laying his hand on the breast of the foremost. "Take it back this instant!

"What the devil do you mean? Once again I ask you, where is your warrant?" shouted the furious Peters, his big red face glaring over the farther end of the coffin.

"The warrant is on its way. This coffin shall remain in the house until it comes."

The authority in Holmes's voice had its effect upon the bearers. Peters had suddenly vanished into the house, and they obeyed these new orders. "Quick, Watson, quick! Here is a screw-driver!" he shouted, as the coffin was replaced upon the table. "Here's one for you, my man! A sovereign if the lid comes off in a minute! Ask no questions—work away! That's good! Another! And another! Now pull all together! It's giving! It's giving! Ah, that does it at last!"

With a united effort we tore off the coffin-lid. As we did so there came from the inside a stupefying and overpowering smell of chloroform. A body lay within, its head all wreathed in cotton-wool, which had been soaked in the narcotic. Holmes plucked it off and disclosed the statuesque face of a handsome and spiritual woman of middle age. In an instant he had passed his arm round the figure and raised her to a sitting position.

"Is she gone, Watson? Is there a spark left? Surely we are not too late!"

For half an hour it seemed that we were. What with actual suffocation, and what with the poisonous fumes of the chloroform, the Lady Frances seemed to have passed the last point of recall. And then, at last, with artificial respiration, with injected ether, with every device that science could suggest, some flutter of life, some quiver of the eyelids, some dimming of a mirror, spoke of the slowly returning life. A cab had driven up, and Holmes, parting the blind, looked out at it. "Here is Lestrade with his warrant," said he. "He will find that his birds have flown. And here," he added, as a heavy step hurried along the passage, "is someone who has a better right to nurse this lady than we have. Good morning, Mr. Green; I think that the sooner we can move the Lady Frances the better. Meanwhile, the funeral may proceed, and the poor old woman who still lies in that coffin may go to her last resting-place alone."

"Should you care to add the case to your annals, my dear Watson," said Holmes that evening, "it can only be as an example of that temporary eclipse to which even the best-balanced mind may be exposed. Such slips are common to all mortals, and the greatest is he who can recognize and repair them. To this modified credit I may, perhaps, make some claim. My night was haunted by the thought that somewhere a clue, a strange sentence, a curious observation, had come under my notice and had been too easily dismissed. Then, suddenly, in the grey of the morning, the words came back to me. It was the remark of the undertaker's wife, as reported by Philip Green. She had said, 'It should be there before now. It took longer, being out of the ordinary.' It was the coffin of which she spoke. It had been out of the ordinary. That could only mean that it had been made to some special measurement. But why? Why? Then in an instant I remembered the deep sides, and the little wasted figure at the bottom. Why so large a coffin for so small a body? To leave room for another body. Both would be buried under the one certificate. It had all been so clear, if only my own sight had not been dimmed. At eight the Lady Frances would be buried. Our one chance was to stop the coffin before it left the house.

"It was a desperate chance that we might find her alive, but it *was* a chance, as the result showed. These people had never, to my knowledge, done a murder. They might shrink from actual violence at the last. They could bury her with no sign of how she met her end, and even if she were exhumed there was a chance for them. I hoped that such considerations might prevail with them. You can reconstruct the scene well enough. You saw the horrible den upstairs, where the poor lady had been kept so long. They rushed in and overpowered her with their chloroform, carried her down, poured more into the coffin to insure against her wakening, and then screwed

"HOLMES DARTED FORWARD AND BARRED THEIR WAY."

down the lid. A clever device, Watson. It is new to me in the annals of crime. If our ex-missionary friends escape the clutches of Lestrade, I shall expect to hear of some brilliant incidents in their future career."

A NEW
SHERLOCK HOLMES
STORY

The Adventure of the Dying Detective.

By A. CONAN DOYLE.

Illustrated by Wal. Paget.

MRS. HUDSON, the landlady of Sherlock Holmes, was a long-suffering woman. Not only was her first-floor flat invaded at all hours by throngs of singular and often undesirable characters, but her remarkable lodger showed an eccentricity and irregularity in his life which must have sorely tried her patience. His incredible untidiness, his addiction to music at strange hours, his occasional revolver practice within doors, his weird and often malodorous scientific experiments, and the atmosphere of violence and danger which hung around him made him the very worst tenant in London. On the other hand, his payments were princely. I have no doubt that the house might have been purchased at the price which Holmes paid for his rooms during the years that I was with him.

The landlady stood in the deepest awe of him, and never dared to interfere with him, however outrageous his proceedings might seem. She was fond of him, too, for he had a remarkable gentleness and courtesy in his dealings with women. He disliked and distrusted the sex, but he was always a chivalrous opponent. Knowing how genuine was her regard for him, I listened earnestly to her story when she came to my rooms in the second year of my married life and told me of the sad condition to which my poor friend was reduced.

"He's dying, Dr. Watson," said she. "For three days he has been sinking, and I doubt if he will last the day. He would not let me get a doctor. This morning when I saw his bones sticking out of his face and his great bright eyes looking at me I could stand no more of it. 'With your leave or without it, Mr. Holmes, I am going for a doctor this very hour,' said I. 'Let it be Watson, then,' said he. I wouldn't waste an hour in coming to him, sir, or you may not see him alive."

I was horrified, for I had heard nothing of his illness. I need not say that I rushed for my coat and my hat. As we drove back I asked for the details.

"There is little I can tell you, sir. He has been working at a case down at Rotherhithe, in an alley near the river, and he has brought this illness back with him. He took to his bed on Wednesday afternoon and has never moved since. For these three days neither food nor drink has passed his lips."

"Good God! Why did you not call in a doctor?"

"He wouldn't have it, sir. You know how masterful he is. I didn't dare to disobey him. But he's not long for this world, as you'll see for yourself the moment that you set eyes on him."

He was indeed a deplorable spectacle. In

"PUT IT DOWN! DOWN, THIS INSTANT, WATSON—THIS INSTANT, I SAY!"

the dim light of a foggy November day the sick-room was a gloomy spot, but it was that gaunt, wasted face staring at me from the bed which sent a chill to my heart. His eyes had the brightness of fever, there was a hectic flush upon either cheek, and dark crusts clung to his lips ; the thin hands upon the coverlet twitched incessantly, his voice was croaking and spasmodic. He lay listlessly as I entered the room, but the sight of me brought a gleam of recognition to his eyes.

" Well, Watson, we seem to have fallen upon evil days," said he, in a feeble voice, but with something of his old carelessness of manner.

" My dear fellow ! " I cried, approaching him.

" Stand back ! Stand right back ! " said he, with the sharp imperiousness which I had associated only with moments of crisis. " If you approach me, Watson, I shall order you out of the house."

" But why ? "

" Because it is my desire. Is that not enough ? "

Yes, Mrs. Hudson was right. He was more masterful than ever. It was pitiful, however, to see his exhaustion.

" I only wished to help," I explained.

" Exactly ! You will help best by doing what you are told."

" Certainly, Holmes."

He relaxed the austerity of his manner.

" You are not angry ? " he asked, gasping for breath.

Poor devil, how could I be angry when I saw him lying in such a plight before me ?

" It's for your own sake, Watson," he croaked.

" For *my* sake ? "

" I know what is the matter with me. It is a coolie disease from Sumatra—a thing that the Dutch know more about than we, though they have made little of it up to date. One thing only is certain. It is infallibly deadly, and it is horribly contagious."

He spoke now with a feverish energy, the long hands twitching and jerking as he motioned me away.

" Contagious by touch, Watson—that's it, by touch. Keep your distance and all is well."

" Good heavens, Holmes ! Do you suppose that such a consideration weighs with me for an instant ? It would not affect me in the case of a stranger. Do you imagine it would prevent me from doing my duty to so old a friend ? "

Again I advanced, but he repulsed me with a look of furious anger.

" If you will stand there I will talk. If you do not you must leave the room."

I have so deep a respect for the extraordinary qualities of Holmes that I have always deferred to his wishes, even when I least understood them. But now all my professional instincts were aroused. Let him be my master elsewhere, I at least was his in a sick-room.

" Holmes," said I, " you are not yourself. A sick man is but a child, and so I will treat you. Whether you like it or not, I will examine your symptoms and treat you for them."

He looked at me with venomous eyes.

" If I am to have a doctor whether I will or not, let me at least have someone in whom I have confidence," said he.

" Then you have none in me ? "

" In your friendship, certainly. But facts are facts, Watson, and after all you are only a general practitioner with very limited experience and mediocre qualifications. It is painful to have to say these things, but you leave me no choice."

I was bitterly hurt.

" Such a remark is unworthy of you, Holmes. It shows me very clearly the state of your own nerves. But if you have no confidence in me I would not intrude my services. Let me bring Sir Jasper Meek or Penrose Fisher, or any of the best men in London. But someone you *must* have, and that is final. If you think that I am going to stand here and see you die without either helping you myself or bringing anyone else to help you, then you have mistaken your man."

" You mean well, Watson," said the sick man, with something between a sob and a groan. " Shall I demonstrate your own ignorance ? What do you know, pray, of Tapanuli fever ? What do you know of the black Formosa corruption ? "

" I have never heard of either."

" There are many problems of disease, many strange pathological possibilities, in the East, Watson." He paused after each sentence to collect his failing strength. " I have learned so much during some recent researches which have a medico-criminal aspect. It was in the course of them that I contracted this complaint. You can do nothing."

" Possibly not. But I happen to know that Dr. Ainstree, the greatest living authority upon tropical disease, is now in London. All remonstrance is useless, Holmes. I am going this instant to fetch him." I turned resolutely to the door.

"I HEARD THE SHARP SNAP OF A TWISTED KEY."

Never have I had such a shock! In an instant, with a tiger-spring, the dying man had intercepted me. I heard the sharp snap of a twisted key. The next moment he had staggered back to his bed, exhausted and panting after his one tremendous outflame of energy.

"You won't take the key from me by force, Watson. I've got you, my friend. Here you are, and here you will stay until I will otherwise. But I'll humour you." (All this in little gasps, with terrible struggles for breath between.) "You've only my own good at heart. Of course, I know that very well. You shall have your way, but give me time to get my strength. Not now, Watson, not now. It's four o'clock. At six you can go."

"This is insanity, Holmes."

"Only two hours, Watson. I promise you will go at six. Are you content to wait?"

"I seem to have no choice."

"None in the world, Watson. Thank you, I need no help in arranging the clothes. You will please keep your distance. Now, Watson, there is one other condition that I would make. You will seek help, not from the man you mention, but from the one that I choose."

"By all means."

"The first three sensible words that you have uttered since you entered this room, Watson. You will find some books over there. I am somewhat exhausted; I wonder how a battery feels when it pours electricity into a non-conductor? At six, Watson, we resume our conversation."

But it was destined to be resumed long before that hour, and in circumstances which gave me a shock hardly second to that caused by his spring to the door. I had stood for some minutes looking at the silent figure in the bed. His face was almost covered by the clothes and he appeared to be asleep. Then, unable to settle down to reading, I walked slowly round the room, examining the pictures of celebrated criminals with which every wall was adorned. Finally, in my aimless perambulation, I came to the mantelpiece. A litter of pipes, tobacco-pouches, syringes, penknives, revolver cartridges, and other *débris* was scattered over it. In the midst of these was a small black and white ivory box with a sliding lid. It was a neat little thing, and I had stretched out my hand to examine it more closely, when——

It was a dreadful cry that he gave—a yell which might have been heard down the street. My skin went cold and my hair bristled at that horrible scream. As I turned I caught a glimpse of a convulsed face and frantic eyes. I stood paralyzed, with the little box in my hand.

"Put it down! Down, this instant, Watson—this instant, I say!" His head sank back upon the pillow and he gave a deep sigh of relief as I replaced the box upon the mantelpiece. "I hate to have my things touched, Watson. You know that I hate it. You fidget me beyond endurance. You, a doctor—you are enough to drive a patient into an asylum. Sit down, man, and let me have my rest!"

The incident left a most unpleasant impression upon my mind. The violent and causeless excitement, followed by this brutality of speech, so far removed from his usual suavity, showed me how deep was the disorganization of his mind. Of all ruins, that of a noble mind is the most deplorable. I sat in silent dejection until the stipulated time had passed. He seemed to have been watching the clock as well as I, for it was hardly six before he began to talk with the same feverish animation as before.

"Now, Watson," said he. "Have you any change in your pocket?"

"Yes."

"Any silver?"

"A good deal."

"How many half-crowns?"

"I have five."

"Ah, too few! Too few! How very unfortunate, Watson! However, such as they are you can put them in your watch-pocket. And all the rest of your money in your left trouser-pocket. Thank you. It will balance you so much better like that."

This was raving insanity. He shuddered, and again made a sound between a cough and a sob.

"You will now light the gas, Watson, but you will be very careful that not for one instant shall it be more than half on. I implore you to be careful, Watson. Thank you, that is excellent. No, you need not draw the blind. Now you will have the kindness to place some letters and papers upon this table within my reach. Thank you. Now some of that litter from the mantelpiece. Excellent, Watson! There is a sugar-tongs there. Kindly raise that small ivory box with its assistance. Place it here among the papers. Good! You can now go and fetch Mr. Culverton Smith, of 13, Lower Burke Street."

To tell the truth, my desire to fetch a doctor had somewhat weakened, for poor Holmes was so obviously delirious that it seemed dangerous to leave him. However, he was as eager now to consult the person named as he had been obstinate in refusing.

" I never heard the name," said I.

" Possibly not, my good Watson. It may surprise you to know that the man upon earth who is best versed in this disease is not a medical man, but a planter. Mr. Culverton Smith is a well-known resident of Sumatra, now visiting London. An outbreak of the disease upon his plantation, which was distant from medical aid, caused him to study it himself, with some rather far-reaching consequences. He is a very methodical person, and I did not desire you to start before six because I was well aware that you would not find him in his study. If you could persuade him to come here and give us the benefit of his unique experience of this disease, the investigation of which has been his dearest hobby, I cannot doubt that he could help me."

I give Holmes's remarks as a consecutive whole, and will not attempt to indicate how they were interrupted by gaspings for breath and those clutchings of his hands which indicated the pain from which he was suffering. His appearance had changed for the worse during the few hours that I had been with him. Those hectic spots were more pronounced, the eyes shone more brightly out of darker hollows, and a cold sweat glimmered upon his brow. He still retained, however, the jaunty gallantry of his speech. To the last gasp he would always be the master.

" You will tell him exactly how you have left me," said he. " You will convey the very impression which is in your own mind—a dying man—a dying and delirious man. Indeed, I cannot think why the whole bed of the ocean is not one solid mass of oysters, so prolific the creatures seem. Ah, I am wandering! Strange how the brain controls the brain! What was I saying, Watson ? "

" My directions for Mr. Culverton Smith."

" Ah, yes, I remember. My life depends upon it. Plead with him, Watson. There is no good feeling between us. His nephew, Watson—I had suspicions of foul play and I allowed him to see it. The boy died horribly. He has a grudge against me. You will soften him, Watson. Beg him, pray him, get him here by any means. He can save me—only he ! "

" I will bring him in a cab, if I have to carry him down to it."

" You will do nothing of the sort. You will persuade him to come. And then you

will return in front of him. Make any excuse so as not to come with him. Don't forget, Watson. You won't fail me. You never did fail me. No doubt there are natural enemies which limit the increase of the creatures. You and I, Watson, we have done our part. Shall the world, then, be overrun by oysters ? No, no ; horrible ! You'll convey all that is in your mind."

I left him full of the image of this magnificent intellect babbling like a foolish child. He had handed me the key, and with a happy thought I took it with me lest he should lock himself in. Mrs. Hudson was waiting, trembling and weeping, in the passage. Behind me as I passed from the flat I heard Holmes's high, thin voice in some delirious chant. Below, as I stood whistling for a cab, a man came on me through the fog.

" How is Mr. Holmes, sir ? " he asked.

It was an old acquaintance, Inspector Morton, of Scotland Yard, dressed in unofficial tweeds.

" He is very ill," I answered.

He looked at me in a most singular fashion. Had it not been too fiendish, I could have imagined that the gleam of the fanlight showed exultation in his face.

" I heard some rumour of it," said he.

The cab had driven up, and I left him.

Lower Burke Street proved to be a line of fine houses lying in the vague borderland between Notting Hill and Kensington. The particular one at which my cabman pulled up had an air of smug and demure respectability in its old-fashioned iron railings, its massive folding-door, and its shining brasswork. All was in keeping with a solemn butler who appeared framed in the pink radiance of a tinted electric light behind him.

" Yes, Mr. Culverton Smith is in. Dr. Watson ! Very good, sir, I will take up your card."

My humble name and title did not appear to impress Mr. Culverton Smith. Through the half-open door I heard a high, petulant, penetrating voice.

" Who is this person ? What does he want ? Dear me, Staples, how often have I said that I am not to be disturbed in my hours of study ? "

There came a gentle flow of soothing explanation from the butler.

" Well, I won't see him, Staples. I can't have my work interrupted like this. I am not at home. Say so. Tell him to come in the morning if he really must see me."

Again the gentle murmur.

" Well, well, give him that message. He

can come in the morning, or he can stay away. My work must not be hindered."

I thought of Holmes tossing upon his bed of sickness, and counting the minutes, perhaps, until I should bring help to him. It was not a time to stand upon ceremony. His life depended upon my promptness. Before the apologetic butler had delivered his message I had pushed past him and was in the room.

With a shrill cry of anger a man rose from a reclining chair beside the fire. I saw a great yellow face, coarse-grained and greasy, with heavy double chin, and two sullen, menacing grey eyes which glared at me from under tufted and sandy brows. A high bald head had a small velvet smoking-cap poised coquettishly upon one side of its pink curve. The skull was of enormous capacity, and yet, as I looked down, I saw to my amazement that the figure of the man was small and frail, twisted in the shoulders and back like one who has suffered from rickets in his childhood.

"What's this?" he cried, in a high, screaming voice. "What is the meaning of this intrusion? Didn't I send you word that I would see you to-morrow morning?"

"I am sorry," said I, "but the matter cannot be delayed. Mr. Sherlock Holmes——"

The mention of my friend's name had an extraordinary effect upon the little man. The look of anger passed in an instant from his face. His features became tense and alert.

"Have you come from Holmes?" he asked.

"I have just left him."

"What about Holmes? How is he?"

"He is desperately ill. That is why I have come."

The man motioned me to a chair, and turned to resume his own. As he did so I caught a glimpse of his face in the mirror over the mantelpiece. I could have sworn that it was set in a malicious and abominable smile. Yet I persuaded myself that it must have been some nervous contraction which I had surprised, for he turned to me an instant later with genuine concern upon his features.

"I am sorry to hear this," said he. "I only know Mr. Holmes through some business dealings which we have had, but I have every respect for his talents and his character. He is an amateur of crime, as I am of disease. For him the villain, for me the microbe. There are my prisons," he continued, pointing to a row of bottles and jars which stood upon a side table. "Among those gelatine cultivations some of the very worst offenders in the world are now doing time."

"It was on account of your special knowledge that Mr. Holmes desired to see you. He has a high opinion of you, and thought that you were the one man in London who could help him."

The little man started, and the jaunty smoking-cap slid to the floor.

"Why?" he asked. "Why should Mr. Holmes think that I could help him in his trouble?"

"Because of your knowledge of Eastern diseases."

"But why should he think that this disease which he has contracted is Eastern?"

"Because, in some professional inquiry, he has been working among Chinese sailors down in the docks."

Mr. Culverton Smith smiled pleasantly and picked up his smoking-cap.

"Oh, that's it, is it?" said he. "I trust the matter is not so grave as you suppose. How long has he been ill?"

"About three days."

"Is he delirious?"

"Occasionally."

"Tut, tut! This sounds serious. It would be inhuman not to answer his call. I very much resent any interruption to my work, Dr. Watson, but this case is certainly exceptional. I will come with you at once."

I remembered Holmes's injunction.

"I have another appointment," said I.

"Very good. I will go alone. I have a note of Mr. Holmes's address. You can rely upon my being there within half an hour at most."

It was with a sinking heart that I re-entered Holmes's bedroom. For all that I knew the worst might have happened in my absence. To my enormous relief, he had improved greatly in the interval. His appearance was as ghastly as ever, but all trace of delirium had left him and he spoke in a feeble voice, it is true, but with even more than his usual crispness and lucidity.

"Well, did you see him, Watson?"

"Yes; he is coming."

"Admirable, Watson! Admirable! You are the best of messengers."

"He wished to return with me."

"That would never do, Watson. That would be obviously impossible. Did he ask what ailed me?"

"I told him about the Chinese in the East-end."

"Exactly! Well, Watson, you have done all that a good friend could. You can now disappear from the scene."

"I must wait and hear his opinion, Holmes."

"'WHAT'S THIS?' HE CRIED, IN A HIGH, SCREAMING VOICE. 'WHAT IS THE MEANING OF THIS INTRUSION?'"

Watson. Quick, man, if you love me! And don't budge, whatever happens—whatever happens, do you hear? Don't speak! Don't move! Just listen with all your ears." Then in an instant his sudden access of strength departed, and his masterful, purposeful talk droned away into the low, vague murmurings of a semi-delirious man.

From the hiding-place into which I had been so swiftly hustled I heard the footfalls upon the stair, with the opening and the closing of the bedroom door. Then, to my surprise, there came a long silence, broken only by the heavy breathings and gaspings of the sick man. I could imagine that our visitor was standing by the bedside and looking down at the sufferer. At last that strange hush was broken.

"Holmes!" he cried. "Holmes!" in the insistent tone of one who awakens a sleeper. "Can't you hear me, Holmes?" There was a rustling, as if he had shaken the sick man roughly by the shoulder.

"Is that you, Mr. Smith?" Holmes whispered. "I hardly dared hope that you would come."

The other laughed.

"I should imagine not," he said. "And yet, you see, I am here. Coals of fire, Holmes—coals of fire!"

"It is very good of you—very noble of you. I appreciate your special knowledge."

"Of course you must. But I have reasons to suppose that this opinion would be very much more frank and valuable if he imagines that we are alone. There is just room behind the head of my bed, Watson."

"My dear Holmes!"

"I fear there is no alternative, Watson. The room does not lend itself to concealment, which is as well, as it is the less likely to arouse suspicion. But just there, Watson, I fancy that it could be done." Suddenly he sat up with a rigid intentness upon his haggard face. "There are the wheels,

Our visitor sniggered.

"You do. You are, fortunately, the only man in London who does. Do you know what is the matter with you?"

"The same," said Holmes.

"Ah! You recognize the symptoms?"

"Only too well."

"Well, I shouldn't be surprised, Holmes. I shouldn't be surprised if it *were* the same. A bad look-out for you if it is. Poor Victor was a dead man on the fourth day—a strong, hearty young fellow. It was certainly, as you said, very surprising that he should have contracted an out-of-the-way Asiatic disease in the heart of London—a disease, too, of which I had made such a very special study. Singular coincidence, Holmes. Very smart of you to notice it, but rather uncharitable to suggest that it was cause and effect."

"I knew that you did it."

"Oh, you did, did you? Well, you couldn't prove it, anyhow. But what do you think of yourself spreading reports about me like that, and then crawling to me for help the moment you are in trouble? What sort of a game is that—eh?"

I heard the rasping, laboured breathing of the sick man. "Give me the water!" he gasped.

"You're precious near your end, my friend, but I don't want you to go till I have had a word with you. That's why I give you water. There, don't slop it about! That's right. Can you understand what I say?"

Holmes groaned.

"Do what you can for me. Let bygones be bygones," he whispered. "I'll put the words out of my head—I swear I will. Only cure me, and I'll forget it."

"Forget what?"

"Well, about Victor Savage's death. You as good as admitted just now that you had done it. I'll forget it."

"You can forget it or remember it, just as you like. I don't see you in the witness-box. Quite another shaped box, my good Holmes, I assure you. It matters nothing to me that you should know how my nephew died. It's not him we are talking about. It's you."

"Yes, yes."

"The fellow who came for me—I've forgotten his name—said that you contracted it down in the East-end among the sailors."

"I could only account for it so."

"You are proud of your brains, Holmes, are you not? Think yourself smart, don't you? You came across someone who was smarter this time. Now cast your mind back, Holmes. Can you think of no other way you could have got this thing?"

"I can't think. My mind is gone. For Heaven's sake help me!"

"Yes, I will help you. I'll help you to understand just where you are and how you got there. I'd like you to know before you die."

"Give me something to ease my pain."

"Painful, is it? Yes, the coolies used to do some squealing towards the end. Takes you as cramp, I fancy."

"Yes, yes; it is cramp."

"Well, you can hear what I say, anyhow. Listen now! Can you remember any unusual incident in your life just about the time your symptoms began?"

"No, no; nothing."

"Think again."

"I'm too ill to think."

"Well, then, I'll help you. Did anything come by post?"

"By post?"

"A box by chance?"

"I'm fainting—I'm gone!"

"Listen, Holmes!" There was a sound as if he was shaking the dying man, and it was all that I could do to hold myself quiet in my hiding-place. "You must hear me. You *shall* hear me. Do you remember a box —an ivory box? It came on Wednesday. You opened it—do you remember?"

"Yes, yes, I opened it. There was a sharp spring inside it. Some joke——"

"It was no joke, as you will find to your cost. You fool, you would have it and you have got it. Who asked you to cross my path? If you had left me alone I would not have hurt you."

"I remember," Holmes gasped. "The spring! It drew blood. This box—this on the table."

"The very one, by George! And it may as well leave the room in my pocket. There goes your last shred of evidence. But you have the truth now, Holmes, and you can die with the knowledge that I killed you. You knew too much of the fate of Victor Savage, so I have sent you to share it. You are very near your end, Holmes. I will sit here and I will watch you die."

Holmes's voice had sunk to an almost inaudible whisper.

"What is that?" said Smith. "Turn up the gas? Ah, the shadows begin to fall, do they? Yes, I will turn it up, that I may see you the better." He crossed the room and the light suddenly brightened. "Is there any other little service that I can do you, my friend?"

"A match and a cigarette."

I nearly called out in my joy and my

"'YOU'LL ONLY GET YOURSELF HURT,' SAID THE INSPECTOR. 'STAND STILL, WILL YOU?'"

amazement. He was speaking in his natural voice—a little weak, perhaps, but the very voice I knew. There was a long pause, and I felt that Culverton Smith was standing in silent amazement looking down at his companion.

"What's the meaning of this?" I heard him say at last, in a dry, rasping tone.

"The best way of successfully acting a part is to be it," said Holmes. "I give you my word that for three days I have tasted neither food nor drink until you were good enough to pour me out that glass of water. But it is the tobacco which I find most irksome. Ah, here *are* some cigarettes." I heard the striking of a match. "That is very much better. Halloa! halloa! Do I hear the step of a friend?"

There were footfalls outside, the door opened, and Inspector Morton appeared.

"All is in order and this is your man," said Holmes.

The officer gave the usual cautions.

"I arrest you on the charge of the murder of one Victor Savage," he concluded.

"And you might add of the attempted murder of one Sherlock Holmes," remarked my friend with a chuckle. "To save an invalid trouble, inspector, Mr. Culverton Smith was good enough to give our signal by turning up the gas. By the way, the prisoner has a small box in the right-hand pocket of his coat which it would be as well to remove. Thank you. I would handle it gingerly if I were you. Put it down here. It may play its part in the trial."

There was a sudden rush and a scuffle, followed by the clash of iron and a cry of pain.

"You'll only get yourself hurt," said the inspector. "Stand still, will you?" There was the click of the closing handcuffs.

"A nice trap!" cried the high, snarling voice. "It will bring *you* into the dock, Holmes, not me. He asked me to come here to cure him. I was sorry for him and I came. Now he will pretend, no doubt, that I have said anything which he may invent which will corroborate his insane suspicions. You can lie as you like, Holmes. My word is always as good as yours."

"Good heavens!" cried Holmes. "I had totally forgotten him. My dear Watson, I owe you a thousand apologies. To think that I should have overlooked you! I need not introduce you to Mr. Culverton Smith, since I understand that you met somewhat earlier in the evening. Have you the cab below? I will follow you when I am dressed, for I may be of some use at the station."

"I never needed it more," said Holmes, as he refreshed himself with a glass of claret and some biscuits in the intervals of his toilet. "However, as you know, my habits are irregular, and such a feat means less to me than to most men. It was very essential that I should impress Mrs. Hudson with the reality of my condition, since she was to convey it to you, and you in turn to him. You won't be offended, Watson? You will realize that among your many talents dissimulation finds no place, and that if you had shared my secret you would never have been able to impress Smith with the urgent necessity of his presence, which was the vital point of the whole scheme. Knowing his vindictive nature, I was perfectly certain that he would come to look upon his handiwork."

"But your appearance, Holmes—your ghastly face?"

"Three days of absolute fast does not improve one's beauty, Watson. For the rest, there is nothing which a sponge may not cure. With vaseline upon one's forehead, belladonna in one's eyes, rouge over the cheek-bones, and crusts of beeswax round one's lips, a very satisfying effect can be produced. Malingering is a subject upon which I have sometimes thought of writing a monograph. A little occasional talk about half-crowns, oysters, or any other extraneous subject produces a pleasing effect of delirium."

"But why would you not let me near you, since there was in truth no infection?"

"Can you ask, my dear Watson? Do you imagine that I have no respect for your medical talents? Could I fancy that your astute judgment would pass a dying man who, however weak, had no rise of pulse or temperature? At four yards I could deceive you. If I failed to do so, who would bring my Smith within my grasp? No, Watson, I would not touch that box. You can just see if you look at it sideways where the sharp spring like a viper's tooth emerges as you open it. I dare say it was by some such device that poor Savage, who stood between this monster and a reversion, was done to death. My correspondence, however, is, as you know, a varied one, and I am somewhat upon my guard against any packages which reach me. It was clear to me, however, that by pretending that he had really succeeded in his design I might surprise a confession. That pretence I have carried out with the thoroughness of the true artist. Thank you, Watson, you must help me on with my coat. When we have finished at the police-station I think that something nutritious at Simpson's would not be out of place."

THE VALLEY OF FEAR

Facsimile from the Strand Magazine, Volumes XLVIII and XLIX, September 1914 – May 1915.

THE CIPHER AND THE MAN WHO SOLVED IT.

THE STRAND
MAGAZINE.

SEPTEMBER, 1914.
Vol. xlviii.   No. 285.

The VALLEY *of* FEAR

A NEW
SHERLOCK HOLMES
STORY
By
A. CONAN DOYLE

Illustrated by FRANK WILES
PART ·I·
THE TRAGEDY OF
BIRLSTONE

CHAPTER I.
THE WARNING.

I AM inclined to think——" said I.

"I should do so," Sherlock Holmes remarked, impatiently.

I believe that I am one of the most long-suffering ot mortals, but I admit that I was annoyed at the sardonic interruption.

"Really, Holmes," said I, severely, "you are a little trying at times."

He was too much absorbed with his own thoughts to give any immediate answer to my remonstrance. He leaned upon his hand, with his untasted breakfast before him, and he stared at the slip of paper which he had just drawn from its envelope. Then he took the envelope itself, held it up to the light, and very carefully studied both the exterior and the flap.

"It is Porlock's writing," said he, thoughtfully. "I can hardly doubt that it is Porlock's writing, though I have only seen it twice before. The Greek 'e' with the peculiar top flourish is distinctive. But if it is from Porlock, then it must be something of the very first importance."

He was speaking to himself rather than to me, but my vexation disappeared in the interest which the words awakened.

"Who, then, is Porlock?" I asked.

"Porlock, Watson, is a *nom de plume*, a mere identification mark, but behind it lies a shifty and evasive personality. In a former letter he frankly informed me that the name was not his own, and defied me ever to trace him among the teeming millions of this great city. Porlock is important, not for himself, but for the great man with whom he is in touch. Picture to yourself the pilot-fish with the shark, the jackal with the lion—anything that is insignificant in companionship with what is formidable. Not only formidable, Watson, but sinister—in the highest degree sinister. That is where he comes within my purview. You have heard me speak of Professor Moriarty ? "

" The famous scientific criminal, as famous among crooks as——"

" My blushes, Watson," Holmes murmured, in a deprecating voice.

" I was about to say 'as he is unknown to the public.'"

" A touch—a distinct touch ! " cried Holmes. " You are developing a certain unexpected vein of pawky humour, Watson, against which I must learn to guard myself. But in calling Moriarty a criminal you are uttering libel in the eyes of the law, and there lies the glory and the wonder of it. The greatest schemer of all time, the organizer of every devilry, the controlling brain of the underworld—a brain which might have made or marred the destiny of nations. That's the man. But so aloof is he from general suspicion—so immune from criticism—so admirable in his management and self-effacement, that for those very words that you have uttered he could hale you to a court and emerge with your year's pension as a solatium for his wounded character. Is he not the celebrated author of ' The Dynamics of an Asteroid '—a book which ascends to such rarefied heights of pure mathematics that it is said that there was no man in the scientific press capable of criticizing it ? Is this a man to traduce ? Foul-mouthed doctor and slandered professor—such would be your respective *rôles*. That's genius, Watson. But if I am spared by lesser men our day will surely come."

" May I be there to see ! " I exclaimed, devoutly. " But you were speaking of this man Porlock."

" Ah, yes—the so-called Porlock is a link in the chain some little way from its great attachment. Porlock is not quite a sound link, between ourselves. He is the only flaw in that chain so far as I have been able to test it."

" But no chain is stronger than its weakest link."

" Exactly, my dear Watson. Hence the extreme importance of Porlock. Led on by some rudimentary aspirations towards right, and encouraged by the judicious stimulation of an occasional ten-pound note sent to him by devious methods, he has once or twice given me advance information which has been of value—that highest value which anticipates and prevents rather than avenges crime. I cannot doubt that if we had the cipher we should find that this communication is of the nature that I indicate."

Again Holmes flattened out the paper upon his unused plate. I rose and, leaning over him, stared down at the curious inscription, which ran as follows :—

534 C2 13 127 36 31 4 17 21 41
DOUGLAS 109 293 5 37 BIRLSTONE
26 BIRLSTONE 9 13 171

" What do you make of it, Holmes ? "

" It is obviously an attempt to convey secret information."

" But what is the use of a cipher message without the cipher ? "

" In this instance, none at all."

" Why do you say ' in this instance ' ? "

" Because there are many ciphers which I would read as easily as I do the apocrypha of the agony column. Such crude devices amuse the intelligence without fatiguing it. But this is different. It is clearly a reference to the words in a page of some book. Until I am told which page and which book I am powerless."

" But why ' Douglas ' and ' Birlstone ' ? "

" Clearly because those are words which were not contained in the page in question."

" Then why has he not indicated the book ? "

" Your native shrewdness, my dear Watson, that innate cunning which is the delight of your friends, would surely prevent you from enclosing cipher and message in the same envelope. Should it miscarry you are undone. As it is, both have to go wrong before any harm comes from it. Our second post is now overdue, and I shall be surprised if it does not bring us either a further letter of explanation or, as is more probable, the very volume to which these figures refer."

Holmes's calculation was fulfilled within a very few minutes by the appearance of Billy, the page, with the very letter which we were expecting.

" The same writing," remarked Holmes, as he opened the envelope, " and actually signed," he added, in an exultant voice, as he unfolded the epistle. " Come, we are getting on, Watson."

His brow clouded, however, as he glanced over the contents.

" Dear me, this is very disappointing ! I fear, Watson, that all our expectations come to nothing. I trust that the man Porlock will come to no harm.

" ' Dear Mr. Holmes,' he says, ' I will go no further in this matter. It is too dangerous. He suspects me. I can see that he suspects me. He came to me quite unexpectedly after I had actually addressed this envelope with the intention of sending you the key to the cipher. I was able to cover it up. If he had seen it, it would have gone hard with me. But I read suspicion in his eyes. Please burn the cipher message, which can now be of no use to you.—FRED PORLOCK.' "

Holmes sat for some little time twisting this letter between his fingers, and frowning, as he stared into the fire.

" After all," he said at last, " there may be nothing in it. It may be only his guilty conscience. Knowing himself to be a traitor, he may have read the accusation in the other's eyes."

" The other being, I presume, Professor Moriarty ? "

" No less. When any of that party talk about ' he,' you know whom they mean. There is one predominant 'he' for all of them."

" But what can he do ? "

" Hum ! That's a large question. When you have one of the first brains of Europe up against you and all the powers of darkness at his back, there are infinite possibilities. Anyhow, friend Porlock is evidently scared out of his senses. Kindly compare the writing in the note with that upon its envelope, which was done, he tells us, before this ill-omened visit. The one is clear and firm ; the other hardly legible."

" Why did he write at all ? Why did he not simply drop it ? "

" Because he feared I would make some inquiry after him in that case, and possibly bring trouble on him."

" No doubt," said I. " Of course "—I had picked up the original cipher message and was bending my brows over it—" it's pretty maddening to think that an important secret may lie here on this slip of paper, and that it is beyond human power to penetrate it."

Sherlock Holmes had pushed away his untasted breakfast and lit the unsavoury pipe which was the companion of his deepest meditations.

" I wonder ! " said he, leaning back and staring at the ceiling. " Perhaps there are points which have escaped your Machiavellian intellect. Let us consider the problem in the light of pure reason. This man's reference is to a book. That is our point of departure."

" A somewhat vague one."

" Let us see, then, if we can narrow it down. As I focus my mind upon it, it seems rather less impenetrable. What indications have we as to this book ? "

" None."

" Well, well, it is surely not quite so bad as that. The cipher message begins with a large 534, does it not ? We may take it as a working hypothesis that 534 is the particular page to which the cipher refers. So our book has already become a *large* book, which is surely something gained. What other indications have we as to the nature of this large book ? The next sign is C2. What do you make of that, Watson ? "

" Chapter the second, no doubt."

" Hardly that, Watson. You will, I am sure, agree with me that if the page be given the number of the chapter is immaterial. Also that if page 534 only finds us in the second chapter, the length of the first one must have been really intolerable."

" Column ! " I cried.

" Brilliant, Watson. You are scintillating this morning. If it is not column, then I am very much deceived. So now, you see, we begin to visualize a large book, printed in double columns, which are each of a considerable length, since one of the words is numbered in the document as the two hundred and ninety-third. Have we reached the limits of what reason can supply ? "

" I fear that we have."

" Surely you do yourself an injustice. One more coruscation, my dear Watson. Yet another brain-wave. Had the volume been an unusual one he would have sent it to me. Instead of that he had intended, before his plans were nipped, to send me the clue in this envelope. He says so in his note. This would seem to indicate that the book is one which he thought that I would have no difficulty in finding for myself. He had it, and he imagined that I would have it too. In short, Watson, it is a very common book."

" What you say certainly sounds plausible."

" So we have contracted our field of search to a large book, printed in double columns and in common use."

" The Bible ! " I cried, triumphantly.

" Good, Watson, good ! But not, if I may

"HOLMES'S EYES WERE GLEAMING WITH EXCITEMENT, AND HIS THIN, NERVOUS FINGERS TWITCHED
AS HE COUNTED THE WORDS—'DANGER.' 'HA! HA! CAPITAL! PUT THAT DOWN, WATSON.'"

say so, quite good enough. Even if I accepted the compliment for myself, I could hardly name any volume which would be less likely to lie at the elbow of one of Moriarty's associates. Besides, the editions of Holy Writ are so numerous that he could hardly suppose that two copies would have the same pagination. This is clearly a book which is standardized. He knows for certain that his page 534 will exactly agree with my page 534."

"But very few books would correspond with that."

"Exactly. Therein lies our salvation. Our search is narrowed down to standardized books which anyone may be supposed to possess."

"'Bradshaw'!"

"There are difficulties, Watson. The vocabulary of 'Bradshaw' is nervous and terse, but limited. The selection of words would hardly lend itself to the sending of general messages. We will eliminate 'Bradshaw.' The dictionary is, I fear, inadmissible for the same reason. What, then, is left?"

"An almanack."

"Excellent, Watson! I am very much mistaken if you have not touched the spot. An almanack! Let us consider the claims of 'Whitaker's Almanack.' It is in common use. It has the requisite number of pages. It is in double column. Though reserved in its earlier vocabulary, it becomes, if I remember right, quite garrulous towards the end." He picked the volume from his desk. "Here is page 534, column two, a substantial block of print dealing, I perceive, with the trade and resources of British India. Jot down the words, Watson. Number thirteen is 'Mahratta.' Not, I fear, a very auspicious beginning. Number one hundred and twenty-seven is 'Government,' which at least makes sense, though somewhat irrelevant to ourselves and Professor Moriarty. Now let us try again. What does the Mahratta Government do? Alas! the next word is 'pigs'-bristles.' We are undone, my good Watson! It is finished."

He had spoken in jesting vein, but the twitching of his bushy eyebrows bespoke his disappointment and irritation. I sat helpless and unhappy, staring into the fire. A long silence was broken by a sudden exclamation from Holmes, who dashed at a cupboard, from which he emerged with a second yellow-covered volume in his hand.

"We pay the price, Watson, for being too up-to-date," he cried. "We are before our time, and suffer the usual penalties. Being

the seventh of January, we have very properly laid in the new almanack. It is more than likely that Porlock took his message from the old one. No doubt he would have told us so had his letter of explanation been written. Now let us see what page 534 has in store for us. Number thirteen is 'There,' which is much more promising. Number one hundred and twenty-seven is 'is'—'There is'"—Holmes's eyes were gleaming with excitement, and his thin, nervous fingers twitched as he counted the words—"'danger.' Ha! ha! Capital! Put that down, Watson. 'There is danger—may—come—very—soon—one.' Then we have the name 'Douglas'—'rich—country—now—at—Birlstone—House—Birlstone—confidence—is—pressing.' There, Watson! what do you think of pure reason and its fruits? If the greengrocer had such a thing as a laurel-wreath I should send Billy round for it."

I was staring at the strange message which I had scrawled, as he deciphered it, upon a sheet of foolscap on my knee.

"What a queer, scrambling way of expressing his meaning!" said I.

"On the contrary, he has done quite remarkably well," said Holmes. "When you search a single column for words with which to express your meaning, you can hardly expect to get everything you want. You are bound to leave something to the intelligence of your correspondent. The purport is perfectly clear. Some devilry is intended against one Douglas, whoever he may be, residing as stated, a rich country gentleman. He is sure—'confidence' was as near as he could get to 'confident'—that it is pressing. There is our result, and a very workmanlike little bit of analysis it was."

Holmes had the impersonal joy of the true artist in his better work, even as he mourned darkly when it fell below the high level to which he aspired. He was still chuckling over his success when Billy swung open the door and Inspector MacDonald of Scotland Yard was ushered into the room.

Those were the early days at the end of the 'eighties, when Alec MacDonald was far from having attained the national fame which he has now achieved. He was a young but trusted member of the detective force, who had distinguished himself in several cases which had been entrusted to him. His tall, bony figure gave promise of exceptional physical strength, while his great cranium and deep-set, lustrous eyes spoke no less clearly of the keen intelligence which twinkled out from behind his bushy eyebrows. He

" THE INSPECTOR WAS STARING WITH A LOOK OF ABSOLUTE AMAZEMENT AT A PAPER UPON THE

TABLE. IT WAS THE SHEET UPON WHICH I HAD SCRAWLED THE ENIGMATIC MESSAGE."

was a silent, precise man, with a dour nature and a hard Aberdonian accent. Twice already in his career had Holmes helped him to attain success, his own sole reward being the intellectual joy of the problem. For this reason the affection and respect of the Scotchman for his amateur colleague were profound, and he showed them by the frankness with which he consulted Holmes in every difficulty. Mediocrity knows nothing higher than itself, but talent instantly recognizes genius, and MacDonald had talent enough for his profession to enable him to perceive that there was no humiliation in seeking the assistance of one who already stood alone in Europe, both in his gifts and in his experience. Holmes was not prone to friendship, but he was tolerant of the big Scotchman, and smiled at the sight of him.

"You are an early bird, Mr. Mac," said he. "I wish you luck with your worm. I fear this means that there is some mischief afoot."

"If you said 'hope' instead of 'fear' it would be nearer the truth, I'm thinking, Mr. Holmes," the inspector answered, with a knowing grin. "Well, maybe a wee nip would keep out the raw morning chill. No, I won't smoke, I thank you. I'll have to be pushing on my way, for the early hours of a case are the precious ones, as no man knows better than your own self. But—but——"

The inspector had stopped suddenly, and was staring with a look of absolute amazement at a paper upon the table. It was the sheet upon which I had scrawled the enigmatic message.

"Douglas!" he stammered. "Birlstone! What's this, Mr. Holmes? Man, it's witchcraft! Where in the name of all that is wonderful did you get those names?"

"It is a cipher that Dr. Watson and I have had occasion to solve. But why—what's amiss with the names?"

The inspector looked from one to the other of us in dazed astonishment.

"Just this," said he, "that Mr. Douglas, of Birlstone Manor House, was horribly murdered this morning."

CHAPTER II.

MR. SHERLOCK HOLMES DISCOURSES.

IT was one of those dramatic moments for which my friend existed. It would be an over-statement to say that he was shocked or even excited by the amazing announcement. Without having a tinge of cruelty in his singular composition, he was undoubtedly callous from long over-stimulation. Yet, if his emotions were dulled, his intellectual perceptions were exceedingly active. There was no trace then of the horror which I had myself felt at this curt declaration, but his face showed rather the quiet and interested composure of the chemist who sees the crystals falling into position from his over-saturated solution.

"Remarkable!" said he; "remarkable!"

"You don't seem surprised."

"Interested, Mr. Mac, but hardly surprised. Why should I be surprised? I receive an anonymous communication from a quarter which I know to be important, warning me that danger threatens a certain person. Within an hour I learn that this danger has actually materialized, and that the person is dead. I am interested, but, as you observe, I am not surprised."

In a few short sentences he explained to the inspector the facts about the letter and the cipher. MacDonald sat with his chin on his hands, and his great sandy eyebrows bunched into a yellow tangle.

"I was going down to Birlstone this morning," said he. "I had come to ask you if you cared to come with me—you and your friend here. But from what you say we might perhaps be doing better work in London."

"I rather think not," said Holmes.

"Hang it all, Mr. Holmes!" cried the inspector. "The papers will be full of the Birlstone Mystery in a day or two, but where's the mystery if there is a man in London who prophesied the crime before ever it occurred? We have only to lay our hands on that man and the rest will follow."

"No doubt, Mr. Mac. But how did you propose to lay your hands on the so-called Porlock?"

MacDonald turned over the letter which Holmes had handed him.

"Posted in Camberwell—that doesn't help us much. Name, you say, is assumed. Not much to go on, certainly. Didn't you say that you have sent him money?"

"Twice."

"And how?"

"In notes to Camberwell post-office."

"Did you never trouble to see who called for them?"

"No."

The inspector looked surprised and a little shocked.

"Why not?"

"Because I always keep faith. I had promised when he first wrote that I would not try to trace him."

" You think there is someone behind him ? "

" I *know* there is."

" This Professor that I have heard you mention ? "

" Exactly."

Inspector MacDonald smiled, and his eyelid quivered as he glanced towards me.

" I won't conceal from you, Mr. Holmes, that we think in the C.I.D. that you have a wee bit of a bee in your bonnet over this Professor. I made some inquiries myself about the matter. He seems to be a very respectable, learned, and talented sort of man."

" I'm glad you've got as far as to recognize the talent."

" Man, you can't but recognize it. After I heard your view, I made it my business to see him. I had a chat with him on eclipses —how the talk got that way I canna think— but he had out a reflector lantern and a globe and made it all clear in a minute. He lent me a book, but I don't mind saying that it was a bit above my head, though I had a good Aberdeen upbringing. He'd have made a grand meenister, with his thin face and grey hair and solemn-like way of talking. When he put his hand on my shoulder as we were parting, it was like a father's blessing before you go out into the cold, cruel world."

Holmes chuckled and rubbed his hands.

" Great ! " he said ; " great ! Tell me, friend MacDonald ; this pleasing and touching interview was, I suppose, in the Professor's study?"

" That's so."

" A fine room, is it not ? "

" Very fine—very handsome indeed, Mr. Holmes."

" You sat in front of his writing-desk ? "

" Just so."

" Sun in your eyes and his face in the shadow ? "

" Well, it was evening, but I mind that the lamp was turned on my face."

" It would be. Did you happen to observe a picture over the Professor's head ? "

" I don't miss much, Mr. Holmes. Maybe I learned that from you. Yes, I saw the picture—a young woman with her head on her hands, keeking at you sideways."

" That painting was by Jean Baptiste Greuze."

The inspector endeavoured to look interested.

" Jean Baptiste Greuze," Holmes continued, joining his finger-tips and leaning well back in his chair, " was a French artist who flourished between the years 1750 and 1800. I allude, of course, to his working career. Modern criticism has more than endorsed the high opinion formed of him by his contemporaries."

The inspector's eyes grew abstracted.

" Hadn't we better——" he said.

" We are doing so," Holmes interrupted. " All that I am saying has a very direct and vital bearing upon what you have called the Birlstone Mystery. In fact, it may in a sense be called the very centre of it."

MacDonald smiled feebly, and looked appealingly to me.

" Your thoughts move a bit too quick for me, Mr. Holmes. You leave out a link or two, and I can't get over the gap. What in the whole wide world can be the connection between this dead painting man and the affair at Birlstone ? "

" All knowledge comes useful to the detective," remarked Holmes. " Even the trivial fact that in the year 1865 a picture by Greuze, entitled ' La Jeune Fille à l'agneau,' fetched one million two hundred thousand francs— more than forty thousand pounds—at the Portalis sale, may start a train of reflection in your mind."

It was clear that it did. The inspector looked honestly interested.

" I may remind you," Holmes continued, " that the Professor's salary can be ascertained in several trustworthy books of reference. It is seven hundred a year."

" Then how could he buy——"

" Quite so. How could he ? "

" Aye, that's remarkable," said the inspector, thoughtfully. " Talk away, Mr. Holmes. I'm just loving it. It's fine."

Holmes smiled. He was always warmed by genuine admiration—the characteristic of the real artist.

" What about Birlstone ? " he asked.

" We've time yet," said the inspector, glancing at his watch. " I've a cab at the door, and it won't take us twenty minutes to Victoria. But about this picture—I thought you told me once, Mr. Holmes, that you had never met Professor Moriarty."

" No, I never have."

" Then how do you know about his rooms ? "

" Ah, that's another matter. I have been three times in his rooms, twice waiting for him under different pretexts and leaving before he came. Once—well, I can hardly tell about the once to an official detective. It was on the last occasion that I took the liberty of running over his papers, with the most unexpected results."

" You found something compromising ? "

" Absolutely nothing. That was what amazed me. However, you have now seen the point of the picture. It shows him to be a very wealthy man. How did he acquire wealth ? He is unmarried. His younger brother is a station-master in the West of England. His chair is worth seven hundred a year. And he owns a Greuze."

" Well ? "

" Surely the inference is plain."

" You mean that he has a great income, and that he must earn it in an illegal fashion ? "

" Exactly. Of course, I have other reasons for thinking so—dozens of exiguous threads which lead vaguely up towards the centre of the web where the poisonous motionless creature is lurking. I only mention the Greuze because it brings the matter within the range of your own observation."

" Well, Mr. Holmes, I admit that what you say is interesting. It's more than interesting—it's just wonderful. But let us have it a little clearer if you can. Is it forgery, coining, burglary ? Where does the money come from ? "

" Have you ever read of Jonathan Wild ? "

" Well, the name has a familiar sound. Someone in a novel, was he not ? I don't take much stock of detectives in novels— chaps that do things and never let you see how they do them. That's just inspiration, not business."

" Jonathan Wild wasn't a detective, and he wasn't in a novel. He was a master criminal, and he lived last century—1750 or thereabouts."

" Then he's no use to me. I'm a practical man."

" Mr. Mac, the most practical thing that ever you did in your life would be to shut yourself up for three months and read twelve hours a day at the annals of crime. Everything comes in circles, even Professor Moriarty. Jonathan Wild was the hidden force of the London criminals, to whom he sold his brains and his organization on a fifteen per cent. commission. The old wheel turns and the same spoke comes up. It's all been done before and will be again. I'll tell you one or two things about Moriarty which may interest you."

" You'll interest me right enough."

" I happen to know who is the first link in his chain—a chain with this Napoleon-gone-wrong at one end and a hundred broken fighting men, pickpockets, blackmailers, and card-sharpers at the other, with every sort of crime in between. His chief of the staff is Colonel Sebastian Moran, as aloof and guarded and inaccessible to the law as himself. What do you think he pays him ? "

" I'd like to hear."

" Six thousand a year. That's paying for brains, you see—the American business principle. I learned that detail quite by chance. It's more than the Prime Minister gets. That gives you an idea of Moriarty's gains and of the scale on which he works. Another point. I made it my business to hunt down some of Moriarty's cheques lately —just common innocent cheques that he pays his household bills with. They were drawn on six different banks. Does that make any impression on your mind ? "

" Queer, certainly. But what do you gather from it ? "

" That he wanted no gossip about his wealth. No single man should know what he had. I have no doubt that he has twenty banking accounts—the bulk of his fortune abroad in the Deutsche Bank or the Crédit Lyonnais as likely as not. Some time when you have a year or two to spare I commend to you the study of Professor Moriarty."

Inspector MacDonald had grown steadily more impressed as the conversation proceeded. He had lost himself in his interest. Now his practical Scotch intelligence brought him back with a snap to the matter in hand.

" He can keep, anyhow," said he. " You've got us side-tracked with your interesting anecdotes, Mr. Holmes. What really counts is your remark that there is some connection between the Professor and the crime. That you get from the warning received through the man Porlock. Can we for our present practical needs get any farther than that ? "

" We may form some conception as to the motives of the crime. It is, as I gather from your original remarks, an inexplicable, or at least an unexplained, murder. Now, presuming that the source of the crime is as we suspect it to be, there might be two different motives. In the first place, I may tell you that Moriarty rules with a rod of iron over his people. His discipline is tremendous. There is only one punishment in his code. It is death. Now, we might suppose that this murdered man—this Douglas, whose approaching fate was known by one of the arch-criminal's subordinates—had in some way betrayed the chief. His punishment followed and would be known to all, if only to put the fear of death into them."

" Well, that is one suggestion, Mr. Holmes."

"LEANING FORWARD IN THE CAB, HOLMES LISTENED INTENTLY TO MAC DONALD'S SHORT SKETCH
OF THE PROBLEM WHICH AWAITED US IN SUSSEX."

" The other is that it has been engineered by Moriarty in the ordinary course of business. Was there any robbery ? "

" I have not heard."

" If so it would, of course, be against the first hypothesis and in favour of the second. Moriarty may have been engaged to engineer it on a promise of part spoils, or he may have been paid so much down to manage it. Either is possible. But, whichever it may be, or if it is some third combination, it is down at Birlstone that we must seek the solution. I know our man too well to suppose that he has left anything up here which may lead us to him."

" Then to Birlstone we must go ! " cried MacDonald, jumping from his chair. " My word ! it's later than I thought. I can give you gentlemen five minutes for preparation, and that is all."

" And ample for us both," said Holmes, as he sprang up and hastened to change from his dressing-gown to his coat. " While we are on our way, Mr. Mac, I will ask you to be good enough to tell me all about it."

" All about it " proved to be disappointingly little, and yet there was enough to assure us that the case before us might well be worthy of the expert's closest attention. He brightened and rubbed his thin hands together as he listened to the meagre but remarkable details. A long series of sterile weeks lay behind us, and here, at last, there was a fitting object for those remarkable powers which, like all special gifts, become irksome to their owner when they are not in use. That razor brain blunted and rusted with inaction. Sherlock Holmes's eyes glistened, his pale cheeks took a warmer hue, and his whole eager face shone with an inward light when the call for work reached him. Leaning forward in the cab, he listened intently to MacDonald's short sketch of the problem which awaited us in Sussex. The inspector was himself dependent, as he explained to us, upon a scribbled account forwarded to him by the milk train in the early hours of the morning. White Mason, the local officer, was a personal friend, and hence MacDonald had been notified very much more promptly than is usual at Scotland Yard when provincials need their assistance. It is a very cold scent upon which the Metropolitan expert is generally asked to run.

" Dear Inspector MacDonald," said the letter which he read to us, " official requisition for your services is in separate envelope. This is for your private eye. Wire me what train in the morning you can get for Birlstone, and I will meet it—or have it met if I am too occupied. This case is a snorter. Don't waste a moment in getting started. If you can bring Mr. Holmes, please do so, for he will find something after his own heart. You would think the whole thing had been fixed up for theatrical effect, if there wasn't a dead man in the middle of it. My word, it *is* a snorter ! "

" Your friend seems to be no fool," remarked Holmes.

" No, sir ; White Mason is a very live man, if I am any judge."

" Well, have you anything more ? "

" Only that he will give us every detail when we meet."

" Then how did you get at Mr. Douglas and the fact that he had been horribly murdered ? "

" That was in the enclosed official report. It didn't say ' horrible.' That's not a recognized official term. It gave the name John Douglas. It mentioned that his injuries had been in the head, from the discharge of a shotgun. It also mentioned the hour of the alarm, which was close on to midnight last night. It added that the case was undoubtedly one of murder, but that no arrest had been made, and that the case was one which presented some very perplexing and extraordinary features. That's absolutely all we have at present, Mr. Holmes."

" Then, with your permission, we will leave it at that, Mr. Mac. The temptation to form premature theories upon insufficient data is the bane of our profession. I can only see two things for certain at present : a great brain in London and a dead man in Sussex. It's the chain between that we are going to trace."

THE STRAND
MAGAZINE.

OCTOBER, 1914.
Vol. xlviii.   No. 286.

The
VALLEY of FEAR

A NEW
SHERLOCK HOLMES
STORY

By

A. CONAN DOYLE

Illustrated by FRANK WILES

PART · I ·
THE TRAGEDY OF
BIRLSTONE

The opening chapters of this new and thrilling adventure of Sherlock Holmes, which commenced in our last issue, described the receipt by Holmes of a cipher message, from which he deduces that some devilry is intended against a man named Douglas, a rich country gentleman living at Birlstone in Sussex, and that the danger is a pressing one.   Almost as soon as he has deciphered the message he is visited by Inspector MacDonald, of Scotland Yard, who brings the news that Mr. Douglas has been murdered that morning.   He asks Sherlock Holmes and Dr. Watson to accompany him to the scene of the crime, and the three go off together.

CHAPTER III.
THE TRAGEDY OF BIRLSTONE.

AND now for a moment I will ask leave to remove my own insignificant personality and to describe events which occurred before we arrived upon the scene by the light of knowledge which came to us afterwards.   Only in this way can I make the reader appreciate the people concerned and the strange setting in which their fate was cast.

The village of Birlstone is a small and very ancient cluster of half-timbered cottages on the northern border of the county of Sussex.   For centuries it had remained unchanged, but within the last few years its picturesque appearance and situation have attracted a number of well-to-do residents, whose villas

"THE DOCTOR KNELT BESIDE HIM, AND HELD DOWN THE HAND-LAMP. ONE GLANCE WAS ENOUGH TO SHOW THE HEALER THAT HIS PRESENCE COULD BE DISPENSED WITH."

peep out from the woods around. These woods are locally supposed to be the extreme fringe of the great Weald forest, which thins away until it reaches the northern chalk downs. A number of small shops have come into being to meet the wants of the increased population, so that there seems some prospect that Birlstone may soon grow from an ancient village into a modern town. It is the centre for a considerable area of country, since Tunbridge Wells, the nearest place of importance, is ten or twelve miles to the eastward, over the borders of Kent.

About half a mile from the town, standing in an old park famous for its huge beech trees, is the ancient Manor House of Birlstone. Part of this venerable building dates back to the time of the first Crusade, when Hugo de Capus built a fortalice in the centre of the estate, which had been granted to him by the Red King. This was destroyed by fire in 1543, and some of its smoke-blackened corner-stones were used when, in Jacobean times, a brick country house rose upon the ruins of the feudal castle. The Manor House, with its many gables and its small, diamond-paned windows, was still much as the builder had left it in the early seventeenth century. Of the double moats which had guarded its more warlike predecessor the outer had been allowed to dry up, and served the humble function of a kitchen garden. The inner one was still there, and lay, forty feet in breadth, though now only a few feet in depth, round the whole house. A small stream fed it and continued beyond it, so that the sheet of water, though turbid, was never ditch-like or unhealthy. The ground-floor windows were within a foot of the surface of the water. The only approach to the house was over a drawbridge, the chains and windlass of which had long been rusted and broken. The latest tenants of the Manor House had, however, with characteristic energy, set this right, and the drawbridge was not only capable of being raised, but actually was raised every evening and lowered every morning. By thus renewing the custom of the old feudal days the Manor House was converted into an island during the night—a fact which had a very direct bearing upon the mystery which was soon to engage the attention of all England.

The house had been untenanted for some years, and was threatening to moulder into a picturesque decay when the Douglases took possession of it. This family consisted of only two individuals, John Douglas and his wife. Douglas was a remarkable man both in character and in person ; in age he may

have been about fifty, with a strong-jawed, rugged face, a grizzling moustache, peculiarly keen grey eyes, and a wiry, vigorous figure which had lost nothing of the strength and activity of youth. He was cheery and genial to all, but somewhat offhand in his manners, giving the impression that he had seen life in social strata on some far lower horizon than the county society of Sussex. Yet, though looked at with some curiosity and reserve by his more cultivated neighbours, he soon acquired a great popularity among the villagers, subscribing handsomely to all local objects, and attending their smoking concerts and other functions, where, having a remarkably rich tenor voice, he was always ready to oblige with an excellent song. He appeared to have plenty of money, which was said to have been gained in the Californian gold-fields, and it was clear from his own talk and that of his wife that he had spent a part of his life in America. The good impression which had been produced by his generosity and by his democratic manners was increased by a reputation gained for utter indifference to danger. Though a wretched rider, he turned out at every meet, and took the most amazing falls in his determination to hold his own with the best. When the vicarage caught fire he distinguished himself also by the fearlessness with which he re-entered the building to save property, after the local fire brigade had given it up as impossible. Thus it came about that John Douglas, of the Manor House, had within five years won himself quite a reputation in Birlstone.

His wife, too, was popular with those who had made her acquaintance, though, after the English fashion, the callers upon a stranger who settled in the county without introductions were few and far between. This mattered the less to her as she was retiring by disposition and very much absorbed, to all appearance, in her husband and her domestic duties. It was known that she was an English lady who had met Mr. Douglas in London, he being at that time a widower. She was a beautiful woman, tall, dark, and slender, some twenty years younger than her husband, a disparity which seemed in no wise to mar the contentment of their family life. It was remarked sometimes, however, by those who knew them best that the confidence between the two did not appear to be complete, since the wife was either very reticent about her husband's past life or else, as seemed more likely, was very imperfectly informed about it. It had also been noted and commented upon by a few observant people that there were signs sometimes of some nerve-strain upon the part of Mrs. Douglas, and that she would display acute uneasiness if her absent husband should ever be particularly late in his return. On a quiet countryside, where all gossip is welcome, this weakness of the lady of the Manor House did not pass without remark, and it bulked larger upon people's memory when the events arose which gave it a very special significance.

There was yet another individual whose residence under that roof was, it is true, only an intermittent one, but whose presence at the time of the strange happenings which will now be narrated brought his name prominently before the public. This was Cecil James Barker, of Hales Lodge, Hampstead. Cecil Barker's tall, loose-jointed figure was a familiar one in the main street of Birlstone village, for he was a frequent and welcome visitor at the Manor House. He was the more noticed as being the only friend of the past unknown life of Mr. Douglas who was ever seen in his new English surroundings. Barker was himself an undoubted Englishman, but by his remarks it was clear that he had first known Douglas in America, and had there lived on intimate terms with him. He appeared to be a man of considerable wealth, and was reputed to be a bachelor. In age he was rather younger than Douglas, forty-five at the most, a tall, straight, broad-chested fellow, with a clean-shaven prize-fighter face, thick, strong, black eyebrows, and a pair of masterful black eyes which might, even without the aid of his very capable hands, clear a way for him through a hostile crowd. He neither rode nor shot, but spent his days in wandering round the old village with his pipe in his mouth, or in driving with his host, or in his absence with his hostess, over the beautiful countryside. "An easy-going, free-handed gentleman," said Ames, the butler. "But, my word, I had rather not be the man that crossed him." He was cordial and intimate with Douglas, and he was no less friendly with his wife, a friendship which more than once seemed to cause some irritation to the husband, so that even the servants were able to perceive his annoyance. Such was the third person who was one of the family when the catastrophe occurred. As to the other denizens of the old building, it will suffice out of a large household to mention the prim, respectable, and capable Ames and Mrs. Allen, a buxom and cheerful person, who relieved the lady of some of her household cares.

The other six servants in the house bear no relation to the events of the night of January 6th.

It was at eleven-forty-five that the first alarm reached the small local police-station in the charge of Sergeant Wilson, of the Sussex Constabulary. Mr. Cecil Barker, much excited, had rushed up to the door and pealed furiously upon the bell. A terrible tragedy had occurred at the Manor House, and Mr. John Douglas had been murdered. That was the breathless burden of his message. He had hurried back to the house, followed within a few minutes by the police-sergeant, who arrived at the scene of the crime a little past twelve o'clock, after taking prompt steps to warn the county authorities that something serious was afoot.

On reaching the Manor House the sergeant had found the drawbridge down, the windows lighted up, and the whole household in a state of wild confusion and alarm. The white-faced servants were huddling together in the hall, with the frightened butler wringing his hands in the doorway. Only Cecil Barker seemed to be master of himself and his emotions. He had opened the door which was nearest to the entrance, and had beckoned to the sergeant to follow him. At that moment there arrived Dr. Wood, a brisk and capable general practitioner from the village. The three men entered the fatal room together, while the horror-stricken butler followed at their heels, closing the door behind him to shut out the terrible scene from the maid-servants.

The dead man lay upon his back, sprawling with outstretched limbs in the centre of the room. He was clad only in a pink dressing-gown, which covered his night clothes. There were carpet slippers upon his bare feet. The doctor knelt beside him, and held down the hand-lamp which had stood on the table. One glance at the victim was enough to show the healer that his presence could be dispensed with. The man had been horribly injured. Lying across his chest was a curious weapon, a shot-gun with the barrel sawn off a foot in front of the triggers. It was clear that this had been fired at close range, and that he had received the whole charge in the face, blowing his head almost to pieces. The triggers had been wired together, so as to make the simultaneous discharge more destructive.

The country policeman was unnerved and troubled by the tremendous responsibility which had come so suddenly upon him.

"We will touch nothing until my superiors

arrive," he said, in a hushed voice, staring in horror at the dreadful head.

"Nothing has been touched up to now," said Cecil Barker. "I'll answer for that. You see it all exactly as I found it."

"When was that?" The sergeant had drawn out his notebook.

"It was just half-past eleven. I had not begun to undress, and I was sitting by the fire in my bedroom, when I heard the report. It was not very loud—it seemed to be muffled. I rushed down. I don't suppose it was thirty seconds before I was in the room."

"Was the door open?"

"Yes, it was open. Poor Douglas was lying as you see him. His bedroom candle was burning on the table. It was I who lit the lamp some minutes afterwards."

"Did you see no one?"

"No. I heard Mrs. Douglas coming down the stair behind me, and I rushed out to prevent her from seeing this dreadful sight. Mrs. Allen, the housekeeper, came and took her away. Ames had arrived, and we ran back into the room once more."

"But surely I have heard that the drawbridge is kept up all night."

"Yes, it was up until I lowered it."

"Then how could any murderer have got away? It is out of the question. Mr. Douglas must have shot himself."

"That was our first idea. But see." Barker drew aside the curtain, and showed that the long, diamond-paned window was open to its full extent. "And look at this!" He held the lamp down and illuminated a smudge of blood like the mark of a boot-sole upon the wooden sill. "Someone has stood there in getting out."

"You mean that someone waded across the moat?"

"Exactly."

"Then, if you were in the room within half a minute of the crime, he must have been in the water at that very moment."

"I have not a doubt of it. I wish to Heaven that I had rushed to the window. But the curtain screened it, as you can see, and so it never occurred to me. Then I heard the step of Mrs. Douglas, and I could not let her enter the room. It would have been too horrible."

"Horrible enough!" said the doctor, looking at the shattered head and the terrible marks which surrounded it. "I've never seen such injuries since the Birlstone railway smash."

"But, I say," remarked the police-sergeant, whose slow, bucolic common sense was still pondering over the open window. "It's all very well your saying that a man escaped by wading this moat, but what I ask you is—how did he ever get into the house at all if the bridge was up?"

"Ah, that's the question," said Barker.

"At what o'clock was it raised?"

"It was nearly six o'clock," said Ames, the butler.

"I've heard," said the sergeant, "that it was usually raised at sunset. That would be nearer half-past four than six at this time of year."

"Mrs. Douglas had visitors to tea," said Ames. "I couldn't raise it until they went. Then I wound it up myself."

"Then it comes to this," said the sergeant. "If anyone came from outside—*if* they did—they must have got in across the bridge before six and been in hiding ever since, until Mr. Douglas came into the room after eleven."

"That is so. Mr. Douglas went round the house every night the last thing before he turned in to see that the lights were right. That brought him in here. The man was waiting, and shot him. Then he got away through the window and left his gun behind him. That's how I read it—for nothing else will fit the facts."

The sergeant picked up a card which lay beside the dead man upon the floor. The initials V. V., and under it the number 341, were rudely scrawled in ink upon it.

"What's this?" he asked, holding it up.

Barker looked at it with curiosity.

"I never noticed it before," he said. "The murderer must have left it behind him."

"V. V. 341. I can make no sense of that."

The sergeant kept turning it over in his big fingers.

"What's V. V.? Somebody's initials, maybe. What have you got there, Dr. Wood?"

It was a good-sized hammer which had been lying upon the rug in front of the fireplace—a substantial, workmanlike hammer. Cecil Barker pointed to a box of brass-headed nails upon the mantelpiece.

"Mr. Douglas was altering the pictures yesterday," he said. "I saw him myself, standing upon that chair and fixing the big picture above it. That accounts for the hammer."

"We'd best put it back on the rug where we found it," said the sergeant, scratching his puzzled head in his perplexity. "It will want the best brains in the force to get to the bottom of this thing. It will be a London job before it is finished." He raised the hand-lamp and walked slowly round the room. "Halloa!" he cried, excitedly, drawing the window curtain to one side. "What o'clock were those curtains drawn?"

"When the lamps were lit," said the butler. "It would be shortly after four."

"Someone has been hiding here, sure enough." He held down the light, and the marks of muddy boots were very visible in the corner. "I'm bound to say this bears out your theory, Mr. Barker. It looks as if the man got into the house after four, when the curtains were drawn, and before six, when the bridge was raised. He slipped into this room because it was the first that he saw. There was no other place where he could hide, so he popped in behind this curtain. That all seems clear enough. It is likely that his main idea was to burgle the house, but Mr. Douglas chanced to come upon him, so he murdered him and escaped."

"That's how I read it," said Barker. "But, I say, aren't we wasting precious time? Couldn't we start out and scour the country before the fellow gets away?"

The sergeant considered for a moment.

"There are no trains before six in the morning, so he can't get away by rail. If he goes by road with his legs all dripping, it's odds that someone will notice him. Anyhow, I can't leave here myself until I am relieved. But I think none of you should go until we see more clearly how we all stand."

The doctor had taken the lamp and was narrowly scrutinizing the body.

"What's this mark?" he asked. "Could this have any connection with the crime?"

The dead man's right arm was thrust out from his dressing-gown and exposed as high as the elbow. About half-way up the fore-arm was a curious brown design, a triangle inside a circle, standing out in vivid relief upon the lard-coloured skin.

"It's not tattooed," said the doctor, peering through his glasses. "I never saw anything like it. The man has been branded at some time, as they brand cattle. What is the meaning of this?"

"I don't profess to know the meaning of it," said Cecil Barker; "but I've seen the mark on Douglas any time this last ten years."

"And so have I," said the butler. "Many a time when the master has rolled up his sleeves I have noticed that very mark. I've often wondered what it could be."

"Then it has nothing to do with the crime, anyhow," said the sergeant. "But it's a rum thing all the same. Everything about this case is rum. Well, what is it now?"

The butler had given an exclamation of astonishment, and was pointing at the dead man's outstretched hand.

"They've taken his wedding-ring!" he gasped.

"What!"

"Yes, indeed! Master always wore his plain gold wedding-ring on the little finger of his left hand. That ring with the rough nugget on it was above it, and the twisted snake-ring on the third finger. There's the nugget and there's the snake, but the wedding-ring is gone."

"He's right," said Barker.

"Do you tell me," said the sergeant, "that the wedding-ring was *below* the other?"

"Always!"

"Then the murderer, or whoever it was, first took off this ring you call the nugget-ring, then the wedding-ring, and afterwards put the nugget-ring back again."

"That is so."

The worthy country policeman shook his head.

"Seems to me the sooner we get London on to this case the better," said he. "White Mason is a smart man. No local job has ever been too much for White Mason. It won't be long now before he is here to help us. But I expect we'll have to look to London before we are through. Anyhow, I'm not ashamed to say that it is a deal too thick for the likes of me."

CHAPTER IV.
DARKNESS.

AT three in the morning the chief Sussex detective, obeying the urgent call from Sergeant Wilson, of Birlstone, arrived from headquarters in a light dog-cart behind a breathless trotter. By the five-forty train in the morning he had sent his message to Scotland Yard, and he was at the Birlstone station at twelve o'clock to welcome us. Mr. White Mason was a quiet, comfortable-looking person, in a loose tweed suit, with a clean-shaven, ruddy face, a stoutish body, and powerful bandy legs adorned with gaiters, looking like a small farmer, a retired game-keeper, or anything upon earth except a very favourable specimen of the provincial criminal officer.

"A real downright snorter, Mr. Mac-Donald," he kept repeating. "We'll have the pressmen down like flies when they understand it. I'm hoping we will get our work done before they get poking their noses into it and messing up all the trails. There has been nothing like this that I can remember. There are some bits that will come home to you, Mr. Holmes, or I am mistaken. And you also, Dr. Watson, for the medicos will have a word to say before we finish. Your room is at the Westville Arms. There's no other place, but I hear that it is clean and good. The man will carry your bags. This way, gentlemen, if *you* please."

He was a very bustling and genial person, this Sussex detective. In ten minutes we had all found our quarters. In ten more we were seated in the parlour of the inn and being treated to a rapid sketch of those events which have been outlined in the previous chapter. MacDonald made an occasional note, while Holmes sat absorbed with the expression of surprised and reverent admiration with which the botanist surveys the rare and precious bloom.

"Remarkable !" he said, when the story was unfolded. " Most remarkable ! I can hardly recall any case where the features have been more peculiar."

" I thought you would say so, Mr. Holmes," said White Mason, in great delight. " We're well up with the times in Sussex. I've told you now how matters were, up to the time when I took over from Sergeant Wilson between three and four this morning. My word, I made the old mare go ! But I need not have been in such a hurry as it turned out, for there was nothing immediate that I could do. Sergeant Wilson had all the facts. I checked them and considered them, and maybe added a few on my own."

" What were they ? " asked Holmes, eagerly.

" Well, I first had the hammer examined. There was Dr. Wood there to help me. We found no signs of violence upon it. I was hoping that, if Mr. Douglas defended himself with the hammer, he might have left his mark upon the murderer before he dropped it on the mat. But there was no stain."

" That, of course, proves nothing at all," remarked Inspector MacDonald. " There has been many a hammer murder and no trace on the hammer."

" Quite so. It doesn't prove it wasn't used. But there might have been stains, and that would have helped us. As a matter of fact, there were none. Then I examined the gun. They were buck-shot cartridges, and, as Sergeant Wilson pointed out, the triggers were wired together so that if you pulled on the hinder one both barrels were discharged. Whoever fixed that up had made up his mind that he was going to take no

chances of missing his man. The sawn gun was not more than two feet long ; one could carry it easily under one's coat. There was no complete maker's name, but the printed letters ' PEN ' were on the fluting between the barrels, and the rest of the name had been cut off by the saw."

" A big ' P ' with a flourish above it— ' E ' and ' N ' smaller ? " asked Holmes.

" Exactly."

" Pennsylvania Small Arm Company— well-known American firm," said Holmes.

White Mason gazed at my friend as the little village practitioner looks at the Harley Street specialist who by a word can solve the difficulties that perplex him.

" That is very helpful, Mr. Holmes. No doubt you are right. Wonderful—wonderful ! Do you carry the names of all the gunmakers in the world in your memory ? "

Holmes dismissed the subject with a wave.

" No doubt it is an American shot-gun," White Mason continued. " I seem to have read that a sawed-off shot-gun is a weapon used in some parts of America. Apart from the name upon the barrel, the idea had occurred to me. There is some evidence, then, that this man who entered the house and killed its master was an American."

MacDonald shook his head. " Man, you are surely travelling over-fast," said he. " I have heard no evidence yet that any stranger was ever in the house at all."

" The open window, the blood on the sill, the queer card, the marks of boots in the corner, the gun."

" Nothing there that could not have been arranged. Mr. Douglas was an American, or had lived long in America. So had Mr. Barker. You don't need to import an American from outside in order to account for American doings."

" Ames, the butler——"

" What about him ? Is he reliable ? "

" Ten years with Sir Charles Chandos—as solid as a rock. He has been with Douglas ever since he took the Manor House five years ago. He has never seen a gun of this sort in the house."

" The gun was made to conceal. That's why the barrels were sawn. It would fit into any box. How could he swear there was no such gun in the house ? "

" Well, anyhow, he had never seen one."

MacDonald shook his obstinate Scotch head. " I'm not convinced yet that there was ever anyone in the house," said he. " I'm asking you to conseedar "—his accent became more Aberdonian as he lost himself in his argument—"I'm asking you to conseedar what it involves if you suppose that this gun was ever brought into the house and that all these strange things were done by a person from outside. Oh, man, it's just inconceivable! It's clean against common sense. I put it to you, Mr. Holmes, judging it by what we have heard."

"Well, state your case, Mr. Mac," said Holmes, in his most judicial style.

"The man is not a burglar, supposing that he ever existed. The ring business and the card point to premeditated murder for some private reason. Very good. Here is a man who slips into a house with the deliberate intention of committing murder. He knows, if he knows any-

the deed was done, to slip quickly from the window, to wade the moat, and to get away at his leisure. That's understandable. But is it understandable that he should go out of his way to bring with him the most noisy weapon he could select, knowing well that it

will fetch every human being in the house to the spot as quick as they can run, and that it is all odds that he will be seen before he can get across the moat? Is that credible, Mr. Holmes?"

"Well, you put the case strongly," my friend replied, thoughtfully. "It certainly needs a good deal of justification. May I ask, Mr. White Mason, whether you examined the farther side of the moat at once, to see if there were any signs of the man having climbed out from the water?"

"There were no signs, Mr. Holmes. But

"HOLMES EXAMINED THE STONE LEDGE AND THE GRASS BORDER BEYOND IT."

thing, that he will have a deeficulty in making his escape, as the house is surrounded with water. What weapon would he choose? You would say the most silent in the world. Then he could hope, when it is a stone ledge, and one could hardly expect them."

" No tracks or marks ? "

" None."

" Ha ! Would there be any objection, Mr. White Mason, to our going down to the house at once ? There may possibly be some small point which might be suggestive."

" I was going to propose it, Mr. Holmes, but I thought it well to put you in touch with all the facts before we go. I suppose, if anything should strike you——" White Mason looked doubtfully at the amateur.

" I have worked with Mr. Holmes before," said Inspector MacDonald. " He plays the game."

" My own idea of the game, at any rate," said Holmes, with a smile. " I go into a case to help the ends of justice and the work of the police. If ever I have separated myself from the official force, it is because they have first separated themselves from me. I have no wish ever to score at their expense. At the same time, Mr. White Mason, I claim the right to work in my own way and give my results at my own time—complete, rather than in stages."

" I am sure we are honoured by your presence and to show you all we know," said White Mason, cordially. " Come along, Dr. Watson, and when the time comes we'll all hope for a place in your book."

We walked down the quaint village street with a row of pollarded elms on either side of it. Just beyond were two ancient stone pillars, weather-stained and lichen-blotched, bearing upon their summits a shapeless something which had once been the ramping lion of Capus of Birlstone. A short walk along the winding drive, with such sward and oaks around it as one only sees in rural England ; then a sudden turn, and the long, low, Jacobean house of dingy, liver-coloured brick lay before us, with an old-fashioned garden of cut yews on either side of it. As we approached it there were the wooden drawbridge and the beautiful broad moat, as still and luminous as quicksilver in the cold winter sunshine. Three centuries had flowed past the old Manor House, centuries of births and of home-comings, of country dances and of the meetings of fox-hunters. Strange that now in its old age this dark business should have cast its shadow upon the venerable walls. And yet those strange peaked roofs and quaint overhung gables were a fitting covering to grim and terrible intrigue. As I looked at the deep-set windows and the long sweep of the dull-coloured, water-lapped

front I felt that no more fitting scene could be set for such a tragedy.

" That's the window," said White Mason ; " that one on the immediate right of the drawbridge. It's open just as it was found last night."

" It looks rather narrow for a man to pass."

" Well, it wasn't a fat man, anyhow. We don't need your deductions, Mr. Holmes, to tell us that. But you or I could squeeze through all right."

Holmes walked to the edge of the moat and looked across. Then he examined the stone ledge and the grass border beyond it.

" I've had a good look, Mr. Holmes," said White Mason. " There is nothing there ; no sign that anyone has landed. But why should he leave any sign ? "

" Exactly. Why should he ? Is the water always turbid ? "

" Generally about this colour. The stream brings down the clay."

" How deep is it ? "

" About two feet at each side and three in the middle."

" So we can put aside all idea of the man having been drowned in crossing ? "

" No ; a child could not be drowned in it."

We walked across the drawbridge, and were admitted by a quaint, gnarled, dried-up person who was the butler—Ames. The poor old fellow was white and quivering from the shock. The village sergeant, a tall, formal, melancholy man, still held his vigil in the room of fate. The doctor had departed.

" Anything fresh, Sergeant Wilson ? " asked White Mason.

" No, sir."

" Then you can go home. You've had enough. We can send for you if we want you. The butler had better wait outside. Tell him to warn Mr. Cecil Barker, Mrs. Douglas, and the housekeeper that we may want a word with them presently. Now, gentlemen, perhaps you will allow me to give you the views I have formed first, and then you will be able to arrive at your own."

He impressed me, this country specialist. He had a solid grip of fact and a cool, clear, common-sense brain, which should take him some way in his profession. Holmes listened to him intently, with no sign of that impatience which the official exponent too often produced.

" Is it suicide or is it murder—that's our first question, gentlemen, is it not ? If it were suicide, then we have to believe that this man began by taking off his wedding-ring and concealing it ; that he then came

"AMES, I UNDERSTAND THAT YOU HAVE OFTEN SEEN THIS VERY UNUSUAL

MARK, A BRANDED TRIANGLE INSIDE A CIRCLE, UPON MR. DOUGLAS'S FOREARM?"

down here in his dressing-gown, trampled mud into a corner behind the curtain in order to give the idea someone had waited for him, opened the window, put blood on the——"

"We can surely dismiss that," said Mac-Donald.

"So I think. Suicide is out of the question. Then a murder has been done. What we have to determine is whether it was done by someone outside or inside the house."

"Well, let's hear the argument."

"There are considerable difficulties both ways, and yet one or the other it must be. We will suppose first that some person or persons inside the house did the crime. They got this man down here at a time when everything was still, and yet no one was asleep. They then did the deed with the queerest and noisiest weapon in the world, so as to tell everyone what had happened— a weapon that was never seen in the house before. That does not seem a very likely start, does it ? "

"No, it does not."

"Well, then, everyone is agreed that after the alarm was given only a minute at the most had passed before the whole household —not Mr. Cecil Barker alone, though he claims to have been the first, but Ames, and all of them—were on the spot. Do you tell me that in that time the guilty person managed to make footmarks in the corner, open the window, mark the sill with blood, take the wedding-ring off the dead man's finger, and all the rest of it ? It's impossible ! "

"You put it very clearly," said Holmes. "I am inclined to agree with you."

"Well, then, we are driven back to the theory that it was done by someone from outside. We are still faced with some big difficulties, but, anyhow, they have ceased to be impossibilities. The man got into the house between four-thirty and six—that is to say, between dusk and the time when the bridge was raised. There had been some visitors, and the door was open, so there was nothing to prevent him. He may have been a common burglar, or he may have had some private grudge against Mr. Douglas. Since Mr. Douglas has spent most of his life in America, and this shot-gun seems to be an American weapon, it would seem that the private grudge is the more likely theory. He slipped into this room because it was the first he came to, and he hid behind the curtain. There he remained until past eleven at night. At that time Mr. Douglas entered the room. It was a short interview, if there were any interview at all, for Mrs. Douglas declares that her husband had not left her more than a few minutes when she heard the shot."

"The candle shows that," said Holmes.

"Exactly. The candle, which was a new one, is not burned more than half an inch. He must have placed it on the table before he was attacked, otherwise, of course, it would have fallen when he fell. This shows that he was not attacked the instant that he entered the room. When Mr. Barker arrived the lamp was lit and the candle put out."

"That's all clear enough."

"Well, now, we can reconstruct things on those lines. Mr. Douglas enters the room. He puts down the candle. A man appears from behind the curtain. He is armed with this gun. He demands the wedding-ring— Heaven only knows why, but so it must have been. Mr. Douglas gave it up. Then either in cold blood or in the course of a struggle— Douglas may have gripped the hammer that was found upon the mat—he shot Douglas in this horrible way. He dropped his gun and also, it would seem, this queer card, 'V. V. 341,' whatever that may mean, and he made his escape through the window and across the moat at the very moment when Cecil Barker was discovering the crime. How's that, Mr. Holmes ? "

"Very interesting, but just a little unconvincing."

"Man, it would be absolute nonsense if it wasn't that anything else is even worse," cried MacDonald. "Somebody killed the man, and whoever it was I could clearly prove to you that he should have done it some other way. What does he mean by allowing his retreat to be cut off like that ? What does he mean by using a shot-gun when silence was his one chance of escape ? Come, Mr. Holmes, it's up to you to give us a lead, since you say Mr. White Mason's theory is unconvincing."

Holmes had sat intently observant during this long discussion, missing no word that was said, with his keen eyes darting to right and to left, and his forehead wrinkled with speculation.

"I should like a few more facts before I get so far as a theory, Mr. Mac," said he, kneeling down beside the body. "Dear me ! these injuries are really appalling. Can we have the butler in for a moment ? . . . Ames, I understand that you have often seen this very unusual mark, a branded triangle inside a circle, upon Mr. Douglas's forearm ? "

"Frequently, sir."

"You never heard any speculation as to what it meant ? "

"No, sir."

"HOLMES HAD GONE TO THE WINDOW AND WAS EXAMINING WITH HIS LENS THE BLOOD-MARK UPON THE SILL."

"It must have caused great pain when it was inflicted. It is undoubtedly a burn. Now, I observe, Ames, that there is a small piece of plaster at the angle of Mr. Douglas's jaw. Did you observe that in life ? "

"Yes, sir ; he cut himself in shaving yesterday morning."

"Did you ever know him cut himself in shaving before ? "

"Not for a very long time, sir."

"Suggestive ! " said Holmes. "It may, of course, be a mere coincidence, or it may point to some nervousness which would indicate that he had reason to apprehend danger. Had you noticed anything unusual in his conduct yesterday, Ames ? "

"It struck me that he was a little restless and excited, sir."

"Ha ! The attack may not have been entirely unexpected. We do seem to make a little progress, do we not ? Perhaps you would rather do the questioning, Mr. Mac ? "

"No, Mr. Holmes ; it's in better hands."

"Well, then, we will pass to this card— 'V. V. 341.' It is rough cardboard. Have you any of the sort in the house ? "

"I don't think so."

Holmes walked across to the desk and dabbed a little ink from each bottle on to the blotting-paper. "It has not been printed in this room," he said ; "this is black ink, and the other purplish. It has been done by a thick pen, and these are fine. No, it has been done elsewhere, I should say. Can you make anything of the inscription, Ames ? "

"No, sir, nothing."

"What do you think, Mr. Mac ? "

"It gives me the impression of a secret society of some sort. The same with this badge upon the forearm."

"That's my idea, too," said White Mason.

"Well, we can adopt it as a working hypothesis, and then see how far our difficulties disappear. An agent from such a society makes his way into the house, waits for Mr. Douglas, blows his head nearly off with this weapon, and escapes by wading the moat, after leaving a card beside the dead man which will, when mentioned in the papers, tell other members of the society that vengeance has been done. That all hangs together. But why this gun, of all weapons ? "

"Exactly."

"And why the missing ring ? "

"Quite so."

"And why no arrest ? It's past two now. I take it for granted that since dawn every constable within forty miles has been looking out for a wet stranger ? "

"That is so, Mr. Holmes."

"Well, unless he has a burrow close by, or a change of clothes ready, they can hardly miss him. And yet they *have* missed him up to now." Holmes had gone to the window and was examining with his lens the blood-mark upon the sill. "It is clearly the tread of a shoe. It is remarkably broad—a splay foot, one would say. Curious, because, so far as one can trace any footmark in this mud-stained corner, one would say it was a more shapely sole. However, they are certainly very indistinct. What's this under the side-table ? "

"Mr. Douglas's dumb-bells," said Ames.

"Dumb-bell—there's only one. Where's the other ? "

"I don't know, Mr. Holmes. There may have been only one. I have not noticed them for months."

"One dumb-bell——" Holmes said, seriously, but his remarks were interrupted by a sharp knock at the door. A tall, sunburned, capable-looking, clean-shaven man looked in at us. I had no difficulty in guessing that it was the Cecil Barker of whom I had heard. His masterful eyes travelled quickly with a questioning glance from face to face.

"Sorry to interrupt your consultation," said he, "but you should hear the latest."

"An arrest ? "

"No such luck. But they've found his bicycle. The fellow left his bicycle behind him. Come and have a look. It is within a hundred yards of the hall door."

We found three or four grooms and idlers standing in the drive inspecting a bicycle which had been drawn out from a clump of evergreens in which it had been concealed. It was a well-used Rudge-Whitworth, splashed as from a considerable journey. There was a saddle-bag with spanner and oil-can, but no clue as to the owner.

"It would be a grand help to the police," said the inspector, "if these things were numbered and registered. But we must be thankful for what we've got. If we can't find where he went to, at least we are likely to get where he came from. But what in the name of all that is wonderful made the fellow leave it behind ? And how in the world has he got away without it ? We don't seem to get a gleam of light in the case, Mr. Holmes."

"Don't we ? " my friend answered, thoughtfully. "I wonder ! "

THE STRAND
MAGAZINE.

NOVEMBER, 1914.
Vol. xlviii. No. 287.

The
VALLEY of FEAR

A NEW
SHERLOCK HOLMES
STORY

By
A. CONAN DOYLE

Illustrated by FRANK WILES

PART·I·
THE TRAGEDY OF
BIRLSTONE

The opening chapters of this new and thrilling adventure of Sherlock Holmes described the receipt by Holmes of a cipher message, from which he deduces that some devilry is intended against a man named Douglas, a rich country gentleman living at the Manor House, Birlstone, in Sussex, and that the danger is a pressing one. Almost as soon as he has deciphered the message he is visited by Inspector MacDonald, of Scotland Yard, who brings the news that Mr. Douglas has been murdered that morning. He asks Sherlock Holmes and Dr. Watson to accompany him to Birlstone, where they are met by Mr. White Mason, the chief Sussex detective, from whom they learn the details of the crime. The murdered man had been horribly injured, while lying across his chest was a curious weapon—a shot-gun with the barrel sawn off a foot in front of the triggers. Near him was found a card with the initials "V V." and the number " 341 " scrawled on it in ink, and about half-way up the forearm was a curious design—a branded triangle inside a circle. All four then proceed to the Manor House, and, when the present instalment opens, are examining the room in which the crime occurred, accompanied by Mr. Cecil Barker, a friend of the Douglases, who has been staying with them.

CHAPTER V.
THE PEOPLE OF THE DRAMA.

"HAVE you seen all you want of the study?" asked White Mason as we re-entered the house.

"For the time," said the inspector, and Holmes nodded.

"Then perhaps you would now like to hear the evidence of some of the people in the house? We could use the dining-room, Ames. Please come yourself first and tell us what you know."

The butler's account was a simple and a clear one, and he gave a convincing impression of sincerity. He had been engaged five years ago when Mr. Douglas first came to

"HE PLACED THE SLIPPER UPON THE BLOOD-MARK ON THE SILL."

Birlstone. He understood that Mr. Douglas was a rich gentleman who had made his money in America. He had been a kind and considerate employer—not quite what Ames was used to, perhaps, but one can't have everything. He never saw any signs of apprehension in Mr. Douglas—on the contrary, he was the most fearless man he had ever known. He ordered the drawbridge to be pulled up every night because it was the ancient custom of the old house, and he liked to keep the old ways up. Mr. Douglas seldom went to London or left the village, but on the day before the crime he had been shopping at Tunbridge Wells. He, Ames, had observed some restlessness and excitement on the part of Mr. Douglas upon that day, for he had seemed impatient and irritable, which was unusual with him. He had not gone to bed that night, but was in the pantry at the back of the house, putting away the silver, when he heard the bell ring violently. He heard no shot, but it was hardly possible he should, as the pantry and kitchens were at the very back of the house and there were several closed doors and a long passage between. The housekeeper had come out of her room, attracted by the violent ringing of the bell. They had gone to the front of the house together. As they reached the bottom of the stair he had seen Mrs. Douglas coming down it. No, she was not hurrying—it did not seem to him that she was particularly agitated. Just as she reached the bottom of the stair Mr. Barker had rushed out of the study. He had stopped Mrs. Douglas and begged her to go back.

"For God's sake, go back to your room!" he cried. "Poor Jack is dead. You can do nothing. For God's sake, go back!"

After some persuasion upon the stairs Mrs. Douglas had gone back. She did not scream. She made no outcry whatever. Mrs. Allen, the housekeeper, had taken her upstairs and stayed with her in the bedroom. Ames and Mr. Barker had then returned to the study, where they had found everything exactly as the police had seen it. The candle was not lit at that time, but the lamp was burning. They had looked out of the window, but the night was very dark and nothing could be seen or heard. They had then rushed out into the hall, where Ames had turned the windlass which lowered the drawbridge. Mr. Barker had then hurried off to get the police.

Such, in its essentials, was the evidence of the butler.

The account of Mrs. Allen, the housekeeper, was, so far as it went, a corroboration of that of her fellow-servant. The housekeeper's room was rather nearer to the front of the house than the pantry in which Ames had been working. She was preparing to go to bed when the loud ringing of the bell had attracted her attention. She was a little hard of hearing. Perhaps that was why she had not heard the sound of the shot, but in any case the study was a long way off. She remembered hearing some sound which she imagined to be the slamming of a door. That was a good deal earlier—half an hour at least before the ringing of the bell. When Mr. Ames ran to the front she went with him. She saw Mr. Barker, very pale and excited, come out of the study. He intercepted Mrs. Douglas, who was coming down the stairs. He entreated her to go back, and she answered him, but what she said could not be heard.

"Take her up. Stay with her!" he had said to Mrs. Allen.

She had therefore taken her to the bedroom and endeavoured to soothe her. She was greatly excited, trembling all over, but made no other attempt to go downstairs. She just sat in her dressing-gown by her bedroom fire with her head sunk in her hands. Mrs. Allen stayed with her most of the night. As to the other servants, they had all gone to bed, and the alarm did not reach them until just before the police arrived. They slept at the extreme back of the house, and could not possibly have heard anything.

So far the housekeeper—who could add nothing on cross-examination save lamentations and expressions of amazement.

Mr. Cecil Barker succeeded Mrs. Allen as a witness. As to the occurrences of the night before, he had very little to add to what he had already told the police. Personally, he was convinced that the murderer had escaped by the window. The blood-stain was conclusive, in his opinion, upon that point. Besides, as the bridge was up there was no other possible way of escaping. He could not explain what had become of the assassin, or why he had not taken his bicycle, if it were indeed his. He could not possibly have been drowned in the moat, which was at no place more than three feet deep.

In his own mind he had a very definite theory about the murder. Douglas was a reticent man, and there were some chapters in his life of which he never spoke. He had emigrated to America from Ireland when he was a very young man. He had prospered well, and Barker had first met him in California, where they had become partners in a successful mining claim at a place called

"'FOR GOD'S SAKE, GO BACK TO YOUR ROOM!' HE CRIED."

Benito Canyon. They had done very well, but Douglas had suddenly sold out and started for England. He was a widower at that time. Barker had afterwards realized his money and come to live in London. Thus they had renewed their friendship. Douglas had given him the impression that some danger was hanging over his head, and he had always looked upon his sudden departure from California, and also his renting a house in so quiet a place in England, as being connected with this peril. He imagined that some secret society, some implacable organization, was on Douglas's track which would never rest until it killed him. Some remarks of his had given him this idea, though he had never told him what the society was, nor how he had come to offend it. He could only suppose that the legend upon the placard had some reference to this secret society.

"How long were you with Douglas in California?" asked Inspector MacDonald.

"Five years altogether."

"He was a bachelor, you say?"

"A widower."

"Have you ever heard where his first wife came from?"

"No; I remember his saying that she was of Swedish extraction, and I have seen her portrait. She was a very beautiful woman. She died of typhoid the year before I met him."

"You don't associate his past with any particular part of America?"

"I have heard him talk of Chicago. He knew that city well and had worked there. I have heard him talk of the coal and iron districts. He had travelled a good deal in his time."

"Was he a politician? Had this secret society to do with politics?"

"No; he cared nothing about politics."

"You have no reason to think it was a criminal?"

"On the contrary, I never met a straighter man in my life."

"Was there anything curious about his life in California?"

"He liked best to stay and to work at our claim in the mountains. He would never go where other men were if he could help it. That's why I first thought that someone was after him. Then when he left so suddenly for Europe I made sure that it was so. I believe that he had a warning of some sort. Within a week of his leaving half-a-dozen men were inquiring for him."

"What sort of men?"

"Well, they were a mighty hard-looking crowd. They came up to the claim and wanted to know where he was. I told them that he was gone to Europe and that I did not know where to find him. They meant him no good—it was easy to see that."

"Were these men Americans — Californians?"

"Well, I don't know about Californians. They were Americans all right. But they were not miners. I don't know what they were, and was very glad to see their backs."

"That was six years ago?"

"Nearer seven."

"And then you were together five years in California, so that this business dates back not less than eleven years at the least?"

"That is so."

"It must be a very serious feud that would be kept up with such earnestness for as long as that. It would be no light thing that would give rise to it."

"I think it shadowed his whole life. It was never quite out of his mind."

"But if a man had a danger hanging over him, and knew what it was, don't you think he would turn to the police for protection?"

"Maybe it was some danger that he could not be protected against. There's one thing you should know. He always went about armed. His revolver was never out of his pocket. But, by bad luck, he was in his dressing-gown and had left it in the bedroom last night. Once the bridge was up I guess he thought he was safe."

"I should like these dates a little clearer," said MacDonald. "It is quite six years since Douglas left California. You followed him next year, did you not?"

"That is so."

"And he has been married five years. You must have returned about the time of his marriage."

"About a month before. I was his best man."

"Did you know Mrs. Douglas before her marriage?"

"No, I did not. I had been away from England for ten years."

"But you have seen a good deal of her since?"

Barker looked sternly at the detective.

"I have seen a good deal of *him* since," he answered. "If I have seen her, it is because you cannot visit a man without knowing his wife. If you imagine there is any connection——"

"I imagine nothing, Mr. Barker. I am bound to make every inquiry which can bear upon the case. But I mean no offence."

" ' HAVE YOU FOUND OUT

"ANYTHING YET?' SHE ASKED."

" Some inquiries are offensive," Barker answered, angrily.

" It's only the facts that we want. It is in your interest and everyone's interests that they should be cleared up. Did Mr. Douglas entirely approve your friendship with his wife ? "

Barker grew paler, and his great strong hands were clasped convulsively together.

" You have no right to ask such questions ! " he cried. " What has this to do with the matter you are investigating ? "

" I must repeat the question."

" Well, I refuse to answer."

" You can refuse to answer, but you must be aware that your refusal is in itself an answer, for you would not refuse if you had not something to conceal."

Barker stood for a moment with his face set grimly and his strong black eyebrows drawn low in intense thought. Then he looked up with a smile.

" Well, I guess you gentlemen are only doing your clear duty, after all, and that I have no right to stand in the way of it. I'd only ask you not to worry Mrs. Douglas over this matter, for she has enough upon her just now. I may tell you that poor Douglas had just one fault in the world, and that was his jealousy. He was fond of me—no man could be fonder of a friend. And he was devoted to his wife. He loved me to come here and was for ever sending for me. And yet if his wife and I talked together or there seemed any sympathy between us, a kind of wave of jealousy would pass over him and he would be off the handle and saying the wildest things in a moment. More than once I've sworn off coming for that reason, and then he would write me such penitent, imploring letters that I just had to. But you can take it from me, gentlemen, if it was my last word, that no man ever had a more loving, faithful wife —and I can say, also, no friend could be more loyal than I."

It was spoken with fervour and feeling, and yet Inspector MacDonald could not dismiss the subject.

" You are aware," said he, " that the dead man's wedding-ring has been taken from his finger ? "

" So it appears," said Barker.

" What do you mean by ' appears ' ? You know it as a fact."

The man seemed confused and undecided.

" When I said ' appears,' I meant that it was conceivable that he had himself taken off the ring."

" The mere fact that the ring should be absent, whoever may have removed it, would suggest to anyone's mind, would it not, that the marriage and the tragedy were connected ? "

Barker shrugged his broad shoulders.

" I can't profess to say what it suggests," he answered. " But if you mean to hint that it could reflect in any way upon this lady's honour "—his eyes blazed for an instant, and then with an evident effort he got a grip upon his own emotions—" well, you are on the wrong track, that's all."

" I don't know that I've anything else to ask you at present," said MacDonald, coldly.

" There was one small point," remarked Sherlock Holmes. " When you entered the room there was only a candle lighted upon the table, was there not ? "

" Yes, that was so."

" By its light you saw that some terrible incident had occurred ? "

" Exactly."

" You at once rang for help ? "

" Yes."

" And it arrived very speedily ? "

" Within a minute or so."

" And yet when they arrived they found that the candle was out and that the lamp had been lighted. That seems very remarkable."

Again Barker showed some signs of indecision.

" I don't see that it was remarkable, Mr. Holmes," he answered, after a pause. " The candle threw a very bad light. My first thought was to get a better one. The lamp was on the table, so I lit it."

" And blew out the candle ? "

" Exactly."

Holmes asked no further question, and Barker, with a deliberate look from one to the other of us, which had, as it seemed to me, something of defiance in it, turned and left the room.

Inspector MacDonald had sent up a note to the effect that he would wait upon Mrs. Douglas in her room, but she had replied that she would meet us in the dining-room. She entered now, a tall and beautiful woman of thirty, reserved and self-possessed to a remarkable degree, very different from the tragic and distracted figure that I had pictured. It is true that her face was pale and drawn, like that of one who has endured a great shock, but her manner was composed, and the finely-moulded hand which she rested upon the edge of the table was as steady as my own. Her sad, appealing eyes travelled from one to the other of us with a curiously inquisitive expression. That questioning gaze transformed itself suddenly into abrupt speech.

"Have you found out anything yet?" she asked.

Was it my imagination that there was an undertone of fear rather than of hope in the question?

"We have taken every possible step, Mrs. Douglas," said the inspector. "You may rest assured that nothing will be neglected."

"Spare no money," she said, in a dead, even tone. "It is my desire that every possible effort should be made."

"Perhaps you can tell us something which may throw some light upon the matter."

"I fear not, but all I know is at your service."

"We have heard from Mr. Cecil Barker that you did not actually see—that you were never in the room where the tragedy occurred?"

"No; he turned me back upon the stairs. He begged me to return to my room."

"Quite so. You had heard the shot and you had at once come down."

"I put on my dressing-gown and then came down."

"How long was it after hearing the shot that you were stopped on the stair by Mr. Barker?"

"It may have been a couple of minutes. It is so hard to reckon time at such a moment. He implored me not to go on. He assured me that I could do nothing. Then Mrs. Allen, the housekeeper, led me upstairs again. It was all like some dreadful dream."

"Can you give us any idea how long your husband had been downstairs before you heard the shot?"

"No, I cannot say. He went from his dressing-room and I did not hear him go. He did the round of the house every night, for he was nervous of fire. It is the only thing that I have ever known him nervous of."

"That is just the point which I want to come to, Mrs. Douglas. You have only known your husband in England, have you not?"

"Yes. We have been married five years."

"Have you heard him speak of anything which occurred in America and which might bring some danger upon him?"

Mrs. Douglas thought earnestly before she answered.

"Yes," she said at last. "I have always felt that there was a danger hanging over him. He refused to discuss it with me. It

was not from want of confidence in me—there was the most complete love and confidence between us—but it was out of his desire to keep all alarm away from me. He thought I should brood over it if I knew all, and so he was silent."

"How did you know it, then?"

Mrs. Douglas's face lit with a quick smile.

"Can a husband ever carry about a secret all his life and a woman who loves him have no suspicion of it? I knew it in many ways. I knew it by his refusal to talk about some episodes in his American life. I knew it by certain precautions he took. I knew it by certain words he let fall. I knew it by the way he looked at unexpected strangers. I was perfectly certain that he had some powerful enemies, that he believed they were on his track and that he was always on his guard against them. I was so sure of it that for years I have been terrified if ever he came home later than was expected."

"Might I ask," said Holmes, "what the words were which attracted your attention?"

"'The Valley of Fear,'" the lady answered. "That was an expression he has used when I questioned him. 'I have been in the Valley of Fear. I am not out of it yet.' 'Are we never to get out of the Valley of Fear?' I have asked him, when I have seen him more serious than usual. 'Sometimes I think that we never shall,' he has answered."

"Surely you asked him what he meant by the Valley of Fear?"

"I did; but his face would become very grave and he would shake his head. 'It is bad enough that one of us should have been in its shadow,' he said. 'Please God it shall never fall upon you.' It was some real valley in which he had lived and in which something terrible had occurred to him—of that I am certain—but I can tell you no more."

"And he never mentioned any names?"

"Yes; he was delirious with fever once when he had his hunting accident three years ago. Then I remember that there was a name that came continually to his lips. He spoke it with anger and a sort of horror. McGinty was the name — Bodymaster McGinty. I asked him, when he recovered, who Bodymaster McGinty was, and whose body he was master of. 'Never of mine, thank God!' he answered, with a laugh, and that was all I could get from him. But there is a connection between Bodymaster McGinty and the Valley of Fear."

"There is one other point," said Inspector MacDonald. "You met Mr. Douglas in a boarding-house in London, did you not, and became engaged to him there ? Was there any romance, anything secret or mysterious, about the wedding ? "

" There was romance. There is always romance. There was nothing mysterious."

" He had no rival ? "

" No ; I was quite free."

" You have heard, no doubt, that his wedding-ring has been taken. Does that suggest anything to you ? Suppose that some enemy of his old life had tracked him down and committed this crime, what possible reason could he have for taking his wedding-ring ? "

For an instant I could have sworn that the faintest shadow of a smile flickered over the woman's lips.

" I really cannot tell," she answered. " It is certainly a most extraordinary thing."

" Well, we will not detain you any longer, and we are sorry to have put you to this trouble at such a time," said the inspector. " There are some other points, no doubt, but we can refer to you as they arise."

She rose, and I was again conscious of that quick, questioning glance with which she had just surveyed us : " What impression has my evidence made upon you ? " The question might as well have been spoken. Then, with a bow, she swept from the room.

" She's a beautiful woman—a very beautiful woman," said MacDonald, thoughtfully, after the door had closed behind her. " This man Barker has certainly been down here a good deal. He is a man who might be attractive to a woman. He admits that the dead man was jealous, and maybe he knew best himself what cause he had for jealousy. Then there's that wedding-ring. You can't get past that. The man who tears a wedding-ring off a dead man's—— What do you say to it, Mr. Holmes ? "

My friend had sat with his head upon his hands, sunk in the deepest thought. Now he rose and rang the bell.

" Ames," he said, when the butler entered, " where is Mr. Cecil Barker now ? "

" I'll see, sir."

He came back in a moment to say that Mr. Barker was in the garden.

" Can you remember, Ames, what Mr. Barker had upon his feet last night when you joined him in the study ? "

" Yes, Mr. Holmes. He had a pair of bedroom slippers. I brought him his boots when he went for the police."

" Where are the slippers now ? "

" They are still under the chair in the hall."

" Very good, Ames. It is, of course, important for us to know which tracks may be Mr. Barker's and which from outside."

" Yes, sir. I may say that I noticed that the slippers were stained with blood—so, indeed, were my own."

" That is natural enough, considering the condition of the room. Very good, Ames. We will ring if we want you."

A few minutes later we were in the study. Holmes had brought with him the carpet slippers from the hall. As Ames had observed, the soles of both were dark with blood.

" Strange ! " murmured Holmes, as he stood in the light of the window and examined them minutely. " Very strange indeed ! "

Stooping with one of his quick, feline pounces he placed the slipper upon the blood-mark on the sill. It exactly corresponded. He smiled in silence at his colleagues.

The inspector was transfigured with excitement. His native accent rattled like a stick upon railings.

" Man ! " he cried, " there's not a doubt of it ! Barker has just marked the window himself. It's a good deal broader than any boot-mark. I mind that you said it was a splay foot, and here's the explanation. But what's the game, Mr. Holmes—what's the game ? "

" Aye, what's the game ? " my friend repeated, thoughtfully.

White Mason chuckled and rubbed his fat hands together in his professional satisfaction.

" I said it was a snorter ! " he cried. " And a real snorter it is ! "

THE STRAND
MAGAZINE.

DECEMBER, 1914
Vol. xlviii. No. 288.

The VALLEY *of* FEAR

A NEW SHERLOCK HOLMES STORY

By

A. CONAN DOYLE

Illustrated by FRANK WILES

PART·I·
THE TRAGEDY OF BIRLSTONE

The opening chapters of this new and thrilling adventure of Sherlock Holmes described the receipt by Holmes of a cipher message, from which he deduces that some devilry is intended against a man named Douglas, a rich country gentleman living at the Manor House, Birlstone, in Sussex, and that the danger is a pressing one. Almost as soon as he has deciphered the message he is visited by Inspector MacDonald, of Scotland Yard, who brings the news that Mr. Douglas has been murdered that morning.

Holmes, Dr. Watson, and the inspector proceed to the scene of the tragedy, where they are met by Mr. White Mason, the chief Sussex detective. The murdered man had been horribly injured, while lying across his chest was a curious weapon—a shot-gun with the barrel sawn off a foot in front of the triggers. Near him was found a card with the initials "V. V."

and the number "341" scrawled on it in ink, and about half-way up the forearm was a curious design—a branded triangle inside a circle. His wedding-ring had been removed and the ring above it replaced.

There is no clue to the murderer except a bloody footprint on the window-sill, and he had apparently made his escape by wading across the moat. Holmes is much struck by the fact that one of Douglas's dumb-bells is missing.

Cecil Barker, Douglas's most intimate friend, is considerably flustered while being cross-examined by the detectives, and confesses that Douglas had been jealous on account of his attentions to Mrs. Douglas. Holmes ascertains from Ames, the butler, that on the previous evening Barker was wearing a pair of bed-room slippers which were stained with blood. The last instalment ends with the following dialogue, which takes place in the study, Holmes having brought with him the blood-stained slippers from the hall:—

"Strange!" murmured Holmes, as he stood in the light of the window and examined them minutely. "Very strange indeed!"

Stooping with one of his quick, feline pounces he placed the slipper upon the blood-mark on the sill. It exactly corresponded. He smiled in silence at his colleagues.

The inspector was transfigured with excitement.

"Man!" he cried, "there's not a doubt of it! Barker has just marked the window himself. It's a good deal broader than any boot-mark. I mind that you said it was a splay foot, and here's the explanation. But what's the game, Mr. Holmes—what's the game?"

"Aye, what's the game?" my friend repeated, thoughtfully.

White Mason chuckled and rubbed his fat hands together in his professional satisfaction.

"I said it was a snorter!" he cried. "And a real snorter it is!"

CHAPTER VI.
A DAWNING LIGHT.

THE three detectives had many matters of detail into which to inquire, so I returned alone to our modest quarters at the village inn; but before doing so I took a stroll in the curious old-world garden which flanked the house. Rows of very ancient yew trees, cut into strange designs, girded it round. Inside was a beautiful stretch of lawn with an old sundial in the middle, the whole effect so soothing and restful that it was welcome to my somewhat jangled nerves. In that deeply peaceful atmosphere one could forget or remember only as some fantastic nightmare that darkened study with the sprawling, blood-stained figure upon the floor. And yet as I strolled round it and tried to steep my soul in its gentle balm, a strange incident occurred which brought me back to the tragedy and left a sinister impression in my mind.

I have said that a decoration of yew trees circled the garden. At the end which was farthest from the house they thickened into a continuous hedge. On the other side of this hedge, concealed from the eyes of anyone approaching from the direction of the house, there was a stone seat. As I approached the spot I was aware of voices, some remark in the deep tones of a man, answered by a little ripple of feminine laughter. An instant later I had come round the end of the hedge, and my eyes lit upon Mrs. Douglas and the man Barker before they were aware of my presence. Her appearance gave me a shock. In the dining-room she had been demure and discreet. Now all pretence of grief had passed away from her. Her eyes shone with the joy of living, and her face still quivered with amusement at some remark of her companion. He sat forward, his hands clasped and his forearms on his knees, with an answering smile upon his bold, handsome face. In an instant—but it was just one instant too late—they resumed their solemn masks as my figure came into view. A hurried word or two passed between them, and then Barker rose and came towards me.

"Excuse me, sir," said he, "but am I addressing Dr. Watson?"

I bowed with a coldness which showed, I daresay, very plainly the impression which had been produced upon my mind.

"We thought that it was probably you, as your friendship with Mr. Sherlock Holmes is so well known. Would you mind coming over and speaking to Mrs. Douglas for one instant?"

I followed him with a dour face. Very clearly I could see in my mind's eye that shattered figure upon the floor. Here within a few hours of the tragedy were his wife and his nearest friend laughing together behind a bush in the garden which had been his. I greeted the lady with reserve. I had grieved with her grief in the dining-room. Now I met her appealing gaze with an unresponsive eye.

"I fear that you think me callous and hard-hearted?" said she.

I shrugged my shoulders.

"It is no business of mine," said I.

"Perhaps some day you will do me justice. If you only realized——"

"There is no need why Dr. Watson should realize," said Barker, quickly. "As he has himself said, it is no possible business of his."

"Exactly," said I, "and so I will beg leave to resume my walk."

"One moment, Dr. Watson," cried the woman, in a pleading voice. "There is one question which you can answer with more authority than anyone else in the world, and it may make a very great difference to me. You know Mr. Holmes and his relations with the police better than anyone else can do. Supposing that a matter were brought confidentially to his knowledge, is it absolutely necessary that he should pass it on to the detectives?"

"Yes, that's it," said Barker, eagerly. "Is he on his own or is he entirely in with them?"

" ' MR. HOLMES IS AN INDEPENDENT INVESTIGATOR,' I SAID. ' HE IS HIS OWN MASTER.' "

" I really don't know that I should be justified in discussing such a point."

" I beg—I implore that you will, Dr.
Watson. I assure you that you will be
helping us—helping me greatly if you will
guide us on that point."

There was such a ring of sincerity in the
woman's voice that for the instant I forgot
all about her levity and was moved only to
do her will.

" Mr. Holmes is an independent investigator," I said. " He is his own master,

and would act as his own judgment directed. At the same time he would naturally feel loyalty towards the officials who were working on the same case, and he would not conceal from them anything which would help them in bringing a criminal to justice. Beyond this I can say nothing, and I would refer you to Mr. Holmes himself if you wanted fuller information."

So saying I raised my hat and went upon my way, leaving them still seated behind that concealing hedge. I looked back as I rounded the far end of it, and saw that they were still talking very earnestly together, and, as they were gazing after me, it was clear that it was our interview that was the subject of their debate.

"I wish none of their confidences," said Holmes, when I reported to him what had occurred. He had spent the whole afternoon at the Manor House in consultation with his two colleagues, and returned about five with a ravenous appetite for a high tea which I had ordered for him. "No confidences, Watson, for they are mighty awkward if it comes to an arrest for conspiracy and murder."

"You think it will come to that?"

He was in his most cheerful and *débonnaire* humour.

"My dear Watson, when I have exterminated that fourth egg I will be ready to put you in touch with the whole situation. I don't say that we have fathomed it—far from it—but when we have traced the missing dumb-bell——"

"The dumb-bell!"

"Dear me, Watson, is it possible that you have not penetrated the fact that the case hangs upon the missing dumb-bell? Well, well, you need not be downcast, for, between ourselves, I don't think that either Inspector Mac or the excellent local practitioner has grasped the overwhelming importance of this incident. One dumb-bell, Watson! Consider an athlete with one dumb-bell. Picture to yourself the unilateral development—the imminent danger of a spinal curvature. Shocking, Watson; shocking!"

He sat with his mouth full of toast and his eyes sparkling with mischief, watching my intellectual entanglement. The mere sight of his excellent appetite was an assurance of success, for I had very clear recollections of days and nights without a thought of food, when his baffled mind had chafed before some problem whilst his thin, eager features became more attenuated with the asceticism of complete mental concentration. Finally he lit his pipe and, sitting in the ingle-nook of the old village inn, he talked slowly and at random about his case, rather as one who thinks aloud than as one who makes a considered statement.

"A lie, Watson—a great big, thumping, obtrusive, uncompromising lie—that's what meets us on the threshold. There is our starting point. The whole story told by Barker is a lie. But Barker's story is corroborated by Mrs. Douglas. Therefore she is lying also. They are both lying and in a conspiracy. So now we have the clear problem—why are they lying, and what is the truth which they are trying so hard to conceal? Let us try, Watson, you and I, if we can get behind the lie and reconstruct the truth.

"How do I know that they are lying? Because it is a clumsy fabrication which simply *could* not be true. Consider! According to the story given to us the assassin had less than a minute after the murder had been committed to take that ring, which was under another ring, from the dead man's finger, to replace the other ring—a thing which he would surely never have done—and to put that singular card beside his victim. I say that this was obviously impossible. You may argue—but I have too much respect for your judgment, Watson, to think that you will do so—that the ring may have been taken before the man was killed. The fact that the candle had only been lit a short time shows that there had been no lengthy interview. Was Douglas, from what we hear of his fearless character, a man who would be likely to give up his wedding-ring at such short notice, or could we conceive of his giving it up at all? No, no, Watson, the assassin was alone with the dead man for some time with the lamp lit. Of that I have no doubt at all. But the gunshot was apparently the cause of death. Therefore the gunshot must have been fired some time earlier than we are told. But there could be no mistake about such a matter as that. We are in the presence, therefore, of a deliberate conspiracy upon the part of the two people who heard the gunshot—of the man Barker and of the woman Douglas. When on the top of this I am able to show that the blood-mark upon the window-sill was deliberately placed there by Barker in order to give a false clue to the police, you will admit that the case grows dark against him.

"Now we have to ask ourselves at what hour the murder actually did occur. Up to half-past ten the servants were moving about the house, so it was certainly not before that time. At a quarter to eleven they had all gone to their rooms with the exception of Ames, who was in the pantry. I have been trying some experiments after you left us this afternoon, and I find that no noise which MacDonald can make in the study can penetrate to me in the pantry when the doors are all shut. It is otherwise, however, from the housekeeper's room. It is not so far down the corridor, and from it I could vaguely hear a voice when it was very loudly raised. The sound from

past eleven, when they rang the bell and summoned the servants. What were they doing, and why did they not instantly give the alarm? That is the question which faces us, and when it has been answered we will surely have gone some way to solve our problem."

"YOU THINK, THEN, DEFINITELY, THAT BARKER AND MRS. DOUGLAS ARE GUILTY OF THE MURDER?"

a shot-gun is to some extent muffled when the discharge is at very close range, as it undoubtedly was in this instance. It would not be very loud, and yet in the silence of the night it should have easily penetrated to Mrs. Allen's room. She is, as she has told us, somewhat deaf, but none the less she mentioned in her evidence that she did hear something like a door slamming half an hour before the alarm was given. Half an hour before the alarm was given would be a quarter to eleven. I have no doubt that what she heard was the report of the gun, and that this was the real instant of the murder. If this is so, we have now to determine what Mr. Barker and Mrs. Douglas, presuming that they are not the actual murderers, could have been doing from a quarter to eleven, when the sound of the gun-shot brought them down, until a quarter

"I am convinced myself," said I, "that there is an understanding between those two people. She must be a heartless creature to sit laughing at some jest within a few hours of her husband's murder."

"Exactly. She does not shine as a wife even in her own account of what occurred. I am not a whole-souled admirer of womankind, as you are aware, Watson, but my experience of life has taught me that there are few wives having any regard for their husbands who would let any man's spoken word stand between them and that husband's dead body. Should I ever marry, Watson, I should hope to inspire my wife with some feeling which would prevent her from being walked off by a housekeeper when my corpse was lying within a few yards of her. It was badly stage-managed, for even the rawest of investigators must be struck by the absence of the usual feminine ululation. If there had been nothing else, this incident alone would have suggested a prearranged conspiracy to my mind."

"You think, then, definitely, that Barker and Mrs. Douglas are guilty of the murder?"

"There is an appalling directness about your questions, Watson," said Holmes, shaking his pipe at me. "They come at me like bullets. If you put it that Mrs. Douglas and Barker know the truth about the murder and are conspiring to conceal it, then I can give you a whole-souled answer. I am sure they do. But your more deadly proposition is not so clear. Let us for a moment consider the difficulties which stand in the way.

"We will suppose that this couple are united by the bonds of a guilty love and that they have determined to get rid of the man who stands between them. It is a large supposition, for discreet inquiry among servants and others has failed to corroborate it in any way. On the contrary, there is a good deal of evidence that the Douglases were very attached to each other."

"That I am sure cannot be true," said I, thinking of the beautiful, smiling face in the garden.

"Well, at least they gave that impression. However, we will suppose that they are an extraordinarily astute couple, who deceive everyone upon this point and who conspire to murder the husband. He happens to be a man over whose head some danger hangs——"

"We have only their word for that."

Holmes looked thoughtful.

"I see, Watson. You are sketching out a theory by which everything they say from the beginning is false. According to your idea, there was never any hidden menace or secret society or Valley of Fear or Boss MacSomebody or anything else. Well, that is a good, sweeping generalization. Let us see what that brings us to. They invent this theory to account for the crime. They then play up to the idea by leaving this bicycle in the park as a proof of the existence of some outsider. The stain on the window-sill conveys the same idea. So does the card upon the body, which might have been prepared in the house. That all fits into your hypothesis, Watson. But now we come on the nasty angular, uncompromising bits which won't slip into their places. Why a cut-off shotgun of all weapons—and an American one at that? How could they be so sure that the sound of it would not bring someone on to them? It's a mere chance, as it is, that Mrs.

Allen did not start out to inquire for the slamming door. Why did your guilty couple do all this, Watson?"

"I confess that I can't explain it."

"Then, again, if a woman and her lover conspire to murder a husband, are they going to advertise their guilt by ostentatiously removing his wedding-ring after his death? Does that strike you as very probable, Watson?"

"No, it does not."

"And once again, if the thought of leaving a bicycle concealed outside had occurred to you, would it really have seemed worth doing when the dullest detective would naturally say this is an obvious blind, as the bicycle is the first thing which the fugitive needed in order to make his escape?"

"I can conceive of no explanation."

"And yet there should be no combination of events for which the wit of man cannot conceive an explanation. Simply as a mental exercise, without any assertion that it is true, let me indicate a possible line of thought. It is, I admit, mere imagination, but how often is imagination the mother of truth?

"We will suppose that there *was* a guilty secret, a really shameful secret, in the life of this man Douglas. This leads to his murder by someone who is, we will suppose, an avenger—someone from outside. This avenger, for some reason which I confess I am still at a loss to explain, took the dead man's wedding-ring. The vendetta might conceivably date back to the man's first marriage and the ring be taken for some such reason. Before this avenger got away Barker and the wife had reached the room. The assassin convinced them that any attempt to arrest him would lead to the publication of some hideous scandal. They were converted to this idea and preferred to let him go. For this purpose they probably lowered the bridge, which can be done quite noiselessly, and then raised it again. He made his escape, and for some reason thought that he could do so more safely on foot than on the bicycle. He therefore left his machine where it would not be discovered until he had got safely away. So far we are within the bounds of possibility, are we not?"

"Well, it is possible, no doubt," said I, with some reserve.

"We have to remember, Watson, that whatever occurred is certainly something very extraordinary. Well now, to continue our supposititious case, the couple—not necessarily a guilty couple—realize after the murderer is gone that they have placed themselves in a position in which it may be difficult for them to prove that they did not themselves either do the deed or connive at it. They rapidly and rather clumsily met the situation. The mark was put by Barker's blood-stained slipper upon the window-sill to suggest how the fugitive got away. They obviously were the two who must have heard the sound of the gun, so they gave the alarm exactly as they would have done, but a good half-hour after the event."

"And how do you propose to prove all this ? "

"Well, if there were an outsider he may be traced and taken. That would be the most effective of all proofs. But if not—well, the resources of science are far from being exhausted. I think that an evening alone in that study would help me much."

"An evening alone ! "

"I propose to go up there presently. I have arranged it with the estimable Ames, who is by no means whole-hearted about Barker. I shall sit in that room and see if its atmosphere brings me inspiration. I'm a believer in the *genius loci.* You smile, friend Watson. Well, we shall see. By the way, you have that big umbrella of yours, have you not ? "

"It is here."

"Well, I'll borrow that, if I may."

"Certainly—but what a wretched weapon ! If there is danger——"

"Nothing serious, my dear Watson, or I should certainly ask for your assistance. But I'll take the umbrella. At present I am only awaiting the return of our colleagues from Tunbridge Wells, where they are at present engaged in trying for a likely owner to the bicycle."

It was nightfall before Inspector Mac-Donald and White Mason came back from their expedition, and they arrived exultant, reporting a great advance in our investigation.

"Man, I'll admeet that I had my doubts if there was ever an outsider," said MacDonald, "but that's all past now. We've had the bicycle identified and we have a description of our man, so that's a long step on our journey."

"It sounds to me like the beginning of the end," said Holmes; "I'm sure I congratulate you both with all my heart."

"Well, I started from the fact that Mr. Douglas had seemed disturbed since the day before, when he had been at Tunbridge Wells. It was at Tunbridge Wells, then, that he had become conscious of some danger. It was clear, therefore, that if a man had come over with a bicycle it was from Tunbridge Wells that he might be expected to have come. We took the bicycle over with us and showed it at the hotels. It was identified at once by the manager of the Eagle Commercial as belonging to a man named Hargrave who had taken a room there two days before. This bicycle and a small valise were his whole belongings. He had registered his name as coming from London, but had given no address. The valise was London-made and the contents were British, but the man himself was undoubtedly an American."

"Well, well," said Holmes, gleefully, "you have indeed done some solid work whilst I have been sitting spinning theories with my friend. It's a lesson in being practical, Mr. Mac."

"Aye, it's just that, Mr. Holmes," said the inspector with satisfaction.

"But this may all fit in with your theories," I remarked.

"That may or may not be. But let us hear the end, Mr. Mac. Was there nothing to identify this man ? "

"So little that it was evident he had carefully guarded himself against identification. There were no papers or letters and no marking upon the clothes. A cycle-map of the county lay upon his bedroom table. He had left the hotel after breakfast yesterday morning upon his bicycle, and no more was heard of him until our inquiries."

"That's what puzzles me, Mr. Holmes," said White Mason. "If the fellow did not want the hue and cry raised over him, one would imagine that he would have returned and remained at the hotel as an inoffensive tourist. As it is, he must know that he will be reported to the police by the hotel manager, and that his disappearance will be connected with the murder."

"So one would imagine. Still he has been justified of his wisdom up to date at any rate, since he has not been taken. But his description—what of that ? "

MacDonald referred to his notebook.

"Here we have it so far as they could give it. They don't seem to have taken any very particular stock of him, but still the porter, the clerk, and the chambermaid are all agreed that this about covers the points. He was a man about five foot nine in height, fifty or so years of age, his hair slightly grizzled, a greyish moustache, a curved nose, and a face which all of them described as fierce and forbidding."

"Well, bar the expression, that might almost be a description of Douglas himself," said Holmes. "He is just over fifty, with grizzled hair and moustache and about the same height. Did you get anything else?"

"He was dressed in a heavy grey suit with a reefer jacket, and he wore a short yellow overcoat and a soft cap."

"What about the shot-gun?"

"It is less than two feet long. It could very well have fitted into his valise. He could have carried it inside his overcoat without difficulty."

"And how do you consider that all this bears upon the general case?"

"Well, Mr. Holmes," said MacDonald, "when we have got our man— and you may be sure that I had his description on the wires within five minutes of hearing it—we shall be better able to judge. But even as it stands, we have surely gone a long way. We know that an American calling himself Hargrave came to Tunbridge Wells two days ago with bicycle and valise. In the latter was a sawn-off shot-gun, so he came with the deliberate purpose of crime. Yesterday morning he set off for this place upon his bicycle with his gun concealed in his overcoat. No one saw him arrive, so far as we can learn, but he need not pass through the village to reach the park gates, and there are many cyclists upon the road. Presumably he at once concealed his cycle among the laurels, where it was found, and possibly lurked there himself, with his eye on the house waiting for Mr. Douglas to come out. The shot-gun is a strange weapon to use inside a house, but he had intended to use it outside, and then it has very obvious advantages, as it would be impossible to miss with it, and the sound of shots is so common in an English sporting neighbourhood that no particular notice would be taken."

"That is all very clear!" said Holmes.

"Well, Mr. Douglas did not appear. What was he to do next? He left his bicycle and

approached the house in the twilight. He found the bridge down and no one about. He took his chance, intending, no doubt, to make some excuse if he met anyone. He met no one. He slipped into the first room that he saw and concealed himself behind the curtain. From thence he could see the drawbridge go up

"'IT SOUNDS TO ME LIKE THE BEGINNING OF THE END,'
SAID HOLMES; 'I'M SURE I CONGRATULATE YOU BOTH
WITH ALL MY HEART.'"

and he knew that his only escape was through the moat. He waited until a quarter past eleven, when Mr. Douglas, upon his usual nightly round, came into the room. He shot him and escaped, as arranged. He was aware that the bicycle would be described by the hotel people and be a clue against him, so he left it there and made his way by some other means to London or to some safe hiding-place which he had already arranged. How is that, Mr. Holmes?"

"Well, Mr. Mac, it is very good and very clear so far as it goes. That is your end of the story. My end is that the crime was comthe common cause."

"Can we help you, Mr. Holmes?"

"No, no! Darkness and Dr. Watson's umbrella. My wants are simple. And Ames—the faithful Ames—no doubt he will stretch a point for me. All my lines of thought lead me back invariably to the one basic question—why should an athletic man develop his frame upon so unnatural an instrument as a single dumb-bell?"

It was late that night when Holmes returned from his solitary excursion. We slept in a double-bedded room, which was the best that the little country inn could do for us. I was already asleep when I was partly awakened by his entrance.

"Well, Holmes," I murmured, "have you found out anything?"

He stood beside me in silence, his candle in his hand. Then the tall lean figure inclined towards me.

"I say, Watson," he whispered, "would you be afraid to sleep in the same room as a lunatic, a man with softening of the brain, an idiot whose mind has lost its grip?"

"Not in the least," I answered in astonishment.

"Ah, that's lucky," he said, and not another word would he utter that night.

mitted half an hour earlier than reported; that Mrs. Douglas and Mr. Barker are both in a conspiracy to conceal something; that they aided the murderer's escape—or at least, that they reached the room before he escaped—and that they fabricated evidence of his escape through the window, whereas in all probability they had themselves let him go by lowering the bridge. That's *my* reading of the first half."

The two detectives shook their heads.

"Well, Mr. Holmes, if this is true we only tumble out of one mystery into another," said the London inspector.

"And in some ways a worse one," added White Mason. "The lady has never been in America in her life. What possible connection could she have with an American assassin which would cause her to shelter him?"

"I freely admit the difficulties," said Holmes. "I propose to make a little investigation of my own to-night, and it is just possible that it may contribute something to

CHAPTER VII.
THE SOLUTION.

NEXT morning, after breakfast, we found Inspector MacDonald and Mr. White Mason seated in close consultation in the small parlour of the local police-sergeant. Upon the table in front of them were piled a number of letters and telegrams, which they were carefully sorting and docketing. Three had been placed upon one side.

" Still on the track of the elusive bicyclist ? " Holmes asked, cheerfully. " What is the latest news of the ruffian ? "

MacDonald pointed ruefully to his heap of correspondence.

" He is at present reported from Leicester, Nottingham, Southampton, Derby, East Ham, Richmond, and fourteen other places. In three of them—East Ham, Leicester, and Liverpool—there is a clear case against him and he has actually been arrested. The country seems to be full of fugitives with yellow coats."

" Dear me ! "- said Holmes, sympathetically. " Now, Mr. Mac, and you, Mr. White Mason, I wish to give you a very earnest piece of advice. When I went into this case with you I bargained, as you will no doubt remember, that I should not present you with half-proved theories, but that I should retain and work out my own ideas until I had satisfied myself that they were correct. For this reason I am not at the present moment telling you all that is in my mind. On the other hand, I said that I would play the game fairly by you, and I do not think it is a fair game to allow you for one unnecessary moment to waste your energies upon a profitless task. Therefore I am here to advise you this morning, and my advice to you is summed up in three words : Abandon the case."

MacDonald and White Mason stared in amazement at their celebrated colleague.

" You consider it hopeless ? " cried the inspector.

" I consider *your* case to be hopeless. I do not consider that it is hopeless to arrive at the truth."

" But this cyclist. He is not an invention. We have his description, his valise, his bicycle. The fellow must be somewhere. Why should we not get him ? "

" Yes, yes ; no doubt he is somewhere, and no doubt we shall get him, but I would not have you waste your energies in East Ham or Liverpool. I am sure that we can find some shorter cut to a result."

" You are holding something back. It's hardly fair of you, Mr. Holmes." The inspector was annoyed.

" You know my methods of work, Mr. Mac. But I will hold it back for the shortest time possible. I only wish to verify my details in one way, which can very readily be done, and then I make my bow and return to London, leaving my results entirely at your service. I owe you too much to act otherwise,

for in all my experience I cannot recall any more singular and interesting study."

" This is clean beyond me, Mr. Holmes. We saw you when we returned from Tunbridge Wells last night, and you were in general agreement with our results. What has happened since then to give you a completely new idea of the case ? "

" Well, since you ask me, I spent, as I told you that I would, some hours last night at the Manor House."

" Well, what happened ? "

" Ah ! I can only give you a very general answer to that for the moment. By the way, I have been reading a short, but clear and interesting, account of the old building, purchasable at the modest sum of one penny from the local tobacconist." Here Holmes drew a small tract, embellished with a rude engraving of the ancient Manor House, from his waistcoat pocket. " It immensely adds to the zest of an investigation, my dear Mr. Mac, when one is in conscious sympathy with the historical atmosphere of one's surroundings. Don't look so impatient, for I assure you that even so bald an account as this raises some sort of picture of the past in one's mind. Permit me to give you a sample. ' Erected in the fifth year of the reign of James I., and standing upon the site of a much older building, the Manor House of Birlstone presents one of the finest surviving examples of the moated Jacobean residence——' "

" You are making fools of us, Mr. Holmes."

" Tut, tut, Mr. Mac !—the first sign of temper I have detected in you. Well, I won't read it verbatim, since you feel so strongly upon the subject. But when I tell you that there is some account of the taking of the place by a Parliamentary colonel in 1644, of the concealment of Charles for several days in the course of the Civil War, and finally of a visit there by the second George, you will admit that there are various associations of interest connected with this ancient house."

" I don't doubt it, Mr. Holmes, but that is no business of ours."

" Is it not ? Is it not ? Breadth of view, my dear Mr. Mac, is one of the essentials of our profession. The inter-play of ideas and the oblique uses of knowledge are often of extraordinary interest. You will excuse these remarks from one who, though a mere connoisseur of crime, is still rather older and perhaps more experienced than yourself."

" I'm the first to admit that," said the detective, heartily. " You get to your point,

"'WELL, HOLMES,' I MURMURED, 'HAVE YOU FOUND OUT ANYTHING?'"

I admit, but you have such a deuced round-the-corner way of doing it."

"Well, well, I'll drop past history and get down to present-day facts. I called last night, as I have already said, at the Manor House. I did not see either Mr. Barker or Mrs. Douglas. I saw no necessity to disturb them, but I was pleased to hear that the lady was not visibly pining and that she had partaken of an excellent dinner. My visit was specially made to the good Mr. Ames, with whom I exchanged some amiabilities which culminated in his allowing me, without reference to anyone else, to sit alone for a time in the study."

"What! With that!" I ejaculated.

"No, no; everything is now in order. You gave permission for that, Mr. Mac, as I am informed. The room was in its normal state, and in it I passed an instructive quarter of an hour."

"What were you doing?"

"Well, not to make a mystery of so simple a matter, I was looking for the missing dumb-bell. It has always bulked rather large in my estimate of the case. I ended by finding it."

"Where?"

"Ah! There we come to the edge of the unexplored. Let me go a little farther, a very little farther, and I will promise that you shall share everything that I know."

"Well, we're bound to take you on your own terms," said the inspector; "but when it comes to telling us to abandon the case——Why, in the name of goodness, should we abandon the case?"

"For the simple reason, my dear Mr. Mac, that you have not got the first idea what it is that you are investigating."

"We are investigating the murder of Mr. John Douglas, of Birlstone Manor."

"Yes, yes; so you are. But don't trouble to trace the mysterious gentleman upon the bicycle. I assure you that it won't help you."

"Then what do you suggest that we do?"

"I will tell you exactly what to do, if you will do it."

"Well, I'm bound to say I've always found you had reason behind all your queer ways. I'll do what you advise."

"And you, Mr. White Mason?"

The country detective looked helplessly from one to the other. Mr. Holmes and his methods were new to him.

"Well, if it is good enough for the inspector it is good enough for me," he said, at last.

"Capital!" said Holmes. "Well, then, I should recommend a nice, cheery country walk for both of you. They tell me that the views from Birlstone Ridge over the Weald are very remarkable. No doubt lunch could be got at some suitable hostelry, though my ignorance of the country prevents me from recommending one. In the evening, tired but happy——"

"Man, this is getting past a joke!" cried MacDonald, rising angrily from his chair.

"Well, well, spend the day as you like," said Holmes, patting him cheerfully upon the shoulder. "Do what you like and go where you will, but meet me here before dusk without fail—without fail, Mr. Mac."

"That sounds more like sanity."

"All of it was excellent advice, but I don't insist, so long as you are here when I need you. But now, before we part, I want you to write a note to Mr. Barker."

"Well?"

"I'll dictate it, if you like. Ready?

"'DEAR SIR,—It has struck me that it is our duty to drain the moat, in the hope that we may find some——'"

"It's impossible," said the inspector; "I've made inquiry."

"Tut, tut, my dear sir! Do, please, do what I ask you."

"Well, go on."

"'——in the hope that we may find something which may bear upon our investigation. I have made arrangements, and the workmen will be at work early to-morrow morning diverting the stream——'"

"Impossible!"

"'——diverting the stream, so I thought it best to explain matters beforehand.'
Now sign that, and send it by hand about four o'clock. At that hour we shall meet again in this room. Until then we can each do what we like, for I can assure you that this inquiry has come to a definite pause."

THE STRAND
MAGAZINE.

JANUARY, 1915.
Vol. xlix. No. 289.

The VALLEY *of* FEAR

A NEW SHERLOCK HOLMES STORY

By

A. CONAN DOYLE

Illustrated by FRANK WILES

PART · I ·

THE TRAGEDY OF BIRLSTONE

The opening chapters of this new and thrilling adventure of Sherlock Holmes described the receipt by Holmes of a cipher message, from which he deduces that some devilry is intended against a man named Douglas, a rich country gentleman living at the Manor House, Birlstone, in Sussex, and that the danger is a pressing one. Almost as soon as he has deciphered the message he is visited by Inspector MacDonald, of Scotland Yard, who brings the news that Mr. Douglas has been murdered that morning.

Holmes, Dr. Watson, and the inspector proceed to the scene of the tragedy, where they are met by Mr. White Mason, the chief Sussex detective. The murdered man had been horribly injured, while lying across his chest was a curious weapon—a shot-gun with the barrel sawn off a foot in front of the triggers.

Near him was found a card with the initials "V. V." and the number "341" scrawled on it in ink, and about half-way up the forearm was a curious design— a branded triangle inside a circle. His wedding-ring had been removed and the ring above it replaced.

There is no clue to the murderer except a bloody footprint on the window-sill, and he had apparently made his escape by wading across the moat. Holmes is much struck by the fact that one of Douglas's dumb-bells is missing.

Cecil Barker, Douglas's most intimate friend, is considerably flustered while being cross-examined by the detectives, and confesses that Douglas had been jealous on account of his attentions to Mrs. Douglas. Holmes ascertains from Ames, the butler, that on the previous evening Barker was wearing a pair of

"THEN SUDDENLY HE HAULED SOMETHING IN AS A FISHERMAN LANDS A FISH."

bedroom slippers which were stained with blood, and, on comparing them with the footprints on the window-sill, finds that they correspond.

Holmes gives Watson his reasons for believing that Mrs. Douglas and Barker know all about the murder. He advises the other detectives to abandon the case and asks them to meet him that same evening, when he promises they shall share everything he knows. The last instalment ends with the dispatch, at Holmes's suggestion, of the following letter to Barker:—

"It has struck me that it is our duty to drain the moat, in the hope that we may find something which may bear upon our investigation. I have made arrangements, and the workmen will be at work early to - morrow morning diverting the stream, so I thought it best to explain matters beforehand."

CHAPTER VII. (continued).

VENING was drawing in when we reassembled. Holmes was very serious in his manner, myself curious, and the detectives obviously critical and annoyed.

"Well, gentlemen," said my friend, gravely, " I am asking you now to put everything to the test with me, and you will judge for yourselves whether the observations which I have made justify the conclusions to which I have come. It is a chill evening, and I do not know how long our expedition may last, so I beg that you will wear your warmest coats. It is of the first importance that we should be in our places before it grows dark, so, with your permission, we will get started at once."

We passed along the outer bounds of the Manor House park until we came to a place where there was a gap in the rails which fenced it. Through this we slipped, and then, in the gathering gloom, we followed Holmes until we had reached a shrubbery which lies nearly opposite to the main door and the drawbridge. The latter had not been raised. Holmes crouched down behind the screen of laurels, and we all three followed his example.

"Well, what are we to do now ? " asked MacDonald, with some gruffness.

"Possess our souls in patience and make as little noise as possible," Holmes answered.

"What are we here for at all ? I really think that you might treat us with more frankness."

Holmes laughed.

"Watson insists that I am the dramatist in real life," said he. " Some touch of the artist wells up within me and calls insistently for a well-staged performance. Surely our profession, Mr. Mac, would be a drab and sordid one if we did not sometimes set the scene so as to glorify our results. The blunt accusation, the brutal tap upon the shoulder —what can one make of such a *dénouement* ? But the quick inference, the subtle trap, the clever forecast of coming events, the triumphant vindication of bold theories—are these not the pride and the justification of our life's work ? At the present moment you thrill with the glamour of the situation and the anticipation of the hunter. Where would be that thrill if I had been as definite as a time-table ? I only ask a little patience, Mr. Mac, and all will be clear to you."

" Well, I hope the pride and justification and the rest of it will come before we all get our death of cold," said the London detective, with comic resignation.

We all had good reason to join in the aspiration, for our vigil was a long and bitter one. Slowly the shadows darkened over the long, sombre face of the old house. A cold, damp reek from the moat chilled us to the bones and set our teeth chattering. There was a single lamp over the gateway and a steady globe of light in the fatal study. Everything else was dark and still.

" How long is this to last ? " asked the inspector, suddenly. " And what is it we are watching for ? "

" I have no more notion than you how long it is to last," Holmes answered with some asperity. " If criminals would always schedule their movements like railway trains it would certainly be more convenient for all of us. As to what it is we—— Well, *that's* what we are watching for."

As he spoke the bright yellow light in the study was obscured by somebody passing to and fro before it. The laurels among which we lay were immediately opposite the window and not more than a hundred feet from it. Presently it was thrown open with a whining of hinges, and we could dimly see the dark outline of a man's head and shoulders looking out into the gloom. For some minutes he peered forth, in a furtive, stealthy fashion, as one who wishes to be assured that he is unobserved. Then he leaned forward, and in the intense silence we were aware of the soft lapping of agitated water. He seemed to be stirring up the moat with something which he held in his hand. Then suddenly he hauled something in as a fisherman lands a fish—some large round object which obscured the light as it was dragged through the open casement.

" Now ! " cried Holmes. " Now ! "

We were all upon our feet, staggering after him with our stiffened limbs, whilst he, with one of those outflames of nervous energy

"MRS. DOUGLAS TURNED, AND IN AN INSTANT HER ARMS WERE ROUND HIM. BARKER HAD
SEIZED HIS OUTSTRETCHED HAND."

which could make him on occasion both the most active and the strongest man that I have ever known, ran swiftly across the bridge and rang violently at the bell. There was the rasping of bolts from the other side, and the amazed Ames stood in the entrance. Holmes brushed him aside without a word and, followed by all of us, rushed into the room which had been occupied by the man whom we had been watching.

The oil lamp on the table represented the glow which we had seen from outside. It was now in the hand of Cecil Barker, who held it towards us as we entered. Its light shone upon his strong, resolute, clean-shaven face and his menacing eyes.

" What the devil is the meaning of all this ? " he cried. " What are you after, anyhow ? "

Holmes took a swift glance round and then pounced upon a sodden bundle tied together with cord which lay where it had been thrust under the writing-table.

" This is what we are after, Mr. Barker. This bundle, weighted with a dumb-bell, which you have just raised from the bottom of the moat."

Barker stared at Holmes with amazement in his face.

" How in thunder came you to know anything about it ? " he asked.

" Simply that I put it there."

" You put it there ! You ! "

" Perhaps I should have said ' replaced it there,' " said Holmes. " You will remember, Inspector MacDonald, that I was somewhat struck by the absence of a dumb-bell. I drew your attention to it, but with the pressure of other events you had hardly the time to give it the consideration which would have enabled you to draw deductions from it. When water is near and a weight is missing it is not a very far-fetched supposition that something has been sunk in the water. The idea was at least worth testing, so with the help of Ames, who admitted me to the room, and the crook of Dr. Watson's umbrella, I was able last night to fish up and inspect this bundle. It was of the first importance, however, that we should be able to prove who placed it there. This we accomplished by the very obvious device of announcing that the moat would be dried to-morrow, which had, of course, the effect that whoever had hidden the bundle would most certainly withdraw it the moment that darkness enabled him to do so. We have no fewer than four witnesses as to who it was who took advantage of the opportunity, and so, Mr. Barker, I think the word lies now with you."

Sherlock Holmes put the sopping bundle upon the table beside the lamp and undid the cord which bound it. From within he extracted a dumb-bell, which he tossed down to its fellow in the corner. Next he drew forth a pair of boots. " American, as you perceive," he remarked, pointing to the toes. Then he laid upon the table a long, deadly, sheathed knife. Finally he unravelled a bundle of clothing, comprising a complete set of underclothes, socks, a grey tweed suit, and a short yellow overcoat.

" The clothes are commonplace," remarked Holmes, " save only the overcoat, which is full of suggestive touches." He held it tenderly towards the light, whilst his long, thin fingers flickered over it. " Here, as you perceive, is the inner pocket prolonged into the lining in such a fashion as to give ample space for the truncated fowling-piece. The tailor's tab is on the neck—Neale, Outfitter, Vermissa, U.S.A. I have spent an instructive afternoon in the rector's library, and have enlarged my knowledge by adding the fact that Vermissa is a flourishing little town at the head of one of the best-known coal and iron valleys in the United States. I have some recollection, Mr. Barker, that you associated the coal districts with Mr. Douglas's first wife, and it would surely not be too far-fetched an inference that the V.V. upon the card by the dead body might stand for Vermissa Valley, or that this very valley, which sends forth emissaries of murder, may be that Valley of Fear of which we have heard. So much is fairly clear. And now, Mr. Barker, I seem to be standing rather in the way of your explanation."

It was a sight to see Cecil Barker's expressive face during this exposition of the great detective. Anger, amazement, consternation, and indecision swept over it in turn. Finally he took refuge in a somewhat acid irony.

" You know such a lot, Mr. Holmes, perhaps you had better tell us some more," he sneered.

" I have no doubt that I could tell you a great deal more, Mr. Barker, but it would come with a better grace from you."

" Oh, you think so, do you ? Well, all I can say is that if there's any secret here it is not my secret, and I am not the man to give it away."

" Well, if you take that line, Mr. Barker," said the inspector, quietly, " we must just keep you in sight until we have the warrant and can hold you."

" You can do what you damn please about that," said Barker, defiantly.

The proceedings seemed to have come to a

definite end so far as he was concerned, for one had only to look at that granite face to realize that no *peine forte et dure* would ever force him to plead against his will. The deadlock was broken, however, by a woman's voice. Mrs. Douglas had been standing listening at the half-opened door, and now she entered the room.

"You have done enough for us, Cecil," said she. "Whatever comes of it in the future, you have done enough."

"Enough and more than enough," remarked Sherlock Holmes, gravely. "I have every sympathy with you, madam, and I should strongly urge you to have some confidence in the common sense of our jurisdiction and to take the police voluntarily into your complete confidence. It may be that I am myself at fault for not following up the hint which you conveyed to me through my friend, Dr. Watson, but at that time I had every reason to believe that you were directly concerned in the crime. Now I am assured that this is not so. At the same time, there is much that is unexplained, and I should strongly recommend that you ask *Mr. Douglas* to tell us his own story."

Mrs. Douglas gave a cry of astonishment at Holmes's words. The detectives and I must have echoed it, when we were aware of a man who seemed to have emerged from the wall, and who advanced now from the gloom of the corner in which he had appeared. Mrs. Douglas turned, and in an instant her arms were round him. Barker had seized his outstretched hand.

"It's best this way, Jack," his wife repeated. "I am sure that it is best."

"Indeed yes, Mr. Douglas," said Sherlock Holmes. "I am sure that you will find it best."

The man stood blinking at us with the dazed look of one who comes from the dark into the light. It was a remarkable face—bold grey eyes, a strong, short-clipped, grizzled moustache, a square, projecting chin, and a humorous mouth. He took a good look at us all, and then, to my amazement, he advanced to me and handed me a bundle of paper.

"I've heard of you," said he, in a voice which was not quite English and not quite American, but was altogether mellow and pleasing. "You are the historian of this bunch. Well, Dr. Watson, you've never had such a story as that pass through your hands before, and I'd lay my last dollar on that. Tell it your own way, but there are the facts, and you can't miss the public so long as you have those. I've been cooped up two days, and I've spent the daylight hours—as much

daylight as I could get in that rat-trap—in putting the thing into words. You're welcome to them—you and your public. There's the story of the Valley of Fear."

"That's the past, Mr. Douglas," said Sherlock Holmes, quietly. "What we desire now is to hear your story of the present."

"You'll have it, sir," said Douglas. "Can I smoke as I talk? Well, thank you, Mr. Holmes; you're a smoker yourself, if I remember right, and you'll guess what it is to be sitting for two days with tobacco in your pocket and afraid that the smell will give you away." He leaned against the mantelpiece and sucked at the cigar which Holmes had handed him.. "I've heard of you, Mr. Holmes ; I never guessed that I would meet you. But before you are through with that " —he nodded at my papers—" you will say I've brought you something fresh."

Inspector MacDonald had been staring at the new-comer with the greatest amazement.

"Well, this fairly beats me ! " he cried at last. "If you are Mr. John Douglas, of Birlstone Manor, then whose death have we been investigating for these two days, and where in the world have you sprung from now ? You seemed to me to come out of the floor like a Jack-in-a-box."

"Ah, Mr. Mac," said Holmes, shaking a reproving forefinger, "you would not read that excellent local compilation which described the concealment of King Charles. People did not hide in those days without reliable hiding-places, and the hiding-place that has once been used may be again. I had persuaded myself that we should find Mr. Douglas under this roof."

"And how long have you been playing this trick upon us, Mr. Holmes ? " said the inspector, angrily. "How long have you allowed us to waste ourselves upon a search that you knew to be an absurd one ? "

"Not one instant, my dear Mr. Mac. Only last night did I form my views of the case. As they could not be put to the proof until this evening, I invited you and your colleague to take a holiday for the day. Pray, what more could I do ? When I found the suit of clothes in the moat at once became apparent to me that the body we had found could not have been the body of Mr. John Douglas at all, but must be that of the bicyclist from Tunbridge Wells. No other conclusion was possible. Therefore I had to determine where Mr. John Douglas himself could be, and the balance of probability was that, with the connivance of his wife and his friend, he was concealed in a house which had such conveniences for a fugitive, and awaiting quieter times, when he could make his final escape."

"Well, you figured it out about right," said Mr. Douglas, approvingly. "I thought I'd dodge your British law, for I was not sure how I stood under it, and also I saw my chance to throw these hounds once for all off my track. Mind you, from first to last I have done nothing to be ashamed of, and nothing that I would not do again, but you'll judge that for yourselves when I tell you my story. Never mind warning me, inspector; I'm ready to stand pat upon the truth.

"I'm not going to begin at the beginning. That's all there"—he indicated my bundle of papers—"and a mighty queer yarn you'll find it. It all comes down to this: that there are some men that have good cause to hate me and would give their last dollar to know that they had got me. So long as I am alive and they are alive, there is no safety in this world for me. They hunted me from Chicago to California; then they chased me out of America; but when I married and settled down in this quiet spot I thought my last years were going to be peaceable. I never explained to my wife how things were. Why should I pull her into it? She would never have a quiet moment again, but would be always imagining trouble. I fancy she knew something, for I may have dropped a word here or a word there—but until yesterday, after you gentlemen had seen her, she never knew the rights of the matter. She told you all she knew, and so did Barker here, for on the night when this thing happened there was mighty little time for explanations. She knows everything now, and I would have been a wiser man if I had told her sooner. But it was a hard question, dear"—he took her hand for an instant in his own—"and I acted for the best.

"Well, gentlemen, the day before these happenings I was over in Tunbridge Wells and I got a glimpse of a man in the street. It was only a glimpse, but I have a quick eye for these things, and I never doubted who it was. It was the worst enemy I had among them all—one who has been after me like a hungry wolf after a caribou all these years. I knew there was trouble coming, and I came home and made ready for it. I guessed I'd fight through it all right on my own. There was a time when my luck was the talk of the whole United States. I never doubted that it would be with me still.

"I was on my guard all that next day and never went out into the park. It's as well, or he'd have had the drop on me with that buck-shot gun of his before ever I could draw on him. After the bridge was up—my mind was always more restful when that bridge was up in the evenings—I put the thing clear out of my head. I never figured on his getting into the house and waiting for me. But when I made my round in my dressing-gown, as my habit was, I had no sooner entered the study than I scented danger. I guess when a man has had dangers in his life—and I've had more than most in my time—there is a kind of sixth sense that waves the red flag. I saw the signal clear enough, and yet I couldn't tell you why. Next instant I spotted a boot under the window curtain, and then I saw why plain enough.

"I'd just the one candle that was in my hand, but there was a good light from the hall lamp through the open door. I put down the candle and jumped for a hammer that I'd left on the mantel. At the same moment he sprang at me. I saw the glint of a knife and I lashed at him with the hammer. I got him somewhere, for the knife tinkled down on the floor. He dodged round the table as quick as an eel, and a moment later he'd got his gun from under his coat. I heard him cock it, but I had got hold of it before he could fire. I had it by the barrel, and we wrestled for it all ends up for a minute or more. It was death to the man that lost his grip. He never lost his grip, but he got it butt downwards for a moment too long. Maybe it was I that pulled the trigger. Maybe we just jolted it off between us. Anyhow, he got both barrels in the face, and there I was, staring down at all that was left of Ted Baldwin. I'd recognized him in the township and again when he sprang for me, but his own mother wouldn't recognize him as I saw him then. I'm used to rough work, but I fairly turned sick at the sight of him.

"I was hanging on to the side of the table when Barker came hurrying down. I heard my wife coming, and I ran to the door and stopped her. It was no sight for a woman. I promised I'd come to her soon. I said a word or two to Barker—he took it all in at a glance—and we waited for the rest to come along. But there was no sign of them. Then we understood that they could hear nothing, and that all that had happened was only known to ourselves.

"It was at that instant that the idea came to me. I was fairly dazzled by the brilliancy of it. The man's sleeve had slipped up and there was the branded mark of the Lodge upon his forearm. See here."

The man whom we knew as Douglas turned up his own coat and cuff to show a

"I HEARD HIM COCK THE GUN, BUT I HAD GOT HOLD OF IT BEFORE HE COULD FIRE."

brown triangle within a circle exactly like that which we had seen upon the dead man.

" It was the sight of that which started me on to it. I seemed to see it all clear at a glance. There was his height and hair and figure about the same as my own. No one could swear to his face, poor devil ! I brought down this suit of clothes, and in a quarter of an hour Barker and I had put my dressing-gown on him and he lay as you found him. We tied all his things into a bundle, and I weighted them with the. only weight I could find and slung them through the window. The card he had meant to lay upon my body was lying beside his own. My rings were put on his finger, but when it came to the wedding-ring " —he held out his muscular hand—" you can see for yourselves that I had struck my limit. I have not moved it since the day I was married, and it would have taken a file to get it off. I don't know, anyhow, that I would have cared to part with it, but if I had wanted to I couldn't. So we just had to leave that detail to take care of itself. On the other hand, I brought a bit of plaster down and put it where I am wearing one myself at this instant. You slipped up there, Mr. Holmes, clever as you are, for if you had chanced to take off that plaster you would have found no cut underneath it.

" Well, that was the situation. If I could lie low for a while and then get away where I would be joined by my wife, we would have a chance at last of living at peace for the rest of our lives. These devils would give me no rest so long as I was aboveground, but if they saw in the papers that Baldwin had got his man there would be an end of all my troubles. I hadn't much time to make it clear to Barker and to my wife, but they understood enough to be able to help me. I knew all about this hiding-place, so did Ames, but it never entered his head to connect it with the matter. I retired into it, and it was up to Barker to do the rest.

" I guess you can fill in for yourselves what he did. He opened the window and made

the mark on the sill to give an idea of how the murderer escaped. It was a tall order, that, but as the bridge was up there was no other way. Then, when everything was fixed, he rang the bell for all he was worth. What happened afterwards you know—and so, gentlemen, you can do what you please, but I've told you the truth and the whole truth, so help me, God ! What I ask you now is, how do I stand by the English law ? "

There was a silence, which was broken by Sherlock Holmes.

" The English law is, in the main, a just law. You will get no worse than your deserts from it. But I would ask you how did this man know that you lived here, or how to get into your house, or where to hide to get you ? "

" I know nothing of this."

Holmes's face was very white and grave.

" The story is not over yet, I fear," said he. " You may find worse dangers than the English law, or even than your enemies from America. I see trouble before you, Mr. Douglas. You'll take my advice and still be on your guard."

And now, my long-suffering readers, I will ask you to come away with me for a time, far from the Sussex Manor House of Birlstone, and far also from the year of grace in which we made our eventful journey which ended with the strange story of the man who had been known as John Douglas. I wish you to journey back some twenty years in time, and westward some thousands of miles in space, that I may lay before you a singular and a terrible narrative—so singular and so terrible that you may find it hard to believe that, even as I tell it, even so did it occur. Do not think that I intrude one story before another is finished. As you read on you will find that this is not so. And when I have detailed those distant events and you have solved this mystery of the past we shall meet once more in those rooms in Baker Street where this, like so many other wonderful happenings, will find its end.

PART II.
THE SCOWRERS.

CHAPTER I.
THE MAN.

It was the fourth of February in the year 1875. It had been a severe winter, and the snow lay deep in the gorges of the Gilmerton Mountains. The steam plough had, however, kept the rail - track open, and the evening train which connects the long

line of coal-mining and iron-working settlements was slowly groaning its way up the steep gradients which lead from Stagville on the plain to Vermissa, the central township which lies at the head of the Vermissa Valley. From this point the track sweeps downwards to Barton's Crossing, Helmdale, and the purely agricultural county of Merton. It was a single-track railroad, but at every siding, and they were numerous, long lines of trucks piled with coal and with iron ore told of the hidden wealth which had brought a rude population and a bustling life to this most desolate corner of the United States of America.

For desolate it was. Little could the first pioneer who had traversed it have ever imagined that the fairest prairies and the most lush water-pastures were valueless compared with this gloomy land of black crag and tangled forest. Above the dark and often scarcely penetrable woods upon their sides, the high, bare crowns of the mountains, white snow and jagged rock, towered upon either flank, leaving a long, winding, tortuous valley in the centre. Up this the little train was slowly crawling.

The oil lamps had just been lit in the leading passenger-car, a long, bare carriage in which some twenty or thirty people were seated. The greater number of these were workmen returning from their day's toil in the lower portion of the valley. At least a dozen, by their grimed faces and the safety lanterns which they carried, proclaimed themselves as miners. These sat smoking in a group, and conversed in low voices, glancing occasionally at two men on the opposite side of the car, whose uniform and badges showed them to be policemen. Several women of the labouring class, and one or two travellers who might have been small local storekeepers, made up the rest of the company, with the exception of one young man in a corner by himself. It is with this man that we are concerned. Take a good look at him, for he is worth it.

He is a fresh-complexioned, middle-sized young man, not far, one would guess, from his thirtieth year. He has large, shrewd, humorous grey eyes which twinkle inquiringly from time to time as he looks round through his spectacles at the people about him. It is easy to see that he is of a sociable and possibly simple disposition, anxious to be friendly to all men. Anyone could pick him at once as gregarious in his habits and communicative in his nature, with a quick wit and a ready smile. And yet the man who studied him more closely might discern a certain firmness of jaw and grim tightness about the lips which would warn him that there were depths beyond, and that this pleasant, brown-haired young Irishman might conceivably leave his mark for good or evil upon any society to which he was introduced.

Having made one or two tentative remarks to the nearest miner, and received only short gruff replies, the traveller resigned himself to uncongenial silence, staring moodily out of the window at the fading landscape. It was not a cheering prospect. Through the growing gloom there pulsed the red glow of the furnaces on the sides of the hills. Great heaps of slag and dumps of cinders loomed up on each side, with the high shafts of the collieries towering above them. Huddled groups of mean wooden houses, the windows of which were beginning to outline themselves in light, were scattered here and there along the line, and the frequent halting-places were crowded with their swarthy inhabitants. The iron and coal valleys of the Vermissa district were no resorts for the leisured òr the cultured. Everywhere there were stern signs of the crudest battle of life, the rude work to be done, and the rude, strong workers who did it.

The young traveller gazed out into this dismal country with a face of mingled repulsion and interest, which showed that the scene was new to him. At intervals he drew from his pocket a bulky letter to which he referred, and on the margins of which he scribbled some notes. Once from the back of his waist he produced something which one would hardly have expected to find in the possession of so mild-mannered a man. It was a navy revolver of the largest size. As he turned it slantwise to the light, the glint upon the rims of the copper shells within the drum showed that it was fully loaded. He quickly restored it to his secret pocket, but not before it had been observed by a working man who had seated himself upon the adjoining bench.

"Halloa, mate!" said he. "You seem heeled and ready."

The young man smiled with an air of embarrassment.

"Yes," said he; "we need them sometimes in the place I come from."

"And where may that be?"

"I'm last from Chicago."

"A stranger in these parts?"

"Yes."

"You may find you need it here," said the workman.

"Ah! Is that so?" The young man seemed interested.

"Have you heard nothing of doings hereabouts?"

"Nothing out of the way."

"Why, I thought the country was full of it. You'll hear quick enough. What made you come here?"

" I heard there was always work for a willing man."

" Are you one of the Labour Union ? "

" Sure."

" Then you'll get your job, I guess. Have you any friends ? "

" Not yet, but I have the means of making them."

" How's that, then ? "

" I am one of the Ancient Order of Freemen. There's no town without a lodge, and where there is a lodge I'll find my friends."

The remark had a singular effect upon his companion. He glanced round suspiciously at the others in the car. The miners were still whispering among themselves. The two police officers were dozing. He came across, seated himself close to the young traveller, and held out his hand.

" Put it there," he said.

A hand-grip passed between the two.

" I see you speak the truth. But it's well to make certain."

He raised his right hand to his right eyebrow. The traveller at once raised his left hand to his left eyebrow.

" Dark nights are unpleasant," said the workman.

" Yes, for strangers to travel," the other answered.

" That's good enough. I'm Brother Scanlan, Lodge 341, Vermissa Valley. Glad to see you in these parts."

" Thank you. I'm Brother John McMurdo, Lodge 29, Chicago. Bodymaster, J. H. Scott. But I am in luck to meet a brother so early."

" Well, there are plenty of us about. You won't find the Order more flourishing anywhere in the States than right here in Vermissa Valley. But we could do with some lads like you. I can't understand a spry man of the Labour Union finding no work to do in Chicago."

" I found plenty of work to do," said McMurdo.

" Then why did you leave ? "

McMurdo nodded towards the policemen and smiled.

" I guess those chaps would be glad to know," he said.

Scanlan groaned sympathetically.

" In trouble ? " he asked, in a whisper.

" Deep."

" A penitentiary job ? "

" And the rest."

" Not a killing ? "

" It's early days to talk of such things," said McMurdo, with the air of a man who had been surprised into saying more than he intended. " I've my own good reason for leaving Chicago, and let that be enough for you. Who are you that you should take it on yourself to ask such things ? "

His grey eyes gleamed with sudden and dangerous anger from behind his glasses.

" All right, mate. No offence meant. The boys will think none the worse of you whatever you may have done. Where are you bound for now ? "

" To Vermissa."

" That's the third halt down the line. Where are you staying ? "

McMurdo took out an envelope and held it close to the murky oil lamp.

" Here is the address—Jacob Shafter, Sheridan Street. It's a boarding-house that was recommended by a man I knew in Chicago."

" Well, I don't know it, but Vermissa is out of my beat. I live at Hobson's Patch, and that's here where we are drawing up. But, say, there's one bit of advice I'll give you before we part. If you're in trouble in Vermissa, go straight to the Union House and see Boss McGinty. He is the bodymaster of Vermissa Lodge, and nothing can happen in these parts unless Black Jack McGinty wants it. So long, mate. Maybe we'll meet in lodge one of these evenings. But mind my words ; if you are in trouble go to Boss McGinty."

Scanlan descended, and McMurdo was left once again to his thoughts. Night had now fallen, and the flames of the frequent furnaces were roaring and leaping in the darkness. Against their lurid background dark figures were bending and straining, twisting and turning, with the motion of winch or of windlass, to the rhythm of an eternal clank and roar.

" I guess hell must look something like that," said a voice.

McMurdo turned and saw that one of the policemen had shifted in his seat and was staring out into the fiery waste.

" For that matter," said the other policeman, " I allow that hell must *be* something like that. If there are worse devils down yonder than some we could name, it's more than I'd expect. I guess you are new to this part, young man ? "

" Well, what if I am ? " McMurdo answered, in a surly voice.

" Just this, mister ; that I should advise you to be careful in choosing your friends. I don't think I'd begin with Mike Scanlan or his gang if I were you."

" What in thunder is it to you who are my friends ? " roared McMurdo, in a voice which brought every head in the carriage round to

"'HUSH, ON YOUR LIFE!' CRIED THE MINER, STANDING STILL IN HIS ALARM, AND GAZING
IN AMAZEMENT AT HIS COMPANION."

witness the altercation. "Did I ask you for your advice, or did you think me such a sucker that I couldn't move without it? You speak when you are spoken to, and by the Lord you'd have to wait a long time if it was me!"

He thrust out his face, and grinned at the patrolmen like a snarling dog.

The two policemen, heavy, good-natured men, were taken aback by the extraordinary vehemence with which their friendly advances had been rejected.

"No offence, stranger," said one. "It was a warning for your own good, seeing that you are, by your own showing, new to the place."

"I'm new to the place, but I'm not new to you and your kind," cried McMurdo, in a cold fury. "I guess you're the same in all places, shoving your advice in when nobody asks for it."

"Maybe we'll see more of you before very long," said one of the patrolmen, with a grin. "You're a real hand-picked one, if I am a judge."

"I was thinking the same," remarked the other. "I guess we may meet again."

"I'm not afraid of you, and don't you think it," cried McMurdo. "My name's Jack McMurdo—see? If you want me you'll find me at Jacob Shafter's, at Sheridan Street, Vermissa, so I'm not hiding from you, am I? Day or night I dare to look the like of you in the face. Don't make any mistake about that."

There was a murmur of sympathy and admiration from the miners at the dauntless demeanour of the new-comer, while the two policemen shrugged their shoulders and renewed a conversation between themselves. A few minutes later the train ran into the ill-lit depot and there was a general clearing, for Vermissa was far the largest township on the line. McMurdo picked up his leather grip-sack, and was about to start off into the darkness when one of the miners accosted him.

"By gosh, mate, you know how to speak to the cops," he said, in a voice of awe.

" It was grand to hear you. Let me carry your grip-sack and show you the road. I'm passing Shafter's on the way to my own shack."

There was a chorus of friendly "Good nights" from the other miners as they passed from the platform. Before ever he had set foot in it, McMurdo the turbulent had become a character in Vermissa.

The country had been a place of terror, but the township was in its way even more depressing. Down that long valley there was at least a certain gloomy grandeur in the huge fires and the clouds of drifting smoke, while the strength and industry of man found fitting monuments in the hills which he had spilled by the side of his monstrous excavations. But the town showed a dead level of mean ugliness and squalor. The broad street was churned up by the traffic into a horrible rutted paste of muddy snow. The side-walks were narrow and uneven. The numerous gas-lamps served only to show more clearly a long line of wooden houses, each with its veranda facing the street, unkempt and dirty. As they approached the centre of the town the scene was brightened by a row of well-lit stores, and even more by a cluster of liquor saloons and gaming-houses, in which the miners spent their hard-earned but generous wages.

" That's the Union House," said the guide, pointing to one saloon which rose almost to the dignity of being an hotel. " Jack McGinty is the Boss there."

" What sort of a man is he ? " asked McMurdo.

" What ! Have you never heard of the Boss ? "

" How could I have heard of him when you know that I am a stranger in these parts ? "

" Well, I thought his name was known right across the Union. It's been in the papers often enough."

" What for ? "

" Well "—the miner lowered his voice— " over the affairs."

" What affairs ? "

" Good Lord, mister, you are queer goods, if I may say it without offence. There's only one set of affairs that you'll hear of in these parts, and that's the affairs of the Scowrers."

" Why, I seem to have read of the Scowrers in Chicago. A gang of murderers, are they not ? "

" Hush, on your life ! " cried the miner, standing still in his alarm, and gazing in amazement at his companion. " Man, you won't live long in these parts if you speak in the open street like that. Many a man has had the life beaten out of him for less."

" Well, I know nothing about them. It's only what I have read."

" And I'm not saying that you have not read the truth." The man looked nervously round him as he spoke, peering into the shadows as if he feared to see some lurking danger. " If killing is murder, then God knows there is murder and to spare. But don't you dare to breathe the name of Jack McGinty in connection with it, stranger, for every whisper goes back to him, and he is not one that is likely to let it pass. Now, that's the house you're after — that one standing back from the street. You'll find old Jacob Shafter that runs it as honest a man as lives in this township."

" I thank you," said McMurdo, and shaking hands with his new acquaintance he plodded, his grip-sack in his hand, up the path which led to the dwelling-house, at the door of which he gave a resounding knock. It was opened at once by someone very different from what he had expected.

It was a woman, young and singularly beautiful. She was of the Swedish type, blonde and fair-haired, with the piquant contrast of a pair of beautiful dark eyes, with which she surveyed the stranger with surprise and a pleasing embarrassment which brought a wave of colour over her pale face. Framed in the bright light of the open doorway, it seemed to McMurdo that he had never seen a more beautiful picture, the more attractive for its contrast with the sordid and gloomy surroundings. A lovely violet growing upon one of those black slag-heaps of the mines would not have seemed more surprising. So entranced was he that he stood staring without a word, and it was she who broke the silence.

" I thought it was father," said she, with a pleasing little touch of a Swedish accent. " Did you come to see him ? He is down town. I expect him back every minute."

McMurdo continued to gaze at her in open admiration until her eyes dropped in confusion before this masterful visitor.

" No, miss," he said at last; " I'm in no hurry to see him. But your house was recommended to me for board. I thought it might suit me, and now I know it will."

" You are quick to make up your mind," said she, with a smile.

" Anyone but a blind man could do as much," the other answered.

She laughed at the compliment.

" Come right in, sir," she said. " I'm Miss Ettie Shafter, Mr. Shafter's daughter. My mother's dead, and I run the house. You can sit down by the stove in the front room until father comes along. Ah, here he is ; so you can fix things with him right away."

A heavy, elderly man came plodding up the path. In a few words McMurdo explained his business. A man of the name of Murphy had given him the address in Chicago. He in turn had had it from someone else. Old Shafter was quite ready. The stranger made no bones about terms, agreed at once to every condition, and was apparently fairly flush of money. For twelve dollars a week, paid in advance, he was to have board and lodging. So it was that McMurdo, the self-confessed fugitive from justice, took up his abode under the roof of the Shafters, the first step which was to lead to so long and dark a train of events, ending in a far distant land.

(To be continued.)

The
VALLEY of FEAR

A NEW
SHERLOCK HOLMES
STORY

By

A. CONAN DOYLE

Illustrated by FRANK WILES

SYNOPSIS OF PREVIOUS INSTALMENTS.

PART I.—THE TRAGEDY OF BIRLSTONE.

The opening chapters of this new and thrilling adventure of Sherlock Holmes described the receipt by Holmes of a cipher message, from which he deduces that some devilry is intended against a man named Douglas, a rich country gentleman living at the Manor House, Birlstone, in Sussex, and that the danger is a pressing one. Almost as soon as he has deciphered the message he is visited by Inspector MacDonald, of Scotland Yard, who brings the news that Mr. Douglas has been murdered that morning.

Holmes, Dr. Watson, and the inspector proceed to the scene of the tragedy, where they are met by Mr. White Mason, the chief Sussex detective. The murdered man had been horribly injured, while lying across his chest was a curious weapon—a shot-gun with the barrel sawn off a foot in front of the triggers. Near him was found a card with the initials "V. V." and the number "341" scrawled on it in ink, and about half-way up the forearm was a curious design— a branded triangle inside a circle. His wedding-ring had been removed and the ring above it replaced.

There is no clue to the murderer except a bloody footprint on the window-sill, and he had apparently made his escape by wading across the moat. Holmes is much struck by the fact that one of Douglas's dumb-bells is missing.

Cecil Barker, Douglas's most intimate friend, is considerably flustered while being cross-examined by the detectives, and confesses that Douglas had been jealous on account of his attentions to Mrs. Douglas. Holmes ascertains from Ames, the butler, that on the previous evening Barker was wearing a pair of bedroom slippers which were stained with blood, and, on comparing them with the footprints on the window-sill, finds that they correspond.

Holmes gives Watson his reasons for believing that Mrs. Douglas and Barker know all about the murder. He advises the other detectives to abandon the case and asks them to meet him that same evening, when he promises they shall share everything he knows. Meanwhile the detectives send a note to Barker saying that they intend to drain the moat on the morrow.

On meeting in the evening they hide near the moat, from which they see Barker drag a large bundle. All thereupon rush into the house, and Holmes extracts from the bundle a pair of boots, a knife, and some clothing of American make—and the missing dumb-bell! Holmes's deductions from this discovery cause much astonishment, which is increased when he recommends that *Mr. Douglas* be asked to tell his own story.

At Holmes's words a man seemed to emerge from the wall. It is Douglas himself, who explains that he has been cooped up since killing, in self-defence, a man who had tried to murder him two days previously. The fact that this man—whom he had known in America, and who had been searching for him for years—was similar in build to himself gave him an idea. He would let it be thought that he (Douglas) had been killed and that the murderer had escaped. The dead man was dressed in Douglas's clothes, and

the fact that each bore a similar brand on his arm made the deception easier. Barker then did his best to help his friend by providing misleading clues, with what result we know.

During his enforced hiding Douglas had written an account of the events leading up to the tragedy. This he hands to Dr. Watson, saying, "There's the story of the Valley of Fear!"

PART II—THE SCOWRERS.

The scene now changes to America some twenty years earlier. In a West-bound train from Chicago John McMurdo, a member of the Ancient Order of Freemen, meets Brother Scanlan, a fellow-member of the Order. McMurdo—who, it appears, is fleeing from justice—tells Scanlan he is bound for Vermissa, where he intends to put up at a boarding-house kept by Jacob Shafter.

CHAPTER II.
THE BODYMASTER.

cMURDO was a man who made his mark quickly. Wherever he was the folk around soon knew it. Within a week he had become infinitely the most important person at Shafter's. There were ten or a dozen boarders there, but they were honest foremen or commonplace clerks from the stores, of a very different calibre to the young Irishman. Of an evening when they gathered together his joke was always the readiest, his conversation the brightest, and his song the best. He was a born boon companion, with a magnetism which drew good humour from all around him. And yet he showed again and again, as he had shown in the railway-carriage, a capacity for sudden, fierce anger which compelled the respect and even fear of those who met him. For the law, too, and all connected with it, he exhibited a bitter contempt which delighted some and alarmed others of his fellow-boarders.

From the first he made it evident, by his open admiration, that the daughter of the house had won his heart from the instant that he had set eyes upon her beauty and her grace. He was no backward suitor. On the second day he told her that he loved her, and from then onwards he repeated the same story with an absolute disregard of what she might say to discourage him.

"Someone else!" he would cry. "Well, the worse luck for someone else! Let him look out for himself! Am I to lose my life's chance and all my heart's desire for someone else? You can keep on saying 'No,' Ettie! The day will come when you will say 'Yes,' and I'm young enough to wait."

He was a dangerous suitor, with his glib Irish tongue and his pretty, coaxing ways. There was about him also that glamour of experience and of mystery which attracts a woman's interest and finally her love. He could talk of the sweet valleys of County Monaghan from which he came, of the lovely distant island, the low hills and green meadows of which seemed the more beautiful when imagination viewed them from this place of grime and snow. Then he was versed in the life of the cities of the North, of Detroit and the lumber-camps of Michigan, of Buffalo, and finally of Chicago, where he had worked in a saw-mill. And afterwards came the hint of romance, the feeling that strange things had happened to him in that great city, so strange and so intimate that they might not be spoken of. He spoke wistfully of a sudden leaving, a breaking of old ties, a flight into a strange world ending in this dreary valley, and Ettie listened, her dark eyes gleaming with pity and with sympathy— those two qualities which may turn so rapidly and so naturally to love.

McMurdo had obtained a temporary job as a bookkeeper, for he was a well-educated man. This kept him out most of the day, and he had not found occasion yet to report himself to the head of the Lodge of the Ancient Order of Freemen. He was reminded of his omission, however, by a visit one evening from Mike Scanlan, the fellow-member whom he had met in the train. Scanlan, a small, sharp-faced, nervous, black-eyed man, seemed glad to see him once more. After a glass or two of whisky, he broached the object of his visit.

"Say, McMurdo," said he, "I remembered your address, so I made bold to call. I'm surprised that you've not reported to the bodymaster. What's amiss that you've not seen Boss McGinty yet ? "

" Well, I had to find a job. I have been busy."

" You must find time for him if you have none for anything else. Good Lord, man, you're mad not to have been down to the Union House and registered your name the first morning after you came here ! If you fall foul of him—well, you *mustn't*—that's all ! "

McMurdo showed mild surprise.

" I've been a member of Lodge for over two years, Scanlan, but I never heard that duties were so pressing as all that."

" Maybe not in Chicago ! "

" Well, it's the same society here."

" Is it ? " Scanlan looked at him long and fixedly. There was something sinister in his eyes.

" Is it not ? "

" You'll tell me that in a month's time. I hear you had a talk with the patrolmen after I left the train."

" How did you know that ? "

" Oh, it got about—things do get about for good and for bad in this district."

" Well, yes. I told the hounds what I thought of them."

" By the Lord, you'll be a man after McGinty's heart ! "

" What—does he hate the police, too ? " Scanlan burst out laughing.

" You go and see him, my lad," said he, as he took his leave. " It's not the police, but you, that he'll hate if you don't ! Now, take a friend's advice and go at once ! "

It chanced that on the same evening McMurdo had another more pressing interview which urged him in the same direction. It may have been that his attentions to Ettie had been more evident than before, or that they had gradually obtruded themselves into the slow mind of his good Swedish host ; but, whatever the cause, the boarding-house-keeper beckoned the young man into his private room and started on to the subject without any circumlocution.

" It seems to me, mister," said he, " dat you are gettin' set on my Ettie. Ain't dat so, or am I wrong ? "

" Yes, that is so," the young man answered.

" Well, I vant to tell you right now dat it ain't no manner of use. There's someone slipped in afore you."

" She told me so."

" Well, you can lay dat she told you truth ! But did she tell you who it vas ? "

" No ; I asked her, but she would not tell."

" I dare say not, the leetle baggage. Perhaps she did not vish to vrighten you avay."

" Frighten ! " McMurdo was on fire in a moment.

" Ah, yes, my vriend ! You need not be ashamed to be vrightened of him. It is Teddy Baldwin."

" And who the devil is he ? "

" He is a Boss of Scowrers."

" Scowrers ! I've heard of them before. It's Scowrers here and Scowrers there, and always in a whisper ! What are you all afraid of ? Who *are* the Scowrers ? "

The boarding-house-keeper instinctively sank his voice, as everyone did who talked about that terrible society.

" The Scowrers," said he, " are the Ancient Order of Freemen."

The young man started.

"Why, I am a member of that Order myself."

" You ! I would never have had you in my house if I had known it—not if you vere to pay me a hundred dollar a veek."

" What's amiss with the Order ? It's for charity and good-fellowship. The rules say so."

" Maybe in some places. Not here ! "

" What is it here ? "

" It's a murder society, dat's vat it is." McMurdo laughed incredulously.

" How do you prove that ? " he asked.

" Prove it ! Are there not vifty murders to prove it ? Vat about Milman and Van Shorst, and the Nicholson vamily, and old Mr. Hyam, and little Billy James, and the others ? Prove it ! Is dere a man or a voman in dis valley dat does not know it ? "

" See here ! " said McMurdo, earnestly. " I want you to take back what you've said or else to make it good. One or the other you must do before I quit this room. Put yourself in my place. Here am I, a stranger in the town. I belong to a society that I know only as an innocent one. You'll find it through the length and breadth of the States, but always as an innocent one. Now, when I am counting upon joining it here, you tell me that it is the same as a murder society called the ' Scowrers.' I guess you owe me either an apology or else an explanation, Mr. Shafter."

" I can but tell you vat the whole vorld knows, mister. The bosses of the one are the bosses of the other. If you offend the one, it is the other dat vill strike you. We have proved it too often."

" That's just gossip ! I want proof ! " said McMurdo.

" If you live here long you vill get your

"MAYBE YOU ARE IN A HUMOUR FOR A FIGHT, MR. BOARDER?"

"'THAT I AM,' CRIED MCMURDO, SPRINGING TO HIS FEET. 'YOU NEVER SAID A MORE WELCOME WORD.'"

proof. But I vorget dat you are yourself one of dem. You vill soon be as bad as the rest. But you will find other lodgings, mister. I cannot have you here. Is it not bad enough dat one of these people come courting my Ettie, and dat I dare not turn him down, but dat I should have another for my boarder? Yes, indeed, you shall not sleep here after to-night!"

So McMurdo found himself under sentence of banishment both from his comfortable quarters and from the girl whom he loved. He found her alone in the sitting-room that same evening, and he poured his troubles into her ear.

"Sure, your father is after giving me notice," he said. "It's little I would care if it was just my room; but indeed, Ettie, though it's only a week that I've known you, you are the very breath of life to me, and I can't live without you."

"Oh, hush, Mr. McMurdo! Don't speak so!" said the girl. "I have told you, have I not, that you are too late? There is another, and if I have not promised to marry him at once, at least I can promise no one else."

"Suppose I had been first, Ettie, would I have had a chance?"

The girl sank her face into her hands.

"I wish to Heaven that you *had* been first," she sobbed.

McMurdo was down on his knees before her in an instant.

"For God's sake, Ettie, let it stand at that!" he cried. "Will you ruin your life and my own for the sake of this promise? Follow your heart, acushla! 'Tis a safer guide than any promise given before you knew what it was that you were saying."

He had seized Ettie's white hand between his own strong brown ones.

"Say that you will be mine and we will face it out together."

"Not here?"

"Yes, here."

"No, no, Jack!" His arms were round her now. "It could not be here. Could you take me away?"

A struggle passed for a moment over McMurdo's face, but it ended by setting like granite.

"No, here," he said. "I'll hold you against the world, Ettie, right here where we are!"

"Why should we not leave together?"

"No, Ettie, I can't leave here."

"But why?"

"I'd never hold my head up again if I felt that I had been driven out. Besides, what is there to be afraid of? Are we not free folk

in a free country? If you love me and I you, who will dare to come between?"

"You don't know, Jack. You've been here too short a time. You don't know this Baldwin. You don't know McGinty and his Scowrers."

"No, I don't know them, and I don't fear them, and I don't believe in them!" said McMurdo. "I've lived among rough men, my darling, and instead of fearing them it has always ended that they have feared me —always, Ettie. It's mad on the face of it! If these men, as your father says, have done crime after crime in the valley, and if everyone knows them by name, how comes it that none are brought to justice? You answer me that, Ettie!"

"Because no witness dares to appear against them. He would not live a month if he did. Also because they have always their own men to swear that the accused one was far from the scene of the crime. But surely, Jack, you must have read all this! I had understood that every paper in the States was writing about it."

"Well, I have read something, it is true, but I had thought it was a story. Maybe these men have some reason in what they do. Maybe they are wronged and have no other way to help themselves."

"Oh, Jack, don't let me hear you speak so! That is how he speaks—the other one!"

"Baldwin—he speaks like that, does he?"

"And that is why I loathe him so. Oh, Jack, now I can tell you the truth, I loathe him with all my heart; but I fear him also. I fear him for myself, but, above all, I fear him for father. I know that some great sorrow would come upon us if I dared to say what I really felt. That is why I have put him off with half-promises. It was in real truth our only hope. But if you would fly with me, Jack, we could take father with us and live for ever far from the power of these wicked men."

Again there was the struggle upon McMurdo's face, and again it set like granite.

"No harm shall come to you, Ettie—nor to your father either. As to wicked men, I expect you may find that I am as bad as the worst of them before we're through."

"No, no, Jack! I would trust you anywhere."

McMurdo laughed bitterly.

"Good Lord, how little you know of me! Your innocent soul, my darling, could not even guess what is passing in mine. But, halloa, who's the visitor?"

The door had opened suddenly and a young

fellow came swaggering in with the air of one who is the master. He was a handsome, dashing young man of about the same age and build as McMurdo himself. Under his broad-brimmed black felt hat, which he had not troubled to remove, a handsome face, with fierce, domineering eyes and a curved, hawk-bill of a nose, looked savagely at the pair who sat by the stove.

Ettie had jumped to her feet, full of confusion and alarm.

" I'm glad to see you, Mr. Baldwin," said she. " You're earlier than I had thought. Come and sit down."

Baldwin stood with his hands on his hips looking at McMurdo.

" Who is this ? " he asked, curtly.

" It's a friend of mine, Mr. Baldwin—a new boarder here. Mr. McMurdo, can I introduce you to Mr. Baldwin ? "

The young men nodded in a surly fashion to each other.

" Maybe Miss Ettie has told you how it is with us ? " said Baldwin.

" I didn't understand that there was any relation between you."

" Did you not ? Well, you can understand it now. You can take it from me that this young lady is mine, and you'll find it a very fine evening for a walk."

" Thank you, I am in no humour for a walk."

" Are you not ? " The man's savage eyes were blazing with anger. " Maybe you are in a humour for a fight, Mr. Boarder ? "

" That I am," cried McMurdo, springing to his feet. " You never said a more welcome word."

" For God's sake, Jack ! Oh, for God's sake ! " cried poor, distracted Ettie. " Oh, Jack, Jack, he will do you a mischief ! "

" Oh, it's ' Jack,' is it ? " said Baldwin, with an oath. " You've come to that already, have you ? "

" Oh, Ted, be reasonable—be kind ! For my sake, Ted, if ever you loved me, be great-hearted and forgiving ! "

" I think, Ettie, that if you were to leave us alone we could get this thing settled," said McMurdo, quietly. " Or maybe, Mr. Baldwin, you will take a turn down the street with me. It's a fine evening, and there's some open ground beyond the next block."

" I'll get even with you without needing to dirty my hands," said his enemy. " You'll wish you had never set foot in this house before I am through with you."

" No time like the present," cried McMurdo.

" I'll choose my own time, mister. You can leave the time to me. See here ! " He suddenly rolled up his sleeve and showed upon his forearm a peculiar sign which appeared to have been branded there. It was a circle with a cross within it. " D'you know what that means ? "

" I neither know nor care ! "

" Well, you will know. I'll promise you that. You won't be much older either. Perhaps Miss Ettie can tell you something about it. As to you, Ettie, you'll come back to me on your knees. D'ye hear, girl ? On your knees ! And then I'll tell you what your punishment may be. You've sowed—and, by the Lord, I'll see that you reap ! " He glared at them both in fury. Then he turned upon his heel, and an instant later the outer door had banged behind him.

For a few moments McMurdo and the girl stood in silence. Then she threw her arms around him.

" Oh, Jack, how brave you were ! But it is no use—you must fly ! To-night—Jack—to-night ! It's your only hope. He will have your life. I read it in his horrible eyes. What chance have you against a dozen of them, with Boss McGinty and all the power of the Lodge behind them ? "

McMurdo disengaged her hands, kissed her, and gently pushed her back into a chair.

" There, acushla, there ! Don't be disturbed or fear for me. I'm a Freeman myself. I'm after telling your father about it. Maybe I am no better than the others, so don't make a saint of me. Perhaps you hate me, too, now that I've told you as much."

" Hate you, Jack ! While life lasts I could never do that. I've heard that there is no harm in being a Freeman anywhere but here, so why should I think the worse of you for that ? But if you are a Freeman, Jack, why should you not go down and make a friend of Boss McGinty ? Oh, hasten, Jack, hasten ! Get your word in first, or the hounds will be on your trail."

" I was thinking the same thing," said McMurdo. " I'll go right now and fix it. You can tell your father that I'll sleep here to-night and find some other quarters in the morning."

The bar of McGinty's saloon was crowded as usual, for it was the favourite lounge of all the rougher elements of the town. The man was popular, for he had a rough, jovial disposition which formed a mask, covering a great deal which lay behind it. But, apart from this popularity, the fear in which he was held throughout the township, and, indeed, down the whole thirty miles of the valley and past the mountains upon either side of it, was enough in itself to fill his bar, for none could afford to neglect his goodwill.

Besides those secret powers which it was universally believed that he exercised in so pitiless a fashion, he was a high public official, a municipal councillor, and a commissioner for roads, elected to the office through the votes of the ruffians who in turn expected to receive favours at his hands. Rates and taxes were enormous, the public works were notoriously neglected, the accounts were slurred over by bribed auditors, and the decent citizen was terrorized into paying public blackmail, and holding his tongue lest some worse thing befall him. Thus it was that, year by year, Boss McGinty's diamond pins became more obtrusive, his gold chains more weighty across a more gorgeous vest, and his saloon stretched farther and farther, until it threatened to absorb one whole side of the Market Square.

McMurdo pushed open the swinging door of the saloon and made his way amid the crowd of men within, through an atmosphere which was blurred with tobacco smoke and heavy with the smell of spirits. The place was brilliantly lighted, and the huge, heavily-gilt mirrors upon every wall reflected and multiplied the garish illumination. There were several bar-tenders in their shirt-sleeves hard at work, mixing drinks for the loungers who fringed the broad, heavily-metalled counter. At the far end, with his body resting upon the bar, and a cigar stuck at an acute angle from the corner of his mouth, there stood a tall, strong, heavily-built man, who could be none other than the famous McGinty himself. He was a black-maned giant, bearded to the cheek-bones, and with a shock of raven hair which fell to his collar. His complexion was as swarthy as that of an Italian, and his eyes were of a strange dead black, which, combined with a slight squint, gave them a particularly sinister appearance. All else in the man, his noble proportions, his fine features, and his frank bearing, fitted in with that jovial man-to-man manner which he affected. Here, one would say, is a bluff, honest fellow, whose heart would be sound, however rude his outspoken words might seem. It was only when those dead dark eyes, deep and remorseless, were turned upon a man that he shrank within himself, feeling that he was face to face with an infinite possibility of latent evil, with a strength and courage and cunning behind it which made it a thousand times more deadly.

Having had a good look at his man, McMurdo elbowed his way forward with his usual careless audacity, and pushed himself through the little group of courtiers who were fawning upon the powerful Boss, laughing uproariously at the smallest of his jokes. The young stranger's bold grey eyes looked back fearlessly through their glasses at the deadly black ones which turned sharply upon him.

"Well, young man, I can't call your face to mind."

"I'm new here, Mr. McGinty."

"You are not so new that you can't give a gentleman his proper title."

"He's Councillor McGinty, young man," said a voice from the group.

"I'm sorry, Councillor. I'm strange to the ways of the place. But I was advised to see you."

"Well, you see me. This is all there is. What d'you think of me?"

"Well, it's early days. If your heart is as big as your body, and your soul as fine as your face, then I'd ask for nothing better," said McMurdo.

"By gosh, you've got an Irish tongue in your head, anyhow," cried the saloon-keeper, not quite certain whether to humour this audacious visitor or to stand upon his dignity. "So you are good enough to pass my appearance?"

"Sure," said McMurdo.

"And you were told to see me?"

"I was."

"And who told you?"

"Brother Scanlan, of Lodge 341, Vermissa. I drink your health, Councillor, and to our better acquaintance." He raised a glass with which he had been served to his lips and elevated his little finger as he drank it.

McGinty, who had been watching him narrowly, raised his thick black eyebrows.

"Oh, it's like that, is it?" said he. "I'll have to look a bit closer into this, Mister——"

"McMurdo."

"A bit closer, Mr. McMurdo, for we don't take folk on trust in these parts, nor believe all we're told neither. Come in here for a moment, behind the bar."

There was a small room there lined round with barrels. McGinty carefully closed the door, and then seated himself on one of them, biting thoughtfully on his cigar, and surveying his companion with those disquieting eyes. For a couple of minutes he sat in complete silence.

McMurdo bore the inspection cheerfully, one hand in his coat-pocket, the other twisting his brown moustache. Suddenly McGinty stooped and produced a wicked-looking revolver.

" WELL, YOUNG MAN, I CAN'T CALL YOUR FACE TO MIND."

"See here, my joker," said he; "if I thought you were playing any game on us, it would be a short shrift for you."

"This is a strange welcome," McMurdo answered, with some dignity, "for the body-master of a Lodge of Freemen to give to a stranger brother."

"Aye, but it's just that same that you have to prove," said McGinty, "and God help you if you fail. Where were you made?"

"Lodge 29, Chicago."

"When?"

"June 24th, 1872."

"What bodymaster?"

"James H. Scott."

"Who is your district ruler?"

"Bartholomew Wilson."

"Hum! You seem glib enough in your tests. What are you doing here?"

"Working, the same as you, but a poorer job."

"You have your back answer quick enough."

"Yes, I was always quick of speech."

"Are you quick of action?"

"I have had that name among those who knew me best."

"Well, we may try you sooner than you think. Have you heard anything of the Lodge in these parts?"

"I've heard that it takes a man to be a brother."

"True for you, Mr. McMurdo. Why did you leave Chicago?"

"I'm hanged if I tell you that."

McGinty opened his eyes. He was not used to being answered in such fashion, and it amused him.

"Why won't you tell me?"

"Because no brother may tell another a lie."

"Then the truth is too bad to tell?"

"You can put it that way if you like."

"See here, mister; you can't expect me, as bodymaster, to pass into the Lodge a man for whose past he can't answer."

McMurdo looked puzzled. Then he took a worn newspaper-cutting from an inner pocket.

"You wouldn't squeal on a fellow?" said he.

"I'll wipe my hand across your face if you say such words to me," cried McGinty, hotly.

"You are right, Councillor," said McMurdo, meekly. "I should apologize. I spoke without thought. Well, I know that I am safe in your hands. Look at that cutting."

McGinty glanced his eyes over the account of the shooting of one Jonas Pinto, in the Lake Saloon, Market Street, Chicago, in the New Year week of '74.

"Your work?" he asked, as he handed back the paper.

McMurdo nodded.

"Why did you shoot him?"

"I was helping Uncle Sam to make dollars. Maybe mine were not as good gold as his, but they looked as well and were cheaper to make. This man Pinto helped me to shove the queer——"

"To do what?"

"Well, it means to pass the dollars out into circulation. Then he said he would split. Maybe he did split. I didn't wait to see. I just killed him and lighted out for the coal country."

"Why the coal country?"

"'Cause I'd read in the papers that they weren't too particular in those parts."

McGinty laughed.

"You were first a coiner and then a murderer, and you came to these parts because you thought you'd be welcome?"

"That's about the size of it," McMurdo answered.

"Well, I guess you'll go far. Say, can you make those dollars yet?"

McMurdo took half-a-dozen from his pocket. "Those never passed the Washington mint," said he.

"You don't say!" McGinty held them to the light in his enormous hand, which was as hairy as a gorilla's. "I can see no difference! Gosh, you'll be a mighty useful brother, I'm thinking. We can do with a bad man or two amongst us, friend McMurdo, for there are times when we have to take our own part. We'd soon be against the wall if we didn't shove back at those that were pushing us."

"Well, I guess I'll do my share of shoving with the rest of the boys."

"You seem to have a good nerve. You didn't flinch when I put this pistol on you."

"It was not me that was in danger."

"Who, then?"

"It was you, Councillor." McMurdo drew a cocked pistol from the side-pocket of his pea-jacket. "I was covering you all the time. I guess my shot would have been as quick as yours."

McGinty flushed an angry red and then burst into a roar of laughter.

"By gosh!" said he. "Say, we've had no such holy terror come to hand this many a year. I reckon the Lodge will learn to be proud of you. Well, what the deuce do you want? And can't I speak alone with a gentleman for five minutes but you must butt in upon us?"

"HIS HAND CLOSED ROUND THE OTHER'S NECK AND HE HURLED HIM ACROSS ONE OF THE
BARRELS."

The bar-tender stood abashed.

"I'm sorry, Councillor, but it's Mr. Ted Baldwin. He says he must see you this very minute."

The message was unnecessary, for the set, cruel face of the man himself was looking over the servant's shoulder. He pushed the bar-tender out and closed the door on him.

"So," said he, with a furious glance at McMurdo, "you got here first, did you? I've a word to say to you, Councillor, about this man."

"Then say it here and now, before my face," cried McMurdo.

"I'll say it at my own time, in my own way."

"Tut, tut!" said McGinty, getting off his barrel. "This will never do. We have a new brother here, Baldwin, and it's not for us to greet him in such a fashion. Hold out your hand, man, and make it up."

"Never!" cried Baldwin, in a fury.

"I've offered to fight him if he thinks I have wronged him," said McMurdo. "I'll fight him with fists, or, if that won't satisfy him, I'll fight him any other way he chooses. Now I'll leave it to you, Councillor, to judge between us as a bodymaster should."

"What is it, then?"

"A young lady. She's free to choose for herself."

"Is she?" cried Baldwin.

"As between two brothers of the Lodge, I should say that she was," said the Boss.

"Oh, that's your ruling, is it?"

"Yes, it is, Ted Baldwin," said McGinty, with a wicked stare. "Is it you that would dispute it?"

"You would throw over one that has stood by you five years in favour of a man that you never saw before in your life? You're not bodymaster for life, Jack McGinty, and, by God, when next it comes to a vote——"

The Councillor sprang at him like a tiger. His hand closed round the other's neck and he hurled him back across one of the barrels. In his mad fury he would have squeezed the life out of him if McMurdo had not interfered.

"Easy, Councillor! For Heaven's sake, go easy!" he cried, as he dragged him back.

McGinty released his hold, and Baldwin, cowed and shaken, gasping for breath, and shivering in every limb, as one who has looked over the very edge of death, sat up on the barrel over which he had been hurled.

"You've been asking for it this many a day, Ted Baldwin. Now you've got it," cried McGinty, his huge chest rising and falling.

"Maybe you think if I were voted down from bodymaster you would find yourself in my shoes. It's for the Lodge to say that. But so long as I am the chief, I'll have no man lift his voice against me or my rulings."

"I have nothing against you," mumbled Baldwin, feeling his throat.

"Well, then," cried the other, relapsing in a moment into a bluff joviality, "we are all good friends again, and there's an end of the matter."

He took a bottle of champagne down from the shelf and twisted out the cork.

"See now," he continued, as he filled three high glasses, "let us drink the quarrelling toast of the Lodge. After that, as you know, there can be no bad blood between us. Now, then, the left hand on the apple of my throat, I say to you, Ted Baldwin, what is the offence, sir?"

"The clouds are heavy," answered Baldwin.

"But they will for ever brighten."

"And this I swear."

The men drank their wine, and the same ceremony was performed between Baldwin and McMurdo.

"There," cried McGinty, rubbing his hands, "that's the end of the black blood. You come under Lodge discipline if it goes farther, and that's a heavy hand in these parts, as Brother Baldwin knows, and as you will very soon find out, Brother McMurdo, if you ask for trouble."

"Faith, I'd be slow to do that," said McMurdo. He held out his hand to Baldwin. "I'm quick to quarrel and quick to forgive. It's my hot Irish blood, they tell me. But it's over for me, and I bear no grudge."

Baldwin had to take the proffered hand, for the baleful eye of the terrible Boss was upon him. But his sullen face showed how little the words of the other had moved him.

McGinty clapped them both on the shoulders.

"Tut! These girls, these girls!" he cried. "To think that the same petticoats should come between two of my boys. It's the devil's own luck. Well, it's the colleen inside of them that must settle the question, for it's outside the jurisdiction of a bodymaster, and the Lord be praised for that. We have enough on us, without the women as well. You'll have to be affiliated to Lodge 341, Brother McMurdo. We have our own ways and methods, different to Chicago. Saturday night is our meeting, and if you come then we'll make you free for ever of the Vermissa Valley."

The VALLEY of FEAR

A NEW SHERLOCK HOLMES STORY

By

A. CONAN DOYLE

Illustrated by FRANK WILES

PART II.
THE SCOWRERS.

CHAPTER III.
LODGE 341, VERMISSA.

ON the day following the evening which had contained so many exciting events McMurdo moved his lodgings from old Jacob Shafter's and took up his quarters at the Widow MacNamara's, on the extreme outskirts of the town. Scanlan, his original acquaintance aboard the train, had occasion shortly afterwards to move into Vermissa, and the two lodged together. There was no other boarder, and the hostess was an easy-going old Irishwoman who left them to themselves, so that they had a freedom for speech and action welcome to men who had secrets in common. Shafter had relented to the extent of letting McMurdo come to his meals there when he liked, so that his intercourse with Ettie was by no means broken. On the contrary, it drew closer and

more intimate as the weeks went by. In his bedroom at his new abode McMurdo felt it to be safe to take out the coining moulds, and under many a pledge of secrecy a number of the brothers from the Lodge were allowed to come in and see them, each of them carrying away in his pocket some examples of the false money, so cunningly struck that there was never the slightest difficulty or danger in passing it. Why, with such a wonderful art at his command, McMurdo should condescend to work at all was a perpetual mystery to his companions, though he made it clear to anyone who asked him that if he lived without any visible means it would very quickly bring the police upon his track.

One policeman was, indeed, after him already, but the incident, as luck would have it, did the adventurer a great deal more good than harm. After the first introduction there were few evenings when he did not find his way to McGinty's saloon, there to make closer acquaintance with "the boys," which was the jovial title by which the dangerous gang who infested the place were known to each other. His dashing manner and fearlessness of speech made him a favourite with them all, while the rapid and scientist way in which he polished off his antagonist in an "all in" bar-room scrap earned the respect of that rough community. Another incident, however, raised him even higher in their estimation.

Just at the crowded hour one night the door opened and a man entered with the quiet blue uniform and peaked cap of the Coal and Iron Police. This was a special body raised by the railways and colliery owners to supplement the efforts of the ordinary civil police, who were perfectly helpless in the face of the organized ruffianism which terrorized the district. There was a hush as he entered, and many a curious glance was cast at him, but the relations between policemen and criminals are peculiar in the States, and McGinty himself, standing behind his counter, showed no surprise when the inspector enrolled himself among his customers.

"A straight whisky, for the night is bitter," said the police-officer. "I don't think we have met before, Councillor?"

"You'll be the new captain?" said McGinty.

"That's so. We're looking to you, Councillor, and to the other leading citizens, to help us in upholding law and order in this township. Captain Marvin is my name—of the Coal and Iron."

"We'd do better without you, Captain Marvin," said McGinty, coldly. "For we have our own police of the township, and no need for any imported goods. What are you but the paid tool of the men of capital, hired by them to club or to shoot your poorer fellow-citizens?"

"Well, well, we won't argue about that," said the police-officer, good-humouredly. "I expect we all do our duty same as we see it, but we can't all see it the same." He had drunk off his glass and had turned to go, when his eyes fell upon the face of Jack McMurdo, who was scowling at his elbow. "Halloa! halloa!" he cried, looking him up and down. "Here's an old acquaintance."

McMurdo shrank away from him.

"I was never a friend to you nor any other cursed copper in my life," said he.

"An acquaintance isn't always a friend," said the police captain, grinning. "You're Jack McMurdo of Chicago, right enough, and don't you deny it."

McMurdo shrugged his shoulders.

"I'm not denying it," said he. "D'ye think I'm ashamed of my own name?"

"You've got good cause to be, anyhow."

"What the devil d'you mean by that?" he roared, with his fists clenched.

"No, no, Jack; bluster won't do with me. I was an officer in Chicago before ever I came to this darned coal-bunker, and I know a Chicago crook when I see one."

McMurdo's face fell.

"Don't tell me that you're Marvin of the Chicago Central!" he cried.

"Just that same old Teddy Marvin, at your service. We haven't forgotten the shooting of Jonas Pinto up there."

"I never shot him."

"Did you not? That's good impartial evidence, ain't it? Well, his death came in uncommon handy for you, or they would have had you for shoving the queer. Well, we can let that be bygones, for, between you and me —and perhaps I'm going farther than my duty in saying it—they could get no clear case against you, and Chicago's open to you to-morrow."

"I'm very well where I am."

"Well, I've given you the office, and you're a sulky dog not to thank me for it."

"Well, I suppose you mean well, and I do thank you," said McMurdo, in no very gracious manner.

"It's mum with me so long as I see you living on the straight," said the captain. "But, by gum, if you get off on the cross after this it's another story! So good-night to you—and good night, Councillor."

He left the bar-room, but not before he had created a local hero. McMurdo's deeds in far Chicago had been whispered before. He had put off all questions with a smile as one who did not wish to have greatness thrust upon him. But now the thing was officially confirmed. The bar-loafers crowded round him and shook him heartily by the hand. He was free of the community from that time on. He could drink hard and show little trace of it, but that evening, had his mate Scanlan not been at hand to lead him home, the fêted hero would surely have spent his night under the bar.

On a Saturday night McMurdo was introduced to the Lodge. He had thought to pass in without ceremony as being an initiate of Chicago; but there were particular rites in Vermissa of which they were proud, and these had to be undergone by every postulant. The assembly met in a large room reserved for such purposes at the Union House. Some sixty members assembled at Vermissa, but

"I WAS AN OFFICER IN CHICAGO BEFORE EVER I CAME TO THIS DARNED COAL-BUNKER, AND I KNOW A CHICAGO CROOK WHEN I SEE ONE."

that by no means represented the full strength of the organization, for there were several other lodges in the valley, and others across the mountains on either side, who exchanged members when any serious business was afoot, so that a crime might be done by men who were strangers to the locality. Altogether, there were not fewer than five hundred scattered over the coal district.

In the bare assembly room the men were gathered round a long table. At the side was a second one laden with bottles and glasses, on which some members of the company were already turning their eyes. McGinty sat at the head with a flat black velvet cap upon his shock of tangled black hair and a coloured purple stole round his neck, so that he seemed to be a priest presiding over some diabolical ritual. To right and left of him were the higher Lodge officials, the cruel, hand-some face of Ted Baldwin among them. Each of these wore some scarf or medallion as emblem of his office. They were, for the most part, men of mature age, but the rest of the company consisted of young fellows from eighteen to twenty-five, the ready and capable agents who carried out the commands of their seniors. Among the older men were many whose features showed the tigerish, lawless souls within, but looking at the rank and file it was difficult to believe that these eager and open-faced young fellows were in very truth a dangerous gang of murderers, whose minds had suffered such complete moral per-version that they took a horrible pride in their proficiency at the business, and looked with the deepest respect at the man who had the reputation for making what they called a "clean job." To their contorted natures it had become a spirited and chivalrous thing to volunteer for service against some man who had never injured them, and whom, in many cases, they had never seen in their lives. The crime committed, they quarrelled as to who had actually struck the fatal blow, and amused each other and the company by de-scribing the cries and contortions of the murdered man. At first they had shown some secrecy in their arrangements, but at the time which this narrative describes their proceed-ings were extraordinarily open, for the re-peated failures of the law had proved to them that, on the one hand, no one would dare to witness against them, and, on the other, they had an unlimited number of staunch witnesses upon whom they could call, and a well-filled treasure chest from which they could draw the funds to engage the best legal talent in the State. In ten long years of outrage there

had been no single conviction, and the only danger that ever threatened the Scowrers lay in the victim himself, who, however out-numbered and taken by surprise, might, and occasionally did, leave his mark upon his assailants.

McMurdo had been warned that some ordeal lay before him, but no one would tell him in what it consisted. He was led now into an outer room by two solemn brothers. Through the plank partition he could hear the murmur of many voices from the assembly within. Once or twice he caught the sound of his own name, and he knew that they were discussing his candidature. Then there entered an inner guard, with a green and gold sash across his chest.

"The bodymaster orders that he shall be trussed, blinded, and entered," said he. The three of them then removed his coat, turned up the sleeve of his right arm, and finally passed a rope round above the elbows and made it fast. They next placed a thick black cap right over his head and the upper part of his face, so that he could see nothing. He was then led into the assembly hall.

It was pitch-dark and very oppressive under his hood. He heard the rustle and murmur of the people round him, and then the voice of McGinty sounded, dull and distant, through the covering of his ears.

"John McMurdo," said the voice, "are you already a member of the Ancient Order of Freemen?"

He bowed in assent.

"Is your lodge No. 29, Chicago?"

He bowed again.

"Dark nights are unpleasant," said the voice.

"Yes, for strangers to travel," he answered.

"The clouds are heavy."

"Yes; a storm is approaching."

"Are the brethren satisfied?" asked the bodymaster.

There was a general murmur of assent.

"We know, brother, by your sign and by your countersign, that you are indeed one of us," said McGinty. "We would have you know, however, that in this county and in other counties of these parts we have certain rites, and also certain duties of our own, which call for good men. Are you ready to be tested?"

"I am."

"Are you of stout heart?"

"I am."

"Take a stride forward to prove it."

As the words were said he felt two hard points in front of his eyes, pressing upon them so that it appeared as if he could not move forward without a danger of losing them. None the less, he nerved himself to step resolutely out, and as he did so the pressure melted away. There was a low murmur of applause.

"He is of stout heart," said the voice. "Can you bear pain ? "

"As well as another," he answered.

"Test him ! "

It was all he could do to keep himself from screaming out, for an agonizing pain shot through his forearm. He nearly fainted at the sudden shock of it, but he bit his lip and clenched his hands to hide his agony.

"I can take more than that," said he.

This time there was loud applause. A finer first appearance had never been made in the Lodge. Hands clapped him on the back, and the hood was plucked from his head. He stood blinking and smiling amid the congratulations of the brothers.

"One last word, Brother McMurdo," said McGinty. "You have already sworn the oath of secrecy and fidelity, and you are aware that the punishment for any breach of it is instant and inevitable death ? "

"I am," said McMurdo.

"And you accept the rule of the bodymaster for the time being under all circumstances ? "

"I do."

"Then, in the name of Lodge 341, Vermissa, I welcome you to its privileges and debates. You will put the liquor on the table, Brother Scanlan, and we will drink to our worthy brother."

McMurdo's coat had been brought to him, but before putting it on he examined his right arm, which still smarted heavily. There, on the flesh of the forearm, was a clear-cut circle with a triangle within it, deep and red, as the branding-iron had left it. One or two of his neighbours pulled up their sleeves and showed their own Lodge marks.

"We've all had it," said one, "but not all as brave as you over it."

"Tut ! It was nothing," said he ; but it burned and ached all the same.

When the drinks which followed the ceremony of initiation had all been disposed of, the business of the Lodge proceeded. McMurdo, accustomed only to the prosaic performances of Chicago, listened with open ears, and more surprise than he ventured to show, to what followed.

"The first business on the agenda paper," said McGinty, "is to read the following letter from Division Master Windle, of Merton County, Lodge 249. He says :—

DEAR SIR,—There is a job to be done on Andrew Rae, of Rae and Sturmash, coal-owners near this place. You will remember that your Lodge owes us a return, having had the services of two brethren in the matter of the patrolman last fall. If you will send two good men they will be taken charge of by Treasurer Higgins of this Lodge, whose address you know. He will show them when to act and where.—Yours in freedom,

J. W. WINDLE, D.M.A.O.F.

Windle has never refused us when we have had occasion to ask for the loan of a man or two, and it is not for us to refuse him." McGinty paused and looked round the room with his dull, malevolent eyes. "Who will volunteer for the job ? "

Several young fellows held up their hands. The bodymaster looked at them with an approving smile.

"You'll do, Tiger Cormac. If you handle it as well as you did the last you won't be amiss. And you, Wilson."

"I've no pistol," said the volunteer, a mere boy in his teens.

"It's your first, is it not ? Well, you have to be blooded some time. It will be a great start for you. As to the pistol, you'll find it waiting for you, or I'm mistaken. If you report yourselves on Monday it will be time enough. You'll get a great welcome when you return."

"Any reward this time ? " asked Cormac, a thick-set, dark-faced, brutal-looking young man, whose ferocity had earned him the nickname of " Tiger."

"Never mind the reward. You just do it for the honour of the thing. Maybe when it is done there will be a few odd dollars at the bottom of the box."

"What has the man done ? " asked young Wilson.

"Sure, it's not for the likes of you to ask what the man has done. He has been judged over there. That's no business of ours. All we have to do is to carry it out for them, same as they would for us. Speaking of that, two brothers from the Merton Lodge are coming over to us next week to do some business in this quarter."

"Who are they ? " asked someone.

"Faith, it is wiser not to ask. If you know nothing you can testify nothing, and no trouble can come of it. But they are men who will make a clean job when they are about it."

"And time, too ! " cried Ted Baldwin. "Folk are getting out of hand in these parts. It was only last week that three of our men were turned off by Foreman Blaker. It's been owing him a long time, and he'll get it full and proper."

"HE NEARLY FAINTED AT THE SUDDEN SHOCK OF IT, BUT HE BIT HIS LIP AND

CLENCHED HIS HANDS TO HIDE HIS AGONY. 'I CAN TAKE MORE THAN THAT,' SAID HE."

" Get what ? " McMurdo whispered to his neighbour.

" The business end of a buck-shot cartridge," cried the man, with a loud laugh. " What think you of our ways, brother ? "

McMurdo's criminal soul seemed to have already absorbed the spirit of the vile association of which he was now a member.

" I like it well," said he. " 'Tis a proper place for a lad of mettle."

Several of those who sat around heard his words and applauded them.

" What's that ? " cried the black-maned bodymaster, from the end of the table.

" 'Tis our new brother, sir, who finds our ways to his taste."

McMurdo rose to his feet for an instant.

" I would say, Worshipful Master, that if a man should be wanted I should take it as an honour to be chosen to help the Lodge."

There was great applause at this. It was felt that a new sun was pushing its rim above the horizon. To some of the elders it seemed that the progress was a little too rapid.

" I would move," said the secretary, Harraway, a vulture-faced old greybeard who sat near the chairman, " that Brother McMurdo should wait until it is the good pleasure of the Lodge to employ him."

" Sure, that was what I meant. I'm in your hands," said McMurdo.

" Your time will come, brother," said the chairman. " We have marked you down as a willing man, and we believe that you will do good work in these parts. There is a small matter to-night in which you may take a hand, if it so please you."

" I will wait for something that is worth while."

" You can come to-night, anyhow, and it will help you to know what we stand for in this community. I will make the announcement later. Meanwhile "—he glanced at his agenda paper—" I have one or two more points to bring before the meeting. First of all, I will ask the treasurer as to our bank balance. There is the pension to Jim Carnaway's widow. He was struck down doing the work of the Lodge, and it is for us to see that she is not the loser."

" Jim was shot last month when they tried to kill Chester Wilcox, of Marley Creek," McMurdo's neighbour informed him.

" The funds are good at the moment," said the treasurer, with the bank-book in front of him. " The firms have been generous of late. Max Linder and Co. paid five hundred to be left alone. Walker Brothers sent in a hundred, but I took it on myself to return it and ask for

five. If I do not hear by Wednesday their winding gear may get out of order. We had to burn their breaker last year before they became reasonable. Then the West Section Coaling Company has paid its annual contribution. We have enough in hand to meet any obligations."

" What about Archie Swindon ? " asked a brother.

" He has sold out and left the district. The old devil left a note for us to say that he had rather be a free crossing-sweeper in New York than a large mine-owner under the power of a ring of blackmailers. By gosh, it was as well that he made a break for it before the note reached us ! I guess he dare not show his face in this valley again."

An elderly, clean-shaven man, with a kindly face and a good brow, rose from the end of the table which faced the chairman.

" Mr. Treasurer," he asked, " may I ask who has bought the property of this man that we have driven out of the district ? "

" Yes, Brother Morris. It has been bought by the State and Merton County Railroad Company."

" And who bought the mines of Todman and of Lee that came into the market in the same way last year ? "

" The same company, Brother Morris."

" And who bought the ironworks of Manson and of Shuman and of Van Deher and of Atwood, which have all been given up of late ? "

" They were all bought by the West Gilmerton General Mining Company."

" I don't see, Brother Morris," said the chairman, " that it matters a nickel to us who buys them, since they can't carry them out of the district."

" With all respect to you, Worshipful Master, I think that it may matter very much to us. This process has been going on now for ten long years. We are gradually driving all the small men out of trade. What is the result ? We find in their places great companies like the Railroad or the General Iron, who have their directors in New York or Philadelphia, and care nothing for our threats. We can take it out of their local bosses, but it only means that others will be sent in their stead. And we are making it dangerous for ourselves. The small men could not harm us. They had not the money nor the power. So long as we did not squeeze them too dry, they would stay on under our power. But if these big companies find that we stand between them and their profits, they will spare no pains and no expense to hunt us down and bring us to court."

There was a hush at these ominous words, and every face darkened as gloomy looks were exchanged. So omnipotent and unchallenged had they been that the very thought that there was possible retribution in the background had been banished from their minds. And yet the idea struck a chill to the most reckless of them.

"It is my advice," the speaker continued, "that we bear less heavily upon the small men. On the day that they have all been driven out the power of this society will have been broken."

Unwelcome truths are not popular. There were angry cries as the speaker resumed his seat. McGinty rose with gloom upon his brow.

"Brother Morris," said he, "you were always a croaker. So long as the members of this Lodge stand together there is no power in this United States that can touch them. Sure, have we not tried it often enough in the law courts? I expect the big companies will find it easier to pay than to fight, same as the little companies do. And now, brethren"—McGinty took off his black velvet cap and his stole as he spoke—"this Lodge has finished its business for the evening, save for one small matter which may be mentioned when we are parting. The time has now come for fraternal refreshment and for harmony."

Strange indeed is human nature. Here were these men to whom murder was familiar, who again and again had struck down the father of the family, some man against whom they had no personal feeling, without one thought of compunction or of compassion for his weeping wife or helpless children, and yet the tender or pathetic in music could move them to tears. McMurdo had a fine tenor voice, and if he had failed to gain the goodwill of the Lodge before, it could no longer have been withheld after he had thrilled them with "I'm Sitting on the Stile, Mary," and "On the Banks of Allan Water." In his very first night the new recruit had made himself one of the most popular of the brethren, marked already for advancement and high office. There were other qualities needed, however, besides those of good fellowship, to make a worthy Freeman, and of these he was given an example before the evening was over. The whisky bottle had passed round many times, and the men were flushed and ripe for mischief, when their bodymaster rose once more to address them.

"Boys," said he, "there's one man in this town that wants trimming up, and it's for you to see that he gets it. I'm speaking of James Stanger, of the *Herald.* You've seen

how he's been opening his mouth against us again?"

There was a murmur of assent, with many a muttered oath. McGinty took a slip of paper from his waistcoat pocket.

"'Law and Order!' That's how he heads it. 'Reign of Terror in the Coal and Iron District. Twelve years have now elapsed since the first assassinations which proved the existence of a criminal organization in our midst. From that day these outrages have never ceased, until now they have reached a pitch which makes us the opprobrium of the civilized world. Is it for such results as this that our great country welcomes to its bosom the alien who flies from the despotisms of Europe? Is it that they shall themselves become tyrants over the very men who have given them shelter, and that a state of terrorism and lawlessness should be established under the very shadow of the sacred folds of the starry flag of freedom which would raise horror in our minds if we read of it as existing under the most effete monarchy of the East? The men are known. The organization is patent and public. How long are we to endure it? Can we for ever live—' Sure, I've read enough of the slush!" cried the chairman, tossing the paper down upon the table. "That's what he says of us. The question I'm asking you is, What shall we say to him?"

"Kill him!" cried a dozen fierce voices.

"I protest against that," said Brother Morris, the man of the good brow and shaven face. "I tell you, brethren, that our hand is too heavy in this valley, and that there will come a point where, in self-defence, every man will unite to crush us out. James Stanger is an old man. He is respected in the township and the district. His paper stands for all that is solid in the valley. If that man is struck down, there will be a stir through this State that will only end with our destruction."

"And how would they bring about our destruction, Mister Stand-back?" cried McGinty. "Is it by the police? Sure, half of them are in our pay and half of them afraid of us. Or is it by the law courts and the judge? Haven't we tried that before now, and what ever came of it?"

"There is a Judge Lynch that might try the case," said Brother Morris.

A general shout of anger greeted the suggestion.

"I have but to raise my finger," cried McGinty, "and I could put two hundred men into this town that would clear it out from end to end." Then, suddenly raising his voice and bending his huge black brows into a terrible frown: "See here, Brother Morris, I have my eye on you, and have had for some time. You've no heart yourself, and you try to take the heart out of others. It will be an ill day for you, Brother Morris, when your own name comes on our agenda paper, and I'm thinking that it's just there that I ought to place it."

Morris had turned deadly pale and his knees seemed to give way under him as he fell back into his chair. He raised his glass in his trembling hand and drank before he could answer.

"I apologize, Worshipful Master, to you and to every brother in this Lodge if I have said more than I should. I am a faithful member—you all know that—and it is my fear lest evil come to the Lodge which makes me speak in anxious words. But I have greater trust in your judgment than in my own, Worshipful Master, and I promise you that I will not offend again."

The bodymaster's scowl relaxed as he listened to the humble words.

"Very good, Brother Morris. It's myself that would be sorry if it were needful to give you a lesson. But so long as I am in this chair we shall be a united Lodge in word and in deed. And now, boys," he continued, looking round at the company, "I'll say this much—that if Stanger got his full deserts there would be more trouble than we need ask for. These editors hang together, and every journal in the State would be crying out for police and troops. But I guess you can give him a pretty severe warning. Will you fix it, Brother Baldwin?"

"Sure!" said the young man, eagerly.

"How many will you take?"

"Half-a-dozen, and two to guard the door. You'll come, Gower, and you, Mansel, and you, Scanlan, and the two Willabys."

"I promised the new brother he should go," said the chairman.

Ted Baldwin looked at McMurdo with eyes which showed that he had not forgotten nor forgiven.

"Well, he can come if he wants," he said, in a surly voice. "That's enough. The sooner we get to work the better."

The company broke up with shouts and yells and snatches of drunken song. The bar was still crowded with revellers, and many of the brethren remained there. The little band who had been told off for duty passed out into the street, proceeding in twos and threes along the sidewalk so as not to provoke attention. It was a bitterly cold night, with a half-moon shining brilliantly in a frosty, star-spangled sky. The men stopped and gathered in a yard which faced a high building. The words "Vermissa Herald" were printed in gold lettering between the brightly-lit windows. From within came the clanking of the printing-press.

"Here, you," said Baldwin to McMurdo; "you can stand below at the door and see that the road is kept open for us. Arthur Willaby can stay with you. You others come with me. Have no fear, boys, for we have a dozen witnesses that we are in the Union bar at this very moment."

It was nearly midnight, and the street was deserted save for one or two revellers upon their way home. The party crossed the road and, pushing open the door of the newspaper office, Baldwin and his men rushed in and up the stair which faced them. McMurdo and another remained below. From the room above came a shout, a cry for help, and then the sound of trampling feet and of falling chairs. An instant later a grey-haired man rushed out on to the landing. He was seized before he could get farther, and his spectacles came tinkling down to McMurdo's feet. There was a thud and a groan. He was on his face and half-a-dozen sticks were clattering together as they fell upon him. He writhed, and his long, thin limbs quivered under the blows. The others ceased at last, but Baldwin, his cruel face set in an infernal smile, was hacking at the man's head, which he vainly endeavoured to defend with his arms. His white hair was dabbled with patches of blood. Baldwin was still stooping over his victim, putting in a short, vicious blow whenever he could see a part exposed, when McMurdo dashed up the stair and pushed him back.

"You'll kill the man," said he. "Drop it!"

Baldwin looked at him in amazement.

"Curse you!" he cried. "Who are you to interfere—you that are new to the Lodge? Stand back!" He raised his stick, but McMurdo had whipped his pistol out of his hip pocket.

"Stand back yourself!" he cried. "I'll blow your face in if you lay a hand on me. As to the Lodge, wasn't it the order of the bodymaster that the man was not to be killed, and what are you doing but killing him?"

"It's truth he says," remarked one of the men.

"By gosh, you'd best hurry yourselves!" cried the man below. "The windows are all lighting up and you'll have the whole township on your back inside of five minutes."

"'STAND BACK YOURSELF!' HE CRIED. 'I'LL BLOW YOUR FACE IN IF YOU LAY A HAND ON ME.'"

There was indeed the sound of shouting in the street, and a little group of compositors and typesetters was forming in the hall below and nerving itself to action. Leaving the limp and motionless body of the editor at the head of the stair, the criminals rushed down and made their way swiftly along the street.

Having reached the Union House, some of them mixed with the crowd in McGinty's saloon, whispering across the bar to the Boss that the job had been well carried through. Others, and among them McMurdo, broke away into side-streets, and so by devious paths to their own homes.

(To be continued.)

The Valley of Fear.

By

A. CONAN DOYLE.

Illustrated by Frank Wiles.

PART II.

THE SCOWRERS.

CHAPTER IV.

THE VALLEY OF FEAR.

WHEN McMurdo awoke next morning he had good reason to remember his initiation into the Lodge. His head ached with the effect of the drink, and his arm, where he had been branded, was hot and swollen. Having his own peculiar source of income, he was irregular in his attendance at his work, so he had a late breakfast and remained at home for the morning, writing a long letter to a friend. Afterwards he read the *Daily Herald*. In a special column, put in at the last moment, he read, " Outrage at the *Herald* Office. Editor seriously injured." It was a short account of the facts with which he was himself more familiar than the writer could have been. It ended with the statement :—

The matter is now in the hands of the police, but it can hardly be hoped that their exertions will be attended by any better results than in the past. Some of the men were recognized, and there is hope that a conviction may be obtained. The source of the outrage was, it need hardly be said, that infamous society which has held this community in bondage for so long a period, and against which the *Herald* has taken so uncompromising a stand. Mr. Stanger's many friends will rejoice to hear that, though he has been cruelly and brutally beaten and has sustained severe injuries about the head, there is no immediate danger to his life.

Below, it stated that a guard of Coal and Iron Police, armed with Winchester rifles, had been requisitioned for the defence of the office.

McMurdo had laid down the paper, and was lighting his pipe with a hand which was shaky from the excesses of the previous evening, when there was a knock outside, and his landlady brought to him a note which had just been handed in by a lad. It was unsigned, and ran thus :—

I should wish to speak to you, but had rather not do so in your house. You will find me beside the flagstaff upon Miller Hill. If you will come there now I have something which it is important for you to hear and for me to say.

McMurdo read the note twice with the utmost surprise, for he could not imagine what it meant or who was the author of it. Had it been in a feminine hand he might have imagined that it was the beginning of one of those adventures which had been familiar enough in his past life. But it was the writing of a man, and of a well-educated one, too. Finally, after some hesitation, he determined to see the matter through.

Miller Hill is an ill-kept public park in the very centre of the town. In summer it is a favourite resort of the people, but in winter it is desolate enough. From the top of it one has a view not only of the whole grimy, straggling town, but of the winding valley beneath, with its scattered mines and factories blackening the snow on either side of it, and of the wooded and white-capped ranges which flank it. McMurdo strolled up the winding path hedged in with evergreen until he reached the deserted restaurant which forms the centre of summer gaiety. Beside it was a bare flagstaff, and underneath it a man, his hat drawn down and the collar of his overcoat raised up. When he turned his face McMurdo saw that it was Brother Morris, he who had incurred the anger of the bodymaster the night before. The Lodge sign was given and exchanged as they met.

"I wanted to have a word with you, Mister McMurdo," said the older man, speaking with a hesitation which showed that he was on delicate ground. "It was kind of you to come."

"Why did you not put your name to the note?"

"One has to be cautious, mister. One never knows in times like these how a thing may come back to one. One never knows either who to trust or who not to trust."

"Surely one may trust brothers of the Lodge?"

"No, no; not always," cried Morris, with vehemence. "Whatever we say, even what we think, seems to go back to that man, McGinty."

"Look here," said McMurdo, sternly; "it was only last night, as you know well, that I swore good faith to our bodymaster. Would you be asking me to break my oath?"

"If that is the view you take," said Morris, sadly, "I can only say that I am sorry I gave you the trouble to come to meet me. Things have come to a bad pass when two free citizens cannot speak their thoughts to each other."

McMurdo, who had been watching his companion very narrowly, relaxed somewhat in his bearing.

"Sure, I spoke for myself only," said he. "I am a new-comer, as you know, and I am strange to it all. It is not for me to open my mouth, Mr. Morris, and if you think well to say anything to me I am here to hear it."

"And to take it back to Boss McGinty," said Morris, bitterly.

"Indeed, then, you do me injustice there," cried McMurdo. "For myself I am loyal to the Lodge, and so I tell you straight, but I would be a poor creature if I were to repeat to any other what you might say to me in confidence. It will go no farther than me, though I warn you that you may get neither help nor sympathy."

"I have given up looking for either the one or the other," said Morris. "I may be putting my very life in your hands by what I say, but, bad as you are—and it seemed to me last night that you were shaping to be as bad as the worst—still you are new to it, and your conscience cannot yet be as hardened as theirs. That was why I thought to speak with you."

"Well, what have you to say?"

"If you give me away, may a curse be on you!"

"Sure, I said I would not."

"I would ask you, then, when you joined the Freemen's Society in Chicago, and swore vows of charity and fidelity, did ever it cross your mind that you might find it would lead you to crime?"

"If you call it crime," McMurdo answered.

"Call it crime!" cried Morris, his voice vibrating with passion. "You have seen little of it if you can call it anything else. Was it crime last night when a man, old enough to be your father, was beaten till the blood dripped from his white hairs? Was that crime—or what else would you call it?"

"There are some would say it was war," said McMurdo. "A war of two classes with all in, so that each struck as best it could."

"Well, did you think of such a thing when you joined the Freemen's Society at Chicago?"

"No, I'm bound to say I did not."

"Nor did I when I joined it at Philadelphia. It was just a benefit club and a meeting-place for one's fellows. Then I heard of this place—curse the hour that the name first fell upon my ears!—and I came to better myself. My God, to better myself! My wife and three children came with me. I started a dry goods store in Market Square, and I prospered well. The word had gone round that I was a Freeman, and I was forced to join the local Lodge, same as you did last night. I've the badge of shame on my forearm, and something worse branded on my heart. I found that I was under the orders of a black villain, and caught in a meshwork of crime. What could I do? Every word I said to make things better was taken as treason, same as it was last night. I can't get away, for all I have in the world is in my store. If I leave the society, I know well that it means murder to me, and God knows what to my wife and children. Oh, man, it is awful—awful!" He put his hands to his face, and his body shook with convulsive sobs.

McMurdo shrugged his shoulders.

"You were too soft for the job," said he. "You are the wrong sort for such work."

"I had a conscience and a religion, but they made me a criminal among them. I was chosen for a job. If I backed down I knew well what would come to me. Maybe I'm a coward. Maybe it's the thought of my poor little woman and the children that makes me one. Anyhow, I went. I guess it will haunt me for ever. It was a lonely house, twenty miles from here, over the range yonder. I was told off for the door, same as you were last night. They could not trust me with the job. The others went in. When they came out their hands were crimson to the wrists. As we turned away a child was screaming out of the house behind us. It was a boy of five who had seen his father murdered. I nearly fainted with the horror of it, and yet I had to keep a bold and smiling face, for well I knew that if I did not it would be out of my house that they would come next with their bloody hands, and it would be my little Fred that would be screaming for his father. But I was a criminal then—part sharer in a murder, lost for ever in this world, and lost also in the next. I am a good Catholic, but the priest would have no word with me when he heard I was a Scowrer, and I am excommunicated from my faith. That's how it stands with me. And I see you going down the same road, and I ask you what the end is to be? Are you ready to be a cold-blooded murderer also, or can we do anything to stop it?"

"What would you do?" asked McMurdo, abruptly. "You would not inform?"

"God forbid!" cried Morris. "Sure, the very thought would cost me my life."

"That's well," said McMurdo. "I'm thinking that you are a weak man, and that you make too much of the matter."

"Too much! Wait till you have lived here longer. Look down the valley. See the cloud of a hundred chimneys that overshadows it. I tell you that the cloud of murder hangs thicker and lower than that over the heads of the people. It is the Valley of Fear—the Valley of Death. The terror is in the hearts of the people from the dusk to the dawn. Wait, young man, and you will learn for yourself."

"Well, I'll let you know what I think when I have seen more," said McMurdo, carelessly. "What is very clear is that you are not the man for the place, and that the sooner you sell out—if you only get a dime a dollar for what the business is worth—the better it will be for you. What you have said is safe with me, but, by gosh! if I thought you were an informer——"

"No, no!" cried Morris, piteously.

"Well, let it rest at that. I'll bear what you have said in mind, and maybe some day I'll come back to it. I expect you meant kindly by speaking to me like this. Now I'll be getting home."

"One word before you go," said Morris. "We may have been seen together. They may want to know what we have spoken about."

"Ah, that's well thought of."

"I offer you a clerkship in my store."

"And I refuse it. That's our business.

Well, so long, Brother Morris, and may you find things go better with you in the future."

That same afternoon, as McMurdo sat smoking, lost in thought, beside the stove of his sitting-room, the door swung open, and its framework was filled with the huge figure of Boss McGinty. He passed the sign, and then, seating himself opposite to the young man, he looked at him steadily for some time, a look which was as steadily returned.

"I'm not much of a visitor, Brother McMurdo," he said, at last. "I guess I am too busy over the folk that visit me. But I thought I'd stretch a point and drop down to see you in your own house."

"I'm proud to see you here, Councillor," McMurdo answered, heartily, bringing his whisky-bottle out of the cupboard. "It's an honour that I had not expected."

"How's the arm?" asked the Boss.

McMurdo made a wry face.

"Well, I'm not forgetting it," he said. "But it's worth it."

"Yes, it's worth it," the other answered, "to those that are loyal, and go through with it, and are a help to the Lodge. What were you speaking to Brother Morris about on Miller Hill this morning?"

The question came so suddenly that it was well that he had his answer prepared. He burst into a hearty laugh.

"Morris didn't know I could earn a living here at home. He sha'n't know either, for he has got too much conscience for the likes of me. But he's a good-hearted old chap. It was his idea that I was at a loose end, and that he would do me a good turn by offering me a clerkship in a dry goods store."

"Oh, that was it?""

"Yes, that was it."

"And you refused it?"

"Sure. Couldn't I earn ten times as much in my own bedroom with four hours' work?"

"That's so. But I wouldn't get about too much with Morris."

"Why not?"

"Well, I guess because I tell you not. That's enough for most folk in these parts."

"It may be enough for most folks, but it ain't enough for me, Councillor," said McMurdo, boldly. "If you are a judge of men you'll know that."

The swarthy giant glared at him, and his hairy paw closed for an instant round the glass as though he would hurl it at the head of his companion. Then he laughed in his loud, boisterous, insincere fashion.

" You're a queer card, for sure," said he. " Well, if you want reasons I'll give them. Did Morris say nothing to you against the Lodge ? "

" No."

" Nor against me ? "

" No."

" Well, that's because he daren't trust you. But in his heart he is not a loyal brother. We know that well, so we watch him, and we wait for the time to admonish him. I'm thinking that the time is drawing near. There's no room for scabby sheep in our pen. But if you keep company with a disloyal man, we might think that you were disloyal, too. See ? "

" There's no chance of my keeping company with him, for I dislike the man," McMurdo answered. " As to being disloyal, if it was any man but you, he would not use the word to me twice."

" Well, that's enough," said McGinty, draining off his glass. " I came down to give you a word in season, and you've had it."

" I'd like to know," said McMurdo, " how you ever came to learn that I had spoken with Morris at all."

McGinty laughed.

" It's my business to know what goes on in this township," said he. " I guess you'd best reckon on my hearing all that passes. Well, time's up, and I'll just say——"

But his leave-taking was cut short in a very unexpected fashion. With a sudden crash the door flew open, and three frowning, intent faces glared in at them from under the peaks of police caps. McMurdo sprang to his feet and half drew his revolver, but his arm stopped midway as he became conscious that two Winchester rifles were levelled at his head. A man in uniform advanced into the room, a six-shooter in his hand. It was Captain Marvin, once of Chicago, and now of the Coal and Iron Constabulary. He shook his head with a half smile at McMurdo.

" I thought you'd be getting into trouble, Mr. Crooked McMurdo, of Chicago," said he. " Can't keep out of it, can you ? Take your hat and come along with us."

" I guess you'll pay for this, Captain Marvin," said McGinty. " Who are you, I'd like to know, to break into a house in this fashion, and molest honest, law-abiding men ? "

" You're standing out in this deal, Councillor McGinty," said the police captain. " We are not out after you, but after this man McMurdo. It is for you to help, not to hinder us in our duty."

" He is a friend of mine, and I'll answer for his conduct," said the Boss.

" By all accounts, Mr. McGinty, you may have to answer for your own conduct some of these days," the police captain answered. " This man McMurdo was a crook before ever he came here, and he's a crook still. Cover him, patrolman, while I disarm him."

" There's my pistol," said McMurdo, coolly. " Maybe, Captain Marvin, if you and I were alone and face to face, you would not take me so easy."

" Where's your warrant ? " asked McGinty. " By gosh ! a man might as well live in Russia as in Vermissa while folk like you are running the police. It's a capitalist outrage, and you'll hear more of it, I reckon."

" You do what you think is your duty the best way you can, Councillor. We'll look after ours."

" What am I accused of ? " asked McMurdo.

" Of being concerned in the beating of old Editor Stanger at the *Herald* office. It wasn't your fault that it isn't a murder charge."

" Well, if that's all you have against him," cried McGinty, with a laugh, " you can save yourself a deal of trouble by dropping it right now. This man was with me in my saloon playing poker up to midnight, and I can bring a dozen to prove it."

" That's your affair, and I guess you can settle it in court to-morrow. Meanwhile, come on, McMurdo, and come quietly if you don't want a gun-butt across your head. You stand wide, Mr. McGinty, for I warn you I will brook no resistance when I am on duty."

So determined was the appearance of the captain that both McMurdo and his Boss were forced to accept the situation. The latter managed to have a few whispered words with the prisoner before they parted.

" What about——" he jerked his thumb upwards to signify the coining plant.

" All right," whispered McMurdo, who had devised a safe hiding-place under the floor.

" I'll bid you good-bye," said the Boss, shaking hands. " I'll see Reilly, the lawyer, and take the defence upon myself. Take my word for it that they won't be able to hold you."

" I wouldn't bet on that. Guard the prisoner, you two, and shoot him if he tries any games. I'll search the house before I leave."

Marvin did so, but apparently found no trace of the concealed plant. When he had descended he and his men escorted McMurdo to the headquarters. Darkness had fallen and a keen

"WITH A CRASH THE DOOR FLEW OPEN, AND THREE FROWNING FACES GLARED AT THEM FROM UNDER THE PEAKS OF POLICE CAPS."

blizzard was blowing, so that the streets were nearly deserted, but a few loiterers followed the group and, emboldened by invisibility, shouted imprecations at the prisoner.

"Lynch the cursed Scowrer!" they cried. "Lynch him!" They laughed and jeered as he was pushed into the police depot. After a short formal examination from the inspector-in-charge, he was handed on to the common cell. Here he found Baldwin and three other criminals of the night before, all arrested that afternoon, and waiting their trial next morning.

But even within this inner fortress of the law the long arm of the Freemen was able to extend. Late at night there came a jailer with a straw bundle for their bedding, out of which he extracted two bottles of whisky, some glasses, and a pack of cards. They spent an hilarious night without an anxious thought as to the ordeal of the morning.

Nor had they cause, as the result was to show. The magistrate could not possibly, on the evidence, have brought in the sentence which would have carried the matter to a higher court. On the one hand, the compositors and pressmen were forced to admit that the light was uncertain, that they were themselves much perturbed, and that it was difficult for them to absolutely swear to the identity of the assailants, although they believed that the accused were among them. Cross-examined by the clever attorney who had been engaged by McGinty, they were even more nebulous in their evidence. The injured man had already deposed that he was so taken by surprise by the suddenness of the attack that he could state nothing beyond the fact that the first man who struck him wore a moustache. He added that he knew them to be Scowrers, since no one else in the community could possibly have any enmity to him, and he had long been threatened on account of his outspoken editorials. On the other hand, it was clearly shown by the united and unfaltering evidence of six citizens, including that high municipal official, Councillor McGinty, that the men had been at a card party at the Union House until an hour very much later than the commission of the outrage. Needless to say that they were discharged with something very near to an apology from the Bench for the inconvenience to which they had been put, together with an implied censure of Captain Marvin and the police for their officious zeal.

The verdict was greeted with loud applause by a Court in which McMurdo saw many familiar faces. Brothers of the Lodge smiled and waved. But there were others who sat with compressed lips and brooding eyes as the men filed out of the dock. One of them, a little, dark-bearded, resolute fellow, put the thoughts of himself and comrades into words as the ex-prisoners passed him. "You damned murderers!" he said. "We'll fix you yet."

CHAPTER V.
THE DARKEST HOUR.

IF anything had been needed to give an impetus to Jack McMurdo's popularity among his fellows, it would have been his arrest and acquittal. That a man on the very night of joining the Lodge should have done something which brought him before the magistrate was a new record in the annals of the society. Already he had earned the reputation of a good boon companion, a cheery reveller, and withal a man of high temper, who would not take an insult even from the all-powerful Boss himself. But, in addition to this, he impressed his comrades with the idea that among them all there was not one whose brain was so ready to devise a bloodthirsty scheme, or whose hand would be more capable of carrying it out. "He'll be the boy for the clean job," said the oldsters to each other, and waited their time until they could set him to his work. McGinty had instruments enough already, but he recognized that this was a supremely able one. He felt like a man holding a fierce bloodhound in leash. There were curs to do the smaller work, but some day he would slip this creature upon its prey. A few members of the Lodge, Ted Baldwin among them, resented the rapid rise of the stranger, and hated him for it, but they kept clear of him, for he was as ready to fight as to laugh.

But if he gained favour with his fellows, there was another quarter, one which had become even more vital to him, in which he lost it. Ettie Shafter's father would have nothing more to do with him, nor would he allow him to enter the house. Ettie herself was too deeply in love to give him up altogether, and yet her own good sense warned her of what would come from a marriage with a man who was regarded as a criminal. One morning after a sleepless night she determined to see him, possibly for the last time, and make one strong endeavour to draw him from those evil influences which were sucking him down. She went to his house, as he had often begged her to do, and made her way into the room which he used as his sitting-room. He was seated at a table with his back turned and a letter in front of him. A sudden spirit of girlish mischief came over her—she was still only nineteen. He had not heard her when she pushed open the door. Now she tip-toed forward, and laid her hand lightly upon his bended shoulders.

If she had expected to startle him, she certainly succeeded, but only in turn to be startled herself. With a tiger spring he turned on her, and his right hand was feeling for her throat. At the same instant, with the other hand he crumpled up the paper that lay before him. For a moment he stood glaring. Then astonishment and joy took the place of the ferocity which had convulsed his features—a ferocity which had sent her shrinking back in horror as from something which had never before intruded into her gentle life.

"It's you!" said he, mopping his brow. "And to think that you should come to me, heart of my hearts, and I should find nothing better to do than to want to strangle you! Come then, darling," and he held out his arms. "Let me make it up to you."

But she had not recovered from that sudden glimpse of guilty fear which she had read in the man's face. All her woman's instinct told her that it was not the mere fright of a man who is startled. Guilt—that was it—guilt and fear.

"What's come over you, Jack?" she cried. "Why were you so scared of me? Oh, Jack, if your conscience was at ease, you would not have looked at me like that."

"Sure, I was thinking of other things, and when you came tripping so lightly up those fairy feet of yours——"

"No, no; it was more than that, Jack." Then a sudden suspicion seized her. "Let me see that letter you were writing."

"Ah, Ettie, I couldn't do that."

Her suspicions became certainties.

"It's to another woman!" she cried. "I know it. Why else should you hold it from me? Was it to your wife that you were writing? How am I to know that you are not a married man—you, a stranger, that nobody knows?"

"I am not married, Ettie. See now, I swear it. You're the only one woman on earth to me. By the Cross of Christ, I swear it!"

He was so white with passionate earnestness that she could not but believe him.

"Well, then," she cried, "why will you not show me the letter?"

"I'll tell you, acushla," said he. "I'm under oath not to show it, and just as I wouldn't break my word to you, so I would keep it to those who hold my promise. It's the business of the Lodge, and even to you it's secret. And if I was scared when a hand fell on me, can't you understand it when it might have been the hand of a detective?"

She felt that he was telling the truth. He gathered her into his arms, and kissed away her fears and doubts.

"Sit here by me, then. It's a queer throne for such a queen, but it's the best your poor lover can find. He'll do better for you some of these days, I'm thinking. Now your mind is easy once again, is it not?"

"How can it ever be at ease, Jack, when I know that you are a criminal among criminals—when I never know the day that I may hear that you are in the dock for murder? McMurdo the Scowrer—that was what one of our boarders called you yesterday. It went through my heart like a knife."

"Sure, hard words break no bones."

"But they were true."

"Well, dear, it's not as bad as you think. We are but poor men that are trying in our own way to get our rights."

Ettie threw her arms round her lover's neck.

"Give it up, Jack! For my sake—for God's sake, give it up! It was to ask you that I came here to-day. Oh, Jack, see, I beg it of you on my bended knees. Kneeling here before you, I implore you to give it up."

He raised her, and soothed her with her head against his breast.

"Sure, my darlin', you don't know what it is you are asking. How could I give it up when it would be to break my oath and to desert my comrades? If you could see how things stand with me, you could never ask it of me. Besides, if I wanted to, how could I do it? You don't suppose that the Lodge would let a man go free with all its secrets?"

"I've thought of that, Jack. I've planned it all. Father has saved some money. He is weary of this place, where the fear of these people darkens our lives. He is ready to go. We would fly together to Philadelphia or New York, where we should be safe from them."

McMurdo laughed.

"The Lodge has a long arm. Do you think it could not stretch from here to Philadelphia or New York?"

"Well, then, to the West, or to England, or to Sweden, whence father came. Anywhere to get away from this Valley of Fear."

McMurdo thought of old Brother Morris.

"Sure, it is the second time I have heard the valley so named," said he. "The shadow does indeed seem to lie heavy on some of you."

"It darkens every moment of our lives. Do you suppose that Ted Baldwin has ever forgiven us? If it were not that he fears you, what do you suppose that our chances would be? If you saw the look in those dark, hungry eyes of his when they fall on me!"

"By gosh! I'd teach him better manners if I caught him at it. But see here, little girl. I can't leave here. I can't. Take that from me once and for all. But if you will leave me to find my own way, I will try to prepare a way of getting honourably out of it."

"There is no honour in such a matter."

"GIVE IT UP, JACK! FOR MY SAKE—FOR GOD'S SAKE, GIVE IT UP!'"

"Well, well, it's just how you look at it. But if you'll give me six months I'll work it so as I can leave without being ashamed to look others in the face."

The girl laughed with joy.

"Six months!" she cried. "Is it a promise?"

"Well, it may be seven or eight. But within a year at the farthest we will leave the valley behind us."

It was the most that Ettie could obtain, and yet it was something. There was this distant light to illuminate the gloom of the immediate future. She returned to her father's house more light-hearted than she had ever been since Jack McMurdo had come into her life.

It might be thought that as a member all the doings of the society would be told to him, but he was soon to discover that the organization was wider and more complex than the simple Lodge. Even Boss McGinty was ignorant as to many things, for there was an official named the county delegate, living at Hobson's Patch, farther down the line, who had power over several different Lodges, which he wielded in a sudden and arbitrary way. Only once did McMurdo see him, a sly little grey-haired rat of a man with a slinking gait and a sidelong glance which was charged with malice. Evans Pott was his name, and even the great Boss of Vermissa felt towards him something of the repulsion and fear which the huge Danton may have felt for the puny but dangerous Robespierre.

One day Scanlan, who was McMurdo's fellow-boarder, received a note from McGinty, enclosing one from Evans Pott, which informed him that he was sending over two good men, Lawler and Andrews, who had instructions to act in the neighbourhood, though it was best for the cause that no particulars as to their objects should be given. Would the bodymaster see to it that suitable arrangements be made for their lodgings and comfort until the time for action should arrive? McGinty added that it was impossible for anyone to remain secret at the Union House, and that, therefore, he would be obliged if McMurdo and Scanlan would put the strangers up for a few days in their boarding-house.

The same evening the two men arrived, each carrying his grip-sack. Lawler was an elderly man, shrewd, silent, and self-contained, clad in an old black frock-coat, which, with his soft felt hat and ragged, grizzled beard, gave him a general resemblance to an itinerant preacher. His companion, Andrews, was little more than a boy, frank-faced and cheerful, with the breezy manner of one who is out for a holiday, and means to enjoy every minute of it. Both of the men were total abstainers, and behaved in all ways as exemplary members of society, with the one single exception that they were assassins who had often proved themselves to be most capable instruments for this Association of murder. Lawler had already carried out fourteen commissions of the kind, and Andrews three.

They were, as McMurdo found, quite ready to converse about their deeds in the past, which they recounted with the half-bashful pride of men who had done good and unselfish service for the community. They were reticent, however, as to the immediate job in hand.

"They chose us because neither I nor the boy here drink," Lawler explained. "They can count on us saying no more than we should. You must not take it amiss, but it is the orders of the county delegate that we obey."

"Sure, we are all in it together," said Scanlan, McMurdo's mate, as the four sat together at supper.

"That's true enough, and we'll talk till the cows come home of the killing of Charlie Williams, or of Simon Bird, or any other job in the past. But till the work is done we say nothing."

"There are half-a-dozen about here that I have a word to say to," said McMurdo, with an oath. "I suppose it isn't Jack Knox, of Ironhill, that you are after? I'd go some way to see him get his deserts."

"No, it's not him yet."

"Or Herman Strauss?"

"No, nor him either."

"Well, if you won't tell us, we can't make you, but I'd be glad to know."

Lawler smiled, and shook his head. He was not to be drawn.

In spite of the reticence of their guests, Scanlan and McMurdo were quite determined to be present at what they called the "fun." When, therefore, at an early hour one morning McMurdo heard them creeping down the stairs, he awakened Scanlan, and the two hurried on their clothes. When they were dressed they found that the others had stolen out, leaving the door open behind them. It was not yet dawn, and by the light of the lamps they could see the two men some distance down the street. They followed them warily, treading noiselessly in the deep snow.

The boarding-house was near the edge of the township, and soon they were at the cross-roads which are beyond its boundary. Here three men were waiting, with whom Lawler and Andrews held a short, eager conversation. Then they all moved on together. It was clearly some notable job which needed numbers. At this point there are several trails which lead to various mines. The strangers took that which led to the Crow Hill, a huge business which was in strong hands, who had been able, thanks to their energetic and fearless New England manager, Josiah H. Dunn, to keep some order and discipline during the long reign of terror.

Day was breaking now, and a line of workmen were slowly making their way, singly and in groups, along the blackened path.

McMurdo and Scanlan strolled on with the others, keeping in sight of the men whom they followed. A thick mist lay over them, and from the heart of it there came the sudden scream of a steam whistle. It was the ten-minute signal before the cages descended and the day's labour began.

When they reached the open space round

"'WHO ARE YOU?' HE ASKED, AS HE ADVANCED. 'WHAT

the mine-shaft there were a hundred miners waiting, stamping their feet and blowing on their fingers, for it was bitterly cold. The strangers stood in a little group under the shadow of the engine-house. Scanlan and McMurdo climbed a heap of slag, from which the whole scene lay before them. They saw the mine engineer, a great bearded Scotsman named Menzies, come out of the engine-house and blow his whistle for the cages to be lowered. At the same instant a tall, loose-framed young man, with a clean-shaven, earnest face, advanced eagerly towards the pit-head. As he came forward his eyes fell upon the group, silent and motionless, under the engine-house. The men had drawn down their hats and turned up their collars to screen their faces. For a moment the

ARE YOU LOITERING THERE FOR?'"

and helpless as if they were paralyzed. The manager clapped his two hands to the wound and doubled himself up. Then he staggered away, but another of the assassins fired, and he went down sideways, kicking and clawing among a heap of clinkers. Menzies, the Scotsman, gave a roar of rage at the sight, and rushed with an iron spanner at the murderers, but was met by two balls in the face, which dropped him dead at their very feet. There was a surge forward of some of the miners, and an inarticulate cry of pity and of anger, but a couple of the strangers emptied their six-shooters over the heads of the crowd, and they broke and scattered, some of them rushing wildly back to their homes in Vermissa. When a few of the bravest had rallied, and there was a return to the mine, the murderous gang had vanished in the mists of the morning without a single witness being able to swear to the identity of these men who in front of a hundred spectators had wrought this double crime.

Scanlan and McMurdo made their way back, Scanlan somewhat subdued, for it was the first murder job that he had seen with his own eyes, and it appeared less funny than he had been led to believe. The horrible screams of the dead manager's wife pursued them as they hurried to the town. McMurdo was absorbed and silent, but he

presentiment of death laid its cold hand upon the manager's heart. At the next he had shaken it off and saw only his duty towards intrusive strangers.

"Who are you?" he asked, as he advanced. "What are you loitering there for?"

There was no answer, but the lad Andrews stepped forward and shot him in the stomach. The hundred waiting miners stood as motionless showed no sympathy for the weakening of his companion.

"Sure, it is like a war," he repeated. "What is it but a war between us and them, and we hit back where we best can?"

There was high revel in the Lodge room at the Union House that night, not only over the killing of the manager and engineer of the Crow Hill mine, which would bring this organization into line with the other black-mailed and terror-stricken companies of the district, but also over a distant triumph which had been wrought by the hands of the Lodge itself. It would appear that when the county delegate had sent over five good men to strike a blow in Vermissa, he had demanded that, in return, three Vermissa men should be secretly selected and sent across to kill William Hales, of Stake Royal, one of the best-known and most popular mine-owners in the Gilmerton district, a man who was believed not to have an enemy in the world, for he was in all ways a pattern employer. He had insisted, however, upon efficiency in the work, and had therefore paid off certain drunken and idle *employés* who were members of the all-powerful society. Coffin notices hung outside his door had not weakened his resolution, and so in a free, civilized country he found himself condemned to death.

The execution had now been duly carried out. Ted Baldwin, who sprawled in the seat of honour beside the bodymaster, had been the chief of the party. His flushed face and glazed, bloodshot eyes told of sleeplessness and drink. He and his two comrades had spent the night before among the mountains. They were unkempt and weather-stained. But no heroes, returning from a forlorn hope, could have had a warmer welcome from their comrades. The story was told and retold amid cries of delight and shouts of laughter. They had waited for their man as he drove home at nightfall, taking their station at the top of a steep hill, where his horse must be at a walk. He was so furred to keep out the cold that he could not lay his hand on his pistol. They had pulled him out and shot him again and again.

None of them knew the man, but there is eternal drama in a killing, and they had shown the Scowrers of Gilmerton that the Vermissa men were to be relied upon. There had been one *contretemps*, for a man and his wife had driven up while they were still emptying their revolvers into the silent body. It had been suggested that they should shoot them both, but they were harmless folk who were not connected with the mines, so they were sternly bidden to drive on and keep silent,

lest a worse thing befall them. And so the blood-mottled figure had been left as a warning to all such hard-hearted employers, and the three noble avengers had hurried off into the mountains, where unbroken Nature comes down to the very edge of the furnaces and the slag-heaps.

It had been a great day for the Scowrers. The shadow had fallen even darker over the valley. But as the wise general chooses the moment of victory in which to redouble his efforts, so that his foes may have no time to steady themselves after disaster, so Boss McGinty, looking out upon the scene of his operations with brooding and malicious eyes, had devised a new attack upon those who opposed him. That very night, as the half-drunken company broke up, he touched McMurdo on the arm and led him aside into that inner room where they had their first interview.

"See here, my lad," said he, "I've got a job that's worthy of you at last. You'll have the doing of it in your own hands."

"Proud I am to hear it," McMurdo answered.

"You can take two men with you—Manders and Reilly. They have been warned for service. We'll never be right in this district until Chester Wilcox has been settled, and you'll have the thanks of every Lodge in the coal-fields if you can down him."

"I'll do my best, anyhow. Who is he, and where shall I find him?"

McGinty took his eternal half-chewed, half-smoked cigar from the corner of his mouth, and proceeded to draw a rough diagram on a page torn from his note-book.

"He's the chief foreman of the Iron Dyke Company. He's a hard citizen, an old colour-sergeant of the war, all scars and grizzle. We've had two tries at him, but had no luck, and Jim Carnaway lost his life over it. Now it's for you to take it over. That's the house, all alone at the Iron Dyke cross-road, same as you see here in the map, without another within earshot. It's no good by day. He's armed, and shoots quick and straight, with no questions asked. But at night—well, there he is, with his wife, three children, and a hired help. You can't pick or choose. It's all or none. If you could get a bag of blasting powder at the front door with a slow match to it——"

"What's the man done?"

"Didn't I tell you he shot Jim Carnaway?"

"Why did he shoot him?"

"What in thunder has that to do with you? Carnaway was about his house at night, and he shot him. That's enough for me and you. You've got to set the thing right."

" There's these two women and the children. Do they go up, too ? "

" They have to, else how can we get him ? "

" It seems hard on them, for they've done nothing amiss."

" What sort of talk is this ? Do you stand back from it ? "

" Easy, Councillor, easy. What have I ever said or done that you should think I would be after standing back from an order of the bodymaster of my own Lodge ? If it's right or if it's wrong it's for you to decide."

" You'll do it, then ? "

" Of course I will do it."

" When ? "

" Well, you had best give me a night or two that I may see the house and make my plans. Then——"

" Very good," said McGinty, shaking him by the hand. " I leave it with you. It will be a great day when you bring us the news. It's just the last stroke that will bring them all to their knees."

McMurdo thought long and deeply over the commission which had been so suddenly placed in his hands. The isolated house in which Chester Wilcox lived was about five miles off in an adjacent valley. That very night he started off all alone to prepare for the attempt. It was daylight before he returned from his reconnaissance. Next day he interviewed his two subordinates, Manders and Reilly, reckless youngsters, who were as elated as if it were a deer hunt. Two nights later they met outside the town, all three armed, and one of them carrying a sack stuffed with the powder which was used in the quarries. It was two in the morning before they came to the lonely house. The night was a windy one, with broken clouds drifting swiftly across the face of a three-quarter moon. They had been warned to be on their guard against bloodhounds, so they moved forward cautiously, with their pistols cocked in their hands. But there was no sound save the howling of the wind and no movement but the swaying branches above them. McMurdo listened at the door of the lonely house, but all was still within. Then he leaned the powder bag against it, ripped a hole in it with his knife, and attached the fuse. When it was well alight, he and his two companions took to their heels, and were some distance off, safe and snug in a sheltering ditch, before the shattering roar of the explosion, with the low, deep rumble of the collapsing building, told them that their work was done. No cleaner job had ever been carried out in the bloodstained annals of the society. But, alas that work so well organized and boldly conceived should all have gone for nothing ! Warned by the fate of the various victims, and knowing that he was marked down for destruction, Chester Wilcox had moved himself and his family only the day before to some safer and less known quarters, where a guard of police should watch over them. It was an empty house which had been torn down by the gunpowder, and the grim old colour-sergeant of the war was still teaching discipline to the miners of Iron Dyke.

" Leave him to me," said McMurdo. " He's my man, and I'll get him sure, if I have to wait a year for him."

A vote of thanks and confidence was passed in full Lodge, and so for the time the matter ended. When a few weeks later it was reported in the papers that Wilcox had been shot at from an ambuscade, it was an open secret that McMurdo was still at work upon his unfinished job.

Such were the methods of the Society of Freemen, and such were the deeds of the Scowrers by which they spread their rule of fear over the great and rich district which was for so long a period haunted by their terrible presence. Why should these pages be stained by further crimes ? Have I not said enough to show the men and their methods ? These deeds are written in history, and there are records wherein one may read the details of them. There one may learn of the shooting of Policemen Hunt and Evans because they had ventured to arrest two members of the society—a double outrage planned at the Vermissa Lodge, and carried out in cold blood upon two helpless and disarmed men. There also one may read of the shooting of Mrs. Larbey whilst she was nursing her husband, who had been beaten almost to death by orders of Boss McGinty. The killing of the elder Jenkins, shortly followed by that of his brother, the mutilation of James Murdoch, the blowing-up of the Staphouse family, and the murder of the Stendals all followed hard upon each other in the same terrible winter. Darkly the shadow lay upon the Valley of Fear. The spring had come with running brooks and blossoming trees. There was hope for all Nature, bound so long in an iron grip ; but nowhere was there any hope for the men and women who lived under the yoke of the terror. Never had the cloud above them been so dark and hopeless as in the early summer of the year '75.

The Valley of Fear.

By

A. CONAN DOYLE.

Illustrated by Frank Wiles.

PART II.

THE SCOWRERS.

CHAPTER VI.

DANGER.

IT was the height of the reign of terror. McMurdo, who had already been appointed inner Deacon, with every prospect of some day succeeding McGinty as bodymaster, was now so necessary to the councils of his comrades that nothing was done without his help and advice. The more popular he became, however, with the Freemen, the blacker were the scowls which greeted him as he passed along the streets of Vermissa. In spite of their terror the citizens were taking heart to bind themselves together against their oppressors. Rumours had reached the Lodge of secret gatherings in the *Herald* office and of distribution of firearms among the law-abiding people. But McGinty and his men were undisturbed by such reports. They were numerous, resolute, and well armed. Their opponents were scattered and powerless. It would all end, as it had done in the past, in aimless talk, and possibly in impotent arrests. So said McGinty, McMurdo, and all the bolder spirits.

It was a Saturday evening in May. Saturday was always the Lodge night, and McMurdo was leaving his house to attend it, when Morris, the weaker brother of the Order, came to see him. His brow was creased with care and his kindly face was drawn and haggard.

"Can I speak with you freely, Mr. McMurdo?"

"Sure."

"I can't forget that I spoke my heart to you once, and that you kept it to yourself, even though the Boss himself came to ask you about it."

"What else could I do if you trusted me? It wasn't that I agreed with what you said."

"I know that well. But you are the one that I can speak to and be safe. I've a secret here"—he put his hand to his breast—" and it is just burning the life out of me. I wish it had come to any one of you but me If I tell it, it will mean murder, for sure. If I don't, it may bring the end of us all. God help me, but I am near out of my wits over it!"

McMurdo looked at the man earnestly. He was trembling in every limb. He poured some whisky into a glass and handed it to him.

"That's the physic for the likes of you," said he. "Now let me hear of it."

Morris drank, and his white face took a tinge of colour.

"I can tell it you all in one sentence," said he. "There's a detective on our trail."

McMurdo stared at him in astonishment.

"Why, man, you're crazy!" he said. "Isn't the place full of police and detectives, and what harm did they ever do us?"

"No, no; it's no man of the district. As you say, we know them, and it is little that they can do. But you've heard of Pinkerton's?"

"I've read of some folk of that name."

"Well, you can take it from me you've no show when they are on your trail. It's not a take-it-or-miss-it Government concern. It's a dead earnest business proposition that's out for results, and keeps out till, by hook or by crook, it gets them. If a Pinkerton man is deep in this business we are all destroyed."

"We must kill him."

"Ah, it's the first thought that came to you! So it will be up at the Lodge. Didn't I say to you that it would end in murder?"

"Sure, what is murder? Isn't it common enough in these parts?"

"It is indeed, but it's not for me to point out the man that is to be murdered. I'd never rest easy again. And yet it's our own necks that may be at stake. In God's name what shall I do?" He rocked to and fro in his agony of indecision.

But his words had moved McMurdo deeply. It was easy to see that he shared the other's opinion as to the danger, and the need for meeting it. He gripped Morris's shoulder and shook him in his earnestness.

"See here, man," he cried, and he almost screeched the words in his excitement, "you won't gain anything by sitting keening like an old wife at a wake. Let's have the facts. Who is the fellow? Where is he? How did you hear of him? Why did you come to me?"

"I came to you, for you are the one man that would advise me. I told you that I had a store in the East before I came here. I left good friends behind me, and one of them is in the telegraph service. Here's a letter that I had from him yesterday. It's this part from the top of the page. You can read it for yourself."

This was what McMurdo read:—

"How are the Scowrers getting on in your parts? We read plenty of them in the papers. Between you and me I expect to hear news from you before long. Five big corporations and the two railroads have taken the thing up in dead earnest. They mean it, and you can bet they'll get there. They are right deep down into it. Pinkerton has taken hold under their orders, and his best man, Birdy Edwards, is operating. The thing has got to be stopped right now."

"Now read the postscript."

"Of course, what I give you is what I learned in business, so it goes no further. It's a queer cipher that you handle by the yard every day and can get no meaning from."

McMurdo sat in silence for some time with the letter in his restless hands. The mist had lifted for a moment, and there was the abyss before him.

"Does anyone else know of this?" he asked.

"I have told no one else."

"But this man—your friend—has he any other person that he would be likely to write to?"

"Well, I dare say he knows one or two more."

"Of the Lodge?"

"It's likely enough."

"I was asking because it is likely that he may have given some description of this fellow, Birdy Edwards. Then we could get on his trail."

"Well, it's possible. But I should not think he knew him. He is just telling me the news that came to him by way of business. How would he know this Pinkerton man?"

McMurdo gave a violent start.

"By gosh!" he cried, "I've got him. What a fool I was not to know it. Lord, but we're in luck! We will fix him before he can do any harm. See here, Morris; will you leave this thing in my hands?"

"Sure, if you will only take it off mine!"

"I'll do that. You can stand right back and let me run it. Even your name need not be mentioned. I'll take it all on myself as if it were to me that this letter has come. Will that content you?"

"It's just what I would ask."

"Then leave it at that and keep your head shut. Now I'll get down to the Lodge, and we'll soon make old man Pinkerton sorry for himself."

"You wouldn't kill this man?"

"The less you know, friend Morris, the easier your conscience will be and the better you will sleep. Ask no questions, and let things settle themselves. I have hold of it now."

Morris shook his head sadly as he left.

"I feel that his blood is on my hands," he groaned.

"Self-protection is no murder, anyhow," said McMurdo, smiling grimly. "It's him or us. I guess this man would destroy us all if we left him long in the valley. Why, Brother Morris, we'll have to elect you body-master yet, for you've surely saved the Lodge."

And yet it was clear from his actions that he thought more seriously of this new intrusion than his words would show. It may have been his guilty conscience; it may have been the reputation of the Pinkerton organization; it may have been the knowledge that great rich corporations had set themselves the task of clearing out the Scowrers; but, whatever his reason, his actions were those of a

"'I CAN TELL IT YOU ALL IN ONE SENTENCE,' SAID HE.   'THERE'S A DETECTIVE ON OUR TRAIL.'"

man who is preparing for the worst. Every paper which could incriminate him was destroyed before he left the house. After that he gave a long sigh of satisfaction, for it seemed to him that he was safe; and yet the danger must still have pressed somewhat upon him, for on his way to the Lodge he stopped at old Shafter's. The house was forbidden him, but when he tapped at the window Ettie came out to him. The dancing Irish devilry had gone from her lover's eyes. She read his danger in his earnest face.

"Something has happened!" she cried. "Oh, Jack, you are in danger!"

"Sure, it is not very bad, my sweetheart. And yet it may be wise that we make a move before it is worse."

"Make a move!"

"I promised you once that I would go some day. I think the time is coming. I had news to-night—bad news—and I see trouble coming."

"The police?"

"Well, a Pinkerton. But, sure, you wouldn't know what that is, acushla, nor what it may mean to the likes of me. I'm too deep in this thing, and I may have to get out of it quick. You said you would come with me if I went."

"Oh, Jack, it would be the saving of you."

"I'm an honest man in some things, Ettie. I wouldn't hurt a hair of your bonnie head for all that the world can give, nor ever pull you down one inch from the golden throne above the clouds where I always see you. Would you trust me?"

She put her hand in his without a word.

"Well, then, listen to what I say and do as I order you, for indeed it's the only way for us. Things are going to happen in this valley. I feel it in my bones. There may be many of us that will have to look out for ourselves. I'm one, anyhow. If I go, by day or night, it's you that must come with me!"

"I'd come after you, Jack."

"No, no; you shall come *with* me. If this valley is closed to me and I can never come back, how can I leave you behind, and me perhaps in hiding from the police with never a chance of a message? It's with me you must come. I know a good woman in the place I come from, and it's there I'd leave you till we can get married. Will you come?"

"Yes, Jack, I will come."

"God bless you for your trust in me. It's a fiend out of hell that I should be if I abused it. Now, mark you, Ettie, it will be just a

word to you, and when it reaches you you will drop everything and come right down to the waiting-hall at the depot and stay there till I come for you."

"Day or night, I'll come at the word, Jack."

Somewhat eased in mind now that his own preparations for escape had been begun, McMurdo went on to the Lodge. It had already assembled, and only by complicated signs and countersigns could he pass through the outer guard and inner guard who close-tiled it. A buzz of pleasure and welcome greeted him as he entered. The long room was crowded, and through the haze of tobacco-smoke he saw the tangled black mane of the bodymaster, the cruel, unfriendly features of Baldwin, the vulture face of Harraway, the secretary, and a dozen more who were among the leaders of the Lodge. He rejoiced that they should all be there to take counsel over his news.

"Indeed, it's glad we are to see you, brother!" cried the chairman. "There's business here that wants a Solomon in judgment to set it right."

"It's Lander and Egan," explained his neighbour, as he took his seat. "They both claim the head-money given by the Lodge for the shooting of old man Crabbe over at Stylestown, and who's to say which fired the bullet?"

McMurdo rose in his place and raised his hand. The expression of his face froze the attention of the audience. There was a dead hush of expectation.

"Worshipful Master," he said, in a solemn voice, "I claim urgency."

"Brother McMurdo claims urgency," said McGinty. "It's a claim that by the rules of this Lodge takes precedence. Now, brother, we attend you."

McMurdo took the letter from his pocket.

"Worshipful Master and brethren," he said, "I am the bearer of ill news this day, but it is better that it should be known and discussed than that a blow should fall upon us without warning which would destroy us all. I have information that the most powerful and richest organizations in this State have bound themselves together for our destruction, and that at this very moment there is a Pinkerton detective, one Birdy Edwards, at work in the valley collecting the evidence which may put a rope round the neck of many of us, and send every man in this room into a felon's cell. That is the situation for the discussion of which I have made a claim of urgency."

There was a dead silence in the room. It was broken by the chairman.

" What is your evidence for this, Brother McMurdo ? " he asked.

" It is in this letter which has come into my hands," said McMurdo. He read the passage aloud. " It is a matter of honour with me that I can give no further particulars about the letter, nor put it into your hands, but I assure you that there is nothing else in it which can affect the interests of the Lodge. I put the case before you as it has reached me."

" Let me say, Mr. Chairman," said one of the older brethren, " that I have heard of Birdy Edwards, and that he has the name of being the best man in the Pinkerton service."

" Does anyone know him by sight ? " asked McGinty.

" Yes," said McMurdo, " I do."

There was a murmur of astonishment through the hall.

" I believe we hold him in the hollow of our hands," he continued, with an exulting smile upon his face. " If we act quickly and wisely we can cut this thing short. If I have your confidence and your help it is little that we have to fear."

" What have we to fear anyhow ? What can he know of our affairs ? "

" You might say so if all were as staunch as you, Councillor. But this man has all the millions of the capitalists at his back. Do you think there is no weaker brother among all our Lodges that could not be bought ? He will get at our secrets—maybe has got them already. There's only one sure cure."

" That he never leaves the valley," said Baldwin.

McMurdo nodded.

" Good for you, Brother Baldwin," he said. " You and I have had our differences, but you have said the true word to-night."

" Where is he, then ? How shall we know him ? "

" Worshipful Master," said McMurdo, earnestly, " I would put it to you that this is too vital a thing for us to discuss in open Lodge. God forbid that I should throw a doubt on anyone here, but if so much as a word of gossip got to the ears of this man there would be an end of any chance of our getting him. I would ask the Lodge to choose a trusty committee, Mr. Chairman—yourself, if I might suggest it, and Brother Baldwin here, and five more. Then I can talk freely of what I know and of what I would advise should be done."

The proposition was at once adopted and

the committee chosen. Besides the chairman and Baldwin, there were the vulture-faced secretary, Harraway ; Tiger Cormac, the brutal young assassin ; Carter, the treasurer ; and the brothers Willaby, who were fearless and desperate men who would stick at nothing.

The usual revelry of the Lodge was short and subdued, for there was a cloud upon the men's spirits, and many there for the first time began to see the cloud of avenging Law drifting up in that serene sky under which they had dwelled so long. The horrors which they had dealt out to others had been so much a part of their settled lives that the thought of retribution had become a remote one, and so seemed the more startling now that it came so closely upon them. They broke up early and left their leaders to their council.

" Now, McMurdo," said McGinty, when they were alone. The seven men sat frozen in their seats.

" I said just now that I knew Birdy Edwards," McMurdo explained. " I need not tell you that he is not here under that name. He's a brave man, I dare bet, but not a crazy one. He passes under the name of Steve Wilson, and he is lodging at Hobson's Patch."

" How do you know this ? "

" Because I fell into talk with him. I thought little of it at the time, nor would have given it a second thought but for this letter, but now I'm sure it's the man. I met him on the cars when I went down the line on Wednesday—a hard case if ever there was one. He said he was a pressman. I believed it for the moment. Wanted to know all he could get about the Scowrers and what he called ' the outrages ' for the *New York Press.* Asked me every kind of question so as to get something for his paper. You bet I was giving nothing away. ' I'd pay for it, and pay well,' said he, ' if I could get some stuff that would suit my editor.' I said what I thought would please him best, and he handed me a twenty-dollar bill for my information. ' There's ten times that for you,' said he, ' if you can find me all that I want.' "

" What did you tell him, then ? "

" Any stuff I could make up."

" How do you know he wasn't a newspaper man ? "

" I'll tell you. He got out at Hobson's Patch, and so did I. I chanced into the telegraph bureau, and he was leaving it.

" ' See here,' said the operator, after he'd gone out, ' I guess we should charge double rates for this.' 'I guess you should,' said I. He had filled the form with stuff that might have been Chinese for all we could make of it. ' He fires a sheet of this off every day,' said the clerk. ' Yes,' said I ; ' it's special news for his paper, and he's scared that the others should tap it.' That was what the operator thought and what I thought at the time, but I think different now."

" By gosh, I believe you are right ! " said McGinty. " But what do you allow that we should do about it ? "

" Why not go right down now and fix him ? " someone suggested.

" Aye, the sooner the better."

" I'd start this next minute if I knew where we could find him," said McMurdo. " He's in Hobson's Patch, but I don't know the house. I've got a plan, though, if you'll only take my advice."

" Well, what is it ? "

" I'll go to the Patch to-morrow morning. I'll find him through the operator. He can locate him, I guess. Well, then, I'll tell him that I'm a Freeman myself. I'll offer him all the secrets of the Lodge for a price. You bet he'll tumble to it. I'll tell him the papers are at my house, and that it's as much as my life would be worth to let him come while folk were about. He'll see that that's horse sense. Let him come at ten o'clock at night, and he shall see everything. That will fetch him, sure."

" Well ? "

" You can plan the rest for yourselves. Widow MacNamara's is a lonely house. She's as true as steel and as deaf as a post. There's only Scanlan and me in the house. If I get his promise—and I'll let you know if I do—I'd have the whole seven of you come to me by nine o'clock. We'll get him in. If ever he gets out alive—well, he can talk of Birdy Edwards's luck for the rest of his days."

" There's going to be a vacancy at Pinkerton's or I'm mistaken," said McGinty. " Leave it at that, McMurdo. At nine to-morrow we shall be with you. You once get the door shut behind him, and you can leave the rest with us."

CHAPTER VII.
THE TRAPPING OF BIRDY EDWARDS.

As McMurdo had said, the house in which he lived was a lonely one and very well suited for such a crime as they had planned. It was on the extreme fringe of the town, and stood well back from the road. In any other case the conspirators would have simply called out their man, as they had many a time

before, and emptied their pistols into his body ; but in this instance it was very necessary to find out how much he knew, how he knew it, and what had been passed on to his employers. It was possible that they were already too late and that the work had been done. If that were indeed so, they could at least have their revenge upon the man who had done it. But they were hopeful that nothing of great importance had yet come to the detective's knowledge, as otherwise, they argued, he would not have troubled to write down and forward such trivial information as McMurdo claimed to have given him. However, all this they would learn from his own lips. Once in their power they would find a way to make him speak. It was not the first time that they had handled an unwilling witness.

McMurdo went to Hobson's Patch as agreed. The police seemed to take a particular interest in him that morning, and Captain Marvin—he who had claimed the old acquaintance with him at Chicago—actually addressed him as he waited at the depot. McMurdo turned away and refused to speak with him. He was back from his mission in the afternoon, and saw McGinty at the Union House.

" He is coming," he said.

" Good ! " said McGinty. The giant was in his shirt-sleeves, with chains and seals gleaming athwart his ample waistcoat and a diamond twinkling through the fringe of his bristling beard. Drink and politics had made the Boss a very rich as well as powerful man. The more terrible, therefore, seemed that glimpse of the prison or the gallows which had risen before him the night before.

" Do you reckon he knows much ? " he asked, anxiously.

McMurdo shook his head gloomily.

" He's been here some time—six weeks at the least. I guess he didn't come into these parts to look at the prospect. If he has been working among us all that time with the railroad money at his back, I should expect that he has got results, and that he has passed them on."

" There's not a weak man in the Lodge," cried McGinty. " True as steel, every man of them. And yet, by the Lord, there is that skunk Morris. What about him ? If any man gives us away it would be he. I've a mind to send a couple of the boys round before evening to give him a beating up and see what they can get from him."

" Well, there would be no harm in that," McMurdo answered. " I won't deny that I

"THEN, WITH A SUDDEN SHIVERING OF GLASS, A BRISTLE OF GLISTENING RIFLE-BARRELS BROKE

"THROUGH EACH WINDOW, WHILST THE CURTAINS WERE TORN FROM THEIR HANGINGS."

have a liking for Morris and would be sorry to see him come to harm. He has spoken to me once or twice over Lodge matters, and though he may not see them the same as you or I, he never seemed the sort that squeals. But still, it is not for me to stand between him and you."

" I'll fix the old devil," said McGinty, with an oath. " I've had my eye on him this year past."

" Well, you know best about that," McMurdo answered. " But whatever you do must be to-morrow, for we must lie low until the Pinkerton affair is settled up. We can't afford to set the police buzzing to-day of all days."

" True for you," said McGinty. " And we'll learn from Birdy Edwards himself where he got his news, if we have to cut his heart out first. Did he seem to scent a trap ? "

McMurdo laughed.

" I guess I took him on his weak point," he said. " If he could get on a good trail of the Scowrers he's ready to follow it home. I took his money," McMurdo grinned as he produced a wad of dollar notes, " and as much more when he has seen all my papers."

" What papers ? "

" Well, there are no papers. But I filled him up about constitutions and books of rules and forms of membership. He expects to get right down to the end of everything before he leaves."

" Faith, he's right there," said McGinty, grimly. " Didn't he ask you why you didn't bring him the papers ? "

" As if I would carry such things, and me a suspected man, and Captain Marvin after speaking to me this very day at the depot ! "

" Aye, I heard of that," said McGinty. " I guess the heavy end of this business is coming on to you. We could put him down an old shaft when we've done with him, but however we work it we can't get past the man living at Hobson's Patch and you being there to-day."

McMurdo shrugged his shoulders.

" If we handle it right they can never prove the killing," said he. " No one can see him come to the house after dark, and I'll lay to it that no one will see him go. Now, see here, Councillor. I'll show you my plan, and I'll ask you to fit the others into it. You will all come in good time. Very well. He comes at ten. He is to tap three times, and me to open the door for him. Then I'll get behind him and shut it. He's our man then."

" That's all easy and plain."

" Yes, but the next step wants considering.

He's a hard proposition. He's heavily armed. I've fooled him proper, and yet he is likely to be on his guard. Suppose I show him right into a room with seven men in it where he expected to fi.d me alone. There is going to be shooting and somebody is going to be hurt."

" That's so."

" And the noise is going to bring every blamed copper in the township on to the top of us."

" I guess you are right."

" This is how I should work it. You will all be in the big room—same as you saw when you had a chat with me. I'll open the door for him, show him into the parlour beside the door, and leave him there while I get the papers. That will give me the chance of telling you how things are shaping. Then I will go back to him with some faked papers. As he is reading them I will jump for him and get my grip on his pistol arm. You'll hear me call, and in you will rush. The quicker the better, for he is as strong a man as I, and I may have more than I can manage. But I allow that I can hold him till you come."

" It's a good plan," said McGinty. " The Lodge will owe you a debt for this. I guess when I move out of the chair I can put a name to the man that's coming after me."

" Sure, Councillor, I am little more than a recruit," said McMurdo, but his face showed what he thought of the great man's compliment.

When he had returned home he made his own preparations for the grim evening in front of him. First he cleaned, oiled, and loaded his Smith and Wesson revolver. Then he surveyed the room in which the detective was to be trapped. It was a large apartment, with a long deal table in the centre and the big stove at one end. At each of the other sides were windows. There were no shutters to these—only light curtains which drew across. McMurdo examined these attentively. No doubt it must have struck him that the apartment was very exposed for so secret a matter. Yet its distance from the road made it of less consequence. Finally he discussed the matter with his fellow-lodger. Scanlan, though a Scowrer, was an inoffensive little man who was too weak to stand against the opinion of his comrades, but was secretly horrified by the deeds of blood at which he had sometimes been forced to assist. McMurdo told him shortly what was intended.

" And if I were you, Mike Scanlan, I would take a night off and keep clear of it. There will be bloody work here before morning."

" Well, indeed, then, Mac," Scanlan answered, " it's not the will but the nerve that is wanting in me. When I saw Manager Dunn go down at the colliery yonder it was just more than I could stand. I'm not made for it, same as you or McGinty. If the Lodge will think none the worse of me, I'll just do as you advise, and leave you to yourselves for the evening."

The men came in good time as arranged. They were outwardly respectable citizens, well-clad and cleanly, but a judge of faces would have read little hope for Birdy Edwards in those hard mouths and remorseless eyes. There was not a man in the room whose hands had not been reddened a dozen times before. They were as hardened to human murder as a butcher to sheep. Foremost, of course, both in appearance and in guilt, was the formidable Boss. Harraway, the secretary, was a lean, bitter man, with a long, scraggy neck and nervous, jerky limbs—a man of incorruptible fidelity where the finances of the Order were concerned, and with no notion of justice or honesty to anyone beyond. The treasurer, Carter, was a middle-aged man with an impassive, rather sulky expression and a yellow parchment skin. He was a capable organizer, and the actual details of nearly every outrage had sprung from his plotting brain. The two Willabys were men of action, tall, lithe young fellows with determined faces, while their companion, Tiger Cormac, a heavy, dark youth, was feared even by his own comrades for the ferocity of his disposition. These were the men who assembled that night under the roof of McMurdo for the killing of the Pinkerton detective.

Their host had placed whisky upon the table, and they had hastened to prime themselves for the work before them. Baldwin and Cormac were already half-drunk, and the liquor had brought out all their ferocity. Cormac placed his hands on the stove for an instant—it had been lighted, for the spring nights were still cold.

" That will do," said he, with an oath.

" Aye," said Baldwin, catching his meaning. " If he is strapped to that we will have the truth out of him."

" We'll have the truth out of him, never fear," said McMurdo. He had nerves of steel, this man, for, though the whole weight of the affair was on him, his manner was as cool and unconcerned as ever. The others marked it and applauded.

" You are the one to handle him," said the Boss, approvingly. " Not a warning

will he get till your hand is on his throat. It's a pity there are no shutters to your windows."

McMurdo went from one to the other and drew the curtains tighter.

" Sure, no one can spy upon us now. It's close upon the hour."

" Maybe he won't come. Maybe he'll get a sniff of danger," said the secretary.

" He'll come, never fear," McMurdo answered. " He is as eager to come as you can be to see him. Hark to that ! "

They all sat like wax figures, some with their glasses arrested half-way to their lips. Three loud knocks had sounded at the door.

" Hush ! "

McMurdo raised his hand in caution. An exulting glance went round the circle and hands were laid upon hidden weapons.

" Not a sound for your lives ! " McMurdo whispered, as he went from the room, closing the door carefully behind him.

With strained ears the murderers waited. They counted the steps of their comrade down the passage. Then they heard him open the outer door. There were a few words as of greeting. Then they were aware of a strange step inside and of an unfamiliar voice. An instant later came the slam of the door and the turning of the key in the lock. Their prey was safe within the trap. Tiger Cormac laughed horribly, and Boss McGinty clapped his great hand across his mouth.

" Be quiet, you fool ! " he whispered. " You'll be the undoing of us yet."

There was a mutter of conversation from the next room. It seemed interminable. Then the door opened and McMurdo appeared, his finger upon his lip.

He came to the end of the table and looked round at them. A subtle change had come over him. His manner was as of one who has great work to do. His face had set into granite firmness. His eyes shone with a fierce excitement behind his spectacles. He had become a visible leader of men. They stared at him with eager interest, but he said nothing. Still with the same singular gaze, he looked from man to man.

" Well," cried Boss McGinty at last, " is he here ? Is Birdy Edwards here ? "

" Yes," McMurdo answered slowly. " Birdy Edwards is here. I am Birdy Edwards ! "

There were ten seconds after that brief speech during which the room might have been empty, so profound was the silence. The hissing of a kettle upon the stove rose sharp and strident to the ear. Seven white faces, all turned upwards to this man who dominated them, were set motionless with utter terror. Then, with a sudden shivering of glass, a bristle of glistening rifle-barrels broke through each window, whilst the curtains were torn from their hangings. At the sight Boss McGinty gave the roar of a wounded bear and plunged for the half-opened door. A levelled revolver met him there, with the stern blue eyes of Captain Marvin of the Coal and Iron Police gleaming behind the sights. The Boss recoiled and fell back into his chair.

"You're safer there, Councillor," said the man whom they had known as McMurdo. "And you, Baldwin, if you don't take your hand off your gun you'll cheat the hangman yet. Pull it out, or, by the Lord that made me—— There, that will do. There are forty armed men round this house, and you can figure it out for yourselves what chance you have. Take their guns, Marvin!"

There was no possible resistance under the menace of those rifles. The men were disarmed. Sulky, sheepish, and very amazed, they still sat round the table.

"I'd like to say a word to you before we separate," said the man who had trapped them. "I guess we may not meet again until you see me on the stand in the courthouse. I'll give you something to think over betwixt now and then. You know me now for what I am. At last I can put my cards on the table. I am Birdy Edwards, of Pinkerton's. I was chosen to break up your gang. I had a hard and a dangerous game to play. Not a soul, not one soul, not my nearest and dearest knew that I was playing it, except Captain Marvin here and my employers. But it's over to-night, thank God, and I am the winner!"

The seven pale, rigid faces looked up at him. There was an unappeasable hatred in their eyes. He read the relentless threat.

"Maybe you think that the game is not over yet. Well, I take my chance on that. Anyhow, some of you will take no further hand, and there are sixty more besides yourselves that will see a jail this night. I'll tell you this, that when I was put upon this job I never believed there was such a society as yours. I thought it was paper talk, and that I would prove it so. They told me it was to do with the Freemen, so I went to Chicago and was made one. Then I was surer than ever that it was just paper talk, for I found no harm in the society, but a deal of good. Still, I had to carry out my job, and I came for the coal valleys. When I reached this place I learned that I was wrong and that

it wasn't a dime novel after all. So I stayed to look after it. I never killed a man in Chicago. I never minted a dollar in my life. Those I gave you were as good as any others, but I never spent money better. I knew the way into your good wishes, and so I pretended to you that the law was after me. It all worked just as I thought.

"So I joined your infernal Lodge and I took my share in your councils. Maybe they will say that I was as bad as you. They can say what they like, so long as I get you. But what is the truth? The night I joined you beat up old man Stanger. I could not warn him, for there was no time, but I held your hand, Baldwin, when you would have killed him. If ever I have suggested things, so as to keep my place among you, they were things which I knew that I could prevent. I could not save Dunn and Menzies, for I did not know enough, but I will see that their murderers are hanged. I gave Chester Wilcox warning, so that when I blew his house in he and his folk were in hiding. There was many a crime that I could not stop, but if you look back and think how often your man came home the other road, or was down in town when you went for him, or stayed indoors when you thought that he would come out, you'll see my work."

"You blasted traitor!" hissed McGinty, through his closed teeth.

"Aye, John McGinty, you may call me that if it eases your smart. You and your like have been the enemy of God and man in these parts. It took a man to get between you and the poor devils of men and women that you held under your grip. There was just one way of doing it, and I did it. You call me a 'traitor,' but I guess there's many a thousand will call me a 'deliverer' that went down into hell to save them. I've had three months of it. I wouldn't have three such months again if they let me loose in the Treasury at Washington for it. I had to stay till I had it all, every man and every secret, right here in this hand. I'd have waited a little longer if it hadn't come to my knowledge that my secret was coming out. A letter had come into the town that would have set you wise to it all. Then I had to act, and act quickly. I've nothing more to say to you, except that when my time comes I'll die the easier when I think of the work I have done in this valley. Now, Marvin, I'll keep you no more. Have them in and get it over."

There is little more to tell. Scanlan had been given a sealed note to be left at the address of Miss Ettie Shafter—a mission which he had accepted with a wink and a knowing smile. In the early hours of the morning a beautiful woman and a much-muffled man boarded a special train which had been sent by the railroad company, and made a swift, unbroken journey out of the land of danger. It was the last time that ever either Ettie or her lover set foot in the Valley of Fear. Ten days later they were married in Chicago, with old Jacob Shafter as witness of the wedding.

The trial of the Scowrers was held far from the place where their adherents might have terrified the guardians of the law. In vain they struggled. In vain the money of the Lodge—money squeezed by blackmail out of the whole country-side—was spent like water in the attempt to save them. That cold, clear, unimpassioned statement from one who knew every detail of their lives, their organization, and their crimes was unshaken by all the wiles of their defenders. At last, after so many years, they were broken and scattered. The cloud was lifted for ever from the valley. McGinty met his fate upon the scaffold, cringing and whining when the last hour came. Eight of his chief followers shared his fate. Fifty odd had various degrees of imprisonment. The work of Birdy Edwards was complete.

And yet, as he had guessed, the game was not over yet. There was another hand to be played, and yet another and another. Ted Baldwin, for one, had escaped the scaffold; so had the Willabys; so had several other of the fiercest spirits of the gang. For ten years they were out of the world, and then came a day when they were free once more—a day which Edwards, who knew his men, was very sure would be an end of his life of peace. They had sworn an oath on all that they thought holy to have his blood as a vengeance for their comrades. And well they strove to keep their vow. From Chicago he was chased, after two attempts so near to success that it was sure that the third would get him. From Chicago he went, under a changed name, to California, and it was there that the light went for a time out of his life when Ettie Edwards died. Once again he was nearly killed, and once again, under the name of Douglas, he worked in a lonely canyon, where, with an English partner named Barker, he amassed a fortune. At last there came a warning to him that the bloodhounds were on his track once more, and he cleared—only just in time—for England. And here came the John Douglas who for a second time married a worthy mate

and lived for five years as a Sussex country gentleman—a life which ended with the strange happenings of which we have heard.

EPILOGUE.

THE police trial had passed, in which the case of John Douglas was referred to a higher court. So had the Quarter Sessions, at which he was acquitted as having acted in self-defence. " Get him out of England at any cost," wrote Holmes to the wife. " There are forces here which may be more dangerous than those he has escaped. There is no safety for your husband in England."

Two months had gone by, and the case had to some extent passed from our minds. Then one morning there came an enigmatic note slipped into our letter-box. " Dear me, Mr. Holmes! Dear me!" said this singular epistle. There was neither superscription nor signature. I laughed at the quaint message, but Holmes showed an unwonted seriousness.

" Devilry, Watson!" he remarked, and sat long with a clouded brow.

Late that night Mrs. Hudson, our landlady, brought up a message that a gentleman wished to see Holmes, and that the matter was of the utmost importance. Close at the heels of his messenger came Mr. Cecil Barker, our friend of the moated Manor House. His face was drawn and haggard.

" I've had bad news—terrible news, Mr. Holmes," said he.

" I feared as much," said Holmes.

" You have not had a cable, have you ? "

" I have had a note from someone who has."

" It's poor Douglas. They tell me his name is Edwards, but he will always be Jack Douglas of Benito Canyon to me. I told you that they started together for South Africa in the *Palmyra* three weeks ago."

" Exactly."

" The ship reached Cape Town last night. I received this cable from Mrs. Douglas this morning :—

" ' Jack has been lost overboard in gale off St. Helena. No one knows how accident occurred.—Ivy Douglas.' "

" Ha ! It came like that, did it' ? " said Holmes, thoughtfully. " Well, I've no doubt it was well stage-managed."

" You mean that you think there was no accident ? "

" None in the world."

" He was murdered ? "

" Surely ! "

"'I'VE HAD BAD NEWS—TERRIBLE NEWS, MR. HOLMES,' SAID HE."

" So I think also. These infernal Scowrers, this cursed vindictive nest of criminals——"

" No, no, my good sir," said Holmes. " There is a master hand here. It is no case of sawed-off shot-guns and clumsy six-shooters. You can tell an old master by the sweep of his brush. I can tell a Moriarty when I see one. This crime is from London, not from America."

" But for what motive ? "

" Because it is done by a man who cannot afford to fail—one whose whole unique position depends upon the fact that all he does must succeed. A great brain and a huge organization have been turned to the extinction of one man. It is crushing the nut with the hammer—an absurd extravagance of energy—but the nut is very effectually crushed all the same."

" How came this man to have anything to do with it ? "

" I can only say that the first word that ever came to us of the business was from one of his lieutenants. These Americans were well advised. Having an English job to do, they took into partnership, as any foreign criminal could do, this great consultant in crime. From that moment their man was doomed. At first he would content himself by using his machinery in order to find their victim. Then he would indicate how the matter might be treated. Finally, when he read in the reports of the failure of this agent, he would step in himself with a master touch. You heard me warn this man at Birlstone Manor House that the coming danger was greater than the past. Was I right ? "

Barker beat his head with his clenched fist in his impotent anger.

" Do you tell me that we have to sit down under this ? Do you say that no one can ever get level with this king-devil ? "

" No, I don't say that," said Holmes, and his eyes seemed to be looking far into the future. " I don't say that he can't be beat. But you must give me time—you must give me time ! "

We all sat in silence for some minutes, while those fateful eyes still strained to pierce the veil.

THE END.

HIS LAST BOW

Facsimile from the Strand Magazine, Volume LVI,
September 1917.

" ' CURSE YOU, YOU DOUBLE TRAITOR ! ' CRIED THE GERMAN, STRAINING
AGAINST HIS BONDS AND GLARING MURDER FROM HIS FURIOUS EYES."

THE STRAND MAGAZINE

Vol. 54.   SEPTEMBER, 1917.   No. 321.

His Last Bow.

THE WAR SERVICE OF SHERLOCK HOLMES.

By

A. CONAN DOYLE.

Illustrated by A. Gilbert.

IT was nine o'clock at night upon the second of August —the most terrible August in the history of the world. One might have thought already that God's curse hung heavy over a degenerate earth, for there was an awesome hush and a feeling of vague expectancy in the sultry and stagnant air. The sun had long set, but one blood-red gash, like an open wound, lay low in the distant west. Above the stars were shining brightly, and below the lights of the shipping glimmered in the bay. The two famous Germans stood beside the stone parapet of the garden walk, with the long, low, heavily-gabled house behind them, and they looked down upon the broad sweep of the beach at the foot of the great chalk cliff on which Von Bork, like some wandering eagle, had perched himself four years before. They stood with their heads close together talking in low, confidential tones. From below the two glowing ends of their cigars might have been the smouldering eyes of some malignant fiend looking down in the darkness.

A remarkable man this Von Bork—a man who could hardly be matched among all the devoted agents of the Kaiser. It was his talents which had first recommended him for the English mission, the most important mission of all, but since he had taken it over those talents had become more and more manifest to the half-dozen people in the world who were really in touch with the truth. One of these was his present companion, Baron Von Herling, the Chief Secretary of the Legation, whose huge hundred-horse-power Benz car was blocking the country lane as it waited to carry its owner back to London.

"Things are moving very fast now and quite in accordance with the time-table. So far as I can judge the trend of events, you will probably be back in Berlin within the week," the secretary was saying. "When you get there, my dear Von Bork, I think you will be surprised at the warm welcome you will receive. I happen to know what is thought in the All-Highest quarters of your work in this country." He was a huge man, the secretary, deep, broad, and tall, with a slow, heavy fashion of speech which had been his main asset in his political career.

Von Bork laughed in a deprecating way.

"They are not very hard to deceive, these Englanders," he remarked. "A more docile, simple folk could not be imagined."

"I don't know about that," said the other, thoughtfully. "They have strange, unexpected limits, and one must learn to allow for them. It is that surface simplicity of theirs which makes a trap for the stranger. One's first impression is that they are entirely soft. Then you come suddenly upon something very hard, and you know that you have reached the limit and must adapt yourself to the fact. They have, for example, their insular conventions, which simply *must* be observed."

"Meaning 'good form' and 'playing the game' and that sort of thing?" Von Bork sighed as one who had suffered much.

"Meaning British prejudice and convention, in all its queer manifestations. As an example I may quote one of my own worst blunders—I can afford to talk of my blunders, for you know my work well enough to be aware of my successes. It was on my first arrival. I was invited to a week-end gathering at the country-house of a Cabinet Minister. The conversation was amazingly indiscreet."

Von Bork nodded. "I've been there," said he, dryly.

"Exactly. Well, I naturally sent a *résumé* of the information to Berlin. Unfortunately, our good Chancellor is a little heavy-handed in these matters, and he transmitted a remark which showed that he was aware of what had been said. This, of course, took the trail straight up to me. You've no idea the harm that it did me. There was nothing soft about our British hosts on that occasion, I can assure you. I was two years living it down. Now you, with this sporting pose of yours——"

"No, no; don't call it a pose. A pose is an artificial thing. This is quite natural. I am a born sportsman. I enjoy it."

"Well, that makes it the more effective. You yacht against them, you hunt with them, you play polo, you match them in every game. Your four-in-hand takes the prize at Olympia—I have even heard that you go the length of boxing with the young officers. What is the result? Nobody takes you seriously. You are 'a good old sport,'

'quite a decent fellow for a German,' a hard-drinking, night-club, knock-about-town, devil-may-care young fellow. And all the time this quiet country-house of yours is the centre of half the mischief in England, and the sporting squire—the most astute secret-service man in Europe. Genius, my dear Von Bork—genius!"

"You flatter me, Baron. But certainly I may claim that my four years in this country have not been unproductive. I've never shown you my little store. Would you mind stepping in for a moment?"

The door of the study opened straight on to the terrace. Von Bork pushed it back, and, leading the way, he clicked the switch of the electric light. He then closed the door behind the bulky form which followed him, and carefully adjusted the heavy curtain over the latticed window. Only when all these precautions had been taken and tested did he turn his sunburned, aquiline face to his guest.

"Some of my papers have gone," said he. "When my wife and the household left yesterday for Flushing they took the less important with them. I must, of course, claim the protection of the Embassy for the others."

"Everything has been most carefully arranged. Your name has already been filed as one of the personal suite. There will be no difficulties for you or your baggage. Of course, it is just possible that we may not have to go. England may leave France to her fate. We are sure that there is no binding treaty between them."

"And Belgium?" He stood listening intently for the answer.

"Yes, and Belgium too."

Von Bork shook his head. "I don't see how that could be. There is a definite treaty there. It would be the end of her—and what an end! She could never recover from such a humiliation."

"She would at least have peace for the moment."

"But her honour?"

"Tut, my dear sir, we live in a utilitarian age. Honour is a mediæval conception. Besides, England is not ready. It is an inconceivable thing, but even our special war-tax of fifty millions, which one would think made our purpose as clear as if we had advertised it on the front page of the *Times*, has not roused these people from their slumbers. Here and there one hears a question. It is my business to find an answer. Here and there also there is irritation. It is my business to soothe it. But I can assure you that so far as the essentials go—the storage of munitions, the preparation for submarine attack, the arrangements for making high explosives—nothing is prepared. How then can England come in, especially when we have stirred her up such a devil's brew of Irish civil war, window-breaking furies, and God knows what to keep her thoughts at home?"

"She must think of her future."

"Ah, that is another matter. I fancy that in the future we have our own very definite plans about England, and that your information will be very vital to us. It is to-day or to-morrow with Mr. John Bull. If he prefers to-day we are perfectly ready, and the readier, my dear Von Bork, for your labours. If it is to-morrow, I need not tell you that we shall be more ready still. I should think they would be wiser to fight with allies than without them, but that is their own affair. This week is their week of destiny. But let us get away from speculation and back to *real-politik*. You were speaking of your papers."

He sat in the armchair with the light shining upon his broad, bald head, while he puffed sedately at his cigar and watched the movements of his companion.

The large oak-panelled, book-lined room had a curtain hung in the farther corner. When this was drawn it disclosed a large brass-bound safe. Von Bork detached a small key from his watch-chain, and after some considerable manipulation of the lock he swung open the heavy door.

"Look!" said he, standing clear, with a wave of his hand.

The light shone vividly into the opened safe, and the secretary of the Embassy gazed with an absorbed interest at the rows of stuffed pigeon-holes with which it was furnished. Each pigeon-hole had its label, and his eyes, as he glanced along them, read a long series of such titles as "Fords," "Harbour-Defences," "Aeroplanes," "Ireland," "Egypt," "Portsmouth Forts," "The Channel," "Rosyth," and a score of others. Each compartment was bristling with papers and plans.

"Colossal!" said the secretary. Putting down his cigar he softly clapped his fat hands.

"And all in four years, Baron. Not such a bad show for the hard-drinking, hard-riding country squire. But the gem of my collection is coming, and there is the setting all ready for it." He pointed to a space over which "Naval Signals" was printed.

"But you have a good *dossier* there already?"

"Out of date and waste paper. The Admiralty in some way got the alarm and every code has been changed. It was a blow, Baron—the worst set-back in my whole campaign. But, thanks to my cheque-book and the good Altamont, all will be well to-night."

The Baron looked at his watch, and gave a guttural exclamation of disappointment.

"Well, I really can wait no longer. You can imagine that things are moving at present in Carlton House Terrace and that we have all to be at our posts. I had hoped to be able to bring news of your great *coup*. Did Altamont name no hour?"

Von Bork pushed over a telegram.

"Will come without fail to-night and bring new sparking-plugs.—ALTAMONT."

"Sparking-plugs, eh?"

"You see, he poses as a motor expert, and I keep a full garage. In our code everything likely to come up is named after some spare part. If he talks of a radiator it is a battleship, of an oil-pump a cruiser, and so on. Sparking-plugs are naval signals."

"From Portsmouth at midday," said the secretary, examining the superscription. "By the way, what do you give him?"

"Five hundred pounds for this particular job. Of course, he has a salary as well."

"The greedy rogue. They are useful, these traitors, but I grudge them their blood-money."

"I grudge Altamont nothing. He is a wonderful worker. If I pay him well, at least he delivers the goods, to use his own phrase. Besides, he is not a traitor. I assure you that our most Pan-Germanic Junker is a peaceful sucking-dove in his feelings towards England as compared with a real bitter Irish-American."

"Oh, an Irish-American?"

"If you heard him talk you would not doubt it. Sometimes I assure you I can hardly understand him. He seems to have declared war on the King's English as well as on the English King. Must you really go? He may be here any moment."

"No; I'm sorry, but I have already overstayed my time. We shall expect you early to-morrow, and when you get that signal-book through the little door on the Duke of York's steps you can put a triumphant *Finis* to your record in England. What! Tokay!" He indicated a heavily-sealed, dust-covered bottle which stood with two high glasses upon a salver.

"May I offer you a glass before your journey?"

"No, thanks. But it looks like revelry."

"Altamont has a nice taste in wines, and he took a fancy to my Tokay. He is a touchy fellow and needs humouring in small things. He is absolutely vital to my plans, and I have to study him, I assure you." They had strolled out on to the terrace again, and along it to the farther end, where, at a touch from the Baron's chauffeur, the great car shivered and chuckled. "Those are the lights of Harwich, I suppose," said the secretary, pulling on his dust-coat. "How still and peaceful it all seems! There may be other lights within the week, and the English coast a less tranquil place! The heavens, too, may not be quite so peaceful, if all that the good Zeppelin promises us comes true. By the way, who is that?"

Only one window showed a light behind them. In it there stood a lamp, and beside it, seated at a table, was a dear old ruddy-faced woman in a country cap. She was bending over her knitting and stopping occasionally to stroke a large black cat upon a stool beside her.

"That is Martha, the only servant I have left."

The secretary chuckled.

"She might almost personify Britannia," said he, "with her complete self-absorption and general air of comfortable somnolence. Well, *au revoir*, Von Bork!" With a final wave of his hand he sprang into the car, and a moment later the two golden cones from the headlights shot forward through the darkness. The secretary lay back in the cushions of the luxurious Limousine with his thoughts full of the impending European tragedy, and hardly observing that as his car swung round the village street it nearly passed over a little Ford coming in the opposite direction.

Von Bork walked slowly back to the study when the last gleams of the motor lamps had faded into the distance. As he passed he observed that his old housekeeper had put out her lamp and retired. It was a new experience to him, the silence and darkness of his widespread house, for his family and household had been a large one. It was a relief to him, however, to think that they were all in safety, and that, but for that one old woman who lingered in the kitchen, he had the whole place to himself. There was a good deal of tidying up to do inside his study, and he set himself to do it until his keen, handsome face was flushed with the heat of the burning papers. A leather valise stood beside his table, and

into this he began to pack very neatly and systematically the precious contents of his safe. He had hardly got started with the work, however, when his quick ears caught the sound of a distant car. Instantly he gave an exclamation of satisfaction, strapped up the valise, shut the safe, locked it, and hurried out on to the terrace. He was just in time to see the lights of a small car come to a halt at the gate. A passenger sprang out of it and advanced swiftly towards him, while the chauffeur, a heavily-built, elderly man with a grey moustache, settled down like one who resigns himself to a long vigil.

"Well?" asked Von Bork, eagerly, running forward to meet his visitor.

For answer the man waved a small brown-paper parcel triumphantly above his head.

"You can give me the glad hand to-night, mister," he cried. "I'm bringin' home the bacon at last."

"The signals?"

"Same as I said in my cable. Every last one of them—semaphore, lamp-code, Marconi —a copy, mind you, not the original. The sucker that sold it would have handed over the book itself. That was too dangerous. But it's the real goods, and you can lay to that." He slapped the German upon the shoulder with a rough familiarity from which the other winced.

"Come in," he said. "I'm all alone in the house. I was only waiting for this. Of course, a copy is better than the original. If an original were missing they would change the whole thing. You think it's all safe about this copy?"

The Irish-American had entered the study and stretched his long limbs from the arm-chair. He was a tall, gaunt man of sixty, with clear-cut features and a small goatee beard, which gave him a general resemblance to the caricatures of Uncle Sam. A half-smoked sodden cigar hung from the corner of his mouth, and as he sat down he struck a match and relit it. "Makin' ready for a move?" he remarked, as he looked round him. "Say, mister," he added, as his eyes fell upon the safe from which the curtain was now removed, "you don't tell me you keep your papers in that?"

"Why not?"

"Gosh, in a wide-open contraption like that! And they reckon you to be some spy. Why, a Yankee crook would be into that with a can-opener. If I'd known that any letter of mine was goin' to lie loose in a thing like that I'd have been a mutt to write to you at all."

" It would puzzle any of your crooks to force that safe," Von Bork answered. " You won't cut that metal with any tool."

" But the lock ? "

" No; it's a double combination lock. You know what that is ? "

" Search me," said the American, with a shrug.

" Well, you need a word as well as a set of figures before you can get the lock to work." He rose and showed a double radiating disc round the keyhole. " This outer one is for the letters, the inner one for the figures."

" Well, well, that's fine."

" So it's not quite so simple as you thought. It was four years ago that I had it made, and what do you think I chose for the word and figures ? "

" It's beyond me."

" Well, I chose ' August' for the word, and ' 1914' for the figures, and here we are."

The American's face showed his surprise and admiration.

" My, but that was smart ! You had it down to a fine thing."

" Yes ;. a few of us even then could have guessed the date. Here it is, and I'm shutting down to-morrow morning."

" Well, I guess you'll have to fix me up too. I'm not stayin' in this goldarned country all on my lonesome. In a week or less, from what I see, John Bull will be on his hind legs and fair rampin'. I'd rather watch him from over the water."

" But you're an American citizen ? "

" Well, so was Jack James an American citizen, but he's doin' time in Portland all the same. It cuts no ice with a British copper to tell him you're an American citizen. ' It's British law and order over here,' says he. By the way, mister, talking of Jack James, it seems to me you don't do much to cover your men."

" What do you mean ? " Von Bork asked, sharply.

" Well, you are their employer, ain't you ? It's up to you to see that they don't fall down. But they do fall down, and when did you ever pick them up ? There's James——"

" It was James's own fault. You know that yourself. He was too self-willed for the job."

" James was a bonehead—I give you that. Then there was Hollis."

" The man was mad."

" Well, he went a bit woozy towards the end. It's enough to make a man bughouse when he has to play a part from mornin' to night, with a hundred guys all ready to set the coppers wise to him. But now there is Steiner——"

Von Bork started violently, and his ruddy face turned a shade paler.

" What about Steiner ? "

" Well, they've pulled him, that's all. They raided his store last night, and he and his papers are all in Portsmouth Jail. You'll go off and he, poor devil, will have to stand the racket, and lucky if he gets clear with his life. That's why I want to get over the salt water as soon as you do."

Von Bork was a strong, self-contained man, but it was easy to see that the news had shaken him.

" How could they have got on to Steiner ? " he muttered. " That's the worst blow yet."

" Well, you nearly had a darned sight worse one, for I believe they are not far off me."

" You don't mean that ! "

" Sure thing. My landlady down Fratton way had some inquiries, and when I heard of it I guessed it was time for me to hustle. But what I want to know, mister, is how the coppers know these things ? Steiner is the fifth man you've lost since I signed on for you, and I know the name of the sixth if I don't get a move on. How do you explain it, and ain't you ashamed to see your men go down like this ? "

Von Bork flushed crimson.

" How dare you speak in such a way ? "

" If I didn't dare things, mister, I wouldn't be in your service. But I'll tell you straight what is in my mind. I've heard that with you German politicians when an agent has done his work you are not very sorry to see him put away where he can't talk too much."

Von Bork sprang to his feet.

" Do you dare to suggest that I have given away my own agents ? "

" I don't stand for that, mister, but there's a stool pigeon or a cross somewhere, and it's up to you to find out where it is. Anyhow, I am taking no more chances. It's me for little Holland, and the sooner the better."

Von Bork had mastered his anger.

" We have been allies too long to quarrel now at the very hour of victory," said he. " You've done splendid work and taken big risks, and I can't forget it. By all means go to Holland, and you can come with us to Berlin or get a boat from Rotterdam to New York. No other line will be safe a week from now, when Von Tirpitz gets to

"HE WAS GRIPPED AT THE BACK OF HIS NECK BY A GRASP OF IRON, AND A CHLOROFORMED
SPONGE WAS HELD IN FRONT OF HIS WRITHING FACE."

work. But let us settle up, Altamont. I'll take that book and pack it with the rest."

The American held the small parcel in his hand, but made no motion to give it up.

"What about the dough ? " he asked.

" The what ? "

" The boodle. The reward. The five hundred pounds. The gunner turned durned nasty at the last, and I had to square him with an extra hundred dollars or it would have been nitsky for you and me. ' Nothin' doin' ! ' says he, and he meant it too, but the last hundred did it. It's cost me two hundred pounds from first to last, so it isn't likely I'd give it up without gettin' my wad."

Von Bork smiled with some bitterness. "You don't seem to have a very high opinion of my honour," said he ; " you want the money before you give up the book."

" Well, mister, it is a business proposition."

" All right. Have your way." He sat down at the table and scribbled a cheque, which he tore from the book, but he refrained from handing it to his companion. " After all, since we are to be on such terms, Mr. Altamont," said he, " I don't see why I should trust you any more than you trust me. Do you understand ? " he added, looking back over his shoulder at the American. " There's the cheque upon the table. I claim the right to examine that parcel before you pick the money up."

The American passed it over without a word. Von Bork undid a winding of string and two wrappers of paper. Then he sat gazing for a moment in silent amazement at a small blue book which lay before him. Across the cover was printed in golden letters, " Practical Handbook of Bee Culture." Only for one instant did the master-spy glare at this strangely-irrelevant inscription. The next he was gripped at the back of his neck by a grasp of iron, and a chloroformed sponge was held in front of his writhing face.

"Another glass, Watson ? " said Mr. Sherlock Holmes, as he extended the dusty bottle of Imperial Tokay. " We must drink to this joyous reunion."

The thick-set chauffeur, who had seated himself by the table, pushed forward his glass with some eagerness.

" It is a good wine, Holmes," he said, when he had drunk heartily to the sentiment.

" A remarkable wine, Watson. Our noisy friend upon the sofa has assured me that it is from Franz Joseph's special cellar at the Schoenbrunn Palace. Might I trouble you to open the window, for chloroform vapour does not help the palate."

The safe was ajar, and Holmes, who was now standing in front of it, was removing *dossier* after *dossier*, swiftly examining each, and then packing it neatly in Von Bork's valise. The German lay upon the sofa sleeping stertorously, with a strap round his upper arms and another round his legs.

" We need not hurry ourselves, Watson. We are safe from interruption. Would you mind touching the bell ? There is no one in the house except old Martha, who has played her part to admiration. I got her the situation here when first I took the matter up. Ah, Martha, you will be glad to hear that all is well."

The pleasant old lady had appeared in the doorway. She curtsied with a smile to Mr. Holmes, but glanced with some apprehension at the figure upon the sofa.

" It is all right, Martha. He has not been hurt at all."

" I am glad of that, Mr. Holmes. According to his lights he has been a kind master. He wanted me to go with his wife to Germany yesterday, but that would hardly have suited your plans, would it, sir ? "

" No, indeed, Martha. So long as you were here I was easy in my mind. We waited some time for your signal to-night."

" It was the secretary, sir ; the stout gentleman from London."

" I know. His car passed ours. But for your excellent driving, Watson, we should have been the very type of Europe under the Prussian juggernaut. What more, Martha ? "

" I thought he would never go. I knew that it would not suit your plans, sir, to find him here."

" No, indeed. Well, it only meant that we waited half an hour or so on the hill until I saw your lamp go out and knew that the coast was clear. You can report to me to-morrow in London, Martha, at Claridge's Hotel."

" Very good, sir."

" I suppose you have everything ready to leave ? "

" Yes, sir. He posted seven letters to-day. I have the addresses, as usual. He received nine ; I have these also."

" Very good, Martha. I will look into them to-morrow. Good-night. These papers," he continued, as the old lady vanished, " are not of very great importance, for, of course, the information which they represent has been sent off long ago to the German

Government. These are the originals, which could not safely be got out of the country."

" Then they are of no use ? "

" I should not go so far as to say that, Watson. They will at least show our people what is known and what is not. I may say that a good many of these documents have come to him through me, and I need not add are thoroughly untrustworthy. It would brighten my declining years to see a German cruiser navigating the Solent according to the mine-field plans which I have furnished. But you, Watson "—he stopped his work and took his old friend by the shoulders—" I've hardly seen you in the light yet. How have the years used you ? You look the same blithe boy as ever."

" I feel twenty years younger, Holmes. I have seldom felt so happy as when I got your wire asking me to meet you at Harwich with the car. But you, Holmes—you have changed very little—save for that horrible goatee."

" Those are the sacrifices one makes for one's country, Watson," said Holmes, pulling at his little tuft. " To-morrow it will be but a dreadful memory. With my hair cut and a few other superficial changes I shall no doubt reappear at Claridge's to-morrow as I was before this American stunt—I beg your pardon, Watson; my well of English seems to be permanently defiled—before this American job came my way."

" But you had retired, Holmes. We heard of you as living the life of a hermit among your bees and your books in a small farm upon the South Downs."

" Exactly, Watson. Here is the fruit of my leisured ease, the *magnum opus* of my latter years ! " He picked up the volume from the table and read out the whole title, " ' Practical Handbook of Bee Culture, with some Observations upon the Segregation of the Queen.' Alone I did it. Behold the fruit of pensive nights and laborious days, when I watched the little working gangs as once I watched the criminal world of London."

" But how did you get to work again ? "

" Ah ! I have often marvelled at it myself. The Foreign Minister alone I could have withstood, but when the Premier also deigned to visit my humble roof——! The fact is, Watson, that this gentleman upon the sofa was a bit too good for our people. He was in a class by himself. Things were going wrong, and no one could understand why they were going wrong. Agents were suspected or even caught, but there was evidence of some strong and secret central

force. It was absolutely necessary to expose it. Strong pressure was brought upon me to look into the matter. It has cost me two years, Watson, but they have not been devoid of excitement. When I say that I started my pilgrimage at Chicago, graduated in an Irish secret society at Buffalo, gave serious trouble to the constabulary at Skibbereen, and so eventually caught the eye of a subordinate agent of Von Bork, who recommended me as a likely man, you will realize that the matter was complex. Since then I have been honoured by his confidence, which has not prevented most of his plans going subtly wrong and five of his best agents being in prison. I watched them, Watson, and I picked them as they ripened. Well, sir, I hope that you are none the worse ? "

The last remark was addressed to Von Bork himself, who, after much gasping and blinking, had lain quietly listening to Holmes's statement. He broke out now into a furious stream of German invective, his face convulsed with passion. Holmes continued his swift investigation of documents, his long, nervous fingers opening and folding the papers while his prisoner cursed and swore.

" Though unmusical, German is the most expressive of all languages," he observed, when Von Bork had stopped from pure exhaustion. " Halloa ! Halloa ! " he added, as he looked hard at the corner of a tracing before putting it in the box. " This should put another bird in the cage. I had no idea that the paymaster was such a rascal, though I have long had an eye upon him. Dear me, Mister Von Bork, you have a great deal to answer for ! "

The prisoner had raised himself with some difficulty upon the sofa and was staring with a strange mixture of amazement and hatred at his captor.

" I shall get level with you, Altamont," he said, speaking with slow deliberation. "If it takes me all my life I shall get level with you."

" The old sweet song," said Holmes. " How often have I heard it in days gone by ! It was a favourite ditty of the late lamented Professor Moriarty. Colonel Sebastian Moran has also been known to warble it. And yet I live and keep bees upon the South Downs."

" Curse you, you double traitor ! " cried the German, straining against his bonds and glaring murder from his furious eyes.

" No, no, it is not so bad as that," said Holmes, smiling. " As my speech surely shows you, Mr. Altamont of Chicago had

"HOLDING EITHER ARM, THE TWO FRIENDS WALKED HIM VERY SLOWLY DOWN THE GARDEN PATH."

no existence in fact. He was a concoction, a myth, an isolated strand from my bundle of personalities. I used him and he is gone."

" Then who are you ? "

" It is really immaterial who I am, but since the matter seems to interest you, Mr. Von Bork, I may say that this is not my

first acquaintance with the members of your family. I have done a good deal of business in Germany in the past, and my name is probably familiar to you."

" I would wish to know it," said the Prussian, grimly.

" It was I who brought about the separation between Irene Adler and the late King of Bohemia when your cousin Heinrich was the Imperial Envoy. It was I also who saved from murder by the Nihilist Klopman, Count Von und Zu Grafenstein, who was your mother's elder brother. It was I——"

Von Bork sat up in amazement.

" There is only one man——" he cried.

" Exactly," said Holmes.

Von Bork groaned and sank back on the sofa. " And most of that information came through you ! " he cried. " What is it worth ? What have I done ? It is my ruin for ever ! "

" It is certainly a little untrustworthy," said Holmes. " It will require some checking, and you have little time to check it. Your admiral may find the new guns rather larger than he expects and the cruisers perhaps a trifle faster."

Von Bork clutched at his own throat in despair.

" There are a good many other points of detail which will no doubt come to light in good time. But you have one quality which is very rare in a German, Mr. Von Bork : you are a sportsman, and you will bear me no ill will when you realize that you, who have outwitted so many other people, have at last been outwitted yourself. After all, you have done your best for your country and I have done my best for mine, and what could be more natural ? Besides," he added, not unkindly, as he laid his hand upon the shoulder of the prostrate man, " it is better than to fall before some more ignoble foe. These papers are now ready, Watson. If you will help me with our prisoner I think that we may get started for London at once."

It was no easy task to move Von Bork, for he was a strong and a desperate man. Finally, holding either arm, the two friends walked him very slowly down the garden path, which he had trod with such proud confidence when he received the congratulations of the famous diplomatist only a few hours before. After a short final struggle he was hoisted, still bound hand and foot, into the spare seat of the little car. His precious valise was wedged in beside him.

" I trust that you are as comfortable as circumstances permit," said Holmes, when the final arrangements were made. " Should I be guilty of a liberty if I lit a cigar and placed it between your lips ? "

But all amenities were wasted upon the angry German.

" I suppose you realize, Mr. Sherlock Holmes," said he, " that if your Government bears you out in this treatment it becomes an act of war ? "

" What about your Government and all this treatment ? " said Holmes, tapping the valise.

" You are a private individual. You have no warrant for my arrest. The whole proceeding is absolutely illegal and outrageous."

" Absolutely," said Holmes.

" Kidnapping a German subject."

" And stealing his private papers."

" Well, you realize your position, you and your accomplice here. If I were to shout for help as we pass through the village——"

" My dear sir, if you did anything so foolish you would probably enlarge the too-limited titles of our village inns by giving us ' The Dangling Prussian ' as a sign-post. The Englishman is a patient creature, but at present his temper is a little inflamed, and it would be as well not to try him too far. No, Mr. Von Bork, you will go with us in a quiet, sensible fashion to Scotland Yard, whence you can send for your friend Baron Von Herling and see if even now you may not fill that place which he has reserved for you in the Ambassadorial suite. As to you, Watson, you are joining up with your old service, as I understand, so London won't be out of your way. Stand with me here upon the terrace, for it may be the last quiet talk that we shall ever have."

The two friends chatted in intimate converse for a few minutes, recalling once again the days of the past, whilst their prisoner vainly wriggled to undo the bonds that held him. As they turned to the car Holmes pointed back to the moonlit sea and shook a thoughtful head.

" There's an east wind coming, Watson."

" I think not, Holmes. It is very warm."

" Good old Watson ! You are the one fixed point in a changing age. There's an east wind coming all the same, such a wind as never blew on England yet. It will be cold and bitter, Watson, and a good many of us may wither before its blast. But it's God's own wind none the less, and a cleaner, better, stronger land will lie in the sunshine when the storm has cleared. Start her up, Watson, for it's time that we were on our way. I have a cheque for five hundred pounds which should be cashed early, for the drawer is quite capable of stopping it, if he can."

THE CASE-BOOK
OF SHERLOCK HOLMES

Facsimile from the Strand Magazine,
Volumes LXII, LXIII, LXV, LXVII, LXIX, LXXII, and LXXIII,
October 1921 – April 1927.

"HIS THICK STICK HALF RAISED, HE WAS CROUCHING FOR HIS FINAL SPRING AND BLOW WHEN A COOL, SARDONIC VOICE GREETED HIM FROM THE OPEN BEDROOM DOOR: 'DON'T BREAK IT, COUNT! DON'T BREAK IT!'"

THE ADVENTURE OF THE MAZARIN STONE

A NEW SHERLOCK HOLMES STORY

BY

A. Conan Doyle

ILLUSTRATED BY
A. GILBERT. R.O.I.

IT was pleasant to Dr. Watson to find himself once more in the untidy room of the first floor in Baker Street which had been the starting-point of so many remarkable adventures. He looked round him at the scientific charts upon the wall, the acid-charred bench of chemicals, the violin-case leaning in the corner, the coal-scuttle, which contained of old the pipes and tobacco. Finally, his eyes came round to the fresh and smiling face of Billy, the young but very wise and tactful page, who had helped a little to fill up the gap of loneliness and isolation which surrounded the saturnine figure of the great detective.

"It all seems very unchanged, Billy. You don't change, either. I hope the same can be said of him?"

Billy glanced, with some solicitude, at the closed door of the bedroom.

"I think he's in bed and asleep," he said.

It was seven in the evening of a lovely summer's day, but Dr. Watson was sufficiently familiar with the irregularity of his old friend's hours to feel no surprise at the idea.

"That means a case, I suppose?"

"Yes, sir; he is very hard at it just now. I'm frightened for his health. He gets paler and thinner, and he eats nothing. 'When will you be pleased to dine, Mr. Holmes?'

Mrs. Hudson asked. 'Seven-thirty, the day after to-morrow,' said he. You know his way when he is keen on a case."

"Yes, Billy, I know."

"He's following someone. Yesterday he was out as a workman looking for a job. To-day he was an old woman. Fairly took me in, he did, and I ought to know his ways by now." Billy pointed with a grin to a very baggy parasol which leaned against the sofa. "That's part of the old woman's outfit," he said.

"But what is it all about, Billy?"

Billy sank his voice, as one who discusses great secrets of State. "I don't mind telling you, sir, but it should go no farther. It's this case of the Crown diamond."

"What—the hundred - thousand - pound burglary?"

"Yes, sir. They must get it back, sir. Why, we had the Prime Minister and the Home Secretary both sitting on that very sofa. Mr. Holmes was very nice to them. He soon put them at their ease and promised he would do all he could. Then there is Lord Cantlemere——"

"Ah!"

"Yes, sir; you know what that means. He's a stiff 'un, sir, if I may say so. I can get along with the Prime Minister, and I've nothing against the Home Secretary, who seemed a civil, obliging sort of man, but I can't stand his lordship. Neither can Mr. Holmes, sir. You see, he don't believe in Mr. Holmes and he was against employing him. He'd *rather* he failed."

" And Mr. Holmes knows it ? "

" Mr. Holmes always knows whatever there is to know."

" Well, we'll hope he won't fail and that Lord Cantlemere will be confounded. But I say, Billy, what is that curtain for across the window ? "

" Mr. Holmes had it put up there three days ago. We've got something funny behind it."

Billy advanced and drew away the drapery which screened the alcove of the bow window.

Dr. Watson could not restrain a cry of amazement. There was a facsimile of his old friend, dressing-gown and all, the face turned three-quarters towards the window and downwards, as though reading an invisible book, while the body was sunk deep in an armchair. Billy detached the head and held it in the air.

" We put it at different angles, so that it may seem more life-like. I wouldn't dare touch it if the blind were not down. But when it's up you can see this from across the way."

" We used something of the sort once before."

' Before my time," said Billy. He drew the window curtains apart and looked out into the street. " There are folk who watch us from over yonder. I can see a fellow now at the window. Have a look for yourself."

WATSON had taken a step forward when the bedroom door opened, and the long, thin form of Holmes emerged, his face pale and drawn, but his step and bearing as active as ever. With a single spring he was at the window, and had drawn the blind once more.

" That will do, Billy," said he. " You were in danger of your life then, my boy, and I can't do without you just yet. Well, Watson, it is good to see you in your old quarters once again. You come at a critical moment."

" So I gather."

" You can go, Billy. That boy is a problem, Watson. How far am I justified in allowing him to be in danger ? "

" Danger of what, Holmes ? "

" Of sudden death. I'm expecting something this evening."

" Expecting what ? "

" To be murdered, Watson."

" No, no ; you are joking, Holmes ! "

" Even my limited sense of humour could evolve a better joke than that. But we may be comfortable in the meantime, may we not ? Is alcohol permitted ? The gasogene

and cigars are in the old place. Let me see you once more in the customary armchair. You have not, I hope, learned to despise my pipe and my lamentable tobacco ? It has to take the place of food these days."

" But why not eat ? "

" Because the faculties become refined when you starve them. Why, surely, as a doctor, my dear Watson, you must admit that what your digestion gains in the way of blood supply is so much lost to the brain. I am a brain, Watson. The rest of me is a mere appendix. Therefore, it is the brain I must consider."

" But this danger, Holmes ? "

" Ah, yes ; in case it should come off, it would perhaps be as well that you should burden your memory with the name and address of the murderer. You can give it to Scotland Yard, with my love and a parting blessing. Sylvius is the name—Count Negretto Sylvius. Write it down, man, write it down ! 136, Moorside Gardens, N.W. Got it ? "

Watson's honest face was twitching with anxiety. He knew only too well the immense risks taken by Holmes, and was well aware that what he said was more likely to be under-statement than exaggeration. Watson was always the man of action, and he rose to the occasion.

" Count me in, Holmes. I have nothing to do for a day or two."

" Your morals don't improve, Watson. You have added fibbing to your other vices. You bear every sign of the busy medical man, with calls on him every hour."

" Not such important ones. But can't you have this fellow arrested ? "

" Yes, Watson, I could. That's what worries him so."

" But why don't you ? "

" Because I don't know where the diamond is."

" Ah ! Billy told me—the missing Crown jewel ! "

" Yes, the great yellow Mazarin stone. I've cast my net and I have my fish. But I have not got the stone. What is the use of taking *them ?* We can make the world a better place by laying them by the heels. But that is not what I am out for. It's the stone I want."

" And is this Count Sylvius one of your fish ? "

" Yes, and he's a shark. He bites. The other is Sam Merton, the boxer. Not a bad fellow, Sam, but the Count has used him. Sam's not a shark. He is a great big silly bull-headed gudgeon. But he is flopping about in my net all the same."

" Where is this Count Sylvius ? "

" I've been at his very elbow all the morning. You've seen me as an old lady,

Watson. I was never more convincing. He actually picked up my parasol for me once. ' By your leave, madame,' said he—half-Italian, you know, and with the Southern graces of manner when in the mood, but a devil incarnate in the other mood. Life is full of whimsical happenings, Watson."

" It might have been tragedy."

" Well, perhaps it might. I followed him to old Straubenzee's workshop in the Minories. Straubenzee made the air-gun—a very pretty bit of work, as I understand, and I rather fancy it is in the opposite window at the present moment. Have you seen the dummy ? Of course, Billy showed it to you. Well, it may get a bullet through its beautiful head at any moment. Ah, Billy, what is it ? "

The boy had re-appeared in the room with a card upon a tray. Holmes glanced at it with raised eyebrows and an amused smile.

" The man himself. I had hardly expected this. Grasp the nettle, Watson ! A man of nerve. Possibly you have heard of his reputation as a shooter of big game. It would indeed be a triumphant ending to his excellent sporting record if he added me to his bag. This is a proof that he feels my toe very close behind his heel."

" Send for the police."

" I probably shall. But not just yet. Would you glance carefully out of the window, Watson, and see if anyone is hanging about in the street ? "

Watson looked warily round the edge of the curtain.

" Yes, there is one rough fellow near the door."

" That will be Sam Merton—the faithful but rather fatuous Sam. Where is this gentleman, Billy ? "

" In the waiting-room, sir."

" Show him up when I ring."

" Yes, sir."

" If I am not in the room, show him in all the same."

" Yes, sir."

Watson waited until the door was closed, and then he turned earnestly to his companion.

" Look here, Holmes, this is simply impossible. This is a desperate man, who sticks at nothing. He may have come to murder you."

" I should not be surprised."

" I insist upon staying with you."

" You would be horribly in the way."

" In his way ? "

" No, my dear fellow—in my way."

" Well, I can't possibly leave you."

" Yes, you can, Watson. And you will, for you have never failed to play the game. I am sure you will play it to the end. This man has come for his own purpose, but he may stay for mine." Holmes took out his note-book and scribbled a few lines. " Take a cab to Scotland Yard and give this to Youghal of the C.I.D. Come back with the police. The fellow's arrest will follow."

" I'll do that with joy."

" Before you return I may have just time enough to find out where the stone is." He touched the bell. " I think we will go out through the bedroom. This second exit is exceedingly useful. I rather want to see my shark without his seeing me, and I have, as you will remember, my own way of doing it."

I T was, therefore, an empty room into which Billy, a minute later, ushered Count Sylvius. The famous game-shot, sportsman, and man-about-town was a big, swarthy fellow, with a formidable dark moustache, shading a cruel, thin-lipped mouth, and surmounted by a long, curved nose, like the beak of an eagle. He was well dressed, but his brilliant necktie, shining pin, and glittering rings were flamboyant in their effect. As the door closed behind him, he looked round him with fierce, startled eyes, like one who suspects a trap at every turn. Then he gave a violent start as he saw the impassive head and the collar of the dressing-gown which projected above the armchair in the window. At first his expression was one of pure amazement. Then the light of a horrible hope gleamed in his dark, murderous eyes. He took one more glance round to see that there were no witnesses, and then, on tiptoe, his thick stick half raised, he approached the silent figure. He was crouching for his final spring and blow when a cool, sardonic voice greeted him from the open bedroom door :—

" Don't break it, Count ! Don't break it ! "

The assassin staggered back, amazement in his convulsed face. For an instant he half raised his loaded cane once more, as if he would turn his violence from the effigy to the original ; but there was something in that steady grey eye and mocking smile which caused his hand to sink to his side.

" It's a pretty little thing," said Holmes, advancing towards the image. " Tavernier, the French modeller, made it. He is as good at waxworks as your friend Straubenzee is at air-guns."

" Air-guns, sir ! What do you mean ? "

" Put your hat and stick on the side table. Thank you ! Pray take a seat. Would you care to put your revolver out also ? Oh, very good, if you prefer to sit upon it. Your visit is really most opportune, for I wanted badly to have a few minutes' chat with you."

The Count scowled, with heavy, threatening eyebrows.

"Billy advanced and drew away the drapery which screened the window. Dr. Watson gown

" I, too, wished to have some words with you, Holmes. That is why I am here. I won't deny that I intended to assault you just now."

Holmes swung his leg on the edge of the table.

" I rather gathered that you had some idea of the sort in your head," said he. ' But why these personal attentions ? "

" Because you have gone out of your way to annoy me. Because you have put your creatures upon my track."

" My creatures ! I assure you no ! "

" Nonsense ! I have had them followed. Two can play at that game, Holmes."

" It is a small point, Count Sylvius, but perhaps you would kindly give me my prefix when you address me. You can understand could not restrain a cry of amazement. There was a facsimile of his old friend, dressing-and all."

that, with my routine of work, I should find myself on familiar terms with half the rogues' gallery, and you will agree that exceptions are invidious."

"Well, *Mr.* Holmes, then."

"Excellent! But I assure you you are mistaken about my alleged agents."

Count Sylvius laughed contemptuously.

"Other people can observe as well as you.

Yesterday there was an old sporting man. To-day it was an elderly woman. They held me in view all day."

"Really, sir, you compliment me. Old Baron Dowson said the night before he was hanged that in my case what the law had gained the stage had lost. And now you give my little impersonations your kindly praise!"

" It was you—you yourself ? "

Holmes shrugged his shoulders. " You can see in the corner the parasol which you so politely handed to me in the Minories before you began to suspect."

" If I had known, you might never——"

" Have seen this humble home again. I was well aware of it. We all have neglected opportunities to deplore. As it happens, you did not know, so here we are ! "

The Count's knotted brows gathered more heavily over his menacing eyes. " What you say only makes the matter worse. It was not your agents, but your play-acting, busy-body self ! You admit that you have dogged me. Why ? "

" Come now, Count. You used to shoot lions in Algeria."

" Well ? "

" But why ? "

"Why ? The sport—the excitement—the danger ! "

" And, no doubt, to free the country from a pest ? "

" Exactly ! "

" My reasons in a nutshell ! "

The Count sprang to his feet, and his hand involuntarily moved back to his hip-pocket.

" Sit down, sir, sit down ! There was another, more practical, reason. I want that yellow diamond ! "

Count Sylvius lay back in his chair with an evil smile.

" Upon my word ! " said he.

" You knew that I was after you for that. The real reason why you are here to-night is to find out how much I know about the matter and how far my removal is absolutely essential. Well, I should say that, from your point of view, it *is* absolutely essential, for I know all about it, save only one thing, which you are about to tell me."

" Oh, indeed ! And, pray, what is this missing fact ? "

" Where the Crown diamond now is."

The Count looked sharply at his companion. " Oh, you want to know that, do you ? How the devil should I be able to tell you where it is ? "

" You can, and you will."

" Indeed ! "

" You can't bluff me, Count Sylvius." Holmes's eyes, as he gazed at him, contracted and lightened until they were like two menacing points of steel. " You are absolute plate-glass. I see to the very back of your mind."

" Then, of course, you see where the diamond is ! "

Holmes clapped his hands with amusement, and then pointed a derisive finger. " Then you do know. You have admitted it ! "

" I admit nothing."

" Now, Count, if you will be reasonable, we can do business. If not, you will get hurt."

Count Sylvius threw up his eyes to the ceiling. " And you talk about bluff ! " said he.

HOLMES looked at him thoughtfully, like a master chess-player who meditates his crowning move. Then he threw open the table drawer and drew out a squat note-book.

" Do you know what I keep in this book ? "

" No, sir, I do not ! "

" You ! "

" Me ? "

" Yes, sir, *you !* You are all here—every action of your vile and dangerous life."

" Damn you, Holmes ! " cried the Count, with blazing eyes. " There are limits to my patience ! "

" It's all here, Count. The real facts as to the death of old Mrs. Harold, who left you the Blymer estate, which you so rapidly gambled away."

" You are dreaming ! "

" And the complete life history of Miss Minnie Warrender."

" Tut ! You will make nothing of that ! "

" Plenty more here, Count. Here is the robbery in the train-de-luxe to the Riviera on February 13th, 1892. Here is the forged cheque in the same year on the Crédit Lyonnais."

" No ; you're wrong there."

" Then I am right on the others ! Now, Count, you are a card-player. When the other fellow has all the trumps, it saves time to throw down your hand."

" What has all this talk to do with the jewel of which you spoke ? "

" Gently, Count. Restrain that eager mind ! Let me get to the points in my own humdrum fashion. I have all this against you ; but, above all, I have a clear case against both you and your fighting bully in the case of the Crown diamond."

" Indeed ! "

" I have the cabman who took you to Whitehall and the cabman who brought you away. I have the Commissionaire who saw you near the case. I have Ikey Sanders, who refused to cut it up for you. Ikey has peached, and the game is up."

The veins stood out on the Count's forehead. His dark, hairy hands were clenched in a convulsion of restrained emotion. He tried to speak, but the words would not shape themselves.

" That's the hand I play from," said Holmes. " I put it all upon the table. But one card is missing. It's the King of Diamonds. I don't know where the stone is."

" You never shall know."

"No? Now, be reasonable, Count. Consider the situation. You are going to be locked up for twenty years. So is Sam Merton. What good are you going to get out of your diamond? None in the world. But if you hand it over—well, I'll compound a felony. We don't want you or Sam. We want the stone. Give that up, and so far as I am concerned you can go free so long as you behave yourself in the future. If you make another slip—well, it will be the last. But this time my commission is to get the stone, not you."

"But if I refuse?"

"Why, then—alas!—it must be you and not the stone."

Billy had appeared in answer to a ring.

"I think, Count, that it would be as well to have your friend Sam at this conference. After all, his interests should be represented. Billy, you will see a large and ugly gentleman outside the front door. Ask him to come up."

"If he won't come, sir?"

"No violence, Billy. Don't be rough with him. If you tell him that Count Sylvius wants him he will certainly come."

"What are you going to do now?" asked the Count, as Billy disappeared.

"My friend Watson was with me just now. I told him that I had a shark and a gudgeon in my net; now I am drawing the net and up they come together."

The Count had risen from his chair, and his hand was behind his back. Holmes held something half protruding from the pocket of his dressing-gown.

"You won't die in your bed, Holmes."

"I have often had the same idea. Does it matter very much? After all, Count, your own exit is more likely to be perpendicular than horizontal. But these anticipations of the future are morbid. Why not give ourselves up to the unrestrained enjoyment of the present?"

A sudden wild-beast light sprang up in the dark, menacing eyes of the master criminal. Holmes's figure seemed to grow taller as he grew tense and ready.

"It is no use your fingering your revolver, my friend," he said, in a quiet voice. "You know perfectly well that you dare not use it, even if I gave you time to draw it. Nasty, noisy things, revolvers, Count. Better stick to air-guns. Ah! I think I hear the fairy footstep of your estimable partner. Good day, Mr. Merton. Rather dull in the street, is it not?"

THE prize-fighter, a heavily built young man with a stupid, obstinate, slab-sided face, stood awkwardly at the door, looking about him with a puzzled expression. Holmes's debonair manner was a new experience, and though he vaguely felt that it was hostile, he did not know how to counter it. He turned to his more astute comrade for help.

"What's the game now, Count? What's this fellow want? What's up?" His voice was deep and raucous.

The Count shrugged his shoulders and it was Holmes who answered.

"If I may put it in a nutshell, Mr. Merton, I should say it was all up."

The boxer still addressed his remarks to his associate.

"Is this cove trying to be funny, or what? I'm not in the funny mood myself."

"No, I expect not," said Holmes. "I think I can promise you that you will feel even less humorous as the evening advances. Now, look here, Count Sylvius. I'm a busy man and I can't waste time. I'm going into that bedroom. Pray make yourselves quite at home in my absence. You can explain to your friend how the matter lies without the restraint of my presence. I shall try over the Hoffmann Barcarole upon my violin. In five minutes I shall return for your final answer. You quite grasp the alternative, do you not? Shall we take you, or shall we have the stone?"

Holmes withdrew, picking up his violin from the corner as he passed. A few moments later the long-drawn, wailing notes of that most haunting of tunes came faintly through the closed door of the bedroom.

"What is it, then?" asked Merton, anxiously, as his companion turned to him. "Does he know about the stone?"

"He knows a damned sight too much about it. I'm not sure that he doesn't know all about it."

"Good Lord!" The boxer's sallow face turned a shade whiter.

"Ikey Sanders has split on us."

"He has, has he? I'll do him down a thick 'un for that if I swing for it."

"That won't help us much. We've got to make up our minds what to do."

"Half a mo'," said the boxer, looking suspiciously at the bedroom door. "He's a leary cove that wants watching. I suppose he's not listening?"

"How can he be listening with that music going?"

"That's right. Maybe somebody's behind a curtain. Too many curtains in this room." As he looked round he suddenly saw for the first time the effigy in the window, and stood staring and pointing, too amazed for words.

"Tut! it's only a dummy," said the Count.

"A fake, is it? Well, strike me! Madame Tussaud ain't in it. It's the living spit of him, gown and all. But them curtains, Count!"

" Oh, confound the curtains ! We are wasting our time, and there is none too much. He can lag us over this stone."

" The deuce he can ! "

" But he'll let us slip if we only tell him where the swag is."

" What ! Give it up ? Give up a hundred thousand quid ? "

" It's one or the other."

Merton scratched his short-cropped pate.

" He's alone in there. Let's do him in. If his light were out we should have nothing to fear."

The Count shook his head.

" He is armed and ready. If we shot him we could hardly get away in a place like this. Besides, it's likely enough that the police know whatever evidence he has got. Hallo ! What was that ? "

There was a vague sound which seemed to come from the window. Both men sprang round, but all was quiet. Save for the one strange figure seated in the chair, the room was certainly empty.

" Something in the street," said Merton. " Now look here, guv'nor, you've got the brains. Surely you can think a way out of it. If slugging is no use, then it's up to you."

" I've fooled better men than he," the Count answered. " The stone is here in my secret pocket. I take no chances leaving it about. It can be out of England to-night and cut into four pieces in Amsterdam before Sunday. He knows nothing of Van Seddar."

" I thought Van Seddar was going next week."

" He was. But now he must get off by the next boat. One or other of us must slip round with the stone to Lime Street and tell him."

" But the false bottom ain't ready."

" Well, he must take it as it is and chance it. There's not a moment to lose." Again, with the sense of danger which becomes an instinct with the sportsman, he paused and looked hard at the window. Yes, it was surely from the street that the faint sound had come.

" As to Holmes," he continued, " we can fool him easily enough. You see, the damned fool won't arrest us if he can get the stone. Well, we'll promise him the stone. We'll put him on the wrong track about it, and before he finds that it *is* the wrong track it will be in Holland and we out of the country."

" That sounds good to me ! " cried Sam Merton, with a grin.

" You go on and tell the Dutchman to get a move on him. I'll see this sucker and fill him up with a bogus confession. I'll tell him that the stone is in Liverpool. Confound that whining music ; it gets on my nerves ! By the time he finds it isn't in Liverpool it

will be in quarters and we on the blue water. Come back here, out of a line with that keyhole. Here is the stone."

" I wonder you dare carry it."

" Where could I have it safer ? If we could take it out of Whitehall someone else could surely take it out of my lodgings."

" Let's have a look at it."

COUNT SYLVIUS cast a somewhat unflattering glance at his associate, and disregarded the unwashed hand which was extended towards him.

' What—d'ye think I'm going to snatch it off you ? See here, mister, I'm getting a bit tired of your ways."

" Well, well ; no offence, Sam. We can't afford to quarrel. Come over to the window if you want to see the beauty properly. Now hold it to the light ! Here ! "

" Thank you ! "

With a single spring Holmes had leaped from the dummy's chair and had grasped the precious jewel. He held it now in one hand, while his other pointed a revolver at the Count's head. The two villains staggered back in utter amazement. Before they had recovered Holmes had pressed the electric bell.

" No violence, gentlemen—no violence, I beg of you ! Consider the furniture ! It must be very clear to you that your position is an impossible one. The police are waiting below."

The Count's bewilderment overmastered his rage and fear.

" But how the deuce—— ? " he gasped.

" Your surprise is very natural. You are not aware that a second door from my bedroom leads behind that curtain. I fancied that you must have heard me when I displaced the figure, but luck was on my side. It gave me a chance of listening to your racy conversation, which would have been painfully constrained had you been aware of my presence."

The Count gave a gesture of resignation.

" We give you best, Holmes. I believe you are the devil himself."

" Not far from him, at any rate," Holmes answered, with a polite smile.

Sam Merton's slow intellect had only gradually appreciated the situation. Now, as the sound of heavy steps came from the stairs outside, he broke silence at last.

" A fair cop ! " said he. " But, I say, what about that bloomin' fiddle ! I hear it yet."

" Tut, tut ! " Holmes answered. " You are perfectly right. Let it play ! These modern gramophones are a remarkable invention."

There was an inrush of police, the handcuffs clicked, and the criminals were led to

" ' I'm going into that bedroom,' said Holmes. 'Pray make yourselves quite at home in my absence. In five minutes I shall return for your final answer.' "

the waiting cab. Watson lingered with Holmes, congratulating him upon this fresh leaf added to his laurels. Once more their conversation was interrupted by the imperturbable Billy with his card-tray.

" Lord Cantlemere, sir."

" Show him up, Billy. This is the eminent peer who represents the very highest interests," said Holmes. " He is an excellent and loyal person, but rather of the old *régime*.

Shall we make him unbend ? Dare we venture upon a slight liberty ? He knows, we may conjecture, nothing of what has occurred."

THE door opened to admit a thin, austere figure with a hatchet face and drooping mid-Victorian whiskers of a glossy blackness which hardly corresponded with the rounded shoulders and feeble gait. Holmes advanced affably, and shook an unresponsive hand.

"How do you do, Lord Cantlemere ? It is chilly, for the time of year, but rather warm indoors. May I take your overcoat ? "

"No, I thank you ; I will not take it off." Holmes laid his hand insistently upon the sleeve.

"Pray allow me ! My friend Dr. Watson would assure you that these changes of temperature are most insidious."

His lordship shook himself free with some impatience.

"I am quite comfortable, sir. I have no need to stay. I have simply looked in to know how your self-appointed task was progressing."

"It is difficult—very difficult."

"I feared that you would find it so."

There was a distinct sneer in the old courtier's words and manner.

"Every man finds his limitations, Mr. Holmes, but at least it cures us of the weakness of self-satisfaction."

"Yes, sir, I have been much perplexed."

"No doubt."

"Especially upon one point. Possibly you could help me upon it ? "

"You apply for my advice rather late in the day. I thought that you had your own all-sufficient methods. Still, I am ready to help you."

"You see, Lord Cantlemere, we can no doubt frame a case against the actual thieves."

"When you have caught them."

"Exactly. But the question is—how shall we proceed against the receiver ? "

"Is this not rather premature ? "

"It is as well to have our plans ready. Now, what would you regard as final evidence against the receiver ? "

"The actual possession of the stone."

"You would arrest him upon that ? "

"Most undoubtedly."

Holmes seldom laughed, but he got as near it as his old friend Watson could remember.

"In that case, my dear sir, I shall be under the painful necessity of advising your arrest."

Lord Cantlemere was very angry. Some of the ancient fires flickered up into his sallow cheeks.

"You take a great liberty, Mr. Holmes. In fifty years of official life I cannot recall such a case. I am a busy man, sir, engaged upon important affairs, and I have no time or taste for foolish jokes. I may tell you frankly, sir, that I have never been a believer in your powers, and that I have always been of the opinion that the matter was far safer in the hands of the regular police force. Your conduct confirms all my conclusions. I have the honour, sir, to wish you good evening."

Holmes had swiftly changed his position and was between the peer and the door.

"One moment, sir," said he. "To actually go off with the Mazarin stone would be a more serious offence than to be found in temporary possession of it."

"Sir, this is intolerable ! Let me pass."

"Put your hand in the right-hand pocket of your overcoat."

"What do you mean, sir ? "

"Come—come ; do what I ask."

An instant later the amazed peer was standing, blinking and stammering, with the great yellow stone on his shaking palm.

"What ! What ! How is this, Mr. Holmes ? "

"Too bad, Lord Cantlemere, too bad ! " cried Holmes. "My old friend here will tell you that I have an impish habit of practical joking. Also that I can never resist a dramatic situation. I took the liberty—the very great liberty, I admit—of putting the stone into your pocket at the beginning of our interview."

The old peer stared from the stone to the smiling face before him.

"Sir, I am bewildered. But—yes—it is indeed the Mazarin stone. We are greatly your debtors, Mr. Holmes. Your sense of humour may, as you admit, be somewhat perverted, and its exhibition remarkably untimely, but at least I withdraw any reflection I have made upon your amazing professional powers. But how——"

"The case is but half finished ; the details can wait. No doubt, Lord Cantlemere, your pleasure in telling of this successful result in the exalted circle to which you return will be some small atonement for my practical joke. Billy, you will show his lordship out, and tell Mrs. Hudson that I should be glad if she would send up dinner for two as soon as possible."

"'IT TOOK SOME VIOLENCE TO DO THAT,' SAID HOLMES, GAZING AT THE
CHIP ON THE LEDGE. WITH HIS CANE HE STRUCK THE LEDGE SEVERAL
TIMES WITHOUT LEAVING A MARK. 'YES, IT WAS A HARD KNOCK.'"

A NEW SHERLOCK HOLMES STORY

THE PROBLEM OF THOR BRIDGE

by

A·CONAN DOYLE

ILLUSTRATED BY
A. GILBERT ROI

SOMEWHERE in the vaults of the bank of Cox and Co., at Charing Cross, there is a travel-worn and battered tin despatch-box with my name, John H. Watson, M.D., Late Indian Army, painted upon the lid. It is crammed with papers, nearly all of which are records of cases to illustrate the curious problems which Mr. Sherlock Holmes had at various times to examine. Some, and not the least interesting, were complete failures, and as such will hardly bear narrating, since no final explanation is forthcoming. A problem without a solution may interest the student, but can hardly fail to annoy the casual reader. Among these unfinished tales is that of Mr. James Phillimore, who, stepping back into his own house to get his umbrella, was never more seen in this world. No less remarkable is that of the cutter *Alicia*, which sailed one spring morning into a small patch of mist from which she never again emerged, nor was anything further ever heard of herself and her crew. A third case worthy of note is that of Isadora Persano, the well-known journalist and duellist, who was found stark staring mad with a matchbox in front of him which contained a remarkable worm, said to be unknown to science. Apart from these unfathomed cases, there are some which involve the secrets of private families to an extent which would mean consternation in many exalted quarters if it were thought possible that they might find their way into print. I need not say that such a breach of confidence is unthinkable, and that these records will be separated and destroyed now that my friend has time to turn his energies to the matter. There remain a considerable residue of cases of greater or less interest which I might have edited before had I not feared to give the public a surfeit which might react upon the reputation of the man whom above all others I revere. In some I was myself concerned and can speak as an eye-witness, while in others I was either not present or played so small a part that they could only be told as by a third person. The following narrative is drawn from my own experience.

It was a wild morning in October, and I observed as I was dressing how the last remaining leaves were being whirled from the solitary plane tree which graces the yard behind our house. I descended to breakfast prepared to find my companion in depressed spirits, for, like all great artists, he was easily impressed by his surroundings. On the contrary, I found that he had nearly finished his meal, and that his mood was particularly bright and joyous, with that somewhat sinister cheerfulness which was characteristic of his lighter moments.

" You have a case, Holmes ? " I remarked.

" The faculty of deduction is certainly contagious, Watson," he answered. " It has enabled you to probe my secret. Yes, I have a case. After a month of trivialities and stagnation the wheels move once more."

" Might I share it ? "

" There is little to share, but we may discuss it when you have consumed the two hard-boiled eggs with which our new cook has favoured us. Their condition may not be unconnected with the copy of the *Family Herald* which I observed yesterday upon the hall-table. Even so trivial a matter as cooking an egg demands an attention which is conscious of the passage of time, and incompatible with the love romance in that excellent periodical."

A QUARTER of an hour later the table had been cleared and we were face to face. He had drawn a letter from his pocket.

" You have heard of Neil Gibson, the Gold King ? " he said.

" You mean the American Senator ? "

" Well, he was once Senator for some Western State, but is better known as the greatest gold-mining magnate in the world."

" Yes, I know of him. He has surely lived in England for some time. His name is very familiar."

" Yes ; he bought a considerable estate in Hampshire some five years ago. Possibly you have already heard of the tragic end of his wife ? "

" Of course. I remember it now. That is why the name is familiar. But I really know nothing of the details."

Holmes waved his hand towards some papers on a chair. " I had no idea that the case was coming my way or I should have had my extracts ready," said he. " The fact is that the problem, though exceedingly

sensational, appeared to present no difficulty. The interesting personality of the accused does not obscure the clearness of the evidence. That was the view taken by the coroner's jury and also in the police-court proceedings. It is now referred to the Assizes at Winchester. I fear it is a thankless business. I can discover facts, Watson, but I cannot change them. Unless some entirely new and unexpected ones come to light I do not see what my client can hope for."

" Your client ? "

" Ah, I forgot I had not told you. I am getting into your involved habit, Watson, of telling a story backwards. You had best read this first."

The letter which he handed to me, written in a bold, masterful hand, ran as follows :—

CLARIDGE'S HOTEL,
October 3rd.

DEAR MR. SHERLOCK HOLMES,—

I can't see the best woman God ever made go to her death without doing all that is possible to save her. I can't explain things—I can't even try to explain them, but I know beyond all doubt that Miss Dunbar is innocent. You know the facts—who doesn't ? It has been the gossip of the country. And never a voice raised for her ! It's the damned injustice of it all that makes me crazy. That woman has a heart that wouldn't let her kill a fly. Well, I'll come at eleven to-morrow and see if you can get some ray of light in the dark. Maybe I have a clue and don't know it. Anyhow, all I know and all I have and all I am are for your use if only you can save her. If ever in your life you showed your powers, put them now into this case.

Yours faithfully,
J. NEIL GIBSON.

" There you have it," said Sherlock Holmes, knocking out the ashes of his after-breakfast pipe and slowly refilling it. " That is the gentleman I await. As to the story, you have hardly time to master all these papers, so I must give it to you in a nutshell if you are to take an intelligent interest in the proceedings. This man is the greatest financial power in the world, and a man, as I understand, of most violent and formidable character. He married a wife, the victim of this tragedy, of whom I know nothing save that she was past her prime, which was the more unfortunate as a very attractive governess superintended the education of two young children. These are the three people concerned and the scene is a grand old manor house, the centre of an historical English estate. Then as to the tragedy. The wife was found in the grounds nearly half a mile from the house, late at night, clad in her dinner dress, with a shawl over her shoulders and a revolver bullet through her brain. No weapon was found near her and there was no local clue as to the murder. No weapon near her, Watson—mark that ! The crime seems to have been committed late in the evening, and the body was found by a gamekeeper about eleven o'clock, when it was examined by the police and by a doctor before being carried up to the house. Is this too condensed, or can you follow it clearly ? '

" It is all very clear. But why suspect the governess ? "

' Well, in the first place there is some very direct evidence. A revolver with one discharged chamber and a calibre which corresponded with the bullet was found on the floor of her wardrobe." His eyes fixed and he repeated in broken words, " On—the—floor—of—her—wardrobe." Then he sank into silence, and I saw that some train of thought had been set moving which I should be foolish to interrupt. Suddenly with a start he emerged into brisk life once more.

" Yes, Watson, it was found. Pretty damning, eh ? So the two juries thought. Then the dead woman had a note upon her making an appointment at that very place and signed by the governess. How's that ? Finally, there is the motive. Senator Gibson is an attractive person. If his wife dies, who more likely to succeed her than the young lady who had already by all accounts received pressing attentions from her employer ? Love, fortune, power, all depending upon one middle-aged life. Ugly, Watson—very ugly ! "

deny it, for some passing villager had seen her there."

' That really seems final."

" And yet, Watson—and yet ! This bridge —a single broad span of stone with balustraded sides—carries the drive over the narrowest part of a long, deep, reed-girt sheet of water. Thor Mere it is called. In the mouth of the bridge lay the dead woman. Such are the main facts. But here, if I mistake not, is our client, considerably before his time."

Billy had opened the door, but the name which he announced was an unexpected one. Mr. Marlow Bates was a stranger to both of us. He was a thin, nervous wisp of a man with frightened eyes, and a twitching, hesitating manner—a man whom my own professional eye would judge to be on the brink of an absolute nervous breakdown.

' You seem agitated, Mr. Bates," said Holmes. " Pray sit down. I fear I can only give you a short time, for I have an appointment at eleven."

' I know you have," our visitor gasped, shooting out short sentences like a man who is out of breath. " Mr. Gibson is coming. Mr. Gibson is my employer. I am manager of his estate. Mr. Holmes, he is a villain—an infernal villain."

" Yes, indeed, Holmes."

Nor could she prove an alibi. On the contrary, she had to admit that she was down near Thor Bridge—that was the scene of the tragedy—about that hour. She couldn't

" The wife was found in the grounds, late at night, with a revolver bullet through her brain."

" Strong language, Mr. Bates."

" I have to be emphatic, Mr. Holmes, for the time is so limited. I would not have him find me here for the world. He is almost due now. But I was so situated that I could not come earlier. His secretary, Mr. Ferguson, only told me this morning of his appointment with you."

" And you are his manager ? "

" I have given him notice. In a couple of weeks I shall have shaken off his accursed slavery. A hard man, Mr. Holmes, hard to all about him. Those public charities are a screen to cover his private iniquities. But his wife was his chief victim. He was brutal to her—yes, sir, brutal ! How she came by her death I do not know, but I am sure that he had made her life a misery to her. She was a creature of the Tropics, a Brazilian by birth, as no doubt you know ? "

" No ; it had escaped me."

" Tropical by birth and tropical by nature. A child of the sun and of passion. She had loved him as such women can love, but when her own physical charms had faded—I am told that they once were great—there was nothing to hold him. We all liked her and felt for her and hated him for the way that he treated her. But he is plausible and cunning. That is all I have to say to you. Don't take him at his face value. There is more behind. Now I'll go. No, no, don't detain me ! He is almost due."

With a frightened look at the clock our strange visitor literally ran to the door and disappeared.

" Well ! well ! " said Holmes, after an interval of silence. " Mr. Gibson seems to have a nice loyal household. But the warning is a useful one, and now we can only wait till the man himself appears."

SHARP at the hour we heard a heavy step upon the stairs and the famous millionaire was shown into the room. As I looked upon him I understood not only the fears and dislike of his manager, but also the execrations which so many business rivals have heaped upon his head. If I were a sculptor and desired to idealize the successful man of affairs, iron of nerve and leathery of conscience, I should choose Mr. Neil Gibson as my model. His tall, gaunt, craggy figure had a suggestion of hunger and rapacity. An Abraham Lincoln keyed to base uses instead of high ones would give some idea of the man. His face might have been chiselled in granite, hard-set, craggy, remorseless, with deep lines upon it, the scars of many a crisis. Cold grey eyes, looking shrewdly out from under bristling brows, surveyed us each in turn. He bowed in perfunctory fashion as Holmes mentioned my name, and then with a masterful air of possession he

drew a chair up to my companion and seated himself with his bony knees almost touching him.

" Let me say right here, Mr. Holmes," he began, " that money is nothing to me in this case. You can burn it if it's any use in lighting you to the truth. This woman is innocent and this woman has to be cleared, and it's up to you to do it. Name your figure ! "

" My professional charges are upon a fixed scale," said Holmes, coldly. " I do not vary them, save when I remit them altogether."

" Well, if dollars make no difference to you, think of the reputation. If you pull this off every paper in England and America will be booming you. You'll be the talk of two continents."

" Thank you, Mr. Gibson, I do not think that I am in need of booming. It may surprise you to know that I prefer to work anonymously, and that it is the problem itself which attracts me. But we are wasting time. Let us get down to the facts."

" I think that you will find all the main ones in the Press reports. I don't know that I can add anything which will help you. But if there is anything you would wish more light upon—well, I am here to give it."

" Well, there is just one point."

" What is it ? "

" What were the exact relations between you and Miss Dunbar ? "

The Gold King gave a violent start, and half rose from his chair. Then his massive calm came back to him.

" I suppose you are within your rights— and maybe doing your duty—in asking such a question, Mr. Holmes."

" We will agree to suppose so," said Holmes.

" Then I can assure you that our relations were entirely and always those of an employer towards a young lady whom he never conversed with, or even saw, save when she was in the company of his children."

Holmes rose from his chair.

" I am a rather busy man, Mr. Gibson," said he, " and I have no time or taste for aimless conversations. I wish you good morning."

Our visitor had risen also and his great loose figure towered above Holmes. There was an angry gleam from under those bristling brows and a tinge of colour in the sallow cheeks.

" What the devil do you mean by this, Mr. Holmes ? Do you dismiss my case ? "

" Well, Mr. Gibson, at least I dismiss you. I should have thought my words were plain."

" Plain enough, but what's at the back of it ? Raising the price on me, or afraid to tackle it, or what ? I've a right to a plain answer "

"I sprang to my feet, for the expression upon the millionaire's face was fiendish in its intensity, and he had raised his great knotted fist. Holmes smiled languidly and reached his hand out for his pipe."

" Well, perhaps you have," said Holmes. " I'll give you one. This case is quite sufficiently complicated to start with, without the further difficulty of false information."

" Meaning that I lie."

" Well, I was trying to express it as delicately as I could, but if you insist upon the word I will not contradict you."

I sprang to my feet, for the expression upon the millionaire's face was fiendish in its intensity, and he had raised his great knotted fist. Holmes smiled languidly and reached his hand out for his pipe.

" Don't be noisy, Mr. Gibson. I find that after breakfast even the smallest argument is unsettling. I suggest that a stroll in the morning air and a little quiet thought will be greatly to your advantage."

With an effort the Gold King mastered his fury. I could not but admire him, for by a supreme self-command he had turned in a minute from a hot flame of anger to a frigid and contemptuous indifference.

" Well, it's your choice. I guess you know how to run your own business. I can't make you touch the case against your will. You've done yourself no good this morning, Mr. Holmes, for I have broken stronger men than you. No man ever crossed me and was the better for it."

" So many have said so, and yet here I am," said Holmes, smiling. " Well, good morning, Mr. Gibson. You have a good deal yet to learn."

Our visitor made a noisy exit, but Holmes smoked in imperturbable silence, with dreamy eyes fixed upon the ceiling.

" ANY views, Watson ? " he asked at last. " Well, Holmes, I must confess that when I consider that this is a man who would certainly brush any obstacle from his path, and when I remember that his wife may have been an obstacle and an object of dislike, as that man Bates plainly told us, it seems to me——"

" Exactly. And to me also."

" But what were his relations with the governess and how did you discover them ? "

" Bluff, Watson, bluff ! When I considered the passionate, unconventional, unbusinesslike tone of his letter, and contrasted it with his self-contained manner and appearance, it was pretty clear that there was some deep emotion which centred upon the accused woman rather than upon the victim. We've got to understand the exact relations of those three people if we are to reach the truth. You saw the frontal attack which I made upon him and how imperturbably he received it. Then I bluffed him by giving him the impression that I was absolutely certain, when in reality I was only extremely suspicious."

" Perhaps he will come back ? "

" He is sure to come back. He *must* come back. He can't leave it where it is. Ha ! isn't that a ring ? Yes, there is his footstep. Well, Mr. Gibson, I was just saying to Dr. Watson that you were somewhat overdue."

The Gold King had re-entered the room in a more chastened mood than he had left it. His wounded pride still showed in his resentful eyes, but his common sense had shown him that he must yield if he would attain his end.

" I've been thinking it over, Mr. Holmes, and I feel that I have been hasty in taking your remarks amiss. You are justified in getting down to the facts, whatever they may be, and I think the more of you for it. I can assure you, however, that the relations between Miss Dunbar and me don't really touch this case."

" That is for me to decide, is it not ? "

" Yes, I guess that is so. You're like a surgeon who wants every symptom before he can give his diagnosis."

" Exactly. That expresses it. And it is only a patient who has an object in deceiving his surgeon who would conceal the facts of his case."

" That may be so, but you will admit, Mr. Holmes, that most men would shy off a bit when they are asked point-blank what their relations with a woman may be—if there is really some serious feeling in the case. I guess most men have a little private reserve of their own in some corner of their souls where they don't welcome intruders. But the object excuses you, since it was to try and save her. Well, the stakes are down and the reserve open and you can explore where you will. What is it you want ? "

" The truth."

The Gold King paused for a moment as one who marshals his thoughts. His grim, deep-lined face had become even sadder and more grave.

" I can give it to you in a very few words, Mr. Holmes," said he at last. " There are some things that are painful as well as difficult to say, so I won't go deeper than is needful. I met my wife when I was gold-hunting in Brazil. Maria Pinto was the daughter of a Government official at Manaos, and she was very beautiful. I was young and ardent in those days, but even now, as I look back with colder blood and a more critical eye, I can see that she was rare and wonderful in her beauty. It was a deep rich nature, too, passionate, whole-hearted, tropical, ill-balanced, very different from the American women whom I had known. Well, to make a long story short, I loved her and I married her. It was only when the romance had passed—and it lingered for years—that

I realized that we had nothing—absolutely nothing—in common. My love faded. If hers had faded also it might have been easier. But you know the wonderful way of women ! Do what I might nothing could turn her from me. If I have been harsh to her, even brutal as some have said, it has been because I knew that if I could kill her love, or if it turned to hate, it would be easier for both of us. But nothing changed her. She adored me in those English woods as she had adored me twenty years ago on the banks of the Amazon. Do what I might, she was as devoted as ever.

"Then came Miss Grace Dunbar. She answered our advertisement and became governess to our two children. Perhaps you have seen her portrait in the papers. The whole world has proclaimed that she also is a very beautiful woman. Now, I make no pretence to be more moral than my neighbours, and I will admit to you that I could not live under the same roof with such a woman and in daily contact with her without feeling a passionate regard for her. Do you blame me, Mr. Holmes ? "

" I do not blame you for feeling it. I should blame you if you expressed it, since this young lady was in a sense under your protection."

" Well, maybe so," said the millionaire, though for a moment the reproof had brought the old angry gleam into his eyes. " I'm not pretending to be any better than I am. I guess all my life I've been a man that reached out his hand for what he wanted, and I never wanted anything more than the love and possession of that woman. I told her so."

" Oh, you did, did you ? "

Holmes could look very formidable when he was moved.

" I said to her that if I could marry her I would, but that it was out of my power. I said that money was no object and that all I could do to make her happy and comfortable would be done."

" Very generous, I am sure," said Holmes, with a sneer.

" See here, Mr. Holmes. I came to you on a question of evidence, not on a question of morals. I'm not asking for your criticism."

" It is only for the young lady's sake that I touch your case at all," said Holmes, sternly. " I don't know that anything she is accused of is really worse than what you have yourself admitted, that you have tried to ruin a defenceless girl who was under your roof. Some of you rich men have to be taught that all the world cannot be bribed into condoning your offences."

To my surprise the Gold King took the reproof with equanimity.

" That's how I feel myself about it now.

I thank God that my plans did not work out as I intended. She would have none of it, and she wanted to leave the house instantly."

" Why did she not ? "

" Well, in the first place, others were dependent upon her, and it was no light matter for her to let them all down by sacrificing her living. When I had sworn—as I did—that she should never be molested again, she consented to remain. But there was another reason. She knew the influence she had over me, and that it was stronger than any other influence in the world. She wanted to use it for good."

" How ? "

" Well, she knew something of my affairs. They are large, Mr. Holmes—large beyond the belief of an ordinary man. I can make or break—and it is usually break. It wasn't individuals only. It was communities, cities, even nations. Business is a hard game, and the weak go to the wall. I played the game for all it was worth. I never squealed myself and I never cared if the other fellow squealed. But she saw it different. I guess she was right. She believed and said that a fortune for one man that was more than he needed should not be built on ten thousand ruined men who were left without the means of life. That was how she saw it, and I guess she could see past the dollars to something that was more lasting. She found that I listened to what she said, and she believed she was serving the world by influencing my actions. So she stayed—and then this came along."

" Can you throw any light upon that ? "

THE Gold King paused for a minute or more, his head sunk in his hands, lost in deep thought.

" It's very black against her. I can't deny that. And women lead an inward life and may do things beyond the judgment of a man. At first I was so rattled and taken aback that I was ready to think she had been led away in some extraordinary fashion that was clean against her usual nature. One explanation came into my head. I give it to you, Mr. Holmes, for what it is worth. There is no doubt that my wife was bitterly jealous. There is a soul-jealousy that can be as frantic as any body-jealousy, and though my wife had no cause—and I think she understood this—for the latter, she was aware that this English girl exerted an influence upon my mind and my acts that she herself never had. It was an influence for good, but that did not mend the matter. She was crazy with hatred, and the heat of the Amazon was always in her blood. She might have planned to murder Miss Dunbar —or we will say to threaten her with a gun and so frighten her into leaving us. Then there might have been a scuffle and the gun gone off and shot the woman who held it."

"That possibility had already occurred to me," said Holmes. "Indeed, it is the only obvious alternative to deliberate murder."

"But she utterly denies it."

"Well, that is not final—is it ? One can understand that a woman placed in so awful a position might hurry home still in her bewilderment holding the revolver. She might even throw it down among her clothes, hardly knowing what she was doing, and when it was found she might try to lie her way out by a total denial, since all explanation was impossible. What is against such a supposition ? "

"Miss Dunbar herself."

"Well, perhaps."

Holmes looked at his watch. "I have no doubt we can get the necessary permits this morning and reach Winchester by the evening train. When I have seen this young lady, it is very possible that I may be of more use to you in the matter, though I cannot promise that my conclusions will necessarily be such as you desire."

THERE was some delay in the official pass, and instead of reaching Winchester that day we went down to Thor Place, the Hampshire estate of Mr. Neil Gibson. He did not accompany us himself, but we had the address of Sergeant Coventry, of the local police, who had first examined into the affair. He was a tall, thin, cadaverous man, with a secretive and mysterious manner, which conveyed the idea that he knew or suspected a very great deal more than he dared say. He had a trick, too, of suddenly sinking his voice to a whisper as if he had come upon something of vital importance, though the information was usually commonplace enough. Behind these tricks of manner he soon showed himself to be a decent, honest fellow who was not too proud to admit that he was out of his depth and would welcome any help.

"Anyhow, I'd rather have you than Scotland Yard, Mr. Holmes," said he. "If the Yard gets called into a case, then the local loses all credit for success and may be blamed for failure. Now, you play straight, so I've heard."

"I need not appear in the matter at all," said Holmes, to the evident relief of our melancholy acquaintance. "If I can clear it up I don't ask to have my name mentioned."

"Well, it's very handsome of you, I am sure. And your friend, Dr. Watson, can be trusted, I know. Now, Mr. Holmes, as we walk down to the place there is one question I should like to ask you. I'd breathe it to no soul but you." He looked round as though he hardly dare utter the words

"Don't you think there might be a case against Mr. Neil Gibson himself ? "

"I have been considering that."

"You've not seen Miss Dunbar. She is a wonderful fine woman in every way. He may well have wished his wife out of the road. And these Americans are readier with pistols than our folk are. It was *his* pistol, you know."

"Was that clearly made out ? "

"Yes, sir. It was one of a pair that he had."

"One of a pair ? Where is the other ? "

"Well, the gentleman has a lot of firearms of one sort and another. We never quite matched that particular pistol—but the box was made for two."

"If it was one of a pair you should surely be able to match it."

"Well, we have them all laid out at the house if you would care to look them over."

"Later, perhaps. I think we will walk down together and have a look at the scene of the tragedy."

This conversation had taken place in the little front room of Sergeant Coventry's humble cottage, which served as the local police-station. A walk of half a mile or so across a wind-swept heath, all gold and bronze with the fading ferns, brought us to a side gate opening into the grounds of the Thor Place estate. A path led us through the pheasant preserves, and then from a clearing we saw the widespread, half-timbered house, half Tudor and half Georgian, upon the crest of the hill. Beside us there was a long, reedy pool, constricted in the centre where the main carriage drive passed over a stone bridge, but swelling into small lakes on either side. Our guide paused at the mouth of this bridge, and he pointed to the ground.

"That was where Mrs. Gibson's body lay. I marked it by that stone."

"I understand that you were there before it was moved ? "

"Yes ; they sent for me at once."

"Who did ? "

"Mr. Gibson himself. The moment the alarm was given and he had rushed down with others from the house, he insisted that nothing should be moved until the police should arrive."

"That was sensible. I gathered from the newspaper report that the shot was fired from close quarters."

"Yes, sir, very close."

"Near the right temple ? "

"Just behind it, sir."

"How did the body lie ? "

"On the back, sir. No trace of a struggle. No marks. No weapon. The short note from Miss Dunbar was clutched in her left hand "

"Clutched, you say?"

"Yes, sir; we could hardly open the fingers."

"That is of great importance. It excludes the idea that anyone could have placed the note there after death in order to furnish a false clue. Dear me! The note, as I remember, was quite short. 'I will be at Thor Bridge at nine o'clock.— G. Dunbar.' Was that not so?"

"Yes, sir."

"Did Miss Dunbar admit writing it?"

"Yes, sir."

"What was her explanation?"

"Her defence was reserved for the Assizes. She would say nothing."

"The problem is certainly a very interesting one. The point of the letter is very obscure, is it not?"

"Well, sir," said the guide, "it seemed, if I may be so bold as to say so, the only really clear point in the whole case."

Holmes shook his head.

"Granting that the letter is genuine and was really written, it was certainly received some time before—say one hour or two. Why, then, was this lady still clasping it in her left hand? Why should she carry it so carefully? She did not need to refer to it in the interview. Does it not seem remarkable?"

"Well, sir, as you put it, perhaps it does."

"I think I should like to sit quietly for a few minutes and think it out." He seated himself upon the stone ledge of the bridge, and I could see his quick grey eyes darting their questioning glances in every direction. Suddenly he sprang up again and ran across to the opposite parapet, whipped his lens from his pocket, and began to examine the stonework.

"This is curious," said he.

"Yes, sir; we saw the chip on the ledge. I expect it's been done by some passer-by."

The stonework was grey, but at this one point it showed white for a space not larger than a sixpence. When examined closely one could see that the surface was chipped as by a sharp blow.

"It took some violence to do that," said

"Our guide pointed to the ground. 'That was where Mrs. Gibson's body lay.'"

Holmes, thoughtfully. With his cane he struck the ledge several times without leaving a mark. "Yes, it was a hard knock. In a curious place, too. It was not from above but from below, for you see that it is on the *lower* edge of the parapet."

"But it is at least fifteen feet from the body."

"Yes, it is fifteen feet from the body. It may have nothing to do with the matter, but it is a point worth noting. I do not think that we have anything more to learn here. There were no footsteps, you say?"

"The ground was iron hard, sir. There were no traces at all."

"Then we can go. We will go up to the house first and look over these weapons of which you speak. Then we shall get on to Winchester, for I should desire to see Miss Dunbar before we go farther."

MR. NEIL GIBSON had not returned from town, but we saw in the house the neurotic Mr. Bates who had called upon us in the morning. He showed us with a sinister relish the formidable array of firearms of various shapes and sizes which his employer had accumulated in the course of an adventurous life.

"Mr. Gibson has his enemies, as anyone would expect who knew him and his methods," said he. 'He sleeps with a loaded revolver in the drawer beside his bed. He is a man of violence, sir, and there are times when all of us are afraid of him. I am sure that the poor lady who has passed was often terrified."

"Did you ever witness physical violence towards her?"

"No, I cannot say that. But I have heard words which were nearly as bad—words of cold, cutting contempt, even before the servants."

"Our millionaire does not seem to shine in private life," remarked Holmes, as we made our way to the station. "Well, Watson, we have come on a good many facts, some of them new ones, and yet I seem some way from my conclusion. In spite of the very evident dislike which Mr. Bates has to his employer, I gather from him that when the alarm came he was undoubtedly in his library. Dinner was over at eight-thirty and all was normal up to then. It is true that the alarm was somewhat late in the evening, but the tragedy certainly occurred about the hour named in the note. There is no evidence at all that Mr. Gibson had been out of doors since his return from town at five o'clock. On the other hand, Miss Dunbar, as I understand it, admits that she had made an appointment to meet Mrs. Gibson at the bridge. Beyond this she would say nothing, as her lawyer had advised her to reserve her defence. We have several very vital questions to ask that young lady, and my mind will not be easy until we have seen her. I must confess that the case would seem to me to be very black against her if it were not for one thing."

"And what is that, Holmes?"

"The finding of the pistol in her wardrobe."

"Dear me, Holmes!" I cried, "that seemed to me to be the most damning incident of all."

"Not so, Watson. It had struck me even at my first perfunctory reading as very strange, and now that I am in closer touch with the case it is my only firm ground for hope. We must look for consistency. Where there is a want of it we must suspect deception."

"I hardly follow you."

"Well now, Watson, suppose for a moment that we visualize you in the character of a woman who, in a cold, premeditated fashion, is about to get rid of a rival. You have planned it. A note has been written. The victim has come. You have your weapon. The crime is done. It has been workmanlike and complete. Do you tell me that after carrying out so crafty a crime you would now ruin your reputation as a criminal by forgetting to fling your weapon into those adjacent reed-beds which would for ever cover it, but you must needs carry it carefully home and put it in your own wardrobe, the very first place that would be searched? Your best friends would hardly call you a schemer, Watson, and yet I could not picture you doing anything so crude as that."

"In the excitement of the moment——"

"No, no, Watson, I will not admit that it is possible. Where a crime is coolly premeditated, then the means of covering it are coolly premeditated also. I hope, therefore, that we are in the presence of a serious misconception."

"But there is so much to explain."

"Well, we shall set about explaining it. When once your point of view is changed, the very thing which was so damning becomes a clue to the truth. For example, there is this revolver. Miss Dunbar disclaims all knowledge of it. On our new theory she is speaking truth when she says so. Therefore, it was placed in her wardrobe. Who placed it there? Someone who wished to incriminate her. Was not that person the actual criminal? You see how we come at once upon a most fruitful line of inquiry."

A NEW
SHERLOCK HOLMES STORY

THE PROBLEM OF THOR BRIDGE

by
A·CONAN DOYLE

ILLUSTRATED BY
A.GILBERT·R·O·I·

SYNOPSIS OF THE FIRST PART OF THE STORY.

The three leading figures in this Adventure are Neil Gibson, a famous gold-mining magnate, his wife, and their children's young governess, the attractive Miss Dunbar. The wife was found in the grounds of Thor Place, nearly half a mile from the house, late at night, clad in her dinner dress, with a revolver bullet through her brain. No weapon was found near her. There was no trace of a struggle, but in her left hand was clutched a note reading: "I will be at Thor Bridge at nine o'clock.—G. Dunbar." Later, the police discovered on the floor of the wardrobe in the governess's room a revolver with one discharged chamber and a calibre which corresponded with the bullet. Miss Dunbar, when arrested, could prove no alibi—on the contrary, she admitted she was near Thor Bridge, the scene of the tragedy, about the time of Mrs. Gibson's death. She also admitted writing the note, but would say no more.

Gibson urges Sherlock Holmes to spare neither trouble nor expense to clear Miss Dunbar. "It's very black against her," he admits. "I can't deny that. . . . And there is no doubt that my wife was bitterly jealous."

The revolver is found to belong to Gibson, but there is no evidence that he had been out of doors since his return from town at five o'clock. Miss Dunbar, on the other hand, admitted making the appointment with Mrs. Gibson.

On viewing the scene of the tragedy, Sherlock Holmes's careful examination of the bridge reveals a small and apparently recently-made chip on the parapet. "It took some violence to do that," said Holmes, thoughtfully. "It was a hard knock. In a curious place, too. It was not from above but from below, for you see that it is on the lower edge of the parapet."

As the following instalment shows, this apparently insignificant chip in the stone was really the clue to the solution of the mystery.

W E were compelled to spend the night at Winchester, as the formalities had not yet been completed, but next morning, in the company of Mr. Joyce Cummings, the rising barrister who was entrusted with the defence, we were allowed to see the young lady in her cell. I had expected from all that we had heard to see a beautiful woman, but I can

never forget the effect which Miss Dunbar produced upon me. It was no wonder that even the masterful millionaire had found in her something more powerful than himself—something which could control and guide him. One felt, too, as one looked at that strong, clear-cut, and yet sensitive face, that even should she be capable of some impetuous deed, none the less there was an innate nobility of character which would make her influence always for the good. She was a brunette, tall, with a noble figure and commanding presence, but her dark eyes had in them the appealing, helpless expression of the hunted creature who feels the nets around it, but can see no way out from the toils. Now, as she realized the presence and the help of my famous friend, there came a touch of colour in her wan cheeks and a light of hope began to glimmer in the glance which she turned upon us.

" Perhaps Mr. Neil Gibson has told you something of what occurred between us ? " she asked, in a low, agitated voice.

" Yes," Holmes answered ; " you need not pain yourself by entering into that part of the story. After seeing you, I am prepared to accept Mr. Gibson's statement both as to the influence which you had over him and as to the innocence of your relations with him. But why was the whole situation not brought out in court ? "

" It seemed to me incredible that such a charge could be sustained. I thought that if we waited the whole thing must clear itself up without our being compelled to enter into painful details of the inner life of the family. But I understand that far from clearing it has become even more serious."

" My dear young lady," cried Holmes, earnestly, " I beg you to have no illusions upon the point. Mr. Cummings here would assure you that all the cards are at present against us, and that we must do everything that is possible if we are to win clear. It would be a cruel deception to pretend that you are not in very great danger. Give me all the help you can, then, to get at the truth."

" I will conceal nothing."

" Tell us, then, of your true relations with Mr. Gibson's wife."

" She hated me, Mr. Holmes. She hated me with all the fervour of her tropical nature. She was a woman who would do nothing by halves, and the measure of her love for her husband was the measure also of her hatred for me. It is probable that she misunderstood our relations. I would not wish to wrong her, but she loved so vividly in a physical sense that she could hardly under-

stand the mental, and even spiritual, tie which held her husband to me, or imagine that it was only my desire to influence his power to good ends which kept me under his roof. I can see now that I was wrong. Nothing could justify me in remaining where I was a cause of unhappiness, and yet it is certain that the unhappiness would have

"She poured her whole wild fury out in burning and horrible words—

remained even if I had left the house."

" Now, Miss Dunbar," said Holmes, " I beg you to tell us exactly what occurred that evening."

" I can tell you the truth so far as I know it, Mr. Holmes, but I am in a position to prove nothing, and there are points—the most vital points—which I can neither explain nor can I imagine any explanation."

" If you will find the facts, perhaps others may find the explanation."

" With regard, then, to my presence at Thor Bridge that night, I received a note from Mrs. Gibson in the morning. It lay on the table of the schoolroom, and it may have been left there by her own hand. It implored me to see her there after dinner, said she had something important to say to me, and asked me to leave an answer on the sundial in the garden, as she desired no one to be in our confidence. I saw no reason for such secrecy, but I did as she asked, accepting the appointment. She asked me to destroy her note and I burned it in the schoolroom grate. She was very much afraid of her husband, who treated her with a harshness for which I frequently reproached him, and I could only imagine that she acted in this way because she did not wish him to know of our interview. '

" Yet she kept your reply very carefully ? "

" Yes. I was surprised to hear that she had it in her hand when she died."

" Well, what happened then ? "

" I went down as I had promised. When I reached the bridge she was waiting for me. Never did I realize till that moment how this poor creature hated me. She was like a mad woman—indeed, I think she *was* a mad woman, subtly mad with the deep power of deception which insane people may have. How else could she have met me with unconcern every day and yet had so raging a hatred of me in her heart ? I will not say what she said. She poured her whole wild fury out in burning and horrible words. I did not even answer—I could not. It was dreadful to see her. I put my hands to my ears and rushed away. When I left her she was standing still shrieking out her curses at me, in the mouth of the bridge."

" Where she was afterwards found ? "

" Within a few yards from the spot."

" And yet, presuming that she met her death shortly after you left her, you heard no shot ? "

" No, I heard nothing. But, indeed, Mr. Holmes, I was so agitated and horrified by

—I put my hands to my ears
and rushed away."

this terrible outbreak that I rushed to get back to the peace of my own room, and I was incapable of noticing anything which happened."

" You say that you returned to your room. Did you leave it again before next morning ? "

" Yes; when the alarm came that the poor creature had met her death I ran out with the others."

" Did you see Mr. Gibson ? "

" Yes; he had just returned from the bridge when I saw him. He had sent for the doctor and the police."

" Did he seem to you much perturbed ? "

" Mr. Gibson is a very strong, self-contained man. I do not think that he would ever show his emotions on the surface. But I, who knew him so well, could see that he was deeply concerned."

" Then we come to the all-important point. This pistol that was found in your room. Had you ever seen it before ? "

" Never, I swear it."

" When was it found ? "

" Next morning, when the police made their search."

" Among your clothes ? "

" Yes; on the floor of my wardrobe under my dresses."

" You could not guess how long it had been there ? "

" It had not been there the morning before."

" How do you know ? "

" Because I tidied out the wardrobe."

" That is final. Then someone came into your room and placed the pistol there in order to inculpate you."

" It must have been so."

" And when ? "

" It could only have been at meal-time, or else at the hours when I would be in the schoolroom with the children."

" As you were when you got the note ? "

" Yes; from that time onwards, for the whole morning."

" Thank you, Miss Dunbar. Is there any other point which could help me in the investigation ? "

" I can think of none."

" There was some sign of violence on the stone-work of the bridge—a perfectly fresh chip just opposite the body. Could you suggest any possible explanation of that ? "

" Surely it must be a mere coincidence."

" Curious, Miss Dunbar, very curious. Why should it appear at the very time of the tragedy and why at the very place ? "

" But what could have caused it ? Only great violence could have such an effect."

Holmes did not answer. His pale, eager face had suddenly assumed that tense, far-away expression which I had learned to associate with the supreme manifestations of his genius. So evident was the crisis in his mind that none of us dared to speak, and we sat, barrister, prisoner, and myself, watching him in a concentrated and absorbed silence. Suddenly he sprang from his chair, vibrating with nervous energy and the pressing need for action.

" Come, Watson, come ! " he cried.

" What is it, Mr. Holmes ? "

" Never mind, my dear lady. You will hear from me, Mr. Cummings. With the help of the God of justice I will give you a case which will make England ring. You will get news by to-morrow, Miss Dunbar, and meanwhile take my assurance that the clouds are lifting and that I have every hope that the light of truth is breaking through."

IT was not a long journey from Winchester to Thor Place, but it was long to me in my impatience, while for Holmes it was evident that it seemed endless ; for, in his nervous restlessness, he could not sit still, but paced the carriage or drummed with his long, sensitive fingers upon the cushions beside him.

Suddenly, however, as we neared our destination he seated himself opposite to me —we had a first-class carriage to ourselves— and laying a hand upon each of my knees he looked into my eyes with the peculiarly mischievous gaze which was characteristic of his more imp-like moods.

" Watson," said he, " I have some recollection that you go armed upon these excursions of ours."

It was as well for him that I did so, for he took little care for his own safety when his mind was once absorbed by a problem, so that more than once my revolver had been a good friend in need. I reminded him of the fact.

" Yes, yes, I am a little absent-minded in such matters. But have you your revolver on you ? "

I produced it from my hip-pocket, a short, handy, but very serviceable little weapon. He undid the catch, shook out the cartridges, and examined it with care.

" It's heavy—remarkably heavy," said he.

" Yes, it is a solid bit of work."

He mused over it for a minute.

" Do you know, Watson," said he, " I believe your revolver is going to have a very intimate connection with the mystery which we are investigating."

" My dear Holmes, you are joking."

" No, Watson, I am very serious. There is a test before us. If the test comes off, all will be clear. And the test will depend upon the conduct of this little weapon. One cartridge out. Now we will replace the other five and put on the safety-catch. So ! That increases the weight and makes it a better reproduction."

"Suddenly Holmes sprang from his chair. 'Come, Watson, come!' he said. 'With the help of the God of justice I will give you a case which will make England ring.'"

I had no glimmer of what was in his mind nor did he enlighten me, but sat lost in thought until we pulled up in the little Hampshire station. We secured a ramshackle trap, and in a quarter of an hour were at the house of our confidential friend, the sergeant.

" A clue, Mr. Holmes ? What is it ? "

" It all depends upon the behaviour of Dr. Watson's revolver," said my friend. " Here it is. Now, officer, can you give me ten yards of string ? "

The village shop provided a ball of stout twine.

" I think that this is all we will need," said Holmes. " Now, if you please, we will get off on what I hope is the last stage of our journey."

The sun was setting and turning the rolling Hampshire moor into a wonderful autumnal panorama. The sergeant, with many critical and incredulous glances, which showed his deep doubts of the sanity of my companion, lurched along beside us. As we approached the scene of the crime I could see that my friend under all his habitual coolness was in truth deeply agitated.

" Yes," he said, in answer to my remark, " you have seen me miss my mark before, Watson. I have an instinct for such things, and yet it has sometimes played me false. It seemed a certainty when first it flashed across my mind in the cell at Winchester, but one drawback of an active mind is that one can always conceive alternative explanations which would make our scent a false one. And yet—and yet—— Well, Watson, we can but try."

As he walked he had firmly tied one end of the string to the handle of the revolver. We had now reached the scene of the tragedy. With great care he marked out under the guidance of the policeman the exact spot where the body had been stretched. He then hunted among the heather and the ferns until he found a considerable stone. This he secured to the other end of his line of string, and he hung it over the parapet of the bridge so that it swung clear above the water. He then stood on the fatal spot, some distance from the edge of the bridge, with my revolver in his hand, the string being taut between the weapon and the heavy stone on the farther side.

" Now for it ! " he cried.

At the words he raised the pistol to his head, and then let go his grip. In an instant it had been whisked away by the weight of the stone, had struck with a sharp crack against the parapet, and had vanished over the side into the water. It had hardly gone before Holmes was kneeling beside the stonework, and a joyous cry showed that he had found what he expected.

" Was there ever a more exact demonstration ? " he cried. " See, Watson, your revolver has solved the problem ! " As he spoke he pointed to a second chip of the exact size and shape of the first which had appeared on the under edge of the stone balustrade.

" We'll stay at the inn to-night," he continued, as he rose and faced the astonished sergeant. " You will, of course, get a grappling hook and you will easily restore my friend's revolver. You will also find beside it the revolver, string, and weight with which this vindictive woman attempted to disguise her own crime and to fasten a charge of murder upon an innocent victim. You can let Mr. Gibson know that I will see him in the morning, when steps can be taken for Miss Dunbar's vindication."

LATE that evening, as we sat together smoking our pipes in the village inn, Holmes gave me a brief review of what had passed.

" I fear, Watson," said he, " that you will not improve any reputation which I may have acquired by adding the Case of the Thor Bridge Mystery to your annals. I have been sluggish in mind and wanting in that mixture of imagination and reality which is the basis of my art. I confess that the chip in the stonework was a sufficient clue to suggest the true solution, and that I blame myself for not having attained it sooner.

" It must be admitted that the workings of this unhappy woman's mind were deep and subtle, so that it was no very simple matter to unravel her plot. I do not think that in our adventures we have ever come across a stranger example of what perverted love can bring about. Whether Miss Dunbar was her rival in a physical or in a merely mental sense seems to have been equally unforgivable in her eyes. No doubt she blamed this innocent lady for all those harsh dealings and unkind words with which her husband tried to repel her too demonstrative affection. Her first resolution was to end her own life. Her second was to do it in such a way as to involve her victim in a fate which was worse far than any sudden death could be.

" We can follow the various steps quite clearly, and they show a remarkable subtlety of mind. A note was extracted very cleverly from Miss Dunbar which would make it appear that she had chosen the scene of the crime. In her anxiety that it should be discovered she somewhat overdid it, by holding it in her hand to the last. This alone should have excited my suspicions earlier than it did.

" Then she took one of her husband's revolvers—there was, as you saw, an arsenal in the house—and kept it for her own use. A similar one she concealed that morning in Miss Dunbar's wardrobe after discharging one barrel, which she could easily do in the woods without attracting attention. She then went down to the bridge where she had contrived this exceedingly ingenious method for getting rid of her weapon. When Miss Dunbar appeared she used her last breath in pouring out her hatred, and then, when she was out of hearing, carried out her terrible purpose. Every link is now in its place and the chain is complete. The papers may ask why the mere was not dragged in the first instance, but it is easy to be wise after the event, and in any case the expanse of a reed-filled lake is no easy matter to drag unless you have a clear perception of what you are looking for and where. Well, Watson, we have helped a remarkable woman, and also a formidable man. Should they in the future join their forces, as seems not unlikely, the financial world may find that Mr. Neil Gibson has learned something in that schoolroom of Sorrow where our earthly lessons are taught."

"Holmes was kneeling beside the stonework, and a joyous cry showed that he had found what he expected."

"AS I LAY WITH MY EYES FIXED UPON THE SQUARE OF LIGHT I WAS AMAZED
TO SEE MY FATHER'S FACE LOOKING IN AT ME"

The Adventure of the Creeping Man

A NEW SHERLOCK HOLMES STORY

BY

A. Conan Doyle

ILLUSTRATED BY
HOWARD ELCOCK

MR. SHERLOCK HOLMES was always of opinion that I should publish the singular facts connected with Professor Presbury, if only to dispel once for all the ugly rumours which some twenty years ago agitated the University and were echoed in the learned societies of London. There were, however, certain obstacles in the way, and the true history of this curious case remained entombed in the tin box which contains so many records of my friend's adventures. Now we have at last obtained permission to ventilate the facts which formed one of the very last cases handled by Holmes before his retirement from practice. Even now a certain reticence and discretion have to be observed in laying the matter before the public.

It was one Sunday evening early in September of the year 1902 that I received one of Holmes's laconic messages : " Come at once if convenient—if inconvenient come all the same.—S. H." The relations between us in those latter days were peculiar. He was a man of habits, narrow and concentrated habits, and I had become one of them. As an institution I was like the violin, the shag tobacco, the old black pipe, the index books, and others perhaps less excusable. When it was a case of active work and a comrade was needed upon whose nerve he could place some reliance, my *rôle* was obvious. But apart from this I had uses. I was a whetstone for his mind. I stimulated him. He liked to think aloud in my presence. His remarks could hardly be said to be made to me—many of them would have been as appropriately addressed to his bedstead—but none the less, having formed the habit, it had become in some way helpful that I should register and interject. If I irritated him by a certain methodical slowness in my mentality, that irritation served only to make his own flame-like intuitions and impressions flash up the more vividly and swiftly. Such was my humble *rôle* in our alliance.

When I arrived at Baker Street I found him huddled up in his arm-chair with up-drawn knees, his pipe in his mouth and his brow furrowed with thought. It was clear that he was in the throes of some vexatious problem. With a wave of his hand he indicated my old arm-chair, but otherwise for half an hour he gave no sign that he was aware of my presence. Then with a start he seemed to come from his reverie, and, with his usual whimsical smile, he greeted me back to what had once been my home.

" You will excuse a certain abstraction of mind, my dear Watson," said he. " Some curious facts have been submitted to me within the last twenty-four hours, and they in turn have given rise to some speculations of a more general character. I have serious thoughts of writing a small monograph upon the uses of dogs in the work of the detective."

" But surely, Holmes, this has been explored," said I. " Bloodhounds—sleuth-hounds——"

" No, no, Watson ; that side of the matter is, of course, obvious. But there is another which is far more subtle. You may recollect that in the case which you, in your sensational way, coupled with the Copper Beeches, I was able, by watching the mind of the child, to form a deduction as to the criminal habits of the very smug and respectable father."

" Yes, I remember it well."

" My line of thoughts about dogs is analogous. A dog reflects the family life. Whoever saw a frisky dog in a gloomy family, or a sad dog in a happy one ? Snarling people have snarling dogs, dangerous people have dangerous ones. And their passing moods may reflect the passing moods of others."

I shook my head. " Surely, Holmes, this is a little far-fetched," said I.

He had refilled his pipe and resumed his seat, taking no notice of my comment.

" The practical application of what I have said is very close to the problem which I am investigating. It is a tangled skein, you understand, and I am looking for a loose end. One possible loose end lies in the question : Why does Professor Presbury's faithful wolf-hound, Roy, endeavour to bite him ? "

I sank back in my chair in some disappointment. Was it for so trivial a question as this that I had been summoned from my work ? Holmes glanced across at me.

" The same old Watson ! " said he. " You never learn that the gravest issues may depend upon the smallest things. But is it not on the face of it strange that a staid, elderly philosopher—you've heard of Presbury, of course, the famous Camford physiologist ?—that such a man, whose friend has been his devoted wolf-hound, should now have been twice attacked by his own dog ? What do you make of it ? "

" The dog is ill."

" Well, that has to be considered. But he attacks no one else, nor does he apparently molest his master, save on very special occasions. Curious, Watson—very curious. But young Mr. Bennett is before his time, if that is his ring. I had hoped to have a longer chat with you before he came."

THERE was a quick step on the stairs, a sharp tap at the door, and a moment later the new client presented himself. He was a tall, handsome youth about thirty, well dressed and elegant, but with something in his bearing which suggested the shyness of the student rather than the self-possession of the man of the world. He shook hands with Holmes, and then looked with some surprise at me.

" This matter is very delicate, Mr. Holmes," he said. " Consider the relation in which I stand to Professor Presbury, both privately and publicly. I really can hardly justify myself if I speak before any third person."

" Have no fear, Mr. Bennett. Dr. Watson is the very soul of discretion, and I can assure you that this is a matter in which I am very likely to need an assistant."

" As you like, Mr. Holmes. You will, I am sure, understand my having some reserves in the matter."

" You will appreciate it, Watson, when I tell you that this gentleman, Mr. Trevor Bennett, is professional assistant to the great scientist, lives under his roof, and is engaged to his only daughter. Certainly we must agree that the Professor has every claim upon his loyalty and devotion. But it may best be shown by taking the necessary steps to clear up this strange mystery."

" I hope so, Mr. Holmes. That is my one object. Does Dr. Watson know the situation ? "

" I have not had time to explain it."

" Then perhaps I had better go over the ground again before explaining some fresh developments."

" I will do so myself," said Holmes, " in order to show that I have the events in their due order. The Professor, Watson, is a man of European reputation. His life has been academic. There has never been a breath of scandal. He is a widower with one daughter, Edith. He is, I gather, a man of very virile and positive, one might almost say combative, character. So the matter stood until a very few months ago.

" Then the current of his life was broken. He is sixty-one years of age, but he became engaged to the daughter of Professor Morphy, his colleague in the chair of Comparative Anatomy. It was not, as I understand, the reasoned courting of an elderly man, but rather the passionate frenzy of youth, for no one could have shown himself a more devoted lover. The lady, Alice Morphy, was a very perfect girl both in mind and body, so that there was every excuse for the Professor's infatuation. None the less, it did not meet with full approval in his own family."

" We thought it rather excessive," said our visitor.

"Exactly. Excessive and a little violent and unnatural. Professor Presbury was rich, however, and there was no objection upon the part of the father. The daughter, however, had other views, and there were already several candidates for her hand, who, if they were less eligible from a worldly point of view, were at least more of an age. The girl seemed to like the Professor in spite of his eccentricities. It was only age which stood in the way.

"About this time a little mystery suddenly clouded the normal routine of the Professor's life. He did what he had never done before. He left home and gave no indication where he was going. He was away a fortnight, and returned looking rather travel-worn. He made no allusion to where he had been, although he was usually the frankest of men. It chanced, however, that our client here, Mr. Bennett,

received a letter from a fellow-student in Prague, who said that he was glad to have seen Professor Presbury there, although he had not been able to talk to him. Only in this way did his own household learn where he had been.

"Now comes the point. From that time onwards a curious change came over the Professor. He became furtive and sly.

There was a sharp tap at the door, and a moment later the new client presented himself.

Those around him had always the feeling that he was not the man that they had known, but that he was under some shadow which had darkened his higher qualities. His intellect was not affected. His lectures were as brilliant as ever. But always there was something new, something sinister and unexpected. His daughter, who was devoted to him, tried again and again to resume the old relations and to penetrate this mask which her father seemed to have put on. You, sir, as I understand, did the same—but all was in vain. And now, Mr. Bennett, tell in your own words the incident of the letters."

"You must understand, Dr. Watson, that the Professor had no secrets from me. If I were his son or his younger brother, I could not have more completely enjoyed his confidence. As his secretary I handled every paper which came to him, and I opened and subdivided his letters. Shortly after his return all this was changed. He told me that certain letters might come to him from London which would be marked by a cross under the stamp. These were to be set aside for his own eyes only. I may say that several of these did pass through my hands, that they had the E.C. mark, and were in an illiterate handwriting. If he answered them at all the answers did not pass through my hands nor into the letter-basket in which our correspondence was collected."

" And the box," said Holmes.

" Ah, yes, the box. The Professor brought back a little wooden box from his travels. It was the one thing which suggested a Continental tour, for it was one of those quaint carved things which one associates with Germany. This he placed in his instrument cupboard. One day, in looking for a canula, I took up the box. To my surprise he was very angry, and reproved me in words which were quite savage for my curiosity. It was the first time such a thing had happened and I was deeply hurt. I endeavoured to explain that it was a mere accident that I had touched the box, but all the evening I was conscious that he looked at me harshly and that the incident was rankling in his mind." Mr. Bennett drew a little diary book from his pocket. " That was on the 2nd of July," said he.

" You are certainly an admirable witness," said Holmes. " I may need some of these dates which you have noted."

" I learned method among other things from my great teacher. From the time that I observed abnormality in his behaviour I felt that it was my duty to study his case. Thus I have it here that it was on that very day, July 2nd, that Roy attacked the Professor as he came from his study into the hall. Again on July 11th there was

a scene of the same sort, and then I have a note of yet another upon July 20th. After that we had to banish Roy to the stables. He was a dear, affectionate animal—but I fear I weary you."

MR. BENNETT spoke in a tone of reproach, for it was very clear that Holmes was not listening. His face was rigid and his eyes gazed abstractedly at the ceiling. With an effort he recovered himself.

" Singular ! Most singular ! " he murmured. " These details were new to me, Mr. Bennett. I think we have now fairly gone over the old ground, have we not ? But you spoke of some fresh development."

The pleasant, open face of our visitor clouded over, shadowed by some grim remembrance. " What I speak of occurred the night before last," said he. " I was lying awake about two in the morning, when I was aware of a dull muffled sound coming from the passage. I opened my door and peeped out. I should explain that the Professor sleeps at the end of the passage——"

" The date being—— ? " asked Holmes.

Our visitor was clearly annoyed at so irrelevant an interruption.

" I have said, sir, that it was the night before last—that is, September 4th."

Holmes nodded and smiled.

" Pray continue," said he.

" He sleeps at the end of the passage, and would have to pass my door in order to reach the staircase. It was a really terrifying experience, Mr. Holmes. I think that I am as strong-nerved as my neighbours, but I was shaken by what I saw. The passage was dark save that one window half-way along it threw a patch of light. I could see that something was coming along the passage, something dark and crouching. Then suddenly it emerged into the light, and I saw that it was he. He was crawling, Mr. Holmes—crawling ! He was not quite on his hands and knees. I should rather say on his hands and feet, with his face sunk between his hands. Yet he seemed to move with ease. I was so paralysed by the sight that it was not until he had reached my door that I was able to step forward and ask if I could assist him. His answer was extraordinary. He sprang up, spat out some atrocious word at me, and hurried on past me and down the staircase. I waited about for an hour, but he did not come back. It must have been daylight before he regained his room."

" Well, Watson, what make you of that ? " asked Holmes, with the air of the pathologist who presents a rare specimen.

" Lumbago, possibly. I have known a

severe attack make a man walk in just such a way, and nothing would be more trying to the temper."

" Good, Watson ! You always keep us flat-footed on the ground. But we can hardly accept lumbago, since he was able to stand erect in a moment."

" He was never better in health," said Bennett. " In fact, he is stronger than I have known him for years. But there are the facts, Mr. Holmes. It is not a case in which we can consult the police, and yet we are utterly at our wits' end as to what to do, and we feel in some strange way that we are drifting towards disaster. Edith—Miss Presbury—feels as I do, that we cannot wait passively any longer."

" It is certainly a very curious and suggestive case. What do you think, Watson ? "

" Speaking as a medical man," said I, " it appears to be a case for an alienist. The old gentleman's cerebral processes were disturbed by the love affair. He made a journey abroad in the hope of breaking himself of the passion. His letters and the box may be connected with some other private transaction—a loan, perhaps, or share certificates, which are in the box."

" And the wolf-hound no doubt disapproved of the financial bargain. No, no, Watson, there is more in it than this. Now, I can only suggest——"

WHAT Sherlock Holmes was about to suggest will never be known, for at this moment the door opened and a young lady was shown into the room. As she appeared Mr. Bennett sprang up with a cry and ran forward with his hands out to meet those which she had herself outstretched.

" Edith, dear ! Nothing the matter, I hope ? "

" I felt I must follow you. Oh, Jack, I have been so dreadfully frightened ! It is awful to be there alone."

" Mr. Holmes, this is the young lady I spoke of. This is my fiancée."

" We were gradually coming to that conclusion, were we not, Watson ? " Holmes answered, with a smile. " I take it, Miss Presbury, that there is some fresh development in the case, and that you thought we should know ? "

Our new visitor, a bright, handsome girl of a conventional English type, smiled back at Holmes as she seated herself beside Mr. Bennett.

" When I found Mr. Bennett had left his hotel I thought I should probably find him here. Of course, he had told me that he would consult you. But, oh, Mr. Holmes, can you do nothing for my poor father ? "

" I have hopes, Miss Presbury, but the case is still obscure. Perhaps what you have to say may throw some fresh light upon it."

" It was last night, Mr. Holmes. He had been very strange all day. I am sure that there are times when he has no recollection of what he does. He lives as in a strange dream. Yesterday was such a day. It was not my father with whom I lived. His outward shell was there, but it was not really he."

" Tell me what happened."

" I was awakened in the night by the dog barking most furiously. Poor Roy, he is chained now near the stable. I may say that I always sleep with my door locked ; for, as Jack—as Mr. Bennett—will tell you, we all have a feeling of impending danger. My room is on the second floor. It happened that the blind was up in my window, and there was bright moonlight outside. As I lay with my eyes fixed upon the square of light, listening to the frenzied barkings of the dog, I was amazed to see my father's face looking in at me. Mr. Holmes, I nearly died of surprise and horror. There it was pressed against the window-pane, and one hand seemed to be raised as if to push up the window. If that window had opened, I think I should have gone mad. It was no delusion, Mr. Holmes. Don't deceive yourself by thinking so. I dare say it was twenty seconds or so that I lay paralysed and watched the face. Then it vanished, but I could not—I could not spring out of bed and look out after it. I lay cold and shivering till morning. At breakfast he was sharp and fierce in manner, and made no allusion to the adventure of the night. Neither did I, but I gave an excuse for coming to town—and here I am."

Holmes looked thoroughly surprised at Miss Presbury's narrative.

" My dear young lady, you say that your room is on the second floor. Is there a long ladder in the garden ? "

" No, Mr. Holmes ; that is the amazing part of it. There is no possible way of reaching the window—and yet he was there."

" The date being September 4th," said Holmes. " That certainly complicates matters."

It was the young lady's turn to look surprised. " This is the second time that you have alluded to the date, Mr. Holmes," said Bennett. " Is it possible that it has any bearing upon the case ? "

" It is possible—very possible—and yet I have not my full material at present."

" Possibly you are thinking of the connection between insanity and phases of the moon ? "

" No, I assure you. It was quite a different line of thought. Possibly you can

The Professor spat out some atrocious word at me and hurried on down
the staircase.

leave your note-book with me and I will check the dates. Now I think, Watson, that our line of action is perfectly clear. This young lady has informed us—and I have the greatest confidence in her intuition—that her father remembers little or nothing which occurs upon certain dates. We will therefore call upon him as if he had given us an appointment upon such a date. He will put it down to his own lack of memory. Thus we will open our campaign by having a good close view of him."

"That is excellent," said Mr. Bennett. "I warn you, however, that the Professor is irascible and violent at times."

Holmes smiled. "There are reasons why we should come at once—very cogent reasons if my theories hold good. To-morrow, Mr. Bennett, will certainly see us in Camford. There is, if I remember right, an inn called the Chequers where the port used to be above mediocrity, and the linen was above reproach. I think, Watson, that our lot for the next few days might lie in less pleasant places."

Monday morning found us on our way to the famous University town—an easy effort on the part of Holmes, who had no roots to pull up, but one which involved frantic planning and hurrying on my part, as my practice was by this time not inconsiderable. Holmes made no allusion to the case until after we had deposited our suit-cases at the ancient hostel of which he had spoken.

"I think, Watson, that we can catch the Professor just before lunch. He lectures at eleven, and should have an interval at home."

"What possible excuse have we for calling ? "

Holmes glanced at his note-book.

"There was a period of excitement upon August 26th. We will assume that he is a little hazy as to what he does at such times. If we insist that we are there by appointment I think he will hardly venture to contradict us. Have you the effrontery necessary to put it through ? "

"We can but try."

"Excellent, Watson ! Compound of the Busy Bee and Excelsior. We can but try—the motto of the firm. A friendly native will surely guide us."

Such a one on the back of a smart hansom swept us past a row of ancient colleges, and finally turning into a tree-lined drive pulled up at the door of a charming house, girt round with lawns and covered with purple wistaria. Professor Presbury was certainly surrounded with every sign not only of comfort but of luxury. Even as we pulled up a grizzled head appeared at the front window, and we were aware of a pair of keen eyes from under shaggy brows which surveyed us through large horn glasses. A moment later we were actually in his sanctum, and the mysterious scientist, whose vagaries had brought us from London, was standing before us. There was certainly no sign of eccentricity either in his manner or appearance, for he was a portly, large-featured man, grave, tall, and frock-coated, with the dignity of bearing which a lecturer needs. His eyes were his most remarkable feature, keen, observant, and clever to the verge of cunning.

He looked at our cards. "Pray sit down, gentlemen. What can I do for you ? "

Mr. Holmes smiled amiably.

" It was the question which I was about to put to you, Professor."

" To me, sir ! "

" Possibly there is some mistake. I heard through a second person that Professor Presbury of Camford had need of my services."

" Oh, indeed ! " It seemed to me that there was a malicious sparkle in the intense grey eyes. " You heard that, did you ? May I ask the name of your informant ? "

" I am sorry, Professor, but the matter was rather confidential. If I have made a mistake there is no harm done. I can only express my regret."

" Not at all. I should wish to go further into this matter. It interests me. Have you any scrap of writing, any letter or telegram, to bear out your assertion ? "

" No, I have not."

" I presume that you do not go so far as to assert that I summoned you ? "

" I would rather answer no questions," said Holmes.

" No, I dare say not," said the Professor, with asperity. " However, that particular one can be answered very easily without your aid."

HE walked across the room to the bell. Our London friend, Mr. Bennett, answered the call.

" Come in, Mr. Bennett. These two gentlemen have come from London under the impression that they have been summoned. You handle all my correspondence. Have you a note of anything going to a person named Holmes ? "

" No, sir," Bennett answered, with a flush.

" That is conclusive," said the Professor, glaring angrily at my companion. " Now, sir "—he leaned forward with his two hands upon the table—" it seems to me that your position is a very questionable one."

Holmes shrugged his shoulders.

" I can only repeat that I am sorry that we have made a needless intrusion."

" Hardly enough, Mr. Holmes ! " the old man cried, in a high screaming voice, with extraordinary malignancy upon his face. He got between us and the door as he spoke, and he shook his two hands at us with furious passion. " You can hardly get out of it so easily as that." His face was convulsed and he grinned and gibbered at us in his senseless rage. I am convinced that we should have had to fight our way out of the room if Mr. Bennett had not intervened.

" My dear Professor," he cried, " consider your position ! Consider the scandal at

the University ! Mr. Holmes is a well-known man. You cannot possibly treat him with such discourtesy."

Sulkily our host—if I may call him so—cleared the path to the door. We were glad to find ourselves outside the house, and in the quiet of the tree-lined drive. Holmes seemed greatly amused by the episode.

" Our learned friend's nerves are somewhat out of order," said he. " Perhaps our intrusion was a little crude, and yet we have gained that personal contact which I desired. But, dear me, Watson, he is surely at our heels. The villain still pursues us."

There were the sounds of running feet behind, but it was, to my relief, not the formidable Professor but his assistant who appeared round the curve of the drive. He came panting up to us.

" I am so sorry, Mr. Holmes. I wished to apologize."

" My dear sir, there is no need. It is all in the way of professional experience."

" I have never seen him in a more dangerous mood. But he grows more sinister. You can understand now why his daughter and I are alarmed. And yet his mind is perfectly clear."

" Too clear ! " said Holmes. " That was my miscalculation. It is evident that his memory is much more reliable than I had thought. By the way, can we, before we go, see the window of Miss Presbury's room ? "

Mr. Bennett pushed his way through some shrubs and we had a view of the side of the house.

" It is there. The second on the left."

" Dear me, it seems hardly accessible. And yet you will observe that there is a creeper below and a water pipe above which give some foothold."

" I could not climb it myself," said Mr. Bennett.

" Very likely. It would certainly be a dangerous exploit for any normal man."

" There was one other thing I wished to tell you, Mr. Holmes. I have the address of the man in London to whom the Professor writes. He seems to have written this morning and I got it from his blotting paper. It is an ignoble position for a trusted secretary, but what else can I do ? "

Holmes glanced at the paper and put it into his pocket.

" Dorak—a curious name. Slavonic, I imagine. Well, it is an important link in the chain. We return to London this afternoon, Mr. Bennett. I see no good purpose to be served by our remaining. We cannot arrest the Professor because he has done no crime, nor can we place him under constraint, for he cannot be proved to be mad. No action is as yet possible."

"Then what on earth are we to do?"

"A little patience, Mr. Bennett. Things will soon develop. Unless I am mistaken next Tuesday may mark a crisis. Certainly we shall be in Camford on that day. Meanwhile, the general position is undeniably unpleasant, and if Miss Presbury can prolong her visit——"

"That is easy."

"Then let her stay till we can assure her that all danger is past. Meanwhile let him have his way and do not cross him. So long as he is in a good humour all is well."

"There he is!" said Bennett, in a startled whisper. Looking between the branches we saw the tall, erect figure emerge from the hall door and look around him. He stood leaning forward, his hands swinging straight before him, his head turning from side to side. The secretary with a last wave slipped off among the trees, and we saw him presently rejoin his employer, the two entering the house together in what seemed to be animated and even excited conversation.

"I expect the old gentleman has been putting two and two together," said Holmes, as we walked hotel-wards. "He struck me as having a particularly clear and logical brain, from the little I saw of him. Explosive, no doubt, but then from his point of view he has something to explode about if detectives are put on his track and he suspects his own household of doing it. I rather fancy that friend Bennett is in for an uncomfortable time."

Holmes stopped at a post-office and sent off a telegram on our way. The answer reached us in the evening, and he tossed it across to me. "Have visited the Commercial Road and seen Dorak. Suave person, Bohemian, elderly. Keeps large general store.—Mercer."

"Mercer is since your time," said Holmes. "He is my general utility man who looks up routine business. It was important to know something of the man with whom our Professor was so secretly corresponding. His nationality connects up with the Prague visit."

"Thank goodness that something connects with something," said I. "At present we seem to be faced by a long series of inexplicable incidents with no bearing upon each other. For example, what possible connection can there be between an angry wolf-hound and a visit to Bohemia, or either of them with a man crawling down a passage at night? As to your dates, that is the biggest mystification of all."

Holmes smiled and rubbed his hands. We were, I may say, seated in the old sitting-room of the ancient hotel, with a bottle of the famous vintage of which Holmes had spoken on the table between us.

"Well, now, let us take the dates first," said he, his finger-tips together and his manner as if he were addressing a class. "This excellent young man's diary shows that there was trouble upon July 2nd, and from then onwards it seems to have been at nine-day intervals, with, so far as I remember, only one exception. Thus the last outbreak upon Friday was on September 3rd, which also falls into the series, as did August 26th, which preceded it. The thing is beyond coincidence."

I was forced to agree.

"Let us, then, form the provisional theory that every nine days the Professor takes some strong drug which has a passing but highly poisonous effect. His naturally violent nature is intensified by it. He learned to take this drug while he was in Prague, and is now supplied with it by a Bohemian intermediary in London. This all hangs together, Watson!"

"But the dog, the face at the window, the creeping man in the passage?"

"Well, well, we have made a beginning. I should not expect any fresh developments until next Tuesday. In the meantime we can only keep in touch with friend Bennett and enjoy the amenities of this charming town."

IN the morning Mr. Bennett slipped round to bring us the latest report. As Holmes had imagined, times had not been easy with him. Without exactly accusing him of being responsible for our presence, the Professor had been very rough and rude in his speech, and evidently felt some strong grievance. This morning he was quite himself again, however, and had delivered his usual brilliant lecture to a crowded class. "Apart from his queer fits," said Bennett, "he has actually more energy and vitality than I can ever remember, nor was his brain ever clearer. But it's not he—it's never the man whom we have known."

"I don't think you have anything to fear now for a week at least," Holmes answered. "I am a busy man, and Dr. Watson has his patients to attend to. Let us agree that we meet here at this hour next Tuesday, and I shall be surprised if before we leave you again we are not able to explain, even if we cannot perhaps put an end to, your troubles. Meanwhile, keep us posted in what occurs."

I SAW nothing of my friend for the next few days, but on the following Monday evening I had a short note asking me to meet him next day at the train. From

what he told me as we travelled up to
Camford all was well, the peace of the
Professor's house had been unruffled, and
his own conduct perfectly normal.   This
also was the report which was given us by
Mr. Bennett himself when he called upon
us that evening at our old quarters in the
Chequers.   "He heard from his London
correspondent to-day.   There was a letter
and there was a small packet, each with the
cross under the stamp which warned me
not to touch them.   There has been nothing
else."

   "That may prove quite enough," said
Holmes, grimly.   "Now, Mr. Bennett, we
shall, I think, come to some conclusion
to-night.   If my deductions are correct we
should have an opportunity of bringing
matters to a head.   In order to do so it is
necessary to hold the Professor under
observation.   I would suggest, therefore,
that you remain awake and on the look-out.
Should you hear him pass your door do not

grinned and gibbered at us in his senseless
would have had to fight our way out of the
had not intervened.

interrupt him, but follow him as discreetly
as you can. Dr. Watson and I will not be
far off. By the way, where is the key of
that little box of which you spoke ? "

"Upon his watch-chain "

"I fancy our researches must lie in that
direction. At the worst the lock should not
be very formidable. Have you any other
able-bodied man on the premises ? "

"There is the coach-
man, Macphail."

"Where does he sleep ? "

"Over the stables."

"We might possibly want him. Well, we
can do no more until we see how things
develop. Good-bye—but I expect that we
shall see you before morning."

IT was nearly midnight before we took our
station among some bushes immediately
opposite the hall door of the Professor.
It was a fine night, but chilly, and we were
glad of our warm overcoats. There was a
breeze and clouds were scudding across the

sky, obscuring from time to time the half-moon. It would have been a dismal vigil were it not for the expectation and excitement, which carried us along, and the assurance of my comrade that we had probably reached the end of the strange sequence of events which had engaged our attention.

" If the cycle of nine days holds good then we shall have the Professor at his worst to-night," said Holmes. " The fact that these strange symptoms began after his visit to Prague, that he is in secret correspondence with a Bohemian dealer in London, who presumably represents someone in Prague, and that he received a packet from him this very day, all point in one direction. What he takes and why he takes it are still beyond our ken, but that it emanates in some way from Prague is clear enough. He takes it under definite directions which regulate this ninth day system, which was the first point which attracted my attention. But his symptoms are most remarkable. Did you observe his knuckles ? "

I had to confess that I did not.

" Thick and horny in a way which is quite new in my experience. Always look at the hands first, Watson. Then cuffs, trouser-knees, and boots. Very curious knuckles which can only be explained by the mode of progression observed by——" Holmes paused, and suddenly clapped his hand to his forehead. " Oh, Watson, Watson, what a fool I have been ! It seems incredible, and yet it must be true. All points in one direction. How could I miss seeing the connection of ideas ? Those knuckles—how could I have passed those knuckles ? And the dog ! And the ivy ! It's surely time that I disappeared into that little farm of my dreams. Look out, Watson ! Here he is ! We shall have the chance of seeing for ourselves."

THE hall door had slowly opened, and against the lamp-lit background we saw the tall figure of Professor Presbury. He was clad in his dressing-gown. As he stood outlined in the doorway he was erect but leaning forward with dangling arms, as when we saw him last.

Now he stepped forward into the drive, and an extraordinary change came over him. He sank down into a crouching position, and moved along upon his hands and feet, skipping every now and then as if he were overflowing with energy and vitality. He moved along the face of the house and then round the corner. As he disappeared Bennett slipped through the hall door and softly followed him.

" Come, Watson, come ! " cried Holmes, and we stole as softly as we could through

the bushes until we had gained a spot whence we could see the other side of the house, which was bathed in the light of the half-moon. The Professor was clearly visible crouching at the foot of the ivy-covered wall. As we watched him he suddenly began with incredible agility to ascend it. From branch to branch he sprang, sure of foot and firm of grasp, climbing apparently in mere joy at his own powers, with no definite object in view. With his dressing-gown flapping on each side of him he looked like some huge bat glued against the side of his own house, a great square dark patch upon the moonlit wall. Presently he tired of this amusement, and, dropping from branch to branch, he squatted down into the old attitude and moved towards the stables, creeping along in the same strange way as before. The wolf-hound was out now, barking furiously, and more excited than ever when it actually caught sight of its master. It was straining on its chain, and quivering with eagerness and rage. The Professor squatted down very deliberately just out of reach of the hound, and began to provoke it in every possible way. He took handfuls of pebbles from the drive and threw them in the dog's face, prodded him with a stick which he had picked up, flicked his hands about only a few inches from the gaping mouth, and endeavoured in every way to increase the animal's fury, which was already beyond all control. In all our adventures I do not know that I have ever seen a more strange sight than this impassive and still dignified figure crouching frog-like upon the ground and goading to a wilder exhibition of passion the maddened hound, which ramped and raged in front of him, by all manner of ingenious and calculated cruelty.

And then in a moment it happened ! It was not the chain that broke, but it was the collar that slipped, for it had been made for a thick-necked Newfoundland. We heard the rattle of falling metal, and the next instant dog and man were rolling on the ground together, the one roaring in rage, the other screaming in a strange shrill falsetto of terror. It was a very narrow thing for the Professor's life. The savage creature had him fairly by the throat, its fangs had bitten deep, and he was senseless before we could reach them and drag the two apart. It might have been a dangerous task for us, but Bennett's voice and pressure brought the great wolf-hound instantly to reason. The uproar had brought the sleepy and astonished coachman from his room above the stables. " I'm not surprised," said he, shaking his head. " I've seen him at it before. I knew the dog would get him sooner or later."

Dog and man were rolling on the ground together, the one roaring in rage, the other screaming in a strange shrill falsetto of terror.

The hound was secured, and together we carried the Professor up to his room, where Bennett, who had a medical degree, helped me to dress his torn throat. The sharp teeth had passed dangerously near the carotid artery, and the hæmorrhage was serious. In half an hour the danger was past, I had given the patient an injection of morphia, and he had sunk into deep sleep. Then, and only then, were we able to look at each other and to take stock of the situation.

" I think a first-class surgeon should see him," said I.

" For God's sake, no!" cried Bennett. " At present the scandal is confined to our own household. It is safe with us. If it gets beyond these walls it will never stop. Consider his position at the University, his European reputation, the feelings of his daughter."

" Quite so," said Holmes. " I think it may be quite possible to keep the matter to ourselves, and also to prevent its recurrence now that we have a free hand. The key from the watch-chain, Mr. Bennett. Macphail will guard the patient and let us know if there is any change. Let us see what we can find in the Professor's mysterious box."

THERE was not much, but there was enough — an empty phial, another nearly full, a hypodermic syringe, several letters in a crabbed, foreign hand. The marks on the envelopes showed that they were those which had disturbed the routine of the secretary, and each was dated from the Commercial Road and signed " A. Dorak." They were mere invoices to say that a fresh bottle was being sent to Professor Presbury, or receipts to acknowledge money. There was one other envelope, however, in a more educated hand and bearing the Austrian stamp with the postmark of Prague. " Here we have our material!" cried Holmes, as he tore out the enclosure.

" Honoured Colleague," it ran. " Since your esteemed visit I have thought much of your case, and though in your circumstances there are some special reasons for the treatment, I would none the less enjoin caution, as my results have shown that it is not without danger of a kind.

" It is possible that the Serum of Anthropoid would have been better. I have, as I explained to you, used black-faced Langur because a specimen was accessible. Langur is, of course, a crawler and climber, while Anthropoid walks erect, and is in all ways nearer.

" I beg you to take every possible pre-caution that there be no premature revelation of the process. I have one other client in England, and Dorak is my agent for both.

" Weekly reports will oblige.

" Yours with high esteem,
" H. LOWENSTEIN."

Lowenstein! The name brought back to me the memory of some snippet from a newspaper which spoke of an obscure scientist who was striving in some unknown way for the secret of rejuvenescence and the elixir of life. Lowenstein of Prague! Lowenstein with the wondrous strength-giving serum, tabooed by the profession because he refused to reveal its source. In a few words I said what I remembered. Bennett had taken a manual of Zoology from the shelves. " ' Langur,' " he read, " ' the great black-faced monkey of the Himalayan slopes, biggest and most human of climbing monkeys.' Many details are added. Well, thanks to you, Mr. Holmes, it is very clear that we have traced the evil to its source."

" The real source," said Holmes, " lies, of course, in that untimely love affair which gave our impetuous Professor the idea that he could only gain his wish by turning himself into a younger man. When one tries to rise above Nature one is liable to fall below it. The highest type of man may revert to the animal if he leaves the straight road of destiny." He sat musing for a little with the phial in his hand, looking at the clear liquid within. " When I have written to this man and told him that I hold him criminally responsible for the poisons which he circulates, we will have no more trouble. But it may recur. Others may find a better way. There is danger there—a very real danger to humanity. Consider, Watson, that the material, the sensual, the worldly would all prolong their worthless lives. The spiritual would not avoid the call to something higher. It would be the survival of the least fit. What sort of cesspool may not our poor world become?" Suddenly the dreamer disappeared, and Holmes, the man of action, sprang from his chair. " I think there is nothing more to be said, Mr. Bennett. The various incidents will now fit themselves easily into the general scheme. The dog, of course, was aware of the change far more quickly than you. His smell would ensure that. It was the monkey, not the Professor, whom Roy attacked, just as it was the monkey who teased Roy. Climbing was a joy to the creature, and it was a mere chance, I take it, that the pastime brought him to the young lady's window. There is an early train to town, Watson, but I think we shall just have time for a cup of tea at the Chequers before we catch it."

THE 'STRAND' WAR GAME.

THIS game, which is on sale everywhere, is one which we strongly recommend every reader of this magazine to purchase. While easy to learn, it affords an unlimited fund of entertainment, as well as endless opportunities for ingenuity and skill. It is played by two opponents, representing the Allies and the Germans, over a map of the actual territory of the War, and the pieces consist of three kinds—

INFANTRY, CAVALRY, & ARTILLERY,

each with their separate moves and possibilities, it being the object of the player to capture the position of the enemy's capital.

A letter received from a well-known Colonel says : "I think your War Game

THE BEST OF ITS KIND.

I bought one on Saturday and *ten* to-day to give away. It is a combination of Draughts, Chess, and the War Game which must interest all who try it."

The game, like Draughts, Chess, and Bridge, may also give rise to most interesting problem-positions, such, for instance, as

"ALLIES TO PLAY & ENTER BERLIN IN FOUR MOVES."

Perhaps some of our readers may like to invent problems of this kind, and, if so, we shall be glad to see them, and use and pay for any that may be found suitable.

"FOR GOD'S SAKE, MR. HOLMES, GIVE ME SOME ADVICE, FOR I AM AT MY WITS' END."

A NEW SHERLOCK HOLMES STORY

THE ADVENTURE OF THE SUSSEX VAMPIRE

by

A. CONAN DOYLE

ILLUSTRATED BY
H. K. ELCOCK

HOLMES had read carefully a note which the last post had brought him. Then, with the dry chuckle which was his nearest approach to a laugh, he tossed it over to me.

"For a mixture of the modern and the mediæval, of the practical and of the wildly fanciful, I think this is surely the limit," said he. "What do you make of it, Watson?"

I read as follows:—

46, Old Jewry,
Nov. 19th.
Re Vampires.

Sir,

Our client, Mr. Robert Ferguson, of Ferguson and Muirhead, tea brokers, of Mincing Lane, has made some inquiry from us in a communication of even date concerning vampires. As our firm specializes entirely upon the assessment of machinery the matter hardly comes within our purview, and we have therefore recommended Mr. Ferguson to call upon you and lay the matter before you. We have not forgotten your successful action in the case of Matilda Briggs.

We are, Sir,
Faithfully yours,
MORRISON, MORRISON, AND DODD.
per E. J. C.

"Matilda Briggs was not the name of a young woman, Watson," said Holmes, in a reminiscent voice. "It was a ship which is associated with the giant rat of Sumatra, a story for which the world is not yet prepared. But what do we know about vampires? Does it come within our purview either? Anything is better than stagnation, but really we seem to have been switched on to a Grimm's fairy tale. Make a long arm, Watson, and see what V has to say."

I leaned back and took down the great index volume to which he referred. Holmes balanced it on his knee and his eyes moved slowly and lovingly over the record of old cases, mixed with the accumulated information of a lifetime.

"Voyage of the *Gloria Scott*," he read.

" That was a bad business. I have some recollection that you made a record of it, Watson, though I was unable to congratulate you upon the result. Victor Lynch, the forger. Venomous lizard or gila. Remarkable case, that ! Vittoria, the circus belle. Vanderbilt and the Yeggman. Vipers. Vigor, the Hammersmith wonder. Hullo ! Hullo ! Good old index. You can't beat it. Listen to this, Watson. Vampirism in Hungary. And again, Vampires in Transylvania." He turned over the pages with eagerness, but after a short intent perusal he threw down the great book with a snarl of disappointment.

" Rubbish, Watson, rubbish ! What have we to do with walking corpses who can only be held in their grave by stakes driven through their hearts ? It's pure lunacy."

" But surely," said I, " the vampire was not necessarily a dead man ? A living person might have the habit. I have read, for example, of the old sucking the blood of the young in order to retain their youth."

" You are right, Watson. It mentions the legend in one of these references. But are we to give serious attention to such things ? This Agency stands flat-footed upon the ground, and there it must remain. This world is big enough for us. No ghosts need apply. I fear that we cannot take Mr. Robert Ferguson very seriously. Possibly this note may be from him, and may throw some light upon what is worrying him."

He took up a second letter which had lain unnoticed upon the table whilst he had been absorbed with the first. This he began to read with a smile of amusement upon his face which gradually faded away into an expression of intense interest and concentration. When he had finished he sat for some little time lost in thought with the letter dangling from his fingers. Finally, with a start, he aroused himself from his reverie.

" Cheeseman's, Lamberley. Where is Lamberley, Watson ? "

" It is in Sussex, south of Horsham."

" Not very far, eh ? And Cheeseman's ?"

" I know that country, Holmes. It is full of old houses which are named after the men who built them centuries ago. You get Odley's and Harvey's and Carriton's—the folk are forgotten but their names live in their houses."

" Precisely," said Holmes, coldly. It was one of the peculiarities of his proud, self-contained nature that, though he docketed any fresh information very quickly and accurately in his brain, he seldom made any acknowledgment to the giver. " I rather fancy we shall know a good deal more about Cheeseman's, Lamberley, before we

are through. The letter is, as I had hoped, from Robert Ferguson. By the way, he claims acquaintance with you."

" With me ! "

" You had better read it."

He handed the letter across. It was headed with the address quoted.

DEAR MR. HOLMES (it said),—I have been recommended to you by my lawyers, but indeed the matter is so extraordinarily delicate that it is most difficult to discuss. It concerns a friend for whom I am acting. This gentleman married some five years ago a Peruvian lady, the daughter of a Peruvian merchant, whom he had met in connection with the importation of nitrates. The lady was very beautiful, but the fact of her foreign birth and of her alien religion always caused a separation of interests and of feelings between husband and wife, so that after a time his love may have cooled towards her and he may have come to regard their union as a mistake. He felt there were sides of her character which he could never explore or understand. This was the more painful as she was as loving a wife as a man could have—to all appearance absolutely devoted.

Now for the point which I will make more plain when we meet. Indeed, this note is merely to give you a general idea of the situation and to ascertain whether you would care to interest yourself in the matter. The lady began to show some curious traits quite alien to her ordinarily sweet and gentle disposition. The gentleman had been married twice and he had one son by the first wife. This boy was now fifteen, a very charming and affectionate youth, though unhappily injured through an accident in childhood. Twice the wife was caught in the act of assaulting this poor lad in the most unprovoked way. Once she struck him with a stick and left a great weal on his arm.

This was a small matter, however, compared with her conduct to her own child, a dear boy just under one year of age. On one occasion about a month ago this child had been left by its nurse for a few minutes. A loud cry from the baby, as of pain, called the nurse back. As she ran into the room she saw her employer, the lady, leaning over the baby and apparently biting his neck. There was a small wound in the neck, from which a stream of blood had escaped. The nurse was so horrified that she wished to call the husband, but the lady implored her not to do so, and actually gave her five pounds as a price for her silence.

No explanation was ever given, and for the moment the matter was passed over.

It left, however, a terrible impression upon the nurse's mind, and from that time she began to watch her mistress closely, and to keep a closer guard upon the baby, whom she tenderly loved. It seemed to her that even as she watched the mother, so

At last there came one dreadful day when the facts could no longer be concealed from the husband. The nurse's nerve had given way; she could stand the strain no longer, and she made a clean breast of it all to the man. To him it seemed as wild a tale as it may now seem to you. He knew his wife to be a loving wife, and, save for the assaults upon her stepson, a loving mother. Why, then, should she wound her own dear little baby? He

the mother watched her, and that every time she was compelled to leave the baby alone the mother was waiting to get at it. Day and night the nurse covered the child, and day and night the silent, watchful mother seemed to be lying in wait as a wolf waits for a lamb. It must read most incredible to you, and yet I beg you to take it seriously, for a child's life and a man's sanity may depend upon it.

"Hullo! Hullo! Good old index. You can't beat it. Listen to this, Watson."

told the nurse that she was dreaming, that her suspicions were those of a lunatic, and that such libels upon her mistress were not to be tolerated. Whilst they were talking, a sudden cry of pain was heard. Nurse and master rushed together to the nursery. Imagine his feelings, Mr. Holmes, as he saw his wife rise from a kneeling position beside the cot, and saw blood upon the child's exposed neck and upon the sheet. With a cry of horror, he turned his wife's face to the light and saw blood all round her lips. It was she—she beyond all question —who had drunk the poor baby's blood.

So the matter stands. She is now confined to her room. There has been no explanation. The husband is half demented. He knows, and I know, little of Vampirism beyond the name. We had thought it was some wild tale of foreign parts. And yet here in the very heart of the English Sussex—well, all this can be discussed with you in the morning. Will you see me? Will you use your great powers in aiding a distracted man? If so, kindly wire to Ferguson, Cheeseman's, Lamberley, and I will be at your rooms by ten o'clock.

Yours faithfully,
ROBERT FERGUSON.

P.S.—I believe your friend Watson played Rugby for Blackheath when I was three-quarter for Richmond. It is the only personal introduction which I can give.

"Of course I remember him," said I, as I laid down the letter. "Big Bob Ferguson, the finest three-quarter Richmond ever had. He was always a good-natured chap. It is like him to be so concerned over a friend's case."

Holmes looked at me thoughtfully and shook his head.

"I never get your limits, Watson," said he. "There are unexplored possibilities about you. Take a wire down, like a good fellow. 'Will examine your case with pleasure.'"

"_Your_ case!"

"We must not let him think that this Agency is a home for the weak-minded. Of course it is his case. Send him that wire and let the matter rest till morning."

PROMPTLY at ten o'clock next morning Ferguson strode into our room. I had remembered him as a long, slab-sided man with loose limbs and a fine turn of speed, which had carried him round many an opposing back. There is surely nothing in life more painful than to meet the wreck of a fine athlete whom one has known in his prime. His great frame had fallen in, his flaxen hair was scanty, and his shoulders were bowed. I fear that I roused corresponding emotions in him.

"Hullo, Watson," said he, and his voice was still deep and hearty. "You don't look quite the man you did when I threw you over the ropes into the crowd at the Old Deer Park. I expect I have changed a bit also. But it's this last day or two that has aged me. I see by your telegram, Mr. Holmes, that it is no use my pretending to be anyone's deputy."

"It is simpler to deal direct," said Holmes.

"Of course it is. But you can imagine how difficult it is when you are speaking of the one woman whom you are bound to protect and help. What can I do? How am I to go to the police with such a story? And yet the kiddies have got to be protected. Is it madness, Mr. Holmes? Is it something in the blood? Have you any similar case in your experience? For God's sake, give me some advice, for I am at my wits' end."

"Very naturally, Mr. Ferguson. Now sit here and pull yourself together and give me a few clear answers. I can assure you that I am very far from being at my wits' end, and that I am confident we shall find some solution. First of all, tell me what steps you have taken. Is your wife still near the children?"

"We had a dreadful scene. She is a most loving woman, Mr. Holmes. If ever a woman loved a man with all her heart and soul, she loves me. She was cut to the heart that I should have discovered this horrible, this incredible secret. She would not even speak. She gave no answer to my reproaches, save to gaze at me with a sort of wild, despairing look in her eyes. Then she rushed to her room and locked herself in. Since then she has refused to see me. She has a maid who was with her before her marriage, Dolores by name—a friend rather than a servant. She takes her food to her."

"Then the child is in no immediate danger?"

"Mrs. Mason, the nurse, has sworn that she will not leave it night or day. I can absolutely trust her. I am more uneasy about poor little Jack, for, as I told you in my note, he has twice been assaulted by her."

"But never wounded?"

"No; she struck him savagely. It is the more terrible as he is a poor little inoffensive cripple." Ferguson's gaunt features softened as he spoke of his boy. "You would think that the dear lad's condition would soften anyone's heart. A fall in childhood and a twisted spine, Mr. Holmes. But the dearest, most loving heart within."

Holmes had picked up the letter of yesterday and was reading it over. "What other inmates are there in your house, Mr. Ferguson?"

"Two servants who have not been long

with us. One stable hand, Michael, who sleeps in the house. My wife, myself, my boy Jack, baby, Dolores, and Mrs. Mason. That is all."

"I gather that you did not know your wife well at the time of your marriage?"

"I had only known her a few weeks."

"How long had this maid Dolores been with her?"

"Some years."

"Then your wife's character would really be better known by Dolores than by you?"

"Yes, you may say so."

Holmes made a note.

"I fancy," said he, "that I may be of more use at Lamberley than here. It is eminently a case for personal investigation. If the lady remains in her room, our presence could not annoy or inconvenience her. Of course, we would stay at the inn."

Ferguson gave a gesture of relief.

"It is what I hoped, Mr. Holmes. There is an excellent train at two from Victoria, if you could come."

"Of course we could come. There is a lull at present. I can give you my undivided energies. Watson, of course, comes with us. But there are one or two points upon which I wish to be very sure before I start. This unhappy lady, as I understand it, has appeared to assault both the children, her own baby and your little son?"

"That is so."

"But the assaults take different forms, do they not? She has beaten your son."

"Once with a stick and once very savagely with her hands."

"Did she give no explanation why she struck him?"

"None, save that she hated him. Again and again she said so."

"Well, that is not unknown among step-mothers. A posthumous jealousy, we will say. Is the lady jealous by nature?"

"Yes, she is very jealous—jealous with all the strength of her fiery tropical love."

"But the boy—he is fifteen, I understand, and probably very developed in mind, since his body has been circumscribed in action. Did he give you no explanation of these assaults?"

"No; he declared there was no reason."

"Were they good friends at other times?"

"No; there was never any love between them."

"Yet you say he is affectionate?"

"Never in the world could there be so devoted a son. My life is his life. He is absorbed in what I say or do."

Once again Holmes made a note. For some time he sat lost in thought.

"No doubt you and the boy were great comrades before this second marriage. You

were thrown very close together, were you not?"

"Very much so."

"And the boy, having so affectionate a nature, was devoted, no doubt, to the memory of his mother?"

"Most devoted."

"He would certainly seem to be a most interesting lad. There is one other point about these assaults. Were the strange attacks upon the baby and the assaults upon your son at the same period?"

"In the first case it was so. It was as if some frenzy had seized her, and she had vented her rage upon both. In the second case it was Jack who suffered. Mrs. Mason had no complaint to make about the baby."

"That certainly complicates matters."

"I don't quite follow you, Mr. Holmes."

"Possibly not. One forms provisional theories and waits for time or fuller knowledge to explode them. A bad habit, Mr. Ferguson; but human nature is weak. I fear that your old friend here has given an exaggerated view of my scientific methods. However, I will only say at the present stage that your problem does not appear to me to be insoluble, and that you may expect to find us at Victoria at two o'clock."

IT was evening of a dull, foggy November day when, having left our bags at the Chequers, Lamberley, we drove through the Sussex clay of a long winding lane, and finally reached the isolated and ancient farmhouse in which Ferguson dwelt. It was a large, straggling building, very old in the centre, very new at the wings, with towering Tudor chimneys and a lichen-spotted, high-pitched roof of Horsham slabs. The door-steps were worn into curves, and the ancient tiles which lined the porch were marked with the rebus of a cheese and a man, after the original builder. Within, the ceilings were corrugated with heavy oaken beams, and the uneven floors sagged into sharp curves. An odour of age and decay pervaded the whole crumbling building.

There was one very large central room, into which Ferguson led us. Here, in a huge old-fashioned fireplace with an iron screen behind it dated 1670, there blazed and spluttered a splendid log fire.

The room, as I gazed round, was a most singular mixture of dates and of places. The half-panelled walls may well have belonged to the original yeoman farmer of the seventeenth century. They were orna-mented, however, on the lower part by a line of well-chosen modern water-colours; while above, where yellow plaster took the place of oak, there was hung a fine collection of South American utensils and weapons, which

The woman turned her flushed and handsome face towards me. "Where is my husband?" she asked.

had been brought, no doubt, by the Peruvian lady upstairs. Holmes rose, with that quick curiosity which sprang from his eager mind, and examined them with some care. He returned with his eyes full of thought.

"Hullo!" he cried. "Hullo!"

A spaniel had lain in a basket in the corner. It came slowly forward towards its master, walking with difficulty. Its hind legs moved irregularly and its tail was on the ground. It licked Ferguson's hand.

"What is it, Mr. Holmes?"

"The dog. What's the matter with it?"

"That's what puzzled the vet. A sort of paralysis. Spinal meningitis, he thought. But it is passing. He'll be all right soon—won't you, Carlo?"

A shiver of assent passed through the drooping tail. The dog's mournful eyes passed from one of us to the other. He knew that we were discussing his case.

"Did it come on suddenly?"

"In a single night."

"How long ago?"

"It may have been four months ago."

"Very remarkable. Very suggestive."

"What do you see in it, Mr. Holmes?"

"A confirmation of what I had already thought."

"For God's sake, what *do* you think, Mr. Holmes? It may be a mere intellectual puzzle to you, but it is life and death to me! My wife a would-be murderer—my child in constant danger! Don't play with me, Mr. Holmes. It is too terribly serious."

The big Rugby three-quarter was trembling all over. Holmes put his hand soothingly upon his arm.

"I fear that there is pain for you, Mr. Ferguson, whatever the solution may be," said he. "I would spare you all I can. I cannot say more for the instant, but before I leave this house I hope I may have something definite."

"Please God you may! If you will excuse me, gentlemen, I will go up to my wife's room and see if there has been any change."

HE was away some minutes, during which Holmes resumed his examination of the curiosities upon the wall. When our host returned it was clear from his downcast face that he had made no progress. He brought with him a tall, slim, brown-faced girl.

"The tea is ready, Dolores," said Ferguson. "See that your mistress has everything she can wish."

"She verra ill," cried the girl, looking with indignant eyes at her master. "She no ask for food. She verra ill. She need doctor. I frightened stay alone with her without doctor."

Ferguson looked at me with a question in his eyes.

"I should be so glad if I could be of use."

"Would your mistress see Dr. Watson?"

"I take him. I no ask leave. She needs doctor."

"Then I'll come with you at once."

I followed the girl, who was quivering with strong emotion, up the staircase and down an ancient corridor. At the end was an iron-clamped and massive door. It struck me as I looked at it that if Ferguson tried to force his way to his wife he would find it no easy matter. The girl drew a key from her pocket, and the heavy oaken planks creaked upon their old hinges. I passed in and she swiftly followed, fastening the door behind her

On the bed a woman was lying who was clearly in a high fever. She was only half conscious, but as I entered she raised a pair of frightened but beautiful eyes and glared at me in apprehension. Seeing a stranger, she appeared to be relieved, and sank back with a sigh upon the pillow. I stepped up to her with a few reassuring words, and she lay still while I took her pulse and temperature. Both were high, and yet my impression was that the condition was rather that of mental and nervous excitement than of any actual seizure.

"She lie like that one day, two day. I 'fraid she die," said the girl.

The woman turned her flushed and handsome face towards me.

"Where is my husband?"

"He is below, and would wish to see you."

"I will not see him. I will not see him." Then she seemed to wander off into delirium. "A fiend! A fiend! Oh, what shall I do with this devil?"

"Can I help you in any way?"

"No. No one can help. It is finished. All is destroyed. Do what I will, all is destroyed."

The woman must have some strange delusion. I could not see honest Bob Ferguson in the character of fiend or devil.

"Madame," I said, "your husband loves you dearly. He is deeply grieved at this happening."

Again she turned on me those glorious eyes.

"He loves me. Yes. But do I not love him? Do I not love him even to sacrifice myself rather than break his dear heart. That is how I love him. And yet he could think of me—he could speak of me so."

"He is full of grief, but he cannot understand."

"No, he cannot understand. But he should trust."

"Will you not see him?" I suggested.

"No, no; I cannot forget those terrible

my child. I
have a right to
my child. That is the
only message I can send
him." She turned her face
to the wall and would say no
more.

I returned to the room downstairs,
where Ferguson and Holmes still sat
by the fire. Ferguson listened moodily
to my account of the interview.

"How can I send her the child?" he
said. "How do I know what strange

words nor the look upon his face. I will
not see him. Go now. You can do nothing
for me. Tell him only one thing. I want

At this moment I chanced to glance at Holmes, and saw a most singular intentness in his expression. His eyes were fixed with eager curiosity upon something at the other side of the room.

impulse might come upon her? How can I ever forget how she rose from beside it with its blood upon her lips?" He shuddered at the recollection. "The child is safe with Mrs. Mason, and there he must remain."

A smart maid, the only modern thing which we had seen in the house, had brought in some tea. As she was serving it the door opened and a youth entered the room. He was a remarkable lad, pale-faced and fair-haired, with excitable light blue eyes which blazed into a sudden flame of emotion and joy as they rested upon his father. He

rushed forward and threw his arms round his neck with the abandon of a loving girl.

"Oh, daddy," he cried, "I did not know that you were due yet. I should have been here to meet you. Oh, I am so glad to see you!"

Ferguson gently disengaged himself from the embrace with some little show of embarrassment.

"Dear old chap," said he, patting the flaxen head with a very tender hand. "I came early because my friends, Mr. Holmes and Dr. Watson, have been persuaded to come down and spend an evening with us."

"Is that Mr. Holmes, the detective?"

"Yes."

The youth looked at us with a very penetrating and, as it seemed to me, unfriendly gaze.

"What about your other child, Mr. Ferguson?" asked Holmes. "Might we make the acquaintance of the baby?"

"Ask Mrs. Mason to bring baby down," said Ferguson. The boy went off with a curious, shambling gait which told my surgical eyes that he was suffering from a weak spine. Presently he returned, and behind him came a tall, gaunt woman bearing in her arms a very beautiful child, dark-eyed, golden-haired, a wonderful mixture of the Saxon and the Latin. Ferguson was evidently devoted to it, for he took it into his arms and fondled it most tenderly.

"Fancy anyone having the heart to hurt him," he muttered, as he glanced down at the small, angry red pucker upon the cherub throat.

It was at this moment that I chanced to glance at Holmes, and saw a most singular intentness in his expression. His face was as set as if it had been carved out of old ivory, and his eyes, which had glanced for a moment at father and child, were now fixed with eager curiosity upon something at the other side of the room. Following his gaze I could only guess that he was looking out through the window at the melancholy, dripping garden. It is true that a shutter had half-closed outside and obstructed the view, but none the less it was certainly at the window that Holmes was fixing his concentrated attention. Then he smiled and his eyes came back to the baby. On its chubby neck there was this small puckered mark. Without speaking, Holmes examined it with care. Finally he shook one of the dimpled fists which waved in front of him.

"Good-bye, little man. You have made a strange start in life. Nurse, I should wish to have a word with you in private."

He took her aside and spoke earnestly for a few minutes. I only heard the last words, which were : " Your anxiety will soon, I hope, be set at rest." The woman, who seemed to be a sour, silent kind of creature, withdrew with the child.

"What is Mrs. Mason like ? " asked Holmes.

"Not very prepossessing externally, as you can see, but a heart of gold, and devoted to the child."

"Do you like her, Jack ? " Holmes turned suddenly upon the boy. His expressive mobile face shadowed over, and he shook his head.

"Jacky has very strong likes and dislikes," said Ferguson, putting his arm round the boy. "Luckily I am one of his likes."

The boy cooed and nestled his head upon his father's breast. Ferguson gently disengaged him.

"Run away, little Jacky," said he, and he watched his son with loving eyes until he disappeared. "Now, Mr. Holmes," he continued, when the boy was gone, " I really feel that I have brought you on a fool's errand, for what can you possibly do, save give me your sympathy ? It must be an exceedingly delicate and complex affair from your point of view."

"It is certainly delicate," said my friend, with an amused smile, " but I have not been struck up to now with its complexity. It has been a case for intellectual deduction, but when this original intellectual deduction is confirmed point by point by quite a number of independent incidents, then the subjective becomes objective and we can say confidently that we have reached our goal. I had, in fact, reached it before we left Baker Street, and the rest has merely been observation and confirmation."

Ferguson put his big hand to his furrowed forehead.

"For Heaven's sake, Holmes," he said, hoarsely, " if you can see the truth in this matter, do not keep me in suspense. How do I stand ? What shall I do ? I care nothing as to how you have found your facts so long as you have really got them."

"Certainly I owe you an explanation, and you shall have it. But you will permit me to handle the matter in my own way ? Is the lady capable of seeing us, Watson ? "

"She is ill, but she is quite rational."

"Very good. It is only in her presence that we can clear the matter up. Let us go up to her."

"She will not see me," cried Ferguson.

"Oh, yes, she will," said Holmes. He scribbled a few lines upon a sheet of paper. "You at least have the entrée, Watson. Will you have the goodness to give the lady this note ? "

I ASCENDED again and handed the note to Dolores, who cautiously opened the door. A minute later I heard a cry from within, a cry in which joy and surprise seemed to be blended. Dolores looked out.

"She will see them. She will leesten," said she.

At my summons Ferguson and Holmes came up. As we entered the room Ferguson took a step or two towards his wife, who had raised herself in the bed, but she held out her hand to repulse him. He sank into an arm-chair, while Holmes seated himself beside him, after bowing to the lady, who looked at him with wide-eyed amazement.

"I think we can dispense with Dolores," said Holmes. "Oh, very well, madame, if you would rather she stayed I can see no objection. Now, Mr. Ferguson, I am a busy man with many calls, and my methods have to be short and direct. The swiftest surgery is the least painful. Let me first say what will ease your mind. Your wife is a very good, a very loving, and a very ill-used woman."

Ferguson sat up with a cry of joy.

" Prove that, Mr. Holmes, and I am your debtor for ever."

" I will do so, but in doing so I must wound you deeply in another direction."

" I care nothing so long as you clear my wife. Everything on earth is insignificant compared to that."

" Let me tell you, then, the train of reasoning which passed through my mind in Baker Street. The idea of a vampire was to me absurd. Such things do not happen in criminal practice in England. And yet your observation was precise. You had seen the lady rise from beside the child's cot with the blood upon her lips."

" I did."

" Did it not occur to you that a bleeding wound may be sucked for some other purpose than to draw the blood from it ? Was there not a Queen in English history who sucked such a wound to draw poison from it ? "

" Poison ! "

" A South American household. My instinct felt the presence of those weapons upon the wall before my eyes ever saw them. It might have been other poison, but that was what occurred to me. When I saw that little empty quiver beside the small bird-bow, it was just what I expected to see. If the child were pricked with one of those arrows dipped in curare or some other devilish drug, it would mean death if the venom were not sucked out.

" And the dog ! If one were to use such a poison, would one not try it first in order to see that it had not lost its power ? I did not foresee the dog, but at least I understood him and he fitted into my reconstruction.

" Now do you understand ? Your wife feared such an attack. She saw it made and saved the child's life, and yet she shrank from telling you all the truth, for she knew how you loved the boy and feared lest it break your heart."

" Jacky ! "

" I watched him as you fondled the child just now. His face was clearly reflected in the glass of the window where the shutter formed a background. I saw such jealousy, such cruel hatred, as I have seldom seen in a human face."

" My Jacky ! "

" You have to face it, Mr. Ferguson. It is the more painful because it is a distorted love, a maniacal exaggerated love for you, and possibly for your dead mother, which has prompted his action. His very soul is consumed with hatred for this splendid child, whose health and beauty are a contrast to his own weakness."

" Good God ! It is incredible ! "

" Have I spoken the truth, madame ? "

The lady was sobbing, with her face buried in the pillows. Now she turned to her husband.

" How could I tell you, Bob ? I felt the blow it would be to you. It was better that I should wait and that it should come from some other lips than mine. When this gentleman, who seems to have powers of magic, wrote that he knew all, I was glad."

" I think a year at sea would be my prescription for Master Jacky," said Holmes, rising from his chair. " Only one thing is still clouded, madame. We can quite understand your attacks upon Master Jacky. There is a limit to a mother's patience. But how did you dare to leave the child these last two days ? "

" I had told Mrs. Mason. She knew."

" Exactly. So I imagined."

Ferguson was standing by the bed, choking, his hands outstretched and quivering.

" This, I fancy, is the time for our exit, Watson," said Holmes in a whisper. " If you will take one elbow of the too faithful Dolores, I will take the other. There, now," he added, as he closed the door behind him. " I think we may leave them to settle the rest among themselves."

I HAVE only one further note of this case. It is the letter which Holmes wrote in final answer to that with which the narrative begins. It ran thus :—

Baker Street,
Nov. 21st.

Re Vampires.

Sir,

Referring to your letter of the 19th, I beg to state that I have looked into the inquiry of your client, Mr. Robert Ferguson, of Ferguson and Muirhead, tea brokers, of Mincing Lane, and that the matter has been brought to a satisfactory conclusion. With thanks for your recommendation,

I am, Sir,
Faithfully yours,
SHERLOCK HOLMES.

HIS FACE TURNED UPON US WITH A GLARE OF BAFFLED RAGE, WHICH
GRADUALLY SOFTENED INTO A RATHER SHAMEFACED GRIN AS HE
REALIZED THAT TWO PISTOLS WERE POINTED AT HIS HEAD.

THE ADVENTURE OF
THE THREE GARRIDEBS

A NEW
SHERLOCK HOLMES
STORY

BY

A. Conan Doyle

ILLUSTRATED BY
HOWARD ELCOCK

I T may have been a comedy, or it may have been a tragedy. It cost one man his reason, it cost me a blood-letting, and it cost yet another man the penalties of the law. Yet there was certainly an element of comedy. Well, you shall judge for yourselves.

I remember the date very well, for it was in the same month that Holmes refused a knighthood for services which may perhaps some day be described. I only refer to the matter in passing, for in my position of partner and confidant I am obliged to be particularly careful to avoid any indiscretion. I repeat, however, that this enables me to fix the date, which was the latter end of June, 1902, shortly after the conclusion of the South African War. Holmes had spent several days in bed, as was his habit from time to time, but he emerged that morning with a long foolscap document in his hand and a twinkle of amusement in his austere grey eyes.

"There is a chance for you to make some money, friend Watson," said he. "Have you ever heard the name of Garrideb?"

I admitted that I had not.

"Well, if you can lay your hand upon a Garrideb, there's money in it."

"Why?"

"Ah, that's a long story—rather a whimsical one, too. I don't think in all our explorations of human complexities we have ever come upon anything more singular. The fellow will be here presently for cross-examination, so I won't open the matter up till he comes. But meanwhile, that's the name we want."

The telephone directory lay on the table beside me, and I turned over the pages in a rather hopeless quest. But to my amazement there was this strange name in its due place. I gave a cry of triumph.

"Here you are, Holmes! Here it is!"

Holmes took the book from my hand.

"'Garrideb, N.,'" he read, "'136, Little Ryder Street, W.' Sorry to disappoint you, my dear Watson, but this is the man himself. That is the address upon his letter. We want another to match him."

Mrs. Hudson had come in with a card upon a tray. I took it up and glanced at it.

"Why, here it is!" I cried in amazement. "This is a different initial. John Garrideb, Counsellor at Law, Moorville, Kansas, U.S.A."

Holmes smiled as he looked at the card. "I am afraid you must make yet another effort, Watson," said he. "This gentleman is also in the plot already, though I certainly did not expect to see him this morning. However, he is in a position to tell us a good deal which I want to know."

A moment later he was in the room. Mr. John Garrideb, Counsellor at Law, was a short, powerful man with the round, fresh, clean-shaven face characteristic of so many American men of affairs. The general effect was chubby and rather childlike, so that one received the impression of quite a young man with a broad set smile upon his face. His eyes, however, were arresting. Seldom in any human head have I seen a pair which bespoke a more intense inward life, so bright were they, so alert, so responsive to every change of thought. His accent was American, but was not accompanied by any eccentricity of speech.

"Mr. Holmes ? " he asked, glancing from one to the other. "Ah, yes ! Your pictures are not unlike you, sir, if I may say so. I believe you have had a letter from my namesake, Mr. Nathan Garrideb, have you not ? "

"Pray sit down," said Sherlock Holmes. "We shall, I fancy, have a good deal to discuss." He took up his sheets of foolscap. "You are, of course, the Mr. John Garrideb mentioned in this document. But surely you have been in England some time ? "

"Why do you say that, Mr. Holmes ? " I seemed to read sudden suspicion in those expressive eyes.

"Your whole outfit is English."

Mr. Garrideb forced a laugh. " I've read of your tricks, Mr. Holmes, but I never thought I would be the subject of them. Where do you read that ? "

"The shoulder cut of your coat, the toes of your boots—could anyone doubt it ? "

"Well, well, I had no idea I was so obvious a Britisher. But business brought me over here some time ago, and so, as you say, my outfit is nearly all London. However, I guess your time is of value, and we did not meet to talk about the cut of my socks. What about getting down to that paper you hold in your hand ? "

Holmes had in some way ruffled our visitor, whose chubby face had assumed a far less amiable expression.

"Patience ! Patience, Mr. Garrideb ! " said my friend in a soothing voice. " Dr. Watson would tell you that these little digressions of mine sometimes prove in the end to have some bearing on the matter. But why did Mr. Nathan Garrideb not come with you ? "

"Why did he ever drag you into it at all ? " asked our visitor, with a sudden outflame of anger. "What in thunder had you to do with it ? Here was a bit of professional business between two gentlemen, and one of them must needs call in a detective !

I saw him this morning, and he told me this fool-trick he had played me, and that's why I am here. But I feel bad about it, all the same."

"There was no reflection upon you, Mr. Garrideb. It was simply zeal upon his part to gain your end—an end which is, I understand, equally vital for both of you. He knew that I had means of getting information, and, therefore, it was very natural that he should apply to me."

Our visitor's angry face gradually cleared.

"Well, that puts it different," said he. "When I went to see him this morning and he told me he had sent to a detective, I just asked for your address and came right away. I don't want police butting into a private matter. But if you are content just to help us find the man, there can be no harm in that."

"Well, that is just how it stands," said Holmes. "And now, sir, since you are here, we had best have a clear account from your own lips. My friend here knows nothing of the details."

Mr. Garrideb surveyed me with not too friendly a gaze.

"Need he know ? " he asked.

"We usually work together."

"Well, there's no reason it should be kept a secret. I'll give you the facts as short as I can make them. If you came from Kansas I would not need to explain to you who Alexander Hamilton Garrideb was. He made his money in real estate, and afterwards in the wheat pit at Chicago, but he spent it in buying up as much land as would make one of your counties, lying along the Arkansas River, west of Fort Dodge. It's grazing land and lumber land and arable land and mineralized land, and just every sort of land that brings dollars to the man that owns it.

"He had no kith nor kin—or, if he had, I never heard of it. But he took a kind of pride in the queerness of his name. That was what brought us together. I was in the law at Topeka, and one day I had a visit from the old man, and he was tickled to death to meet another man with his own name. It was his pet fad, and he was dead set to find out if there were any more Garridebs in the world. ' Find me another ! ' said he. I told him I was a busy man and could not spend my life hiking round the world in search of Garridebs. ' None the less,' said he, ' that is just what you will do if things pan out as I planned them.' I thought he was joking, but there was a powerful lot of meaning in the words, as I was soon to discover.

"For he died within a year of saying them, and he left a will behind him. It was the queerest will that has ever been filed in the

"Why did he ever drag you into it at all, Mr. Holmes?" asked our visitor, with a sudden outflame of anger. "What in thunder had you to do with it?"

State of Kansas. His property was divided into three parts, and I was to have one on condition that I found two Garridebs who would share the remainder. It's five million dollars for each if it is a cent, but we can't lay a finger on it until we all three stand in a row.

"It was so big a chance that I just let my legal practice slide and I set forth looking for Garridebs. There is not one in the United States. I went through it, sir, with a fine-toothed comb and never a Garrideb could I catch. Then I tried the old country. Sure enough there was the name in the London Telephone Directory. I went after him two days ago and explained the whole matter to him. But he is a lone man, like myself, with some women relations, but no men. It says three adult men in the will. So you see we still have a vacancy, and if you can help to fill it we will be very ready to pay your charges."

"Well, Watson," said Holmes, with a smile, "I said it was rather whimsical, did I not? I should have thought, sir, that your obvious way was to advertise in the agony columns of the papers."

"I have done that, Mr. Holmes. No replies."

"Dear me! Well, it is certainly a most curious little problem. I may take a glance at it in my leisure. By the way, it is curious that you should have come from Topeka. I used to have a correspondent—he is dead now—old Dr. Lysander Starr, who was Mayor in 1890."

"Good old Dr. Starr!" said our visitor. "His name is still honoured. Well, Mr. Holmes, I suppose all we can do is to report to you and let you know how we progress. I reckon you will hear within a day or two." With this assurance our American bowed and departed.

HOLMES had lit his pipe, and he sat for some time with a curious smile upon his face.

"Well?" I asked at last.

"I am wondering, Watson—just wondering!"

"At what?"

Holmes took his pipe from his lips.

"I was wondering, Watson, what on earth could be the object of this man in telling us such a rigmarole of lies. I nearly asked him so—for there are times when a brutal frontal attack is the best policy—but I judged it better to let him think he had fooled us. Here is a man with an English coat frayed at the elbow and trousers bagged at the knee with a year's wear, and yet by this document and by his own account he is a provincial American lately landed in London. There have been no advertisements in the agony columns. You know that I miss nothing there. They are my favourite covert for putting up a bird, and I would never have overlooked such a cock pheasant as that. I never knew a Dr. Lysander Starr of Topeka. Touch him where you would he was false. I think the fellow is really an American, but he has worn his accent smooth with years of London. What is his game, then, and what motive lies behind this preposterous search for Garridebs? It's worth our attention, for, granting that the man is a rascal, he is certainly a complex and ingenious one. We must now find out if our other correspondent is a fraud also. Just ring him up, Watson."

I did so, and heard a thin, quavering voice at the other end of the line.

"Yes, yes, I am Mr. Nathan Garrideb. Is Mr. Holmes there? I should very much like to have a word with Mr. Holmes."

My friend took the instrument and I heard the usual syncopated dialogue.

"Yes, he has been here. I understand that you don't know him. . . . How long? . . . Only two days! . . . Yes, yes, of course, it is a most captivating prospect. Will you be at home this evening? I suppose your namesake will not be there? . . . Very good, we will come then, for I would rather have a chat without him. . . . Dr. Watson will come with me. . . . I understood from your note that you did not go out often. . . . Well, we shall be round about six. You need not mention it to the American lawyer. . . . Very good. Good-bye!"

It was twilight of a lovely spring evening, and even Little Ryder Street, one of the smaller offshoots from the Edgware Road, within a stone-cast of old Tyburn Tree of evil memory, looked golden and wonderful in the slanting rays of the setting sun. The particular house to which we were directed was a large, old-fashioned, Early Georgian edifice with a flat brick face broken only by two deep bay windows on the ground floor. It was on this ground floor that our client lived, and, indeed, the low windows proved to be the front of the huge room in which he spent his waking hours. Holmes pointed as we passed to the small brass plate which bore the curious name.

"Up some years, Watson," he remarked, indicating its discoloured surface. "It's *his* real name, anyhow, and that is something to note."

The house had a common stair, and there were a number of names painted in the hall, some indicating offices and some private chambers. It was not a collection of residential flats, but rather the abode of Bohemian bachelors. Our client opened the door for us himself and apologized by saying that the woman in charge left at four o'clock. Mr. Nathan Garrideb proved to be a very tall, loose-jointed, round-backed person, gaunt and bald, some sixty-odd years of age. He had a cadaverous face, with the dull dead skin of a man to whom exercise was unknown. Large round spectacles and a small projecting goat's beard combined with his stooping attitude to give him an expression of peering curiosity. The general effect, however, was amiable, though eccentric.

The room was as curious as its occupant. It looked like a small museum. It was both broad and deep, with cupboards and cabinets all round, crowded with specimens, geological and anatomical. Cases of butterflies and moths flanked each side of the entrance. A large table in the centre was littered with all sorts of *débris*, while the tall brass tube of a powerful microscope bristled up amongst them. As I glanced round I was surprised at the universality of the man's interests. Here was a case of ancient coins. There was a cabinet of flint instruments. Behind his central table was a large cupboard of fossil bones. Above was a line of plaster skulls with such names as "Neanderthal," "Heidelberg," "Cromagnan" printed beneath them. It was clear that he was a student of many subjects.

As he stood in front of us now, he held a piece of chamois leather in his right hand with which he was polishing a coin.

"Syracusan—of the best period," he explained, holding it up. "They degenerated greatly towards the end. At their best I hold them supreme, though some prefer the Alexandrian school. You will find a chair here, Mr. Holmes. Pray allow me to clear these bones. And you, sir—ah, yes, Dr. Watson—if you would have the goodness to put the Japanese vase to one

"Well, we shall be round about six. Dr. Watson will come with me."

side. You see round me my little interests in life. My doctor lectures me about never going out, but why should I go out when I have so much to hold me here ? I can assure you that the adequate cataloguing of one of those cabinets would take me three good months."

Holmes looked round him with curiosity. "But do you tell me that you *never* go out ? " he said.

" Now and again I drive down to Sotheby's or Christie's. Otherwise I very seldom leave my room. I am not too strong, and my researches are very absorbing. But you can imagine, Mr. Holmes, what a terrific shock—pleasant but terrific—it was for me when I heard of this unparalleled good fortune. It only needs one more Garrideb to complete the matter, and surely we can find one. I had a brother, but he is dead, and female relatives are disqualified. But there must surely be others in the world. I had heard that you handled strange cases, and that was why I sent to you. Of course, this American gentleman is quite right, and I should have taken his advice first, but I acted for the best."

" I think you acted very wisely indeed," said Holmes. " But are you really anxious to acquire an estate in America ? "

" Certainly not, sir. Nothing would induce me to leave my collection. But this gentleman has assured me that he will buy me out as soon as we have established our claim. Five million dollars was the sum named. There are a dozen specimens in the market at the present moment which fill gaps in my collection, and which I am unable to purchase for want of a few hundred pounds. Just think what I could do with five million dollars. Why, I have the nucleus of a national collection. I shall be the Hans Sloane of my age."

His eyes gleamed behind his great spectacles. It was very clear that no pains would be spared by Mr. Nathan Garrideb in finding a namesake.

" I merely called to make your acquaintance, and there is no reason why I should interrupt your studies," said Holmes. " I prefer to establish personal touch with those with whom I do business. There are few questions I need ask, for I have your very clear narrative in my pocket, and I filled up the blanks when this American gentleman called. I understand that up to this week you were unaware of his existence."

" That is so. He called last Tuesday."

" Did he tell you of our interview to-day ? "

" Yes, he came straight back to me. He had been very angry."

" Why should he be angry ? "

" He seemed to think it was some re-

flection on his honour. But he was quite cheerful again when he returned."

" Did he suggest any course of action ? "

" No, sir, he did not."

" Has he had, or asked for, any money from you ? "

" No, sir, never ! "

" You see no possible object he has in view ? "

" None, except what he states."

" Did you tell him of our telephone appointment ? "

" Yes, sir, I did."

Holmes was lost in thought. I could see that he was puzzled.

" Have you any articles of great value in your collection ? "

" No, sir. I am not a rich man. It is a good collection, but not a very valuable one."

" You have no fear of burglars ? "

" Not the least."

" How long have you been in these rooms?"

" Nearly five years."

Holmes's cross-examination was interrupted by an imperative knocking at the door. No sooner had our client unlatched it than the American lawyer burst excitedly into the room.

" Here you are ! " he cried, waving a paper over his head. " I thought I should be in time to get you. Mr. Nathan Garrideb, my congratulations ! You are a rich man, sir. Our business is happily finished and all is well. As to you, Mr. Holmes, we can only say we are sorry if we have given you any useless trouble."

He handed over the paper to our client, who stood staring at a marked advertisement. Holmes and I leaned forward and read it over his shoulder. This is how it ran :—

HOWARD GARRIDEB.

Constructor of Agricultural Machinery.

Binders, reapers' steam and hand plows, drills, harrows, farmers' carts, buckboards, and all other appliances.

Estimates for Artesian Wells.

Apply Grosvenor Buildings, Aston.

" Glorious ! " gasped our host. " That makes our third man."

" I had opened up inquiries in Birmingham," said the American, " and my agent there has sent me this advertisement from a local paper. We must hustle and put the thing through. I have written to this man and told him that you will see him in his office to-morrow afternoon at four o'clock."

" You want *me* to see him ? "

" What do you say, Mr. Holmes ? Don't you think it would be wiser ? Here am I,

"Here you are!" he cried, waving a paper over his head. "Mr. Nathan Garrideb, my congratulations! You are a rich man, sir."

a wandering American with a wonderful tale. Why should he believe what I tell him ? But you are a Britisher with solid references, and he is bound to take notice of what you say. I would go with you if you wished, but I have a very busy day to-morrow, and I could always follow you if you are in any trouble."

"Well, I have not made such a journey for years."

"It is nothing, Mr. Garrideb. I have figured out your connections. You leave at twelve and should be there soon after two. Then you can be back the same night. All you have to do is to see this man, explain the matter, and get an affidavit of his existence. By the Lord ! " he added, hotly, "considering I've come all the way from the centre of America, it is surely little enough if you go a hundred miles in order to put this matter through."

"Quite so," said Holmes. "I think what this gentleman says is very true."

Mr. Nathan Garrideb shrugged his shoulders with a disconsolate air. "Well, if you insist I shall go," said he. "It is certainly hard for me to refuse you anything, considering the glory of hope that you have brought into my life."

"Then that is agreed," said Holmes, "and no doubt you will let me have a report as soon as you can."

"I'll see to that," said the American. "Well," he added, looking at his watch, "I'll have to get on. I'll call to-morrow, Mr. Nathan, and see you off to Birmingham. Coming my way, Mr. Holmes ? Well, then, good-bye, and we may have good news for you to-morrow night."

I noticed that my friend's face cleared when the American left the room, and the look of thoughtful perplexity had vanished.

"I wish I could look over your collection, Mr. Garrideb," said he. "In my profession all sorts of odd knowledge comes useful, and this room of yours is a storehouse of it."

Our client shone with pleasure and his eyes gleamed from behind his big glasses.

"I had always heard, sir, that you were a very intelligent man," said he. "I could take you round now, if you have the time."

"Unfortunately, I have not. But these specimens are so well labelled and classified that they hardly need your personal explanation. If I should be able to look in to-morrow, I presume that there would be no objection to my glancing over them ?"

"None at all. You are most welcome. The place will, of course, be shut up, but Mrs. Saunders is in the basement until four o'clock and would let you in with her key."

"Well, I happen to be clear to-morrow afternoon. If you would say a word to

Mrs. Saunders it would be quite in order. By the way, who is your house-agent ?"

Our client was amazed at the sudden question.

"Holloway and Steele, in the Edgware Road. But why ?"

"I am a bit of an archæologist myself when it comes to houses," said Holmes, laughing. "I was wondering if this was Queen Anne or Georgian."

"Georgian, beyond doubt."

"Really. I should have thought a little earlier. However, it is easily ascertained. Well, good-bye, Mr. Garrideb, and may you have every success in your Birmingham journey."

The house-agent's was close by, but we found that it was closed for the day, so we made our way back to Baker Street. It was not till after dinner that Holmes reverted to the subject.

"Our little problem draws to a close," said he. "No doubt you have outlined the solution in your own mind."

"I can make neither head nor tail of it."

"The head is surely clear enough and the tail we should see to-morrow. Did you notice nothing curious about that advertisement ?"

"I saw that the word ' plough ' was mis-spelt."

"Oh, you did notice that, did you ? Come, Watson, you improve all the time. Yes, it was bad English but good American. The printer had set it up as received. Then the buckboards. That is American also. And artesian wells are commoner with them than with us. It was a typical American advertisement, but purporting to be from an English firm. What do you make of that ?"

"I can only suppose that this American lawyer put it in himself. What his object was I fail to understand."

"Well, there are alternative explanations. Anyhow, he wanted to get this good old fossil up to Birmingham. That is very clear. I might have told him that he was clearly going on a wild-goose chase, but, on second thoughts, it seemed better to clear the stage by letting him go. To-morrow, Watson—well, to-morrow will speak for itself."

HOLMES was up and out early. When he returned at lunch-time I noticed that his face was very grave.

"This is a more serious matter than I had expected, Watson," said he. "It is fair to tell you so, though I know it will only be an additional reason to you for running your head into danger. I should know my Watson by now. But there is danger, and you should know it."

"Well, it is not the first we have shared, Holmes. I hope it may not be the last. What is the particular danger this time ?"

" We are up against a very hard case. I have identified Mr. John Garrideb, Counsellor at Law. He is none other than ' Killer ' Evans, of sinister and murderous reputation."

" I fear I am none the wiser."

" Ah, it is not part of your profession to carry about a portable Newgate Calendar in your memory. I have been down to see friend Lestrade at the Yard. There may be an occasional want of imaginative intuition down there, but they lead the world for thoroughness and method. I had an idea that we might get on the track of our American friend in their records. Sure enough, I found his chubby face smiling up at me from the Rogues' Portrait Gallery. James Winter, *alias* Morecroft, *alias* Killer Evans, was the inscription below." Holmes drew an envelope from his pocket. " I scribbled down a few points from his *dossier*. Aged forty-four. Native of Chicago. Known to have shot three men in the States. Escaped from penitentiary through political influence. Came to London in 1893. Shot a man over cards in a night club in the Waterloo Road in January, 1895. Man died, but he was shown to have been the aggressor in the row. Dead man was identified as Rodger Presbury, famous as forger and coiner in Chicago. Killer Evans released in 1901. Has been under police supervision since, but so far as known has led an honest life. Very dangerous man, usually carries arms and is prepared to use them. That is our bird, Watson—a sporting bird, as you must admit."

" But what is his game ? "

" Well, it begins to define itself. I have been to the house-agents. Our client, as he told us, has been there five years. It was unlet for a year before then. The previous tenant was a gentleman at large named Waldron. Waldron's appearance was well remembered at the office. He had suddenly vanished and nothing more been heard of him. He was a tall, bearded man with very dark features. Now, Presbury, the man whom Killer Evans had shot, was, according to Scotland Yard, a tall, dark man with a beard. As a working hypothesis, I think we may take it that Presbury, the American criminal, used to live in the very room which our innocent friend now devotes to his museum. So at last we get a link, you see."

" And the next link ? "

" Well, we must go now and look for that." He took a revolver from the drawer and handed it to me.

" I have my old favourite with me. If our Wild West friend tries to live up to his nickname, we must be ready for him. I'll give you an hour for a siesta, Watson, and then I think it will be time for our Ryder Street adventure."

I T was just four o'clock when we reached the curious apartment of Nathan Garrideb. Mrs. Saunders, the caretaker, was about to leave, but she had no hesitation in admitting us, for the door shut with a spring lock and Holmes promised to see that all was safe before we left. Shortly afterwards the outer door closed, her bonnet passed the bow window, and we knew that we were alone in the lower floor of the house. Holmes made a rapid examination of the premises. There was one cupboard in a dark corner which stood out a little from the wall. It was behind this that we eventually crouched, while Holmes in a whisper outlined his intentions.

" He wanted to get our amiable friend out of his room—that is very clear, and, as the collector never went out, it took some planning to do it. The whole of this Garrideb invention was apparently for no other end. I must say, Watson, that there is a certain devilish ingenuity about it, even if the queer name of the tenant did give him an opening which he could hardly have expected. He wove his plot with remarkable cunning."

" But what did he want ? "

" Well, that is what we are here to find out.. It has nothing whatever to do with our client, so far as I can read the situation. It is something connected with the man who may have been murdered—the man who may have been his confederate in crime. There is some guilty secret in the room. That is how I read it. At first I thought our friend might have something in his collection more valuable than he knew—something worth the attention of a big criminal. But the fact that Rodger Presbury of evil memory inhabited these rooms points to some deeper reason. Well, Watson, we can but possess our souls in patience and see what the hour may bring."

That hour was not long in striking. We crouched closer in the shadow as we heard the outer door open and shut. Then came the sharp, metallic snap of a key, and the American was in the room. He closed the door softly behind him, took a sharp glance around him to see that all was safe, threw off his overcoat, and walked up to the central table with the brisk manner of one who knows exactly what he has to do and how to do it. He pushed the table to one side, tore up the square of carpet on which it rested, rolled it completely back, and then, drawing a jemmy from his inside pocket, he knelt down and worked vigorously upon the floor. Presently we heard the sound of sliding boards, and an instant later a

There was a crash as Holmes's

square had opened in the planks. Killer
Evans struck a match, lit a stump of candle,
and vanished from our view.

Clearly our moment had come. Holmes
touched my wrist as a signal, and together
we stole across to the open trapdoor.

Gently as we moved, however, the old floor
must have creaked under our feet, for the
head of our American, peering anxiously
round, emerged suddenly from the open
space. His face turned upon us with a
glare of baffled rage, which gradually

pistol came down on the man's head.

softened into a rather shamefaced grin as he realized that two pistols were pointed at his head.

"Well, well!" said he, coolly, as he scrambled to the surface. "I guess you have been one too many for me, Mr. Holmes.

Saw through my game, I suppose, and played me for a sucker from the first. Well, sir, I hand it to you; you have me beat and——"

In an instant he had whisked out a revolver from his breast and had fired two shots. I felt a sudden hot sear as if a red-hot iron had been pressed to my thigh. There was a crash as Holmes's pistol came down on the man's head. I had a vision of him sprawling upon the floor with blood running down his face while Holmes rummaged him for weapons. Then my friend's wiry arms were round me and he was leading me to a chair.

"You're not hurt, Watson ? For God's sake, say that you are not hurt ! "

It was worth a wound—it was worth many wounds—to . know the depth of loyalty and love which lay behind that cold mask. The clear, hard eyes were dimmed for a moment, and the firm lips were shaking. For the one and only time I caught a glimpse of a great heart as well as of a great brain. All my years of humble but single-minded service culminated in that moment of revelation.

"It's nothing, Holmes. It's a mere scratch."

He had ripped up my trousers with his pocket-knife.

"You are right," he cried, with an immense sigh of relief. "It is quite superficial." His face set like flint as he glared at our prisoner, who was sitting up with a dazed face. "By the Lord, it is as well for you. If you had killed Watson, you would not have got out of this room alive. Now, sir, what have you to say for yourself ? "

He had nothing to say for himself. He only lay and scowled. I leaned on Holmes's arm, and together we looked down into the small cellar which had been disclosed by the secret flap. It was still illuminated by the candle which Evans had taken down with him. Our eyes fell upon a mass of rusted machinery, great rolls of paper, a litter of bottles, and, neatly arranged upon a small table, a number of neat little bundles.

"A printing press—a counterfeiter's outfit," said Holmes.

"Yes, sir," said our prisoner, staggering slowly to his feet and then sinking into the chair. "The greatest counterfeiter London ever saw. That's Presbury's machine, and those bundles on the table are two thousand of Presbury's notes worth a hundred each and fit to pass anywhere. Help yourselves, gentlemen. Call it a deal and let me beat it."

Holmes laughed.

"We don't do things like that, Mr. Evans. There is no bolt-hole for you in this country. You shot this man, Presbury, did you not ? "

"Yes, sir, and got five years for it, though it was he who pulled on me. Five years—when I should have had a medal the size of a soup plate. No living man could tell a Presbury from a Bank of England, and if I hadn't put him out he would have flooded London with them. I was the only one in the world who knew where he made them. Can you wonder that I wanted to get to the place ? And can you wonder that when I found this crazy boob of a bug-hunter with the queer name squatting right on the top of it, and never quitting his room, I had to do the best I could to shift him ? Maybe I would have been wiser if I had put him away. It would have been easy enough, but I'm a soft-hearted guy that can't begin shooting unless the other man has a gun also. But say, Mr. Holmes, what have I done wrong, anyhow ? I've not used this plant. I've not hurt this old stiff. Where do you get me ? "

"Only attempted murder, so far as I can see," said Holmes. "But that's not our job. They take that at the next stage. What we wanted at present was just your sweet self. Please give the Yard a call, Watson. It won't be entirely unexpected."

So those were the facts about Killer Evans and his remarkable invention of the three Garridebs. We heard later that our poor old friend never got over the shock of his dissipated dreams. When his castle in the air fell down, it buried him beneath the ruins. He was last heard of at a nursing-home in Brixton. It was a glad day at the Yard when the Presbury outfit was discovered, for, though they knew that it existed, they had never been able, after the death of the man, to find out where it was. Evans had indeed done great service, and caused several worthy C.I.D. men to sleep the sounder, for the counterfeiter stands in a class by himself as a public danger. They would willingly have subscribed to that soup-plate medal of which the criminal had spoken, but an unappreciative Bench took a less favourable view, and the Killer returned to those shades from which he had just emerged.

NEXT MONTH :

Another Sherlock Holmes Story :
"THE ADVENTURE OF THE ILLUSTRIOUS CLIENT."